After a while, he noticed that I was getting fidgety, and that there was an edge creeping into my tone when I was repeating myself for the third or fourth time on some minor detail like where I'd been standing when I said X or Y.

"Got somewhere else you need to be?" he asked aggressively.

"Yeah," I agreed. "That's it exactly."

"Oh, right. Hot, is she?" He favored me with the kind of pruriently suggestive leer that cops and squaddies get issued on day one along with their boots.

I really wasn't in the mood. "It's a he," I said. "He's a demonically possessed psychopath, and he tends to run a core temperature about eight degrees higher than the bog standard ninety-eight point four. So yeah, I think you could safely say he's hot."

MacKay put his notebook away, giving me a stare of truculent suspicion: he'd felt the breeze of something going over his head, and he didn't like it. "Well, I don't think we need anything else from you right now," he said sternly. "The sergeant will probably be in touch again later on, though, so you keep yourself available, yeah?"

"It's all right," I said. "I'll contact him on the astral plane."

"Eh?" The suspicion had turned to frank alarm.

"Skip it," I muttered over my shoulder as I walked away. It wasn't MacKay's fault that my Saturday night was up the Swannee. That was down to nobody but me, which is never as much consolation as it ought to be.

The weekend is meant to be a time when you unwind from the stresses of the week that's gone and recharge your batteries for the shitstorm to come. But not for me, not tonight. The place I was going on to now made this God-spurned dump look positively cozy.

"Hugely entertaining...Smart dialogue, good pacing, and offbeat characters keep the pages turning." —*RT Book Reviews*

"Comes at you fast and hard, with a few surprises that will smack you between the eyes, leaving your mouth hanging open and your attention glued to the page." —Nightsandweekends.com

"Felix offers a darkly droll take on the circumstances of his world, which is just as familiar, intricate, and morally tangled as our own." —*Entertainment Weekly*

"[A] deftly crafted, can't-turn-the-page-fast-enough read." —*Kirkus* (starred review)

Dead Men's Boots

"Every bit as good as...Jim Butcher, Carey hits his stride." —*Publishers Weekly* (starred review)

"Fast-paced...riveting...everything a paranormal thriller fan could want." —*Monsters & Critics*

"Fast-paced....Grip[s] the reader from the moment the body of Gittings is interred and never slows down as every move the exorcist makes seems increasingly dangerous." —*Midwest Book Review*

"The Felix Castor novels are splashed with color and texture, their characters are larger than life (or death), and the stories are, well...out of this world. Castor is a remarkably believable character....A wholly engaging blend of the detective and fantasy genres." —*Booklist*

"Witty, sardonic....Leaves the readers breathless....Irresistible." —*Kirkus* (starred review)

Thicker Than Water

"The author has mastered the challenge of incorporating the paranormal into a normal urban setting, and his refusal to pull punches makes this a harder-hitting genre entry than many others."

—*Publishers Weekly*

The Naming of the Beasts

"Carey's unique and eminently readable style, with his excellent command of concise description and dialogue lends itself perfectly to the pacing of the book, one that we found ourselves wanting to re-read as soon as we finished it."

—*SciFiNow*

"Like Humphrey Bogart meets John Constantine, Felix Castor makes for an enjoyably, untrustworthy guide through the undead-filled streets of London, as painted by Mike Carey....Huge verve and energy...engaging and vivacious."

—*SFX*

VICIOUS CIRCLE

By Mike Carey

FELIX CASTOR NOVELS

The Devil You Know
Vicious Circle
Dead Men's Boots
Thicker Than Water
The Naming of the Beasts

(WRITING AS M. R. CAREY)

The Girl With All the Gifts
Fellside
The Boy on the Bridge

VICIOUS CIRCLE

Felix Castor: Book Two

MIKE CAREY

orbit

www.orbitbooks.net

Copyright © 2006 by Mike Carey
Excerpt from *Dead Men's Boots* copyright © 2007 by Mike Carey
Excerpt from *The Last Day's of Jack Sparks* copyright © 2016 by Jason Arnopp

Cover design by Lauren Panepinto
Cover images by Arcangel Images
Cover copyright © 2018 by Hachette Book Group, Inc.

Orbit
Hachette Book Group
1290 Avenue of the Americas
New York, NY 10104
orbitbooks.net

Originally published in Great Britain by Orbit in October 2006
Published in hardcover and ebook by Grand Central Publishing in July 2008
Published in mass market by Orbit in July 2009
First Orbit Trade Paperback Edition: April 2018

Orbit is an imprint of Hachette Book Group.
The Orbit name and logo are trademarks of Little, Brown Book Group Limited.

The publisher is not responsible for websites (or their content) that are not owned by the publisher.

The Hachette Speakers Bureau provides a wide range of authors for speaking events. To find out more, go to www.hachettespeakersbureau.com or call (866) 376-6591.

Library of Congress Control Number: 2017953244

ISBN: 978-0-316-51178-0 (trade paperback), 978-0-446-53760-5 (ebook)

Printed in the United States of America

LSC-C

10 9 8 7 6 5 4 3 2 1

Alphabetically, to Ben, Davey, and Lou;
chronologically, to Lou, Davey, and Ben.
They won't stay where I put them anyway,
thank God, so either way is fine.
May the world be good enough for them.

Chapter One

The incense stick burned with an orange flame and smelled of *Cannabis sativa*. In Southern Africa it grows wild: you can walk through fields of it, waist-high, the five-fronded leaves caressing you like little hands. But in London, where I live, it's mostly encountered in the form of black, compacted lumps of soft, flaky resin. A lot of the magic's gone by then.

Det. Sgt. Gary Coldwood gave me a downright hostile look through the tendrils of the smoke, which curled lazily up through the cavernous interior of the warehouse, the sweet smell dissipating along the aisles of sour dust. The warehouse was on the Edgware Road, on the ragged hinterlands of an old industrial estate: judging from the smashed windows outside and the rows and rows of empty shelves inside, it had been abandoned for a good few years—but Coldwood had invited me to join him and a few uniformed friends for a legally authorized search, so it was a fair bet that appearances were deceptive.

"Have you finished arsing around, Castor?" he asked, fanning the smoke irritably away from his face. I don't know if all this tact and diplomacy is something he was born with or if he just learned it at cop school.

I nodded distantly. "Almost," I said. "I have to intone the mantra another dozen or so times."

Well, Jesus, you know? It was Saturday night, and I already had a heap of my own shit to cope with. When the Met calls, I answer, because they pay on the nose, but that doesn't mean I have to like it. And anyway, I figure that if you give them a little showmanship they'll be more impressed when you come up with the goods. Look, boys, I say in my own devious way, this is magic: it has to be, because it's got smoke and mirrors. So far, Coldwood's the only cop who's ever called me on it, and that's probably why we get along so well: I respect a man who can smell the bullshit through the incense.

But tonight he was in a bad mood. He hadn't found a dead body in the warehouse, and that meant he didn't know what he was dealing with just yet. Could be a murder, could just be their man doing a runner; and if it *was* a murder, that could be either a golden opportunity or six months of covert surveillance going up in aromatic smoke. So he wanted answers, and that made him less than usually tolerant of my sense of theater.

I murmured a few variations on *om mane padme om,* and he kicked the heel of my shoe resonantly with his Met-issue heavy-duty policeman's boot. I was sitting on the floor in front of him with my knees drawn up, so I suppose it could have been worse.

"Just tell me if you can see anything, Castor," he suggested. "Then you can hum away to your heart's content."

I got up, slowly; slowly enough for Coldwood to lose patience and wander across to see if the forensics boys had managed to shag any prints from a battered-looking desk in the far corner of the room. He really wasn't happy: I could tell by the way his angular face—reminiscent of Dick Tracy, if Dick Tracy had joined-up eyebrows and a skin problem—had subsided onto his lower lip, forcing it out into a truculent shelf. His body language was a bit of a giveaway, too: whenever he finished waving and pointing, which he does when he gives orders, his right hand fell to the discreet shoulder holster he wore under his tan leather jacket, as if to check that it was still there. Coldwood hadn't been an armed response unit for very long, and you could tell the novelty hadn't worn off yet.

I ambled across the warehouse toward the door I'd come in through, away from the forensics team, watched curiously by two or three poor bloody infantry constables who were there to maintain a perimeter. Coldwood knows my tricks, and makes allowances for them, but to these guys I was obviously something of a sideshow. Ignoring them, I looked behind the filing cabinets that were ranged along the wall to the right of the door, banged on the cork notice board behind them, which had sheaves of dusty old invoices clinging to it like mangy fur, and turned the girlie calendars over to look at the bits of gray-painted cinder block they were covering. Disappointingly, there was nothing there. No hidden doors, no wall-mounted safes, not even old graffiti.

I looked down at my feet. The floor of the warehouse was bare gray cement, but just here by the notice board and the filing cabinets there was a ragged rectangle of red linoleum—a psychedelic sunburst pattern, very retro-chic unless it had been there since the seventies. I'd noticed another piece, with the same pattern, underneath the desk. Here, though, there were scuff marks in the dust where the lino had been moved in the recent past. I kicked down experimentally with my heel. There was a slightly hollow boom from underneath my feet.

"Coldwood?" I called over my shoulder.

He must have caught something in my voice—or else he'd heard the hollow note, too—because he was suddenly there at my elbow. "What?" he asked suspiciously.

I pointed down at the lino. "Something here," I said. "Does this place have a cellar?"

Coldwood's eyes narrowed slightly. "Not according to the plans," he said. He beckoned to two of the plods and they came over at a half run. "Get this up," he told them, gesturing at the lino.

They had to move the filing cabinets first, and since the cabinets were full they took a bit of manhandling. I could have helped, but I didn't want to get into an argument about demarcation. The linoleum itself rolled up as easy as shelling peas, though, and Coldwood swore under his breath when he saw the trapdoor underneath. It was obviously something he felt his boys should have spotted first.

It was about five feet square, and it lay exactly flush with the floor on three sides. On the fourth side, the hinges were sunk a centimeter or so into the surface, but it was a professional job with the narrowest of joins so no telltale lines would be trodden into the lino above. There was a keyhole on the left-hand side: a lozenge-shaped keyhole with no widening at the shank end, so this was most likely a Sargent and Greenleaf mortice—not an easy nut to crack.

Coldwood didn't even bother to try: he sent two of the uniforms off to get some crowbars. With a great deal of maneuvering, a few false starts, and a hail of splinters as the wood screamed and split, they finally succeeded in levering the entire lock plate out of its housing. Even then the bolt could scarcely be made to bend. The plate stood out of the trapdoor at a thirty-degree angle, rough star shapes of broken wood still gripped by its corner screws: a wounded sentry who'd been sidestepped rather than defeated. Now that their moment in the spotlight was over, the plods stood back deferentially so that the sergeant could open the trapdoor himself. Coldwood did so, with a grunt of effort because the wood of the trap turned out to be a good inch thick.

Inside, there was a space about a foot deep, separated by three vertical plywood dividers into four compartments of roughly equal size. Three of the compartments were filled with identical brown paper bags, about the size of Tate & Lyle sugar bags, all double wrapped in plastic on top of the paper: the fourth was mostly full of black DVD sleeves, but two small notebooks with slightly oil-stained covers were sitting off in one corner. On the cover of the top one, written in thick black felt tip, were the two words "goods in." What the other said I couldn't tell.

At a nod from the detective sergeant, the grab-and-dab boys fished up one of the bags and both of the notebooks with gingerly, plastic-gloved hands and took them away to the desk, looking like kids at Christmas. Coldwood was still looking at me—a look that said the time for teasing was past. He wanted the whole story.

But so did I. I don't prostitute my talents for just anyone, especially anyone with a rank and a uniform, and when I'm dragged into a situation I know sod all about, I like to play just a little coy until I find my feet. So I threw him a question by way of an answer.

"Is your man about six two, stocky, ginger-haired, wearing Armani slacks and one of those poncy collarless jackets in a sort of olive brown?"

Coldwood made a sound in his throat that might have been a laugh if laughter was in his repertoire. "That's him," he said. "Now stop playing Mystic Meg and tell me where he is."

"Tell me *who* he is," I countered.

"Fuck! Castor, you're a civilian adviser, so just do what you're being paid to do, okay? You don't get to look at my fucking case notes."

I waited. This was my fifth or sixth outing with DS Coldwood, and we'd already established a sort of routine; but like I said, he wasn't in the best of tempers right then—hence his attempt to lead me to water and then shove my head under it.

"I could arrest you for withholding evidence and hindering an investigation," he pointed out darkly.

"You could," I agreed. "And I'd wish you joy proving it."

There was a short pause. Coldwood breathed out explosively.

"His name's Lesley Sheehan," he said, his tone flat and his face deadpan. "He deals whatever drugs he can get his hands on, plus some nasty fetish porn on the side as a bit of a hobby. That's probably what those DVDs are all about. He's maybe two steps up the ladder from the mules and the street runners, and he doesn't matter a toss. But he answers to a man named Robin Pauley, who we'd dearly love to get our hands on. So we've spent the last six months watching Sheehan and building up a case against him because we think we can turn him. He narced before, about ten years back, to get out of a conspiracy to murder charge. When they've done it once, you've got a bit more of a handle on them. Only now he's gone missing and we think Pauley may have sussed what we were up to."

"Sheehan won't be talking now, in any case," I said, with calm and absolute conviction.

Coldwood was exasperated. "Castor, you're not qualified even to have a fucking opinion on—" he snarled. Then he got it. "Oh," he muttered, followed a second or so later by a bitter "Fuck!" He was about to say something else, probably equally terse, when one of the lab rats called across to him.

"Sergeant?"

He turned, brisk and expressionless. Always deal with the matter in hand: keep your imagination holstered like your sidearm. Good copping.

"It's heroin," the tech boy said, with stiff formality. "More or less uncut. About ninety-five, ninety-six percent pure."

Coldwood nodded curtly, then turned back to me.

"So I'm assuming Sheehan's somewhere in here, is he?" he asked, for the sake of form.

I nodded, but I needed to spell it out in case he got his hopes up. "His ghost is in here," I said. "That doesn't mean his corpse is. I've told you before how this works."

"I need to see him," said Coldwood.

I nodded again. Of course he did.

Slipping a hand inside my trenchcoat, I took out my tin whistle. Normally it would be a Clarke Original in the key of D, but some exciting events on board a boat a few months prior to this had left me temporarily without an instrument. The boat in question was a trim little yacht named the *Mercedes*, but if you're thinking Henley Regatta, you're way off the mark: "The Wreck of the Hesperus" would probably give you a better mental picture. Or maybe the *Flying Dutchman*. Anyway, as a result of that little escapade I ended up buying a Sweetone, virulently green in color, and that had become my new default instrument. It didn't feel as ready and responsive to my hand as the old Original used to do, and it looked a bit ridiculous, but it was coming along. Give it another year or so and we'd probably be inseparable.

I put the whistle to my lips and blew G, C, A to tune myself in. I was aware that all the eyes in the room were focused on me now: Coldwood's expressionless, most of the others bright with prurient

"That was what I thought, too," I agreed. "But if you take a look at the back view you'll probably want to amend that diagnosis."

Coldwood favored me with another expressive look, but he got up and strolled around the pathetic figure, where he stared with some surprise at the back of Sheehan's head—or to be more accurate, at the place where it had been. It mostly wasn't there anymore. The shade of Lesley Sheehan lost interest in the sergeant as soon as he passed out of sight: he lifted his hands and stared at them for a moment, then frowned and looked around as if he were trying to remember where his car keys were.

"You're the expert," I said, "but I'm guessing a bullet wound from a gun pressed against his temple just in front of the ear, angled a little backwards. If he was shot from behind, presumably most of his face would be an exit wound."

"It wasn't a gun," muttered Coldwood. "It was one of those captive-bolt efforts they use to kill cows." He pointed. "The whole of the left side of the head has caved in, and most of the bone has stayed in the wound. You don't get that pattern of damage with a high-velocity— Hey, if you chuck up in here I'm having you on an effing charge!"

The last words weren't addressed to me, but to the uniformed copper who'd been looking a little peaky earlier. From where he was standing, the poor sod had an intimate perspective on some of Sheehan's most private parts—the ones that had formerly been inside his skull. It didn't seem to be agreeing with him much at all. At a curt nod from Coldwood he ran for the door.

Coldwood turned his attention back to me. "Where's the body?" he asked. "The real, physical body? Where can we find him?"

"I don't have a bastard clue," I answered truthfully. "I can ask him, if you like. But you might as well ask him yourself. He can see you. He could see you even when you couldn't see him."

"But you're the expert," he echoed me, with deft sarcasm.

"Being an exorcist isn't quite the same as being a detective," I shot back, deadpan. "I don't have a badge I can wave at him—and it's really difficult to kick the shit out of a man who's already dead. But I'll

give it a go, if you leave me alone with him. I'm not doing it in front
of your mob."

Coldwood chewed that one over for a long moment. "Okay," he
said, but he thrust a warning finger under my nose. "Touch the evidence and I'll gut you, Castor. Understand me?"

"I don't need drugs," I said. "I can get high on death."

With a muttered profanity, Coldwood signaled to his team to with-
draw. It was nice and quiet after they'd gone, and I decided to let the
new mood settle in for a minute or two before I tackled Mr. Sheehan.
I slipped my whistle into the purpose-built pocket I'd sewn into the
lining of my coat—I go for a Russian army greatcoat because it hides
a multitude of sins—and in another pocket nearby found a silver hip
flask that was full of extremely rough Greek brandy. I took a swig, and
it expanded inside me like a fire inside a derelict building. It's not good.
Really not good at all. But at moments like this it bridges a gap and
keeps me moving.

With a second mouthful swilling around my gums, I took another
look at the calendars. Just the usual lad mag soft porn: Abbie whatsher-
name, Suzie something else. But Sheehan's tastes ran to material that
was less vanilla, Coldwood had said. Well, he'd given up the pleasures
of the flesh now, that was for damn sure. After doing this job for a decade or so, I still don't know much about the afterlife—but I'm willing
to lay long odds that the dead don't get their end away very much.

There was no point in putting it off anymore: Sheehan's memory
was probably as truncated as what was left of his head, so he must have
forgotten Coldwood's merry marching band by now. I pocketed the
flask again and walked over to where the ghost was standing—his feet
a few inches above the brown paper bags, roughly where the floor had
been. Like therapy, death reveals your deepest instincts: he was guarding his stash.

"So," I said to him, conversationally. "You're dead, then. How's that
working out?"

His eyes flicked over me, lingered, wandered off again. He was having
a hard time staying focused, which perhaps wasn't all that surprising.

"Must have been a shock," I offered. "One moment you're walking along, not a care in the world. The next some guy gets a headlock on you, drags you into an alley and *ker-chunk*: you've got daylight hitting your eyes from the back."

Sheehan frowned, made a formless gesture with his right hand. His lips moved.

"Takes a while even to realize what's happened to you," I went on, commiserating. "You think, well, that was bad but here I am, thank God. And then the hours go by, and the doubts start to set in. Why am I still just standing here? How did I get here in the first place? What do I do next?

"And the truth is, mate, you don't get to do anything. Not now. Doing things is a luxury that the living have. The dead—well, mostly they just get to watch."

Sheehan's eyes widened. I didn't know if that was my words getting past his guard or just the dim stirrings of memory in whatever he was using now for a mind. His hands twitched again, and this time when he spoke I could hear a dry whisper, like wind through grass.

"Poor—poor—"

Self-pity is something you often get from the dead, and it's not like you can really blame them for it. It doesn't look like any of the options are all that attractive; even heaven, if you take the majority view, is a state of oneness with God and perpetual praise of his goodness, which must wear pretty thin after the first few hours, let alone the rest of eternity. On the other hand, this guy was a pusher and a porn merchant and fuck alone knew what else: I wasn't wasting any sympathy, because you never know when you're going to run out.

"Yeah," I said. "It's very much a crock of shit. Some bastard really stiffed you, Sheehan. It's almost worth believing in hell so you can have the comfort of imagining him roasting in it."

"Poor—poor—poor—"

"You said that. I agreed."

"Pauley!" The name was barely audible, but I've got good ears and I was listening on all frequencies.

"Pauley." I turned my back on him: best to distract him as little as possible now, because his attention deficit was probably only going to get worse. "Pauley topped you, did he? Well, that's friends for you. Did it hurt, or was it all over too quick for you to notice?"

A long silence; then a hoarse, almost voiceless whisper. "H-h-hurt. Hurt me."

"Was this over at your place, then?" I asked, my tone so relentlessly neutral I must have sounded bored to death with the whole subject. "Knock on the door, *bang*, you're dead, kind of thing? Or were you out on the town?"

There was a very long silence. I let it stretch. It sounded like the kind of silence that might have a payoff at the end of it. "Bronze," Sheehan whispered. "Bronze." He made a sound like a moan stretched thin and hung up to cure—a moan with no bass to it, because the dead tend to have trouble hitting the low notes. "Buried."

The silence after that final exhalation was different. When I turned around, I knew what I'd see: Sheehan was gone. Exhausted by the effort of speech, his physical manifestation had faded into random motes in the air: not matter, nor energy, nor anything that anyone had managed to trap or measure. He'd be back, given that he had nowhere else to go, but it wouldn't be soon.

I went to the door and stepped outside onto the narrow ribbon of asphalt that separated the warehouse from the street. The only cars parked there were Coldwood's tax-deductible Primera and three regular black-and-whites. Coldwood was off to one side by himself, talking on his cell phone. The plods and the backroom boys were in two separate cliques, responding atavistically to each other's pheromones. There was a brisk wind coming down from the north, but at least it wasn't raining anymore. The sun was setting behind the brutalist high-rises of Colindeep Lane, and a huge mass of gun-gray cloud was pouring across the sky behind it like water down a drain.

Coldwood finished his conversation, put his phone away, and came over to me. "Anything?" he asked, in a tone that expected so little it couldn't possibly be disappointed.

"He fingered Pauley," I said. Coldwood's eyebrows shot up his forehead. "At least, I think he did. And when I asked him where he died he said 'bronze.' Then 'buried.'"

"Brondesbury," Coldwood translated. "Brondesbury Auto Parts. Christ, that'd be a bloody kiss on the cheek from God. If the body's still there—" He was already heading for his car at a fast stroll, dialing as he went. The uniformed coppers turned to follow him with their eyes, awaiting orders with a sort of stolid urgency unique to the boys in blue, but Coldwood was talking on the phone again. "The bodywork place," he was snapping. "The one in Brondesbury Park. Get over there now. Yeah. Yes, get a warrant. But don't wait. Get the place surrounded and don't let any bugger in or out!"

"I take it this is good news," I said to Coldwood's back as he hauled the car door open. Sliding into the driver's seat he spared me a microsecond glance. "That shop is in Pauley's name," he said, with a nasty smile. "We've already got probable cause. If we can get a search warrant, and if the body's still there, we can raid all of his other gaffs and really get some action going." His gaze snapped from me to a uniformed constable who'd just stepped up behind me—the one who'd had to run outside to be sick. "MacKay, take Castor's statement and fax it on to DC Tennant at Luke Street." The car window was already sliding closed as he said it, making any reply redundant. Then Coldwood was out onto the road and gone, trailing a whiff of tortured rubber.

Having my statement taken was very much adding insult to injury, but it was an invitation of the kind that's hard to refuse. I went over the events of the evening while Constable MacKay wrote them down in laborious longhand, culminating in what Sheehan's ghost had said to me when I interrogated him in my official capacity as ghostbuster general. Either MacKay was making up for his earlier lapse of professional sangfroid or he was just very slow on the uptake: either way, he was so mind-meltingly leisurely and methodical in his questioning that bludgeoning him to death with his own notebook would probably have counted as justifiable homicide. He wrote slowly, too, requiring several repetitions of all but the shortest sentences. Overall, I reckoned he had the right stuff to be an officer.

Nothing wrong with his observational skills, though: after a while, he noticed that I was getting fidgety, and that there was an edge creeping into my tone when I was repeating myself for the third or fourth time on some minor detail like where I'd been standing when I said X or Y.

"Got somewhere else you need to be?" he asked aggressively.

"Yeah," I agreed. "That's it exactly."

"Oh, right. Hot, is she?" He favored me with the kind of pruriently suggestive leer that cops and squaddies get issued on day one along with their boots.

I really wasn't in the mood. "It's a he," I said. "He's a demonically possessed psychopath, and he tends to run a core temperature about eight degrees higher than the bog standard ninety-eight point four. So yeah, I think you could safely say he's hot."

MacKay put his notebook away, giving me a stare of truculent suspicion: he'd felt the breeze of something going over his head, and he didn't like it. "Well, I don't think we need anything else from you right now," he said sternly. "The sergeant will probably be in touch again later on, though, so you keep yourself available, yeah?"

"It's all right," I said. "I'll contact him on the astral plane."

"Eh?" The suspicion had turned to frank alarm.

"Skip it," I muttered over my shoulder as I walked away. It wasn't MacKay's fault that my Saturday night was up the Swannee. That was down to nobody but me, which is never as much consolation as it ought to be.

The weekend is meant to be a time when you unwind from the stresses of the week that's gone and recharge your batteries for the shitstorm to come. But not for me, not tonight. The place I was going on to now made this God-spurned dump look positively cozy.

Chapter Two

I can drive, when I have to, but I don't own a car. In London, owning a car doesn't seem to help all that much, unless you want somewhere to sit and soak up the sun while you're lazing on the M25. So it was going to take a long haul on the underground to get me to where I was going—into town on one branch of the Northern Line, back out again on the other one.

It was the twilight zone between Saturday afternoon and Saturday night: the football crowds had already faded away like fairy gold, and it was too early yet for the clubbers and the theatergoers. I was able to sit for most of the way, even if the carriage did have a fugitive whiff of stale fat from someone's illicitly consumed Big Mac.

The guy next to me was reading the *Guardian*, so I read it, too, in staccato glimpses over his shoulder as he turned the pages. The Tories were about to slice and dice their latest leader, which has always been my favorite blood sport; the home secretary was denying some spectacular abuse of office while refusing to relax an injunction that would have allowed the news media to describe exactly what it was; and the Post Mortem Rights Bill was about to come back to the Commons for what was expected to be an eventful third reading.

That wasn't what they were calling it, of course. I think the actual title of the proposed act of parliament was the Redefinition of Legal

Status Extraordinary Powers Act—but the tabloids had resorted to various forms of shorthand, and Post Mortem Rights was the one that had stuck. Personally, I tended to think of it as the Alive Until Proven Dead Act.

Basically the government was trying to pull the law up by its own bootstraps so that it could slip a fairly fundamental postscript into every major statute that had ever been written. It wasn't a case of how the law worked, exactly: it was more a case of who it applied to. The aim was to give some measure of legal protection to the dead—and that's where it got to be good clean fun of the kind that could keep a million lawyers happily engaged from now until Doomsday. Because there were more different kinds of dead and undead entity around these days than there were fish in the sea, or reality TV shows on channel 4. Where did you draw the line? Exactly how much of a physical manifestation did you need to count as a productive citizen?

There'd been some spirited batting around of all these issues in the Commons and in the Lords, and the pundits were saying the bill might hit the rocks if it came to a free vote. But even if it did, it seemed like it was only a matter of time: sooner or later we had to grudgingly accept that our old definitions of life and death were no damn use anymore, and that people who refuse to take the hint when their heart's stopped beating and their perishable parts are six feet under still have at least a minimal degree of protection under the law.

Which for a lot of guys in my profession was just flat-out bad news.

———

I guess the dead were always with us, but for a long while they were fairly discreet about it. Or perhaps there just weren't so many of them who bothered to come back.

In my earliest memories, there's no real distinction: some people had laps you could sit on, hands you could hold, while with others you sort of fell right on through. You learned by trial and error who was which—and then later you learned not to talk about it, because grown-ups couldn't always see or hear the silent woman in the freezer aisle at Sainsbury's, the forlorn kid standing out in the middle of the road with the traffic roaring through him, the wild-eyed, cursing vagrant wandering through the living room wall.

It wasn't that much of a burden, really: more bewildering than traumatic. I found out that ghosts were meant to be scary when I heard other kids telling ghost stories, and as far as I can remember my reaction was just "Oh, so that's what they're called."

The first ghost that ever really rattled me was my sister Katie, and that was because I knew her from when she was alive. I'd even been there when my dad had brought her broken body back to the house, sobbing uncontrollably, fighting off the hands that tried to help him lay her down. She was skipping rope in what was nominally a "play street," off-limits to cars (8:00 AM TO SUNSET, EXCEPT FOR ACCESS). A delivery van, going way too fast in the narrow street, hit her a glancing blow and threw her about ten feet through the air. As far as anyone could tell, she died instantly. The van, meanwhile, kept right on going. My dad spent a lot of time after that going round the neighbors' houses asking people if they'd seen what kind of van it was: he was hoping to identify the driver and get to him before the police did. Fortunately for both of them, he got a whole range of different answers—Mother's Pride, Jacob's Biscuits, Metal Box Company Limited—and eventually had to give up.

I was six years old. You don't really grieve at that age, you just sit around trying to figure out what the hell is going on. I sort of got that Katie was dead, but I wasn't all that clear yet on death itself: it was a transition, a change of state, but how permanent it was and where it left you afterward seemed to vary according to whom I asked.

One thing was for sure: Katie wasn't up in heaven with God. The day we buried her, she walked into my bedroom at five past midnight and tried to climb into bed with me—which was where she normally slept, there being only one room and two beds to share between us three kids. I was perturbed by the broad, bloody gash in her forehead, her pulped shoulder, her gravel-sculpted side, and she was upset by my screaming. It went downhill from there.

My mum and dad were falling apart themselves at this stage, so they didn't have much sympathy to spare. They took me to a doctor, who said nightmares were entirely normal after a trauma—especially a trauma like losing a sibling—and prescribed large doses of sweet bugger all. I was left to get on with it.

And that was how I found out that I was an exorcist.

After two weeks of Katie's nightly visits, I started trying to make her go away, running through the whole gamut of gross and offensive behavior that six-year-old boys can come up with. Katie just kept on staring. But when I sang "Build a bonfire, build a bonfire, put your sister on the top," the subdued little ghost made a whimpering sound and started to flicker like a dying lightbulb.

Seeing that I'd made an impact at last, I pushed on through my small repertoire of songs. Katie tried to talk to me, but whatever she was saying I couldn't hear it over my own raucous chanting. By the time my parents stormed in, their patience finally exhausted, she was gone.

She was gone, and I celebrated. My bed was my own again. I was stronger than death, and I knew that whatever death actually turned out to be, I had the stick that would always bring it to heel: music. I became fascinated by the mechanics of the whole thing; I discovered by trial and error that whistling was better than singing, and playing a flute or tin whistle was best of all. It works differently for each of us, but music is the trigger that does the job for me.

It was years before I really thought again about the shy, scrawny little girl who collected elastic bands for no fathomable reason, wrapping them around each other until they formed a huge, solid ball, and who let me share her lunch when I'd swapped my own crisps and sandwiches for *Twilight Zone* bubblegum cards: years before I even asked myself where she went when I made her go away.

I grew up. So did my big brother, Matthew. We'd never had a lot in common, and as we grew we took off in totally opposite directions. He went straight from school to a Catholic seminary in Upholland—the same one that Johnny Vegas trained in, but Matthew stuck to his guns when Vegas ditched the priesthood to become a stand-up comedian. On the other hand Matthew would have been hampered in that job by having a sense of humor so atrophied that he still thought *The Goons Show* was funny.

I went to Oxford to study English, but dropped out in my second year and by devious and twisted routes ended up going into exorcism. For six or seven years I made a living out of doing to other ghosts for money what I'd done to Katie out of pure, naked self-preservation.

There was a real call for exorcists by this time. Something was happening as the old millennium bumped and creaked and trundled its way downhill toward its terminus. The dead were waking in greater and greater numbers, to the point where suddenly they were impossible to ignore. Most were benign, or at least passive, but some had clearly gotten out of the wrong side of the grave—and a few were downright antisocial. The immaterial ones were bad enough, but some of the dead returned in the flesh, as zombies, while other ghosts—known as loup-garous or *were*—were able to possess animal hosts and sculpt them into a more or less human shape. And in some cases, where you got a big concentration of the dead in one place, other things would appear there, too: things that seemed to correspond to what mediaeval grimoires called demons. It seemed like it was chucking-out time in hell, and the whole rowdy bunch had all come surging out onto the streets at the same time. Kind of like eleven o'clock on the Dock Road back home in Liverpool, but with brimstone.

And equally suddenly, there were the exorcists. Or maybe we'd always been there, too; maybe it's part of the genome or something, but it didn't really come into its own until there was something out there worth exorcising. We're a weird, unlikely lot: every one of us has got his own way of doing the job—which is to catch a ghost, tangle it up in something that it can't get free from, and then dispel it.

For me, obviously, that "something" is music. I play some sequence of notes on my tin whistle, which for me perfectly describes—*models*

might be a better word—the ghost as I perceive it. And somehow the
music adheres to the ghost, or becomes part of it, so that when the
tune stops the ghost stops, too. I'm not unique, I have to admit: I've
met more than a few people who use drums in the same way, and
some bat-shit guy I met once in Argentina taps out a rhythm on his
own cheek. Other exorcists I've bumped into along the way have used
pictures, words, dance, even the syncopation of their own breathing.
The religious ones, of course, use prayer, but it all comes down to the
same thing. Most of us are in no position to get all holier-than-thou
about it.

So for a while, by the simple application of the laws of supply and
demand, I was rolling in it: asking for top dollar and getting what I was
asking for (in the positive rather than the ironic sense of that phrase).
And if anyone ever posed the question, or if I allowed myself to wonder where the ghosts I dispelled actually went to, I had a flip answer in
the breech ready to fire.

It's only in the Western tradition, I'd say, sounding like someone
who'd actually finished out his degree, that ghosts are seen as being the
actual spirits of dead people. Other cultures have them down as being
something else. The Navajo think of ghosts as something that congeals
out of the worst parts of your nature while the rest of you goes into
the next world cleansed and fighting fit. In the Far East, they're often
treated as a sort of emotional pollutant whose appearance depends on
who's looking at them, and so on.

Yeah, I know. Given that ghostbusting was my bread and butter,
and given that I'd started with my own sister, it helped a hell of a lot
if I could tell myself and anyone else who'd listen that ghosts were
something different from the people they looked like. I was only talking my conscience to sleep, and while it was asleep I did some pretty
bad things.

One of them was Rafi.

The Charles Stanger Care Home stands just off the North Circular at Muswell Hill, on the smooth bow-bend of Coppetts Road. From the outside, and from a distance, it looks like what it used to be—a row of Victorian workmen's cottages, turn-of-the-century poverty reinvented as tasteful nostalgia.

Closer in, you see the bars over the windows, riveted directly into the original brickwork, and the looming bulk of the new annex protruding backward at an acute angle, dwarfing the cottages themselves. If you're tuned in to stuff like that, maybe you also notice the magical prophylactics that they've put up beside the main door to discourage the dead: a sprig of myrtle for May, a necromantic circle bearing the words HOC FUGERE—flee this place—a crucifix, and an ornate blue enamel mezuzah. One way or another, you're dumped out of the Victorian reverie into an uncomfortable present.

I stepped in out of a night laden with a fresh freight of rain that had yet to fall onto thick carpet and the expertly canned smell of wild honeysuckle. But the Stanger has a hard time putting on a pretty face: as I pushed open the second set of doors and went on through into the lobby, I could already hear a huge commotion from somewhere further inside. Shouting voices, a woman—or maybe a man—crying, crashes of doors opening and closing. It all sat a little oddly with the soothing Vivaldi being played pianissimo over the speaker system. The nurse at the desk, Helen, was staring off down the corridor and looking like she wanted to bolt. She jerked her head around when she saw me, and I gave her a nod.

"Mr. Castor!" she said, checking her start of alarm. "Felix—It's him. Asmodeus. He's—" She pointed, but seemed unable to get any more words out.

"I heard," I said, tersely. "I'll go on through."

I broke into a trot as I went up the main corridor. This was my usual weekly visit: I still called it that, even though these days the interval between them had stretched out to a month or more. I was tied to this place by the loose elastic of ancient guilt, and every so often the pull became too insistent to ignore. But clearly tonight was going to be a departure from routine. There was something going on up ahead of me, and it was a violent, screaming kind of something. I didn't want to be anywhere near it, but Rafi was my responsibility and this was absolutely my job to sort out.

Rafi's room is in the new annex. I sometimes think, with a certain bitterness, that Rafi's room financed the new annex, because it had cost a medium-size fortune to have the walls, floor, and ceiling lined with silver. I went up past the low-security wards, hearing sobs and shouts and swearing from inside each one as I passed: every loud noise at the Stanger stirs up a host of echoes. As I rounded the corner at a jog, I saw a whole crowd of people clustered about ten feet away from Rafi's door, which seemed to be open. I was looking for Pen, and so I saw her first: she was tussling with two nurses, a man and a woman, and cursing like a longshoreman. Looking at Pen head-on, you always get the impression that she's taller than she is; the vividness of her green eyes and red-auburn hair somehow translates into a sense of imposing height, but in fact she stands a little over five feet tall. The two nurses weren't actually holding on to her, they were just blocking her way to the door and moving with her whenever she tried to slide around them—a very effective human wall.

The rest of the scene was like a bar fight taking place under local rules I wasn't familiar with. Webb, the director of the Stanger Home, sweating and red-faced, was trying to lay hands on Pen to pull her away from the door, but at the same time he was fighting shy of doing anything that might be construed as assault—and any time he got close she just smacked him away. The resulting ballet of twittery hand gestures and involuntary cringeing was strange in the extreme. Half a dozen nurses of both sexes jostled around them, none of them relishing a possibly actionable rumble with someone who wasn't an inmate and might have the money to sue. Two other Stanger staffers were down on the floor, apparently wrestling with each other.

I could hear the voices now—some of them, anyway, raised above the background babble.

"You'll kill him! You're going to kill him." This was Pen, shrill and urgent.

"—have a responsibility to the public, and to the other residents of the home, and I'm not going to be intimidated into—" Webb, partway through a sentence that had clearly been going on for a while and wasn't going to end any time soon.

But just as I pushed through the edges of the group, it was ended for him as a body came sailing through the open doorway and hit the corridor's farther wall with a solid, meaty sound before crashing to the carpeted floor. He was faceup, so I was able to recognize him as Paul, another male nurse, and probably the guy I liked best on the Stanger's staff. He was unconscious, his face flushed purple, and the hypodermic syringe that rolled from his hand was sheared off short as if by a samurai sword, clear liquid weeping from the cleanly sliced edge of the plastic ampoule.

Everyone stared at him with varying degrees of awe and alarm, but nobody made a move to help him or assess the damage. I took the opportunity to thread my way through the onlookers, heading for the empty stretch of corridor around the open door—no-man's-land. One of the two nurses who was blocking Pen—the male one—immediately turned his attention to me, clamping a heavy hand on my shoulder.

"Nobody's allowed through here," he told me, brusquely.

"Leave him!" Webb snapped. "That's Castor."

"Oh thank God!" said Pen, seeing me for the first time. She threw herself into my arms, and I gave her a reassuring hug. At the same time I looked down and realized that the two men on the ground weren't wrestling after all: the conscious one was hauling the unconscious one away from the door, leaving a feathery-edged smear of blood on the carpeted floor from some wound I couldn't see.

Pen's eyes were glistening with tears as she turned them pleadingly on me. "Fix, don't let them hurt him! It's not Rafi, it's Asmodeus. He can't help himself!"

"I know that. It's okay, Pen." I put as much conviction into those words as I could muster. "I'm here now. I'll sort this."

"One of my staff is still in there," Webb told me, cutting across Pen as she started to speak again. "We think she may be dead, but we can't get in to find out. Ditko is . . . frenzied, in a hypermanic state. And as you can see he's violent. I think I'm going to have to gas him."

Pen wailed at the word, and I wasn't surprised. The gas Webb was talking about is a mild nerve toxin—a tabun derivative called OPG, developed at Porton Down for military use but now illegal on any battlefield in the world. Ironically it had turned out to have therapeutic effects if you used it in tiny doses on Alzheimer's sufferers: it blocks the breakdown of acetylcholine in the brain, slowing memory loss. Then someone found out that zombies could use it in much larger doses to do more or less the same thing—slow down the inevitable breakdown of their minds as the processes of butyric decay turned complex electrochemical gradients into rancid sludge. So now the gas was legal in psychotherapeutic contexts, and actively recommended for the dead and undead—a loophole that still had half the civil rights lawyers in the world yelling in each other's face. The fact that it had sedative side effects just added to the confusion.

Using it on Rafi was a spiky proposition in any case, though. He was no zombie: just an ordinary living man with a tenacious passenger. And if Asmodeus was in the ascendant, it would take a big hit even to slow him down, which would mean that the side effects would be that much more painful and extreme. Some of them might even be permanent.

"Let me go in first," I suggested. "Maybe I can calm him down with some music."

Webb huffed and puffed, but unlike the big bad wolf he was actually very keen to avoid having the house blown down. He was looking for a way out of this that caused the minimum damage to life and property—especially property—and he had enough sense to see that I was probably it. After all, this wasn't the first time Rafi had played up: I'd proved my usefulness many times before this. "I'm not legally responsible for you," he reminded me. "You signed a waiver, and I've still got it on file. You go in there on your own recognizance, and if you're hurt—"

"You'll deny all knowledge of my activities," I finished, nodding. "And you won't put a penny in the collection box. Let's just take that shit as read, shall we?"

I turned my back on him and took a step toward Rafi's cell.

"I'm coming with you," Pen yelled, and she pushed her way between the two nurses, who weren't sure anymore what their brief was. I put up my hand to block her. "Better not, Pen," I muttered. "Asmodeus needs me alive, and that's the only thing I've got going for me here. Like you said, it's not Rafi. He won't hold back when he sees you: he may even take a smack at you out of pure spite."

She hesitated, still not convinced. I left her there and went forward, hoping she'd see sense: there was really no time to argue about it while I could see Webb plutzing and quivering his way toward ordering a gas attack. I gave the door a shave-and-a-haircut knock as I went through. It would probably have been safer to take a peek round the edge of the doorway first, but I was going to have to go in anyway: this way I went in with a certain amount of panache, even if I came out again on my arse with my head flying separately.

Stepping over the threshold meant going from carpeted floor to naked metal: an amalgam of steel and silver in the ratio of ten parts to one. It's there behind the plasterboard of the walls, too, shining out in a few places where Rafi has punched his fist through in a temper. My feet boomed hollowly on the metal plate, announcing my arrival even more emphatically than the knock. But Rafi didn't seem to notice me in any case: he was on the far side of the bare cell, kicking savagely at a sprawled form on the floor. Not the nurse, thank God: she was lying motionless just inside the door, a spidery trickle of blood on her forehead and her eyes closed. What Rafi was destroying was the meds trolley. Pills in a hundred party colors were strewn all over the floor and they crunched underfoot as I shifted my ground.

Out of the corner of my eye, I saw that Pen was kneeling down to check the nurse's pulse. I took my tin whistle out of my pocket and put it to my lips, but before I could play a note Rafi threw back his head and howled in what sounded like agony. He threw up his hands and pressed both clenched fists to his forehead, jerking spasmodically from side to side. Then with a deep-throated groan he drew his hands down his face from hairline to chin, digging his nails in deep so that he drew blood from eight parallel gashes.

I was going to have to put a wrench in this. I felt for the stops and blew an opening chord, as low as I could. Since he'd been completely ignoring me up to then, I was hoping to get a certain momentum going before he realized I was there; but at the first sound of the whistle, he spun to face me. I hiccupped into unintended silence. Rafi's pale, ascetically handsome face was strained, his thick black hair hanging in sweat-soaked ringlets, his eyes—pupils, whites, and all—were a black so intense they seemed to suck all the light out of the room. I'd seen the effect before, but somehow this was worse than all the other times. It was as though the blackness were brimming there, behind Rafi's eyes, ready to spill out and drown me.

"*Castor!*" he boomed, in a voice that was louder and harsher than a human throat should have been able to make: a voice like the shrieking intake of a jet engine. For a moment another face moved under his, almost surfacing through skull and muscle and red, stretched skin. "*Too sweet! Too fucking sweet!*"

If he hadn't tensed before he jumped, that might have been the last sound I ever heard. As it was, I just about had time to drop down and to the side, out of the reach of his clutching fingers. At the same time I blew a screaming, modulated discord that I'd used before on Rafi, to good and usually immediate effect.

This time I might as well have been playing "God Save the Queen" with my armpit. He turned in the air like a cat and caught me a glancing blow on the side of the head with his closed fist. There was a split second where my visual field shifted into juddering black-and-white: the whistle flew out of my hand, clattered to the floor a long way away. Then Rafi had his feet back under him and he was advancing on me at a brisk walk, grinning a Cheshire cat grin. Pen pressed herself against the wall, out of sight and out of mind, but she was watching everything that happened, looking for a chance to get that nurse out of the line of fire. Great plan: better than mine, anyway. Without my whistle, I was going to have my work cut out even staying alive here.

I threw a punch, which Rafi swatted aside without breaking stride. His response was devastating—his open hands, fingers as rigid as knitting needles, striking out so fast I heard the whiff of displaced air before I felt the agonizing impact. I staggered backward, trying to keep up some kind of a guard, but it was like being in front of a horizontal avalanche. I went sprawling back out into the corridor with Rafi on top of me, his hands now locking around my throat.

I was staring directly into those liquid black eyes, and I saw no mercy there. I broke his grip by punching outward against his wrists, but that didn't make as much difference as I was hoping for. Rafi strobed, his limbs seeming to be in too many places at once, and even though I'd knocked his hands away to left and right, his grip on my throat didn't slacken. I fought to suck in a breath: if I could breathe I could whistle, even without mechanical aids, but there was nothing doing. He squeezed tighter, and darkness bubbled up inside my head to match the two dark wells I was staring into.

Over Rafi's shoulder I saw Pen running toward me. She got a hold on Rafi's right arm, trying to dislodge it, but it slid through her hands somehow, dopplered, seeming once again to be in a lot of places at the same time. Then he shrugged and stiffened, his head snapping backward and thumping hard into her chest so that she tumbled backward, and got on with the serious business of throttling me.

I was probably two seconds or so from passing out, after which all bets would have been canceled and, no doubt, so would I. But suddenly there was a bigger, stockier shape looming up behind Rafi, and a muscular black arm locked around his neck. It was Paul. He looked strained and pale, which was scarcely surprising, but his movements were methodical: he used his greater weight and leverage to bend Rafi backward until his grip started to slacken on my throat. Rafi hissed voicelessly and threw up his hands to tear Paul's grip free.

Weak and dazed as I was, I forced myself to move, because it didn't look as though I'd be getting a second chance. I rolled hard, shifting my weight to throw Rafi further off his center of gravity, and at the same time I punched him with as much force as I could on the point of the jaw. Caught off balance, he slid sideways out of Paul's hands and we both scrambled clear.

I turned around with my arms up ready to defend myself against a renewed attack, but whatever was happening to Rafi now had made him forget all about me. He was still lying on the ground where he'd fallen, and another ululating howl of pain and desolation was pouring without pause out of his gaping mouth. It was as if my punch hadn't registered with him at all: whatever was hurting him, I could see it had nothing to do with me.

Paul knelt down beside Rafi and felt his pulse. He rolled Rafi's eyelids back and inspected his eyes, then extended the examination to gums and teeth, which was a risk I wouldn't have taken myself. Rafi kept on howling, directly into Paul's face: he seemed to have forgotten our existence.

Two more male nurses loomed over us, looking down at Rafi as if they were wondering where it might be safe to take ahold of him. Paul glanced up, saw them, and pointed into the cell. "Karen," he shouted over Rafi's inhuman keening. "She's still inside. Get her out of there." They snapped to attention like soldiers, turned around, and went into the cell.

From where I was kneeling I had a good view through the doorway. I saw the two men kneel beside the fallen nurse, one of them touching a hand to her forehead. Then I saw her move, flinching away from the touch. She was hurt, maybe badly hurt, but she wasn't dead. Caught between relief and delayed shock, I felt a sickly floating sensation rise inside me, filling me like sour gas: I doubled over and threw up copiously. It was a few moments before I could take notice of my surroundings again.

When I did, I realized that Rafi's siren-sharp wail had died away into abrupt silence. Pen had him cradled in her arms, and Paul was kneeling beside her, his forefinger on Rafi's bare wrist again and an abstracted frown on his face.

Dr. Webb approached us with a certain caution, eyeing the mess I'd just made on the carpet. Then his gaze traversed to Rafi, his head in Pen's lap as she murmured reassurances to him and smoothed his sweat-slicked hair off his forehead. Rafi seemed to be asleep now—a profound, exhausted sleep, his chest rising and falling slowly with his long, deep breaths. Still, Webb's eyes continually kept flicking back to him as he snapped out orders to his staff to start putting the place back together.

I stood up, my legs shaky, and pulled my crushed shirt collar back into some kind of shape, wincing at the pain in my equally crushed throat. "What set this off?" I asked Webb, my voice sounding hoarse and flat.

He gave a bleak snort. "Nothing," he said. "Nothing at all. Karen and Paul went in to give him his evening meds, and he took them. One moment he was fine, the next—well, you saw. He started screaming, and when Karen tried to calm him he lashed out at her. We're lucky she wasn't killed."

I nodded dumbly at that. I couldn't think of anything to say. Webb wasn't expecting an answer, though. "Castor," he said, "this brings forward a discussion we were going to have to have in any case. When we took Ditko on, we did so in the belief that we could help him. We clearly can't. He needs dedicated facilities of a kind that we can't offer."

I looked down at Pen. She wasn't hearing this, fortunately. "There aren't any dedicated facilities for what Rafi's got," I pointed out, but that was bullshit and he knew it. There just weren't any that I wanted to deliver him to.

"There's the MOU," Webb said.

"Rafi's not a lab rat."

"He's not mentally ill, either. He doesn't belong here."

"We've got a contract," I pointed out, playing my ace.

Webb trumped it. "'Voidable where the welfare of staff or other inmates is at stake,'" he quoted from memory. "I don't think there's any argument about that."

I shrugged. "We'll talk."

Webb shook his head. "No, we won't. Make alternative arrangements, Castor. You have twenty-eight days."

"You're all heart, Webb," I croaked. "You'll have to toughen up or people will start taking advantage of you."

He gave me an austere, contemptuous look. "Nobody can say you didn't try," he said coldly.

———

Out in the grounds the moon was up, full and huge, turning everything into a Mercurochrome photograph of itself. I took a turn through the rose garden, enjoying the peace and quiet. It was only relative: there were still some shouts and moans from inside the building, but after Rafi's endless, agonizing foghorn howl it sounded a lot like silence. Rafi was sleeping now, but Pen wouldn't let anyone else touch him for the time being. I thought I'd give them half an hour, then go back inside and see if I was needed.

I leaned against the sundial and looked down a trellised avenue canopied with sweet-smelling blooms. It didn't frame much of a view, though: just a high fence with an inward-tilting fringe of razor wire at the top, and beyond that the six lanes of the North Circular, where even at this hour a steady river of headlights flowed on by.

Alternative arrangements. That was really easy for Webb to say, especially with the gods of the small print on his side. Not so easy to do, though: not unless I wanted to take the route that Webb had suggested, and give Rafi over to the tender mercies of the Metamorphic Ontology Unit at Queen Mary's in Paddington. But that was a last-ditch, desperation kind of thing, and I didn't think we were quite there yet. Much as I respected my old sparring partner Jenna-Jane Mulbridge on an intellectual level, I knew better than anyone that she had some shortcomings where bedside manner was concerned. And that her heart and human feelings were in long-term storage underneath a crossroads somewhere.

While I was still propping up the sundial, making the place look untidy, three small figures loped out of the foliage about fifty yards away and flitted across the lawn in absolute silence. They were in a triangle formation, with the largest of the three in front, the other two flanking and following her. There were some trees on the far side of the lawn, but trees didn't slow them down: they raced on unheeding, their slender bodies sliding through wood as though wood were air. When they got to the wall that separated the Stanger from Coldfall Wood, the girl in the lead—she was about thirteen, or rather had been that age when she died—stopped and looked across at me. She tossed back a full head of ash-blond hair and gave me a wave. I waved back. Then she turned and walked on through the wall, where her two younger companions had already gone on before her.

These were the ghosts of three little girls whom the original Charles Stanger had murdered in the late forties—before being sent down for life and endowing the institution that now carries his name. They'd spent the next fifty years tied to the stones of the old cottages like dogs chained up in a yard. Most ghosts are tethered to a particular place, more often than not the place where they died. It was just a cruel irony that in this case it meant the girls had to rub shoulders with the criminally insane for the rest of eternity—or at least, for as long as the Stanger stayed open. But about a year or so ago I'd given them a private concert: used my tin whistle to play a fragment of an exorcism to them in this same garden, so that although they weren't banished from the place, they were free to leave it. Since then I'd heard rumors of sightings as far afield as the Trocadero and Shadwell Stair, but they still seemed to use the Stanger as a base. I guess they were used to the place now: after half a century, it was as close to being home as anywhere they knew. I kept expecting them to move on—I mean, on to whatever else there is when this world has worn out its welcome—but obviously they still hadn't taken that inevitable step.

I walked on through the gardens, eventually circling around to the far side of the building, where they gave out at last onto the asphalt apron of the car park. It was after midnight now, so the place was deserted except for a few staff cars and Pen's old Mondeo. Paul was leaning against the side of an ambulance in lonely splendor, smoking a fairly pungent cigarillo. He was looking glum.

"How's life?" I asked, slowing to a halt.

He blew out smoke, shook his head in disgust. "You should've asked me when I fuckin' had one, man," he said morosely. "My old lady keeps telling me to give this up, and fuck if she ain't right. What do I need it for? My back feels like I did ten rounds with Tyson, my left eye's closing over. Karen's most likely got a concussion. And my man Rafael's righteously fucked, poor bastard."

I was impressed that he could still worry about Rafi when Rafi's evil passenger had just nearly done for the both of us. I was reminded once again of how much there was going on under that tanklike exterior. "Well, I'm glad you put your retirement off until after tonight, anyway," I said, meaning it. "You probably saved my life."

"Yeah, you're welcome."

"Your boss is an arsehole, though."

"Got that right."

I leaned against the side of the ambulance next to him, but upwind of his cigar. "And Rafi will be okay. At least, he'll be none the worse for anything that happened tonight."

Paul raised his eyebrows as he pondered this. "Cuts all over his face," he mused. "Two broken fingers. Maybe a broken jaw. That shit on his chest looked like blisters—like he was catching fire from the inside."

"But you know I'm right. The fingers will reset themselves tonight. The jaw, too, if I actually broke it. The gouges and the burns will already have healed up: if you looked right now, there wouldn't be a damn thing to see. Rafi's got a very healthy immune system. I guess it's all the good food and exercise."

Paul gave me a slightly fish-eyed stare, checking to see if any of that second-rate irony was at his expense. Then he shook his head again, giving it up. "That lady of yours," he said, after taking another deep drag on the cigar, "she's a class act, Castor. About as big as a high-heel shoe, but she just went for Rafael back there like it was a fair fight. Went for Dr. Webb, too." He grinned wickedly. "That was the high-light of the fucking day. Truth."

"Yeah, Pen is one of a kind," I agreed. "She's not mine, though. I mean, she's just a friend." A whole lot of memories surged up from one of the less-frequented areas of my mind: I shoved them right back down again. "She's—she and Rafi used to be—together. When we were all at university, they were"—I groped for a phrase that accurately defined Pen and Rafi's relationship, but there wasn't one— "an item," I finished lamely. "But it didn't last. Rafi was the flit-and-sip type."

We stood in silence for a few seconds.

"He was my best friend," I said, aware of how bizarre and unhealthy all this sounded. "Pen's, too, both before and after the sweat-and-roses stuff. Everybody liked him. You'd like him, too, if you met him."

"If I *met* him?" Paul's intonation was pained.

"You know what I mean."

"Yeah," he admitted. "I guess I do. Kind of. I've always wanted to ask you, though. What exactly is that thing inside him?"

"Asmodeus. He's a demon. A fucking big one, too. A lot of the lit-erature on the subject says—"

"The literature?" Paul shook his head, wondering. "What, like the *Lancet? Scientific American?*"

"Not exactly, no. I'm talking about books written by carpet-chewing natural philosophers five hundred years ago. Grimoires. Magical text-books. Anyway, they put Asmodeus close to the top of the infernal pecking order. Not someone you want to mess with. But Rafi did just that. He tried to summon Asmodeus about two years ago. I think he was looking to do some kind of Faust thing: buy a shitload of forbid-den knowledge from before the world was made. It didn't work out that way, though. Somehow Asmodeus got into him and started to burn him up from the inside."

The words, banal and deadpan as they were, stirred up a series of disconnected impressions in my mind—some of the component parts of a night I still couldn't forget. Because of the way my mind works, it was mostly the sounds that stayed with me. Rafi's breathing, harsh and shallow and with longer and longer gaps between the in breaths. The grating laughter that was coming from his throat, welling up like blood out of the night-black void that showed when his mouth gaped open. The endless mumble and hiss of boiling water: we'd dumped Rafi into a bathtub full of ice because patches of his skin were going from red to black, but after about a minute the ice was water and the water was bubbling like a witch's cauldron.

"You were there?" Paul asked, sounding—to put it politely—a little skeptical. It's not just cops: everyone draws their lines in the sand, sooner or later, and once they're drawn it takes a lot to shift them.

"His girlfriend called me in the middle of the night. She heard him say my name, and it sounded like his own voice, not the voice of the thing inside him, so she found my number in the back of his diary. By the time I got there, it looked like I might already be too late, but I tried anyway."

"Tried what, exactly."

"I played him a tune."

He nodded. I'd already told him over a couple of beers what it is I do for a living, and how I do it. "You see," I went on, reluctantly, "I was assuming it was a *human* spirit inside him. A ghost. I'd never even met a demon back then. So I listened for a human spirit, and when I found it I started to play it out of him. Then about ten minutes in, I realized that what I'd dredged up was Rafi's own soul. I was dispossessing him from his body—finishing what Asmodeus had started.

"I tried to undo the damage I'd already done. I switched keys in mid-tune, played the opposite of what my instincts were telling me to play, in the hope that I could pull Rafi back into his own flesh. And it sort of worked."

"Sort of?"

I nodded bleakly. "Yeah, sort of. I stuck Rafi back together again— and at the same time I stuck Asmodeus to Rafi, which wasn't part of the plan. They've been trapped in there together ever since. That's why

Asmodeus tends to leave me alone, most of the time—he knows he's going to need me sooner or later if he's ever going to get free again. He's just waiting for me to figure out how to do it." I scowled, fingering one of the bruises on my shoulder. "Don't know what the hell went wrong tonight. He knew who I was, but for once he didn't seem to give a fuck. In fact, he really seemed happy to be getting a crack at me. Like he hadn't expected it."

There was a long silence. I could see how a lot of this must strike Paul as total bullshit, even after what he'd seen. It would have sounded ridiculous to me if I hadn't lived through it, if I hadn't lived through worse things since. All those things in heaven and earth that philosophy tries not to dream about.

Eventually he opened his mouth to say something, but we were interrupted by the sound of high heels on wet asphalt. Pen came out from the shadow of the building and headed over to us. I looked a question at her and she managed a weak smile.

"He's sleeping like a baby," she said.

"Good," I answered. "From past experience, he probably won't surface until sometime late morning. Whenever Asmodeus takes over like that, Rafi burns up a hell of a lot of energy all at once. The best thing we can do now is to let him sleep it off in his own good time."

Pen nodded, but I could see from her face that she didn't buy my "time heals all wounds" approach.

"He never has," she said, "taken over in quite that way. Asmodeus is cruel, and spiteful, and a little bit insane, but that—" She finished off the sentence with a shrug.

She was right, too. The berserker fit was a new one in my experience, and I couldn't see what the demon had to gain by it. In the past Asmodeus had told me he was playing a waiting game, in the knowledge that sooner or later I'd figure out a way to undo whatever it was I'd done and set him and Rafi free from each other. Tonight it seemed he'd run out of patience and out of whatever demons have instead of sanity.

I tried to think of something vaguely reassuring to say, but Paul preempted me by throwing down his unfinished cigar, stamping it out, and stretching his shoulders like somebody warming up for a workout.

"Gotta say good night to you people," he said. "I'm on until two a.m., and that's my break over. You take my advice, you should get some sleep yourselves. The both of you look wiped." He gave us a nod and headed back into the building.

"Thanks again," I called to his retreating back.

"No problem. I'll send in a bill."

I turned to Pen. "That sounds like sense to me," I said. "Unless you're up for some chicken vindaloo? The exotic delights of East Finchley are on our doorstep."

Pen shook her head.

"I'm meant to be going out," she said. "With Dylan."

Dylan? Oh yeah, Dylan Forster—Dr. Feelgood. I'd sort of forgotten about him. The truth was, I kept on forgetting about him again every time Pen mentioned him. I'd long ago abandoned any thoughts of rekindling whatever the two of us had had, but on some level it still disturbed me to think of her going out with someone else. She was part of a triangle whose other two corners were me and Rafi. I knew how unfair that was, and I hated myself for having any reservations when Pen tried to scrape up a little happiness for herself, so whenever she mentioned her affluent, passionate, druid-in-training, Lexus-driving, trust-me-I'm-a-doctor new boyfriend, I put a certain amount of effort into sounding more positive and enthusiastic than I felt.

"Well, even better," I said now. "Take your mind off this stuff for a few hours. Hope it's something good."

"I don't think he had anywhere particular in mind. He just said it was going to be a murderous day, and he absolutely had to see me at the end of it so there'd be something to balance out all the shitty stuff. I told him I was going to see Rafi, and he said he'd meet me afterwards."

She gave me a brief but fierce hug and climbed into the car.

"Drop you somewhere?" she asked, holding the door open for a moment so we could go on talking.

I mulled that one over, but not for very long. My mind was still crawling with the dread that I'd felt when I saw the nurse lying crumpled on the floor of Rafi's cell like yesterday's laundry. Right then I wanted to be out in the open for a little while, and by myself.

I shook my head. "Thanks, but I think I need the walk," I said.

"Then I'll see you tomorrow." She slammed the door, revved up, and pulled away, the Mondeo rocking a little on its wheelbase because it was getting on a bit now and the suspension was more or less shot.

The night was mine. Woot.

As it turned out, I needed more than just a walk. I spent the next few hours trying to shake off that sense of unease in a string of pubs and insomniac water holes from Finchley to King's Cross and beyond. Somewhere along the way, chugalugging my fifth or sixth whisky on the rocks in some Irish-themed nowhere on Kentish Town Road, I realized that what I was feeling had nothing to do with what had happened at the Stanger. It was something in the air, hanging over the whole oblivious city like an ectoplasmic slagheap waiting to start its inexorable downhill slide.

I got back home sometime after three a.m. Pen's place is off Turnpike Lane. It's big and old, built in a nameless fin de siècle style that's even heavier than High Victorian, and it's on the side of a hill so that the basement, where Pen lives, becomes ground level at the back of the house and gives out directly onto the garden. I checked for lights, as I always do: if she'd still been up I'd have gone and split a bottle or at least a glass with her. But everything was dark and silent. She was probably staying over with Dylan at his flat out in Pinner—a sign of how besotted she must be, because the house was a lot more than just somewhere where she hung up her boots, it was also the seat of her own very personal religion, the place of her power, the cave where she was high priestess and sibyl in residence.

My room is up in the eaves, as far away from all that earth-mother stuff as I can get, which suits me fine. Apart from anything else, that's a lot of stairs for anyone to climb if they want to come and find me, and I'll usually hear them coming.

I barely managed to shrug out of my clothes, then I hit the bed and was asleep before I bounced.

I don't know about Rafi, but I sure as hell didn't see a lot of Sunday morning. I woke up at the lag end of lunchtime, bright sunlight cutting through the gap in my curtains like a maniac with a chainsaw. I had a furry mouth and a hangover that was as much psychological as physical. Or animistic, maybe: a hangover of the spirit. How the hell do you cure that? A hair of the god that bit you?

Still no sign of Pen. I breakfasted alone in the sun-bleached kitchen, feeling a slight sense of unreality. The night had seemed so dark, the weight of foreboding so real, it was odd and even a little aggravating that nothing had happened. I felt as though reality was impugning my gut instincts.

But if there *was* some severing sword suspended over London, it was pretty firmly attached, and probably conformed to all relevant EU safety standards. I prowled about the house all day like a hermit with hemorrhoids, waiting for that doom-drenched feeling to revisit me. But it didn't, and disaster didn't strike. In the end I was reduced to watching old episodes of *Fawlty Towers* on some cable channel, and I kept forgetting to laugh.

Pen rolled home early in the evening to find me in the basement, feeding strips of fresh sheep's liver to her two ravens, Edgar and Arthur. She was touched.

"You didn't need to do that, Fix," she said, squeezing my hand—a mistake, since it was dripping with blood and oozy bits of tissue. "They don't mind if I'm a bit late. But thanks."

"I'm always afraid that if I don't keep them happy I'm going to be set meal B," I groused. "They're getting to be the size of bloody vultures."

She seemed tired, and not all that happy: normally she came back from dates with Dr. Feelgood walking on air, so I was solicitous—and maybe a little curious.

"How was your night?" I asked, waggling my eyebrows suggestively.

She shrugged, gave a faint smile. "Okay," she said. "It was . . . yeah. It was okay."

I waited for clarification, and after meeting my eyes in silence for a moment or two she shrugged again. "Dylan was really tired," she said. "He'd had an awful shift, clearing up other people's messes. He wasn't supposed to be on duty today, but he said he had to, just for an hour or so—to check up on some of the work he did yesterday. He didn't trust the doctor who was supposed to take over from him. So I went shopping, over at Camden Market, and he joined me there for a late lunch."

"Did you check in on Rafi?"

"Yeah. We went over there this afternoon. But he was still asleep."

"Told you. He'll wake up right as rain."

She nodded glumly—then visibly brightened as another thought struck her. "Dylan says he might be able to prescribe some stuff that will keep Asmodeus under for more of the time. He wants me to have a word with Webb about letting him in to give Rafi some tests."

I raised my eyebrows. "Worth a try," I said. "I thought you said he was a rag-and-bone man."

"Bones and joints," she corrected, looking at me severely. "But he interned in endocrinology."

She followed me as I walked through into her cramped, pie-slice-shaped bathroom and washed my bloody hands in the sink. I was trying to get away from another lecture about how wonderful Dylan is—Pen's favorite theme for the past few weeks—but it wasn't going to be that easy.

"He's really sweet," she said. "You'd think he'd want to stay well away from Rafi, considering—you know—what he means to me. But he just wants to make me happy."

"Ask him for a blank prescription pad before it wears off," I suggested. She punched me in the shoulder and I took it like a man.

I'd already learned the hard way that sarcastic comments about Dr. Feelgood met with terrible retribution. He was an odd guy for Pen to be dating, in some ways; she wasn't drawn to material things, and affluence normally struck her as a sign of spiritual malaise rather than anything to aspire to. But Dylan's wealth and success and smoked silver Lexus were counterbalanced by the fact that he was an ovate—a sort of junior officer in some druidical training system, learning to be one of nature's high priests. That was how she'd met him—at some solstice-related knees-up on a windswept hill in Pembrokeshire. Pen's own flavor of paganism didn't have ranks and hierarchies, but she liked it a lot that this well-to-do young doctor was groping toward spiritual truth rather than just worrying about his backswing. And he understood about Rafi, which most people flat-out don't.

Yeah, the guy was clearly a saint. It was probably just as well I'd never met him: if opposites attract we'd probably fall head over heels in love with each other and leave Pen out in the cold.

"Are you feeling a sense of choking terror that you can't pin down to anything in particular?" I asked her.

It might have seemed like an odd question in some circumstances, but coming from me Pen knows it's like a doctor asking you if you've been off your food. She searched her mind. It's both capacious and somewhat idiosyncratically arranged, so it took a while. "No," she said at last. "Just the usual choking terrors, and I can pretty much account for those. Why, Fix?"

I dried my hands and went back out into the living room. Arthur was clashing his beak and shrugging his wings open and shut—his way of begging for more, but I was all out of goodies. I skirted around him, keeping my distance in case he decided to search me to make sure. Pen leaned in the doorway, arms folded, looking at me with some concern.

"I don't know," I admitted. "Something coming in on channel death. Or maybe nothing. You know how these things go."

Just by reading her face I could see her decide to change the subject. "Grambas called," she said. "Some men tried to deliver something at the office yesterday, but you weren't there. He's got it in the lockup behind the shop."

I grimaced. A pilgrimage out to Harlesden first thing on a Monday morning wasn't a thrilling prospect. On the other hand, that was meant to be my place of work, and since I owe Pen so much back rent that she could probably legally impound both my kidneys and sell them in Hong Kong, she feels fairly strongly that I should spend more time over there than I do.

But she sympathized with my raw mood, and as usual her sympathy took a concrete form. She cleared the table—by tipping all the newspapers, magazines, coasters, and unopened mail onto the floor—and went to get her tarot deck.

"Pen," I said, regretting that I'd said anything, "you know I don't hold with this stuff."

"It never hurts to get a second opinion," she said.

"From who? Whose opinion are we getting? Pieces of laminated cardboard don't know jack shit about what's going down in the world, Pen. Nobody ever tells them anything."

"It's not the cards, Fix. It's you, and it's me, and it's the *weltgeist*—the world-spirit."

I winced and waved her quiet. The world-spirit. Right, because there's a consciousness in back of the universe and it loves all its children: we get daily evidence of that in terms of famine, plague, and flood. I don't buy the tarot for the same reason that I don't buy religion: the hopes and fears of ordinary people stick up out of the miracles like bones out of a spavined horse. My universe doesn't work like that, and the only spirits in it are the ones that are my stock in trade.

She gave me the cards to shuffle. I considered palming death and top-decking him while she wasn't looking, but she hates it when I do that, so I played fair.

She dealt out a triskele spread—three cards in a triangle, two more crossed in the center. Ordinarily she'd have done a full ten-card spread, but she knows my limits, so she was keeping it short and sweet.

She turned over the cover and the cross—the two cards in the middle. They were an inverted ace of wands and the hanged man. Pen blinked, clearly surprised and a little unsettled by the conjunction.

"That's really weird," she said.

"Tall dark stranger?" I hazarded.

"Don't be stupid, Fix. It's just that those two cards, together like that . . . they mean exactly what you just said. Spiritual energy— negative spiritual energy—in a kind of suspension. Blocked. Frozen. Penned up."

I made no comment, but she didn't expect any. She turned over the root card at lower left: the page of swords, again inverted. "A message," Pen interpreted. "News. All the page cards mean something dawning, something being announced. I think . . . because it's upside down . . . a problem that doesn't get solved, or that gets solved in the wrong way. Fix, if someone asks for your help with something, go in carefully. One step at a time."

The bud card at lower right was old death himself, which as we all know doesn't mean death at all. Pen started to make her speech about change and flux, and I made the "wrap it up" gesture that TV floor managers use. "It's another bad combination," she said stubbornly, refusing to be bullied. "The page of wands, and death. Forget what I said about being careful: you're going to trip up and fall on your face. But it's only the bud, it's not the flower."

The flower is the apex of the triangle. Pen turned it over, and we both looked at it. Justice. I never look at those scales without thinking of Hamlet. "Use every man after his desert, and who should 'scape whipping?" I don't want justice: I want to cop a plea.

Pen gave me a look, and I shook my head—but the querent doesn't get to have the last word, even if it's only a gesture.

"Things will balance out," she said. "Actions will have the consequences they were always going to have. For better or worse."

"Which?" I asked. "Better, or worse?"

"We won't know until it happens."

"Christ, I hate these little bastards."

She gave up on spirituality and got the whisky out. On some things, at least, we still see eye to eye.

Chapter Three

Harlesden is like Kilburn without the scenic beauty—the stamping ground of Jamaican gangsters with itchy trigger fingers, predatory minicab drivers whose cars are their offices, and a great nation of feral cats. Oh, and zombies: for some reason, those who've risen in the body seem to congregate in large numbers on the deserted streets of the soon-to-be-demolished Stonehouse Estate. It's a setting that shows them off to very good advantage.

My office is in Craven Park Road, next to the Grambas Kebab House—or rather, my door is next to their door. The actual room where I conduct my meager and occasional business is on the first floor, directly over Grambas's eternally bubbling deep fryers. On bad days I can see an intimation of hell in that image.

The sign over the door still says F. CASTOR ERADICATIONS, which these days is a pretty outrageous lie. I'm not quite as free and easy as I used to be about toasting ghosts: I can't even remember the last time I did it, which on the whole is probably a good thing. But a man needs to have some stock in trade, and God didn't give me the shoulders or the temperament for hard labor. So I'd finally taken a step that I'd been considering for a while now—and it looked like today would be the day that made it official.

At ten on a rain-sodden May morning, Grambas hadn't even hefted the first doner yet. I knocked on his door and waited, wondering if he was awake. I got my answer when the window above and to the right of my head opened and a shiny bald head was thrust out of it. A pair of watery brown eyes stared down at me, taking their time to focus. To the waist, which mercifully was as far as I could see, Grambas was naked.

"Fuck," he said thickly. "It never stops. Come back at noon, Castor."

"Throw me down the keys," I suggested. "I only need to get that package out of the lockup."

He sighed heavily, nodded, and withdrew. The keys came flying out of the window a few moments later, and I almost went under the wheels of an ice cream van as I stepped backward to catch them. I went into the alley alongside the shop and let myself into the backyard through a door whose hinges were only held together by rust. The lockup, though, has a stout steel-reinforced door and three padlocks: Grambas knows his neighbors well, and though he forgives them their vices he doesn't see a need to finance them.

I took the padlocks off and left them hanging open in their eyebolts. It comes naturally to me to assess the professional credentials of any locks I encounter: I learned lock-picking from a master, and though the world has moved on into realms of electronic key-matching and double-redundant combination codes, I'm still okay with the bog-standard stuff that most people use. One of these three locks was generic, without even a manufacturer's mark; the second was a venerable Squire, and the third was a sexy little beast from the Master Lock titanium series. Numbers one and two I could have handled without a key any day of the week, but for number three I'd have needed a very long run-up indeed. I'm not saying I couldn't have done it, but there'd have had to be a damn good reason why I was trying.

Inside, the lockup was obsessively, immaculately clean. One wall was piled almost to the ceiling with neatly stacked boxes: on the other side, three chest freezers stood in a row like coffins. My package lay on the floor in the middle, with the single word "CASTOR" scrawled across it in thick black marker pen. It was five feet long, one foot broad, and only an inch or so thick. I picked it up, and borrowed Grambas's toolbox on my way out. Mine consists of three wrenches and a ball of string, and I last saw it in 1998. I snapped the padlocks back on again behind me and went back around to the street.

I'd had the new sign made to the exact measurements of the old one, so this was a job that was just about within the scope of my meager DIY skills. I could even use the same screws, apart from one that had rusted through and therefore snapped off as I was getting it out. In spite of that minor setback, and the rain coming on heavier while I worked, within the space of about ten minutes F. CASTOR ERADI- CATIONS had become FELIX CASTOR SPIRITUAL SERVICES. I looked at it with a certain satisfaction. It was a circumlocution I was stealing from a dead man, but hey, he'd died trying to kill me and he'd thieved from me on occasion, too, so I wasn't going to beat myself up about that. The important thing was that I wasn't an offense to the Trades Description Act anymore. Now I just had to sit back and wait for the clients to start pouring in.

As to what spiritual services *were*, exactly, I'd worry about that some other time. I was sure I'd know them when I saw them.

When I took Grambas's toolbox back round to the yard, he was coming out of the lockup carrying a gallon drum of frying oil in each hand. He stopped when he saw me, and put them down. "I forgot to tell you," he said. "You got a customer. Two, in fact."

I raised my eyebrows. That was a novelty these days. "When?" I demanded.

"This morning. About seven o'clock. They were standing in the rain out there when Maya came back from the wholesaler. She felt sorry for them. In fact she wouldn't stop feeling sorry for them, and she wouldn't shut up about it, so in the end I put some pants on and went down. They were still there, waiting for you to show. I told them they should leave a number and I'd call them when you turned up." He dug in his pocket, fished out a table napkin, which he handed to me. There was a phone number written across it in Grambas's lopsided, up-and-down handwriting.

"What did they look like?" I asked him.

"Wet."

In the office I did the usual triage on the utilities bills and the usual ruthless cull on the rest of the mail, most of which is of the kind where you can tell it's a scam or a speeding fine without even opening the envelope. The phone messages take longer, and some of those I had to follow up with calls of my own, but none of them were what you could call work. Not paying work, anyway. There was one from Coldwood asking me to call him, but I decided I'd put that off until later in the day. There was one from Pen, telling me that Coldwood had called the house, too, about five minutes after I left.

And there was one from Juliet.

"Hello, Felix." I was rummaging in the filing cabinet, but that voice—plucking on the bass strings of my nervous system—brought me upright and turned me around to face the phone as though she might actually be there. "I want your advice on something. It's a little unusual, and I'd like you to see it for yourself. You'd have to get over to Acton, though, so I'll understand if you say no. Call me."

I did. Juliet, I should point out, is only a professional acquaintance of mine. True, I'd crawl on my belly to Jerusalem to turn that business relationship into something more torrid and sweat-streaked, but so would any other man who meets her and I'd guess more than half of the women. She's a succubus (retired): getting people aroused and not thinking straight is part of how her species hunts and feeds.

Call return didn't work, but I had Juliet's number written down on a card that I carried in my wallet: like I said earlier, I almost never used it, because there was almost never any point. She stayed—nominally—in a room at a women's refuge in Paddington. It had struck me as odd, at first, but it made a crazy kind of sense: men had abused her and controlled her until she got out from under and devoured them body and soul. In reality, though, the room was just a place where she stored her few belongings: she didn't need to sleep, and she liked the open air, so she never spent much time there herself.

Her phone rang for long enough for me to consider giving up, but it's rare enough to get a ring tone rather than the busy signal, so I held out. It's not really her phone at all: it's in the communal kitchen of the refuge, shared by all two dozen or so of the residents. After a minute or so it was finally picked up by Juliet herself, so my luck was in again. I made a mental note to buy a lottery ticket.

"Hello?"

"It's me," I said. "What's the deal?"

"Oh, hello, Felix. Thanks for getting back to me."

"Well, I'm still your sensei, right? Can't leave you running around on your own out there."

This was one of the more ridiculous aspects of our relationship. Juliet—her real name is Ajulutsikael—had originally been raised from hell to kill and devour me because I was asking awkward questions that a pimp named Damjohn didn't want answered. But then she decided that living on earth was preferable to going home to the arse-end of hell, so she bailed out on the job and let me live—on condition that I taught her the exorcism game. So I found myself giving a work experience placement and tax advice to an entity several thousands of years old, who if she ever got the munchies during the working day could suck my soul out through any bodily orifice or appurtenance she chose. It had been interesting. Many years from now I might even get an unbroken night's sleep again.

"So is this work, or what is it?" I went on, pushing those memories firmly back down into the fetid oubliette of my subconscious.

"I have a commission," she said, sidestepping the question. "At a church in West London. St. Michael's, on Du Cane Road—it's right opposite Wormwood Scrubs."

"And—?"

"And I'd like a second opinion on something."

"Are you being deliberately oblique and mysterious?"

"Yes."

"Fair enough. I'll come on over when I'm done here. Is around six okay?"

"Perfect. Thank you, Felix. It's been a long time. I look forward to seeing you."

"Yeah," I said. "Likewise. Catch you later, Jules."

I hung up. Damn if I wasn't sweating. Just her voice, and I was sweating.

I had to get my mind onto another track. Remembering Grambas's napkin I took it out of my pocket: the numbers were slightly smeared by raindrops from when he'd passed it to me in the yard, but still legible. The first digits were "07968," so it was obviously a mobile.

I dialed.

"Hello?" A man's voice, hesitant and over-careful, as if he expected bad news.

"This is Felix Castor," I said. "You called by my office this morning."

"Mr. Castor!" The sudden excitement added a whole new palette of colors to the guy's voice. I wish I could have that effect on some of the women I meet. "Thank you for getting back to us. Thanks so much. Are you at your office now?"

"Yes, I am. If you'd like to arrange an appointment—"

"We'll be right there. I'm sorry, I mean can we come and see you now? We're very close by. Would that be convenient?"

I considered a face-saving lie: it's never a great idea to let a client see that you're instantly available, because they draw all sorts of inferences about your caseload. On the other hand, it didn't sound like I'd be having to work too hard to sell myself here.

So, "Sure," I said. "Come on over."

They introduced themselves as Melanie and Stephen Torrington—Mel and Steve. Nice people. I could see why Grambas's fiancée, Maya, had instinctively sympathized. They both looked to be in their late thirties, well-dressed and well-groomed, affluent but not making a whole big thing out of it. Actually, there might have been one other thing that triggered the sympathy, and I was surprised that Grambas hadn't mentioned it. The whole of the left side of Melanie's face was a purple mass of bruising, her eye swollen half out of its socket.

Stephen was tall and blond with a rich tan that could even have been natural, although he sure as hell hadn't gotten it in Harlesden. His slate-gray eyes could have given his face a hard cast, but the expression—self-effacing, open, slightly nervous—took a lot of the edge off it. He wore a nicely cut dark gray suit—too nice, and with too good a hang, to have come off the rack—and a sky-blue tie with a lacquered tiepin in the shape of a judge's gavel. He also had a black plastic bin-liner full of something or other, clutched tightly in both hands so that he had to put it down to shake my hand. The bin-liner didn't exactly go with the ensemble, but I figured we'd get to it in due course. And the handshake, which I'd hoped might give me some measure of the man underneath the tan, told me almost nothing. Sometimes whatever sense it is that lets me spy on the dead lets me overhear the emotions of the living, too, through skin-to-skin contact. From Stephen Torrington I got nothing but a burning thread of determination that overrode everything else.

Melanie was also blond, and also tall—a match made in heaven, obviously, or at least at some very exclusive country club on the way to heaven—and judging from the intact side, she had a beautifully sculpted face with aristocratic cheekbones and vivid blue eyes dusted with flecks of a lighter shade, like highlights. The ugly, swollen tissue on the left side sort of ruined the effect, though. She looked as though she'd been in a bad car accident—or as though someone had bounced her off a wall.

Like Steve, she was immaculately dressed and exuded wealth and status. Like him, she seemed to be locked inside a sarcophagus of dense emotion that I felt would have rung aloud if I'd tapped it with a finger. She kept her arms rigidly folded, hugging herself as if for comfort. The handshake here revealed complex, overlapping skeins of positive and negative affect: fear, pride, shame, ferocious love, more fear—a cat's cradle of emotions that shouldn't make it into each other's company.

Steve said he was a solicitor for a family firm in Stoke Newington—not quite a partner, but almost there. Melanie was a barrister, which was how they'd met. They'd been married for eighteen years. This paltry small talk was as stiff and awkward as if I'd been asking them where and how they contracted syphilis.

Things were going to be awkward in other ways, too: with three people in it, my office was already feeling a little crowded. Add to that the fact that the milk I'd left in the portable fridge had soured, turned green, and mutated into a new life form since the last time I was here, and I'd had to hide the fungus-sprouting mugs behind the filing cabinet, and my professional facade was hanging even more askew than it usually does. Once I'd got them sitting down I couldn't even offer them coffee.

Straight down to business, then.

"What can I do for you?" I asked.

"Our daughter," Mel mumbled, her voice slurred and thickened slightly by the swelling on the left side of her jaw. Having said that, she seemed to run out of words.

"Abbie," Steve took up. "Abigail. She's gone missing." Where Mel's voice had been carefully, rigidly flat, his was so full of formless emotion it almost sounded strangled. He fished in his wallet and took out something small and rectangular, which he handed to me. I took it and flipped it over so it was right-side up for me: it was a photograph, passport-size, of a girl. About thirteen or fourteen years old, judging by face and build; long, straight blond hair of the kind that gets called "flyaway" on shampoo bottles; an awkward, apologetic smile. Around her neck, a gold pendant shaped like a teardrop. There was something in her eyes . . . something a little sad and haunted. Or maybe there wasn't. Maybe my memory inserted that nuance, in the light of what happened afterward.

"I'm really sorry to hear that," I said, meaning it about as much as anyone does in those circumstances. These were just strangers, after all, and Abigail was just a name. "How long ago?"

That's a stupid habit I've got: when I can't think of anything else to say, I start in with the questions like a doctor looking to make a diagnosis.

Steve looked to Mel to answer, and again she seemed hard put to it to frame words. "Saturday," she said, hesitantly, as if picking her way across some inner minefield. "The day before yesterday. That was the last time we saw her, and there was—something else that happened then. Something that we think might be connected." I registered the "might," which seemed a little odd, and I was about to pin that one down, when Steve spoke up again.

"We want you to find her for us, Mr. Castor."

I'd already jumped to a different conclusion, and I had my mouth open on the first words of a speech I'd made a hundred times before, so I was caught a little off balance. I closed my mouth, looked from the man to the woman and back again while I tried to think of something else to say.

Most people in the Torringtons' position would be looking for some kind of reassurance that Abigail was still on the right side of the grave: that's a service that a lot of exorcists offer, whether they can make good on the promise or not. I was about to say yes: yes, I'd look for Abbie's spirit, try to find out if it was still inside her body, but with a whole long string of caveats and provisos—because even with the wind at my back and the right kind of focus object I can only find a spirit if it's there to be found. Some people depart very quickly after death and never come back, so only the sloppiest of cowboy operators assumes that the absence of a ghost is proof positive that someone is still alive.

Anyway, that had all gone out the window. Now I had a different proposition on my plate—and a different set of options. I could still take the job on, if I was so inclined. There are ways of finding living people that are (putting this as neutrally as I can) only open to members of my profession, but I don't tend to use them. Rafi aside, I don't traffic with demons, and I don't raise the dead so that I can shake them down for information. Generally speaking, if someone's sleeping quietly in the grave I leave them there. That's the closest thing I have to an ethical standard.

So that left the other option: letting the Torringtons down without too much of a bump.

"I don't normally do missing persons work," I said. It sounded lame, I knew, and it sounded cold. I tried again. "You've called the police, I'm sure, and they're already doing all they can. What I could add to that would be—minimal, and pretty haphazard. I think maybe you ought to see what they can turn up before you start putting out feelers of your own. Or at least, you should discuss it with the officer who's in charge of the case. I know that's cold comfort, but they do know what they're doing."

Into the strained silence that followed, Mel made the lips-parting sound that means someone is about to speak, but then she didn't.

Steve filled the gap. "There is no police investigation," he said, looking like he was biting down on something bitter.

I blinked. "There isn't? Well then, I'd say that's the first thing you need to—"

"Abbie is already dead."

Ever the consummate professional, I didn't actually allow my jaw to unravel all the way to the ground. It took a little effort, though, and there was a strained pause during which the statement just hung in the air, disturbing and palpable. "You'd better run that by me again," I said at last.

Melanie shook her head, as if her mind were automatically refusing—even while she spoke—to go back over this ground again. "She died on a school trip to Cumbria, last summer," she said, her voice if anything even deader and harder than before. "An accident. Three girls fell into a river—Abbie, and two of her friends. It was in spate. The current was very strong."

"They were swept away before anyone could get to them," Steve took up, sounding angry, but it sounded like an old anger, much rehearsed now and very much sick of itself. "They shouldn't have been anywhere near the water in the first place. They had no chance. No chance at all."

They both fell into silence, looking away from me and from each other: I could see that this was still raw, after most of a year. It would probably still be raw after most of a life. "But she came back," I prompted. I was starting to get the picture now: it was a bleak and sad one, executed mainly in grays, but then I don't get to see many that are in bright primaries.

Steve nodded. "Yes, she came back. About three months later. We were in her room."

"Cleaning out her things?" I hazarded, but he shook his head fiercely. "Just sitting. In her room. And I—I suddenly felt that we weren't alone. That somebody had come in, and was standing quite close to us. I couldn't see anything, but I just knew." He smiled a very faint, very tired smile. "I turned to Mel, and said 'Can you feel it?' Something like that. She thought I'd gone mad. But then she nodded. Yes. She was getting it, too.

"That was what it was like, at first. You just had to stand in a certain spot, and you could sense her. It was almost as though you could smell her breath. And about a week after that we started seeing her. Always out of the corner of our eye, at first—never when we actually turned to look at her. It was as though she was coming back to us slowly, from a long way away. We kept waiting, and she kept getting closer. Then we could hear her voice, some nights, calling out good night to us from her room when we were getting into bed. We shouted good night back, as though—"

He paused, and Mel came in on cue. I got the impression, just for a moment, that they'd told this story before, and I wondered if they'd tried out many other exorcists before they got to me. "—as though she was still alive. As though nothing had happened."

"It seemed to be the best way to make her stay," said Steve. "I'd stand at the sink, in the evening, washing up from dinner, and she'd start up a conversation from behind me. I didn't look around. I chatted back to her. Told her about what was happening at work, and—and with her friends. Told her jokes."

He closed his eyes for a few seconds, then opened them again and stared at me as if he was expecting some kind of a challenge. After a moment, a single tear made its slow, meandering way down his cheek. He looked like a man who'd find it hard to cry, and I felt, just for a moment, the guilty twinge of a reluctant voyeur. "I know how strange this must sound, Mr. Castor," Steve Torrington said. "But having her back was what stopped us from falling apart after losing her. We went back to being a family again." He shrugged—a minuscule twitch of his shoulders that spoke volumes. I could see exactly how that would work. And given all the other places that ghosts can end up haunting, the bosom of the family seemed close enough to heaven to make no difference.

Which was maybe the point, a clinical, dispassionate voice pointed out from the back of my mind. For ghosts, happiness is a double-edged proposition.

I put it as gently as I could. "Sometimes—I'd even say often—what keeps the dead here on earth is a feeling that there's something they still have to do. Other times it's just the fear and pain of passing over, or some other strong emotion like anger." I was trying to present this to them in a particular way, so that they could see it as what it was—a kind of happy ending. "It usually tends to be something negative, anyway. Most ghosts are hurting, on some level. I think—if you made Abbie feel as safe and welcome and loved as you probably did—she may just have gone on to whatever comes next." I wouldn't bring heaven into the equation: I'm an atheist myself, as I think I may already have mentioned—mostly because I can't handle the contradiction of an omnipotent God coming up with a world as badly thrown together as this one. A couple of CORGI-approved gas fitters could have done a better job. "She may be somewhere else now—somewhere where she should have gone to straightaway, after she died. The extra time you had with her was a gift and, you know, a comfort—but it was never going to last. The dead aren't that durable, most of the time."

I stopped. Steve was shaking his head very emphatically—almost angrily—but he didn't speak. Instead he turned to look expectantly at Mel, whose eyes were on the desk. Evidently this part of the story fell to her, and evidently she knew it.

"There's something else," she said, and swallowed hard. "I met a man. Three years ago." She darted a quick glance at me, to see how much I'd infer just from those words. I stared back at her, deadpan. I prefer to have the "i"-dotting and "t"-crossing done for me. "He was . . . a client. Someone I was representing."

"A man in your line of business," Steve supplied.

"An exorcist?"

"Yes, exactly. An exorcist."

Mel was looking at Steve with a curious expression now: tense, supplicating, submissive. I wondered whether he'd given her that bruise in the course of a marital disagreement that turned ugly. Three years ago . . . did that count as ancient history or current affairs in this marriage? He didn't look like the wife-beater type. But then, most wife-beaters don't.

As if to shame me for having those suspicions, his arm curled around her shoulders and he drew her close, kissing her on the top of her head because the side of her face that was closest to him was the bruised side.

"You don't have to put yourself through this," he said softly—so softly I could barely hear him. "I'm not blaming you. You know I'm not blaming you?"

Mel nodded, eyes on the ground.

"Do you want to go and wait in the car?"

She nodded again, and he removed his arm, kissing her again.

Mel stood. "I hope . . . ," she said, flashing a wild look at me. "I hope you can help us, Mr. Castor." Then she gave a jerky shrug, turned, and walked out of the room, closing the door behind her.

A heavy silence fell. I decided to let Torrington break it.

"The man's name was Dennis Peace," he said at last, his tone mild—but mild with an undertow. "Perhaps you know him?"

I shook my head. Maybe a vague echo, but ghostbusters aren't that community-minded. And even when we do meet up, we don't always bother to exchange names or sniff each other's backside. The echo was an interesting one, though: something about a fight that ended badly. I'd have to try to pin it down later because Steve was still talking.

"He was being sued over an exorcism that had gone wrong: the ghost wasn't bound properly, and it did a lot of damage to the house it was in. He said it had 'gone geist,' and that that happens sometimes, no matter how careful you are."

Firmer ground again: I welcomed it like an old friend. "That's why it's in the standard contract," I agreed. "The exorcist is responsible for any damage he directly causes, but not for the damage that the ghost does in the course of the binding. It should have been open-and-shut, provided he'd given them a contract in the first place." I was a fine one to talk: I never bothered with any of that legal paraphernalia myself, although I knew only too well how important it could be to have a safety net if things went bad.

"If there'd been a contract, I'm sure everything would have been fine, as you say. Mr. Peace preferred to work on a handshake, I gather, so it was a lot tougher than it seemed. Anyway, Mel ended up representing him, and she decided to plead custom and practice: the plaintiff had employed another exorcist before, knew the standard terms, et cetera. She didn't win.

"But she did spend a lot of time with Peace, while she was preparing the case." There was a hardness in Torrington's tone now. "I think, from what she's said since, that she enjoyed talking to him because he belonged to a world she'd never seen before. He was almost like an action hero in some Hollywood blockbuster. She—was attracted to him, and they had a relationship. Briefly. It was the only time. The only time, ever. I'm absolutely convinced of that. And she knew even while she was doing it that it couldn't be right. She ended it after about two months. There was a scene—a very unpleasant, traumatic one— but in the end Peace accepted that she didn't want to see him again. And then, when it was all over and she had time to think about what she'd done—" There was a long pause. "She told me all about it, and she asked me to forgive her. Which I did. Absolutely. Because she'd been absolutely honest. We agreed that we'd never even talk about it again."

I waited. There was presumably a point to this story, but I couldn't see what it was yet.

"After Abbie died—I mean, after she came back—" Steve's voice dropped again, so that I had to strain to hear it. "Mel made the mistake of calling Dennis to ask him what we should do."

"Why was that a mistake?" I asked.

"Because he took it as a hint that she wanted to get back together with him again." He laughed, shaking his head incredulously. "Our daughter had just died, and she was close to a breakdown, and he was asking her to meet up with him. He booked a hotel room in Paddington. He suggested Mel should tell me he was going to hold a séance for Abbie, and then spend the night there with him. She told him to go and fuck himself." The guttural harshness in his voice came out of nowhere, but it seemed to fit the mood of the moment. He blinked very quickly a few times, as if fighting another outburst of tears. "But he wouldn't take no for an answer. He kept on calling her. He booked appointments with her at chambers, which she had to cancel. Then he waited for her after work a few nights. He said they had to talk about their relationship, where it was going. She told him they didn't have a relationship. She told him to leave her alone. He threatened to tell me what had happened between them, but of course she'd already done that, long before."

He locked eyes with me again. "As time went on, she began to be afraid that Peace was having some kind of psychological breakdown," he said, his mouth quirking down at the corners as if with distaste. "She was afraid."

He did something bizarre at this point: he reached down, opened the neck of the black bag, and peered inside, as if checking its contents gave him some kind of reassurance. Then he closed it again and carried on talking as if nothing had happened.

"Mel never hid any of this from me. And when it got to this stage I got one of my colleagues to send him a letter on the firm's paper, telling him that we'd get an injunction against him if he didn't leave Mel alone. In the old days that would have meant a court order, but I was pretty sure I could actually nail him with an antisocial behavior order—which would have meant prison if he didn't play nicely.

"But he wouldn't get the message. He called Mel again, at work and at home, and I knew I was going to have to put my money where my mouth was. We'd already complained to the police, which had gotten us precisely nowhere, but at least it meant we had a case number. With that and an incident log, you can apply for a court order on your own initiative, so that's what I did.

"But then on Saturday—two days ago—he turned up at the house. He seemed drunk. Out of control. But most drunks I've seen are lethargic so perhaps he was high on something else. When I opened the door he pushed past me—he's a much bigger, heavier man than I am—and demanded to talk to Mel. I picked up the phone to call the police: he ripped it out of the wall. Then he headed for the stairs. It wasn't what I was expecting, and I was a little slow to react. But I went after him, and I tackled him.

"Mel was upstairs, in the bedroom, and she heard all this row—Peace shouting, me shouting back, all the thuds and scuffles. She ran out onto the landing and she saw us on the stairs, wrestling with each other. She saw me go down. I'm not much of a fighter, despite my build, and even if I was I couldn't fight the way he fought. He punched me in the stomach, then kicked me in the same place when I went down. Kicked me again and again, until my muscles seemed to lock and I couldn't make myself breathe in. And the pain—I think I passed out.

"Mel says she screamed at that point, and Dennis looked up at her. That may have saved my life, because he forgot all about me and went after her. He climbed over me and went on up the stairs. And he said—I know this is hearsay evidence, Mr. Castor, but I doubt any of this will ever come to court—he said 'You're coming back to me, bitch. You're going to beg to come back to me.'

"She ran back into the bedroom and locked the door. Her bag was in there, and her mobile was in the bag, so she was going to call the police. But she didn't get the chance. Peace pushed the door in with his shoulder—the lock was a flimsy little thing and it just tore right out of the wood. He—he beat—"

Throughout this recitation, Torrington had been getting more and more agitated. Now he faltered into silence, trembling. I stood up, with some idea of offering him a glass of water, but he waved me away: he didn't want my solicitude.

"He beat her," he said. "You saw her face? Her back and side and her left arm all look the same. And then he ransacked the room. Pulling out drawers and tipping the contents onto the floor, hauling all the clothes out of the wardrobes. When Mel tried to reach for her phone again he stamped on it—smashed it into pieces. If she hadn't snatched her hand away he'd have crushed that, too.

"He seemed to be looking for something, and not finding it. And he was getting more and more frustrated, more and more out of control. Eventually he just turned and walked out of the room again. Mel ran after him, and saw him going into Abbie's room.

"We'd never . . . never changed anything in there. Mel tackled him again when he started wrecking Abbie's things, and he turned on her in a rage. He started to strangle her.

"Then he threw her down on the bed, and she thought that he was going to rape her. But he didn't. He just went on searching. And this time he must have found what he was looking for, because he left. Mel was too terrified by now to try to stop him a third time. But as soon as she heard the door slam she called the police, and then she went down onto the stairs to tend to me."

"You said the police weren't involved," I pointed out.

He gave a bitter snort that might have been intended as a laugh. "I said the police weren't looking for Abbie," he corrected me. "We hadn't even realized . . . We told them about the assault, the damage, and we said we could identify the man who'd done it. They said they'd issue a warrant, and we'd hear in due course. Then when they'd gone, and we were trying to put the place back into some kind of order, we noticed . . . that Abbie wasn't there. But we thought she'd just been frightened away by the noise, and the violence, and she'd come back later.

"By the evening, we were really starting to miss her. She didn't answer when we called, and we couldn't feel her the way we usually do. Because she was gone. It was Abbie he was looking for. And he'd taken her. Somehow he'd taken her away with him."

He fell silent, gripping the neck of the bag tightly in both white-knuckled hands. And the silence lengthened, because I couldn't think of a damn thing to say.

I'd never even heard of a ghost being kidnapped before. It sounded so unlikely, so grotesque, that I still resisted the idea. Ghosts can't be packaged and shipped like groceries or worn and carried like accessories. Mostly they can't move at all outside of a fixed compass. Someone here had to be the voice of reason, and it was asking too much to expect that degree of detachment from Torrington himself.

"You assume he took her," I said, as neutrally as I could. "It could be, as I said, that she left because her time here was—"

"Peace called Mel." There was a tremor in Torrington's voice, and he was still looking down at the black bag, still holding on to it as though it were some kind of lifeline. "About two hours later. He wasn't making much sense, but he said 'You'll have to come back to me now, won't you? Because you can't have her if you don't have me. We'll all be together.' She didn't know what he was talking about. She hung up. She just hung up. And afterwards we realized. We knew."

Okay, that was something pretty hefty in the way of circumstantial evidence. My mind flicked off onto an irresistible tangent. Could it be done? Could it be slickly, smoothly done? Breaking and entering, and grand theft spiritual? Ghosts—most ghosts—haunt a particular place. It might be the place where they died, or where they were buried, or it could just be some spot to which they had strong associations in life.

That's their anchor. They can move a little way away from it: in some cases a couple of hundred yards, but except in a few special cases like the little girl ghosts I set free at the Stanger, I've never heard of it being more. So how would you take a ghost away from its anchor and walk away with it? Maybe . . . yeah, maybe there was a way that I could see. But I knew for a fact that it was something I couldn't do myself.

I was getting dangerously interested. The very weirdness of the situation appealed to my varied and prurient curiosities. But I generally hold to Dirty Harry's dictum that a man should know his limitations.

"I still think the police are your best option," I said. "They can find Peace a lot easier than I can. And I think they'll take a complaint seriously. He broke into your house, after all, and he threatened you."

Torrington was staring at me with a bleak, slightly accusing expression on his face. He knew when he was being snowed.

"And what if they do find him?" he asked, his voice harsh. "Will they find Abbie, too? Can they bring her back for us?"

He had me there. All I could do was shrug, which felt pusillanimous even to me. Okay, he was right. Even a relatively good cop like Coldwood, if something like this fell into his lap, would be helpless running a search for something he couldn't see, hear, or touch—*especially* a cop, because there's that whole blind-deaf-and-dumb pragmatism thing I already mentioned. Conversely, if I was anywhere close to where Abbie was, I'd at least have ways of knowing I was close, and maybe taking a bearing. So there *was* a chance that I could help these people: a chance that I'd be able to run down Peace, and that I'd know what I was looking for when I saw it. It wasn't a good chance, but it was there; and if this didn't count as a spiritual service, then what the hell did?

On the other hand, bringing Abbie back was going to be a much tougher proposition than finding her: I doubted I'd be able to appeal to Peace's better nature, assuming he even had one. And since I didn't know exactly how you went about kidnapping a ghost, I didn't know how you went about bringing her safely home, either. And then there was all the collateral stuff: I'd have to check out the Torringtons' story as far as I could before I got any distance into this. And I'd have to decide what the hell I should charge them, because this fell way outside even the fuzzy logic of my usual tariff.

Once I start coming up with commonsensical points like that, it usually means I'm trying to talk myself out of something I've already decided to do. But this time, reality reasserted itself. There was no point in taking on a job I couldn't do, and adding to the Torringtons' trauma by building up their hopes and then kicking them down again.

Steve Torrington was still looking at me, so I had to say something.

"Well," I temporized, "you've probably got a point there. But if it comes to that, I don't know if I can be of any more use to you than the police could."

"No," he agreed. "How could you know, until you've tried?"

Which was throwing the ball back into my court with a vengeance. I tried to lob it back. "It's not that straightforward, Mr. Torrington. Not like changing a car tire, or"—I cast around for a metaphor, found it close to hand—"or measuring you for a suit. Maybe if I had some of her things. I mean, if I could see her room, or—"

As if he'd been waiting for this moment, Steve hefted the black bin-liner and put it down on the desk between us. "These are the things she cared most about," he said, and he looked at me with the slightest hint of smugness. I shouldn't have been surprised. He was a solicitor, after all. Methodical mind, focused mainly on how the rules of any situation work and what the precedents are. He'd done his research.

I gave him a nod, half-admiring, half-resigned. He emptied the bag carefully onto the desk.

There was quite a lot there: enough so that I wondered what was left behind in Abbie's room. Books, CDs, scrunchies, T-shirts; a cloisonné hair slide with a sort of Celtic knot design; teddy bears and dolls; a pair of very elaborate trainers; some posters of male celebrities I didn't recognize, torn at the corners where the Blu-Tack hadn't yielded quickly enough. It was an embarrassment of riches: the desiderata of a young girl's truncated life. If I was in the right mood, I could probably pick out the items that had meant most to Abbie—the ones that would provide the strongest link to her. But the mood is a skittish thing, and getting into it is never easy for me when there are other people around.

So I picked something up, not quite at random. A Victorian doll of the kind where the head is made out of porcelain while the body is stitched and stuffed, its relatively unfinished look hidden by a sewn-on dress. It had the unsettling, subtly aggressive blankness of a lot of old dolls, and it was in a near-terminal state of disrepair. The head was only attached to the body by a few loops of stitching, most of which had already come away. If I wasn't careful with it, I'd decapitate it without even trying.

A childhood toy seemed the best bet: emotions are always strongest when you're young. Not that Abbie had lived to get old.

I closed my eyes and listened to the doll. That's the only way I can put it: it's not like I was expecting the thing to talk to me. But it's a kind of synesthesia, I guess: I don't have a mind's eye, I have a mind's ear. It takes a while, usually, but if I focus my mind and shut out all distractions then most things have a tune, or at least a note or two, attached to them.

This time it didn't take a while: it didn't take any time at all. Raw emotion hit me like a wall. I must have gasped, because Steve was staring at me with surprise and concern—and maybe, underneath that, with something like distaste.

Abbie's emotions when she held her foam-stuffed friend must have been enormously powerful: powerful enough to linger there, like a recording, for me to pick up. Or maybe the power came from the sheer simplicity, because there was really only one impression there: desperate, aching unhappiness, so deep it was like being at the bottom of a well without knowing how you'd fallen into it.

It took an effort not to throw back my head and howl. If I'd been alone that's probably what I would have done, because emotion that strong, even when it's somebody else's to start with, throws you off balance in all kinds of surprising ways if you can't vent it somehow.

It was an equally intense effort to put the doll down again: it seemed welded to my hands. After I'd done it, I took a few seconds to recover before I tried to talk.

So Torrington got in first. "Is there anything there?" he asked.

I nodded wordlessly.

"A—a trail you can follow?"

"It doesn't work like that," I said. It came out more brusquely than I intended—probably the after-effect of all that black misery still sloshing around my system, but in any case I'm lousy at the bedside manner stuff. I hate having to explain myself, even to intelligent people who can meet me more than halfway. I tried anyway. "I'm reading old emotions, not current ones. I'm not reaching out to Abbie wherever she is now, just . . . getting a sense of her, as she was when she was alive. But yes, there's something there. Enough so that I'll recognize her if I ever see her, or get close to her. It's a start."

"A start?" Steve repeated. Solicitors know the importance of a contract, even when it's just a verbal one.

"Can I keep this stuff overnight?" I asked.

"Of course."

I nodded, feeling a weight settle on me that was different from the weight of Abbie's emotion. "Then here's what I'm offering, if you're still interested. I don't know if I can bring Abbie back to you. Like I said, that depends where she is. If her spirit's gone on to the next station on the line, whatever you want to call that, then nobody can find her for you and nobody can get to where she is. But I may be able to give you an answer to that question—let you know what the odds are. And if she *is* still around—still with us—then there are a few things we can try. If she isn't . . ." I shrugged. "Well, at least you'll know where you stand. Is that any use to you, or would you rather shop elsewhere?"

Torrington was nodding emphatically, and he started to discuss payment—which most prospective clients get to at a much earlier stage of the conversation. I decided to dodge that issue for now, because I still wasn't sure how far I could run with this. If I did hit a brick wall I'd want to just tell them that and get away clean: the hassle of returning a deposit would add all kinds of awkwardness to a situation that was already nasty enough. "You can pay me if I decide to take the case on," I said.

Torrington looked alarmed. "But you said—"

"This first part is just triage. Just—testing the ground. Let's keep it on that basis for now. There's no point you laying any money down in case I come up with a blank. But if you leave it with me overnight, we can talk some more tomorrow when I've had a chance to go over this stuff a bit more thoroughly."

Torrington took the hint and stood up to leave.

"Should I call you in the morning?" he asked.

"I've got your number," I countered. "I'll call you." Looking into his eyes, caught in the headlights of his grief, I relented slightly. "Tonight. I'll try to call you tonight. I should have a bit more information for you then."

I saw him to the door, and he started down the stairs. Before he reached the bottom he looked back, as if conscious that I was still watching. Caught out, I closed the door. There's something magnetic about tragedy. What I was doing was the equivalent of slowing down on the motorway to watch a wreck in the opposite carriageway. I felt a brief twinge of unease and self-disgust.

I felt something else, too: a sense of puzzlement that I couldn't quite nail down. The Torringtons had just aired so much dirty linen in front of me, and bared so many wounds—metaphorical and otherwise—that in some ways I felt I knew them a hell of a lot better than I wanted to. But at the same time, I couldn't shake the feeling that there was something about their relationship that I wasn't getting; some point where I'd added two and two and got to five. Maybe it was that barbed-wire tangle of emotions I'd picked up from Mel, and the fact that fear seemed so dominant there. Not just one fear, either: all sorts of fears looping through one another. Her love for her husband was strong, too, and it came through so loud and clear it seemed almost like religious devotion. But the fear wound itself around that, too, like some kind of pathological bindweed.

Well, even if I took the job, I wasn't signing on to give them relationship therapy. No sense in worrying about it.

I went back to the sprawl of objects on the desk, but I knew as I stared down at them that I wasn't ready yet. I needed to fortify myself for that particular journey.

———

Grambas looked up from his sudoku book as I walked into the café. "So," he called out, tucking his pen behind his ear, "you got a job, Castor?"

I shrugged. "Maybe. I told them I'd think about it."

He wiped his clean hands on his dirty apron. "Yeah," he commiserated, "must be tough, your slate being so full. Not knowing whether or not you can squeeze anything else in . . ."

"Double coffee," I grunted. "To go. Hold the sarcasm."

As he was pouring the thick, black Greek coffee into a Styrofoam cup, Maya walked in with a plastic washbowl full of chipped potatoes. "Castor's in a sour mood," he told her.

"Yeah," she said, "I knew that."

"You knew it?"

"Sure."

"How'd you know it?"

"He was awake."

I got out of there before they could start doing old music hall numbers. The rain was letting up so I took the coffee and my Abbie hangover up to the bridge on Acton Lane, where there's a bench that gives a view out over both the railway cutting and an overgrown, factory-backed stretch of the Grand Union Canal. Call me a hopeless romantic. That vista appeals to me somehow: London with her pants down, but still trying to keep her dignity.

I sat and sipped the hyper-caffeinated sludge, trying to rein my black mood in while bringing my nerves' responsiveness up to a point where it might be dangerous to drive. The two goals were probably mutually exclusive, but in the absence of whisky the coffee was what I felt I needed right then.

The painful intensity of Abbie's residual emotions had taken me by surprise. Okay, psychologically speaking, teenagers are perfect storms: when they're sad, they're very, very sad. But still . . . an attractive girl from an affluent, middle-class family? Parents who seemed to dote on her, and clearly couldn't cope with her loss? What was her tragedy? What had made that tide of misery well up inside her to a point where it overflowed into her toys and left a residue that wouldn't fade?

I wanted to know. And I guess, in the end, that was why I'd said maybe instead of no.

I finished up the coffee, which didn't seem to have helped much, and headed back to the office. I could leave this until later, but it was on my mind now. I might as well find out how far Abbie's orphaned treasures would take me. I wasn't going to be thinking about much else if I put it off.

With the door closed and locked and the phone disconnected at the wall, I threw off my coat and sat down at the desk. I put my whistle down on my right-hand side, but I wasn't ready yet to start to play. First I had to remind myself of what I was fishing for.

I touched the doll gingerly, with the tips of my fingers, and pricked up the ears of my soul. Dead Abbie's sorrow was there again: an endless looped tape of long-ago despair, trapped behind the painted-on smile and the oddly flattened shape that time and circumstances had given to the rag-stuffed body. This time I rode with it for a while longer, paying closer attention to the nuances and the expression. With my left hand, at the same time, I picked up the cloisonné hair slide, which looked to be of more recent vintage than the doll. It had a different resonance, but still in the same general key of inexpressible sorrow.

After five minutes or so, I set both things down, picked up my tin whistle, and put it to my lips.

The opening note was low, and I held it for a long time. A second note followed, equally sustained, but then when you thought it might fade, opening out into a plangent trill that finally kicked the tune into gear. It wasn't a tune I'd ever heard before, or one I was consciously composing as I played. My mind was as passive as I could make it, just resonating with the echoes of Abbie's misery that were still in my head. I was turning her into music. Describing her in the medium I knew best. Putting out a psychic APB: *Have you seen this girl?*

In spiritualist circles, this kind of thing usually gets called a summoning, but people in my business just call it the magic lasso. It's the first phase of an exorcism. Before you can send a ghost away, you have to bind it; wrap your will around it like duct tape, although that's actually a very unpleasant image and I wish I hadn't thought of it. In any case, I was telling Abbie, wherever she was, that she had to dance to my tune now. I was telling her to come to heel.

There were two good reasons why this might not work. The first was that I just didn't know her well enough. I'd never met her, in life or in death, and so the music was incomplete—just an unfinished sketch in sound, based on the emotions I'd sensed in the things she used to own. Those emotions were strong, but they were only a single piece from a huge jigsaw puzzle; what I was doing was analogous to trying to intuit the entire picture from that one piece, without the benefit of the box lid.

The second reason was that she could well be too far away in any case. No summoning is going to work if the ghost doesn't hear it, and I'd never done this before for a ghost who wasn't right there in the same space as me.

But the rules are different in all sorts of ways once you're dead. What's space? What's distance? After a few moments, I felt a tremor of response—like a vibration on some strand of a web that I was spinning in the air, invisibly, all around me. I tried to keep my own emotions—satisfaction, excitement, unease—in check as I built that response into the tune, making my approximation of Abbie a little stronger, pulling her in, calling her to me. The vibration became infinitesimally more marked, more insistent.

And then, in an instant, it was gone.

Dead, blank, empty air surrounded me, like the moment after the fridge stops humming and you think the silence is a new sound.

I skipped a beat, swore under my breath, started up again. The music came more readily this time. I had a better grasp of it now, and so I was aiming better: pitching my tent where I knew she'd be.

Again, the most tenuous and hesitant of tugs on the web of sound—from over my left shoulder, which was away to the southwest somewhere. I guess direction isn't any more meaningful than distance, but the sense of the pull coming from that physical quarter was very strong.

But again, when I reached for it, when I tried to move my mind or my soul out onto that part of the web, the sudden, instantaneous collapse—followed by a great deal of nothing at all.

A suspicion was waking up in the back of my mind, like a hibernating bear roused too early and in a foul mood. But God forbid I should jump to any conclusions. I gave it a rest, filed some long-dead paperwork to get my mind back into neutral.

Half an hour later I tried again, building from first principles. I started with the doll just like before, bracing myself as I prepared to dip first my toe, and then the rest of me, into that cold ocean of unhappiness—but the tide was out. This time when I held the unlovely toy in my hands there was nothing there: no emotional trace at all. Amazed and disconcerted, I picked up a teddy bear, a pair of trainers, a book. Finally I buried my hands in the sprawl of teenage treasure trove, fingers spread wide, touching as many different things at once as I could manage. They were all cold and inert.

And now it was the conclusions that were jumping on me.

That just couldn't happen. The residual emotions we leave in the things we touch aren't like fingerprints; they can be overlaid with stronger, later impressions, but they can't be wiped clean. Or at least, that's what I'd always assumed. But somebody had just done it: killed the psychic trail, pulled the rug out from under me and left me sitting on my arse in the middle of nowhere. And once again I had to admit to myself that I didn't have any idea how that could be done.

Kidnapping ghosts. Blindsiding the hunt. I was dealing with someone who was better than me at my own game. My professional pride was piqued, and slightly punctured. I had to see if I could reflate it.

Yeah, that shallow.

On bad days, I have to admit that I deserve everything I get.

Chapter Four

The front door of St. Michael's Church was massive: bivalved, with a lock on each side. Old wood four inches thick, set tight in a slightly narrow, low-arched narthex, and I could tell by the look of it that it had fossilized hard with age. It moved less than half an inch under my hand, and I gave it up as a bad job. I could pick the locks with nothing more than brute force and bloody-mindedness, but there wouldn't be any point. From the feel of it, the doors were anchored at the bottom, too: there was a bolt on the inside.

There are churches that people will travel a thousand miles out of their way to see. St. Michael's wasn't one of those. Don't get me wrong—it was old, and impressive enough in its way. Early Gothic, very early, taking its shape from Abbé Suger's original prescription, which meant that it was straight up and down and plain as a pike. A colossal ecclesiastical doghouse on which the Holy Spirit could sleep like Snoopy until the day of judgment.

Some people would argue that he'd overslept.

This was where Juliet had told me to meet her, but she was nowhere in sight. All I could do was wait—and while I did, I became aware of a very faint presence somewhere close by. It was something immaterial and shifting, so faint that just the act of focusing my attention on it made it roll back out of reach as though my mind were a searchlight. Whatever it was it had strongly negative overtones for me—like the psychic equivalent of some bitter medicine I'd taken long ago and never forgotten.

Curious, I laid my hands on the church door again, closed my eyes, and listened with my extra sense.

Nothing at first—except for the discomfort of the cold wood against the palms of my hands. Maybe I'd been mistaken in the first place, and all I was feeling was the remains of that psychic hangover I'd had the day before. I considered taking out my whistle and seeing if I could refine the search a little, but just then a woman's footsteps stirred a recursive symphony of echoes on the flags behind me. I turned with a witty and slightly obscene quip ready to launch, but it died before I could even open my mouth, because this wasn't Juliet walking toward me. It was a young woman with bookish spectacles and shoulder-length white-blond hair. She was slight and petite, pale-complexioned, and she walked with her shoulders hunched up as if against heavy rain. Except that the rain had rolled away westward: it was a fine night in late spring, and if it weren't for the cold under the shadow of the church I might even be feeling overdressed in my heavy greatcoat. As it was, she clearly felt that her beige two-piece was too skimpy, even though the sleeves were full and the skirt was demurely calf-length; hands folded, she rubbed her upper arms nervously as she approached me.

Lashless black eyes blinked at me from behind those "I am serious" glasses.

"Mr. Castor?" the woman said, tentatively, as if the question might give offense.

"That's me," I said.

"I'm Susan Book, the verger. Umm . . . Miss Salazar is around the back, in the cemetery. She asked me to show you the way."

Her voice had that rising inflection that turns statements into questions. Normally that irritates me a little, but Susan Book was so clearly anxious to please that resenting her, even in the privacy of your own mind, would have felt like taking a hot iron to a puppy. She held out her hand diffidently. I took it and shook it, holding on long enough to listen in on her feelings. They were dark and confused: something was clearly weighing on her mind. I let go, sharpish; I'd had enough of that for one day.

"I'm all yours," I said, and I threw out my arm to indicate that she should lead the way. She started and spun around as though I were pointing to something behind her. Then she recovered, blushed, and darted me a quick, flustered glance.

"Sorry," she said. "I'm really nervous today. All of this—" She shrugged and made a face. Not knowing what she was talking about, all I could do was nod sympathetically. She turned on her heel and walked back the way she'd come. I fell in alongside her.

"She's amazing, isn't she?" she said wistfully.

"Juliet?"

"Yes, Jul—Miss Salazar. She's so strong. I don't mean physically strong, I mean spiritually. The strength of faith. You can tell just by looking at her that nothing can shake her, or make her doubt herself." There was something in her voice that sounded like yearning. "I really admire that."

"Me too," I said. "Well, up to a point. Self-doubt can be useful, too, though."

"Can it?"

"Definitely. Prevents you from jumping straight off a cliff because you think you can fly, for example."

She laughed uncertainly, as though she wasn't entirely sure whether or not I was joking. "The canon says that doubts are like workouts," she said. "If he's right, I ought to be benching two hundred and fifty pounds by now. I seem to get doubts all the time. But this—maybe the—maybe I'll get stronger by dealing with all of this. Good comes out of evil. That's His way."

I caught the capital "H" on "His," which my brother Matthew uses, too, but there was an almost equally weighted emphasis on "all of this," and I was tempted to ask her what the hell it was that had happened here. But I assumed there was some reason why Juliet hadn't briefed me in advance, so I kept my mouth shut. I didn't say a word about

Juliet herself, either, although I wondered what Susan would think if she knew what Miss Salazar's real name was, or where she hailed from. Best to leave her with her illusions intact.

The church stood in its own very narrow grounds on Du Cane Road, almost directly opposite the soul-dampening pile of Wormwood Scrubs—which is angry red chased with white, like bone showing through an open wound. To the left of the church itself, where Susan Book led me, there was a lych-gate, on the far side of which I could see a trim little graveyard like the stage set for a musical of Gray's "Elegy." This gate was locked, too, with a padlock on a chain. Susan took out a small ring of keys from her pocket, sorted through them, and found the right one. It turned in the padlock after a certain amount of fidgeting and ratcheting, and she slid the chain free so that the gate swung open, stepping aside to let me through.

"I'll unlock the vestry door for you," she said. "It's by the west transept, over there. Miss Salazar is—" She pointed, but I'd already seen Juliet. The cemetery was on a slight slope and she was sitting cross-legged on top of a marble monument of some kind, outlined against the sky. A colossal oak that had to be a couple of hundred years old held up half the sky behind her.

"Thanks," I said. "We'll join you in a couple of minutes."

Susan Book stood for a moment staring up the hill at Juliet's silhouetted form. Then she bustled away, casting a wide-eyed look at me over her shoulder as if I'd caught her out in a moment of self-doubt. I waved, reassuringly I hoped, and walked up the hill to join Juliet. She had her head bowed and she didn't look up as I approached. She didn't seem to notice me, although I knew damn well that she'd heard the key rattle in the lock of the lych-gate, smelled my aftershave on the air as I stepped through, and sieved my pheromones by taste to find out what kind of a day I'd had. As soon as she was close enough so that I didn't have to raise my voice to speak to her, I voiced what was uppermost in my mind.

"Why a church? Did you get religion?"

Her head snapped up and she frowned at me, eyes narrowing to slits. I threw up my hands, palms out, in a meant-no-harm panto-mime. Sometimes I go too far. She infallibly lets me know when that happens.

As usual, once I'd started looking at her, the tricky thing was stopping. Juliet is absurdly, unfeasibly beautiful. Her skin is melanin-free, alabaster smooth, as white as any cliché you care to dredge up. If you go for the default option, snow, then think of her eyes as two deep fishing holes, as black as midnight. But if anyone's fishing, it's from the inside of those holes, and you won't feel the hook until it's way, way down in the back of your throat. Her hair is black, too: a waterfall of black that falls almost to the small of her back, texturelessly sheer. Her body . . . I won't try to cover that. You could get lost there. People have: stronger people than you, and most of them never came back.

Because the point—and I know I've said this already—is that Juliet isn't human. She's a demon: of the family of the succubi, whose pre-ferred method of feeding depends on arousing you to the point where your nervous system starts to fuse into slag and then sucking your soul out through your flesh. Even tonight, dressed coyly in black slacks, boots, and a loose white shirt with a red rose embroidered up the left-hand side, you could never mistake her for anything other than what she was. The confidence, the strength that Susan Book had seen in her—that came from being the top carnivore in a food chain that no man or woman alive could even imagine. Except that "carnivore" wasn't quite the right term: you needed something like "noumovore," or "ani-movore." And even more than that, you needed not to go there.

Thank God she's on our side, that's all. And I'm saying that as an atheist.

And taking another step, I came within range of her scent. It hit me in two waves, as it always does. With the first breath, you're gulping in the rank foulness of fox, cloying and earthy; with the second, which you draw shallowly because of the sharpness of that first impression, you inhale a mélange of perfumes so achingly sweet and sensual your body goes on instant all-points alert. I'm used to it and I was braced for it, but even so I felt a wave of dizziness as all the blood in my head rushed down to my crotch in case it was needed there to bulk out my sudden, painful erection. Men limp around Juliet: limp, and go partially blind because taking your eyes off her suddenly seems like a waste of valuable time.

Which is why it's important never to forget what she is. That way, you can maintain a level of good, old-fashioned, pants-wetting terror as a bulwark against the desire. I've found that to be a healthy balance to keep, because obviously if I ever actually had sex with Juliet, my immortal soul would be the cigarette afterward; but still, it's not easy to think logically when she's right there in front of you. It's not easy to think at all.

She unfolded her legs and stepped down off the chunk of marble with unconscious grace. I realized that it was the cover of a family vault: Joseph and Caroline Rybandt, and a bunch of subsidiary Rybandts listed in a smaller font. Death is no more democratic than life is. I also realized that Juliet was carrying a gray plastic bowl half-full of water. It had been resting in her lap, and when I first saw her she must have been peering down into it.

"So how's tricks?" I asked her.

"Good," she said, neutrally. "On the whole."

"Meaning . . . ?"

"It's fine if I don't think about the hunger. It's been a year now since I actually fed. Fed fully on a human being, body and soul. It's hard sometimes to keep the flavor, and the joy of it, out of my mind."

I groped around for a response, but nothing came. "Yeah," I said after slightly too long a pause, "I thought you were looking slim. Think of it as a detox diet."

Juliet frowned, not getting the reference. Now didn't seem like a good time to explain it.

"So you've got a spook?" I said, to move things along. "A graveyard cling-on?" It was one of the commonest scenarios we came across in our profession: ghosts clinging to the place where their mortal remains still rested, anchored in their own flesh and unable to move on. Some of them got the hang of the wiring and rose again as zombies; most just stayed where they were, getting fainter and more wretched as the years went by.

Juliet looked at me severely. "In this graveyard? There hasn't been a burial here in centuries, Castor—look at the dates."

I did. Joseph had bitten the dust in 1782, and Caroline three years later. More to the point, all the stones were leaning at picturesque angles and most were green with moss. Some had even started to sink into the ground so that the lower parts of their eroded messages of grief and pious hope were hidden in the long grass.

"There are no ghosts here," Juliet said, stating the obvious.

"What then?" I said, feeling a little embarrassed and annoyed to have been called on such a basic point by my own apprentice. Few ghosts hung around for more than a decade or so—almost none past fifty or sixty years. There was only one case on record of a soul surviving through more than a century, and she was currently residing a few miles east of us. Her name was Rosie, and she was sort of a friend of mine.

"Something bigger," said Juliet.

"Then holy water is probably just going to piss it off," I said, nodding toward the bowl. She gave me a meaningful look and thrust the bowl into my hands. I took it by reflex, and to stop the contents slopping over my coat.

"I never said it was holy," said Juliet.

"So you were washing your hair? You know, human women tend to do that in the privacy of—"

"Turn around." She pointed toward the church.

"Widdershins or deasil?"

"Just turn around." She put her hands on my shoulders and did it for me, swiveling me 180 degrees without any effort at all. The touch sent a jarring, sensual charge through me and reminded me yet again, as if I needed it, that Juliet had physical strength in spades, as well as the spiritual kind that Susan Book had been talking about. I stared up at the looming bulk of St. Michael's, which now blocked off the setting sun so that it was just a monolithic slab of ink-black shadow.

"My kind have a gift for camouflage," murmured Juliet, her throaty voice suddenly sinister rather than arousing. "We use it when we hunt. We make false faces for ourselves, pretty or harmless seemings, and we flash them in the eyes of those who look at us." She tapped the rim of the bowl and a ripple shot from edge to center of the water within, then from center back to edge in choppy, broken circles. "So the best way to see us is not to look at us at all."

I stared into the bowl as the ripples subsided. I was seeing the inverted image of St. Michael's Church. It didn't look any better upside down. In fact, it looked a whole lot worse: black smoke or steam was roiling off it in waves, downward into the inverted sky. It looked as though it was on fire—on fire without flames.

Startled, I raised my eyes to the building itself. It stood silent and somber. No smoke, no fireworks.

But back down in the bowl, when I looked again, the black steam rolled and eddied off the church's reflection. St. Michael's was the heart of a shadow inferno.

I stared at Juliet, and she shrugged.

"Anyone you know?" I asked, aiming for a flip, casual tone and missing it by about the length of an airport runway.

"That's a good question," she acknowledged. "But for later. Come inside. You need to get the whole picture."

I felt like that was the last thing I needed, but I stayed with her as she set off down the small hill toward the church, taking the same direction in which Susan Book had gone.

The verger was waiting for us at the door of the vestry, a much smaller stone doghouse attached to the wall of the church at the back. She'd already opened the door, but she hadn't gone inside. She looked more nervous and unhappy than ever—and she looked to Juliet for instructions with the same sad hunger that I'd noticed before.

"You can wait here," Juliet told her, sounding almost gentle. "We'll be five minutes. I just think it will be better if Castor sees for himself."

Susan shook her head. "I'll come with you," she said. "In case you've got any questions. The canon told me to give you any help I could."

She visibly steeled herself, and stepped inside first. Juliet nodded me forward, so I went next in line, with her bringing up the rear.

The vestry was about the size of a large toilet, and it was empty apart from a cupboard for ecclesiastical vestments and half a dozen hooks screwed into the wall. We went on through, via a second, wide open door, into the west transept of the church, a low-roofed side tunnel looking toward the majestic main corridor of the nave. It was completely unlit, apart from the last red rays spilling through the stained-glass windows behind us. It made for a fairly forbidding prospect: it was hard to imagine anyone being inspired to devotion by it. Mind you, I wouldn't say a paternoster if you put a gun to my head, so I'm probably not an unbiased witness there.

I felt it before I'd taken three steps: the chill. It was more like December than May, and more like the High Andes than East Acton. It ate into the bone. No wonder I'd felt cold when I was trying the door outside: the chill must have been radiating out through the stone. I suppressed a shudder and moved on.

But another few steps brought an even bigger surprise. I turned and shot a glance at Juliet, who looked keenly back at me. "Tell me what you're feeling now," she said.

I wanted to confirm it first. I walked left, then right, then forward.

"It changes," I muttered. "Son of a bitch. It's like—there are pockets of cold, in the air, not moving."

"Whatever happened here, it happened very quickly. I think that's why it hasn't—"

She hesitated, looking for the right word.

"Hasn't what?"

"Spread evenly."

My laugh was incredulous, and slightly pained.

Susan Book was waiting for us at the end of the transept, and she was looking back toward us, not expectantly but with anxious intensity. She clearly wasn't going to take a step farther without us. So we walked on and joined her.

The shadows were deeper in the nave, because only the windows to the left-hand side were getting any light. The far side, to the east, was a dimensionless black void. The gray flagstones under our feet faded into the dark a scant three or four yards from where we were, as though we stood on a stone outcrop at the edge of a cliff face.

Now that none of us was moving, I was suddenly aware of a sound. It was very low, both in volume and in pitch: very different from the susurration of echoes our footsteps had raised. It rose and fell, rose and fell again over the space of several seconds, dying away so slowly I was left wondering whether I'd imagined it.

Before I could resolve that question, Juliet was on the move again. She crossed the nave into the featureless dark, and came back a few moments later carrying a candle. How she'd even been able to see what she was aiming for was beyond me.

The candle was plain and white, about eight inches long and with a slight taper at the wick end. Susan looked at it with solemn unhappiness. Juliet took a lighter from her pocket and held it over the wick. "That's a votive candle," Susan said, a little plaintively. "You're meant to light it when you say a prayer."

"Then say one," Juliet suggested.

She touched the wick to the lighter flame, and after a moment it flared and caught.

I thought she was going to lead us on up the nave toward the altar, but she just waited, one hand cupped around the candle flame to shield it from any drafts that might gust in from the open door behind us. But the air was as still as the air inside a coffin must be. The flame rose straight and flicker-free, giving off a single wisp of smoke as the wick burned in.

Then it guttered and almost went out. It shriveled, if a flame can be said to shrivel, and it shrank in on itself. It was as though the darkness and the cold were feeding on it, suckling on the tiny pinpoint of warmth and light and in the process killing it. As the flame surrendered and gave ground, the shadows came back deeper and more opaque than before, and the cold seemed to become a little more intense.

In the dead silence, I heard that sound again: the double-spiked, deep-throated murmur at the limit of hearing.

"You were expecting that?" I asked Juliet, my eyes on the beleaguered candle flame.

"It was the first thing I tried. And that was the second." She was pointing to the wall over to my right. Glancing in that direction, I saw a row of six squat shapes that resolved themselves, when I took a step toward them, into black plastic plant pots.

Each pot had something dead in it. Leafless stems; sagging, frost-burned blossoms; desiccated corms.

"The cold will do that," I pointed out. "You don't need anything supernatural."

"True," Juliet agreed. "But not in the space of five minutes. Look at your hand. The skin on your wrist."

I did. It was already starting to pucker and dry: when I ran a finger across it, there was a dull ache.

"The longer you stay in here, the worse it will get. If you lingered long enough, I suppose—" Juliet's gaze flicked across the plant pots with their freeze-dried, gray-green cargoes. She didn't need to finish the sentence. Again, in the hush after she spoke, a bass rumble in the air or in the stone or in the darkness itself rose and peaked and fell, rose and peaked and died away into silence.

"What the hell is that?" I asked. "That noise?"

Juliet seemed surprised. "You mean you don't recognize it?"

"Not so far."

"It'll come to you."

"Yeah, I'm sure," I said, a little piqued. "But probably not before my leaves start to fall off."

I blew out the candle flame, just before it died of its own accord, and headed for the exit.

———

It had happened during the evensong service, Susan Book said, the night before last.

St. Michael's didn't have a resident priest, and there were no services there during the week. It was only open on Saturdays and Sundays, when Canon Ben Coombes came across from Hammersmith to lead the services for a congregation that was only half as big as it was even ten years ago. The rest of the time, Susan looked after the place along with a sexton named Patricks, who mainly tended the graves but could occasionally be prevailed on to clean graffiti off the walls.

Evensong was her favorite service. She liked the hymns, which always started with "Lead us, heavenly father, lead us," and the canticles that sometimes made her cry, they were so beautiful. And she liked the lighting of the candles—especially around this time of year, when they seemed to take up the work of the sun as the sun failed. Like the light of the spirit, picking up the slack for the fallible and beleaguered flesh.

We were out among the gravestones again, warming ourselves on the last red rays of sunset after the midnight chill of the church. I was reclining at my ease, more or less, on MICHAEL MACLEAN GREATLY MISSED HUSBAND AND FATHER. Juliet was perched elegantly on the headstone of ELAINE FARRAH-BEAUMONT, TAKEN FROM US MUCH TOO SOON, and Susan was sitting on the grass between us, unwilling to disturb the rest of the dearly departed. Under the circumstances, I didn't take that as empty sentimentality. Nor did I take it personally that her eyes never wavered from Juliet's face.

There were about eighty people in the church, she went on: a good house, the canon had said jocularly as Susan helped him into his vestments, so we'd better give them a good show. He'd led the responses and read a psalm—just as he did every week. They were into the first of the two canticles, which was the *cantate domino*: "Oh sing unto the Lord a new song, for he hath done marvelous things . . ."

She stared at the ground, remembering.

"There's a place in the *cantate*," she murmured, "where the choir invite the sea and the earth to make a joyous noise . . ." I remembered it as she said it, thinking back without enthusiasm to my own confused religious education. It had never made a hell of a lot of sense to me.

"Let the floods clap their hands." How, exactly? "And let the hills be joyful." Was there any way we'd be able to tell the difference?

But Susan was still talking, and I reined in my jaundiced memories.

When Canon Coombes got to "Let the sea make a noise," there *was* a noise; from outside, in the street. A shriek of brakes, very loud, followed by the sound of an impact: metal crunching against metal, or against something else. The mood was broken. Even the choir faltered into silence, and every eye looked toward the door.

Canon Coombes cleared his throat, and the congregation faced front again. He nodded to the choir, expecting them to take up where they'd left off. But though they opened their mouths to sing, no sound came out.

"It got cold," Susan said, her voice sounding a little ragged at the edges. "All at once, just . . . terribly, terribly cold. I heard people gasp, and everyone was looking at everyone else, or jumping to their feet. Shocked. Scared. Not understanding it, because it was so fast.

"And then there was something a lot worse."

I waited, but she didn't seem to want to say any more. She looked at Juliet, as if she needed to be told to come out with the rest of it. But Juliet just returned the stare with her own unreadable gaze, until eventually, abashed, Susan looked down at the ground.

"Something laughed at us," she said.

It was so incongruous, I didn't take it in. "Laughed at . . . ?"

"Something laughed," Susan repeated stubbornly, defensively. "It came from high up, near the roof, a long way over our heads. And it was loud. It was very, very loud. It filled the church." She glanced across at me, her face set, as though she was certain in her own mind that I thought she was lying. "But I can't describe the tone of it. I can't make you understand what it felt like. People started to run. Or they just . . . fell down, where they were. Some of them seemed to be having fits, because their arms and legs were jerking and their mouths were wide open.

"It was horrible! All I wanted to do was get away from that awful sound, but I couldn't think. I started to run without even knowing where I was going. I bumped into Ben—Canon Coombes—and he didn't even see me, but he's so much bigger and heavier than me that I went flying. I grabbed hold of the altar rail to keep from falling, and then I couldn't seem to let go of it. It was so cold—the cold going right through me, taking my strength away. You know you see skaters on an ice rink, clinging to the side because they're scared to move out onto the ice? That's what I must have looked like. I just leaned against the rail, with my head spinning, and people screaming and running all around me.

"Then when I did manage to get moving again, I almost tripped over a woman who'd fallen down in the aisle right in front of me. Fainted, or perhaps just hit her head on something. I couldn't leave her there. But she was too heavy for me to carry, so I dragged her toward the door, a few feet at a time, with rests in between. The laughter had stopped by then, but there was still a sort of sense of . . . of being *stared* at. I was scared to look up. It really felt as if something enormous— some giant ogre—had taken the roof off the church and was peering in at us."

She swallowed hard, shook her head. "I don't remember getting to the door, but I must have done, because suddenly I was out on the street. The woman I'd been dragging along was still unconscious, lying on the pavement in front of me, and I realized that there was blood all over her white blouse. I thought she was dead, after all—that the laughing thing had managed to kill her somehow. But then I realized . . ."

She held out her hands for us to see. There was scabbed skin on both palms, all the way across in a broad straight line, angry and red at the top and bottom edges.

"It was *my* blood, not hers. It must have happened when I touched the altar rail. The metal was so cold that my skin just stuck to it. That was why it was so hard to let go."

It was a pretty eloquent demonstration. I listened in silence as she wrapped up her story. Everyone got out alive, although some crawled out on their hands and knees: incredibly, very few were even hurt, beyond bruised arms and cut foreheads. The ones who'd gone into fits seemed to recover quite quickly, except that they were still pale and shaking. Canon Coombes had locked up the church there and then, and told Susan to cancel the Sunday services. After which he'd fled, leaving her to call ambulances for the hurt and the traumatized (leaving red smears on the keys of her mobile phone) and to try to talk down those who were still hysterical.

On Sunday he'd called her at home. He'd spoken to the diocese, he said, and they'd authorized him to engage an exorcist—so long as it was a church-approved one. He told Susan to pick someone out of the yellow pages.

But Susan didn't have a yellow pages, so she'd gone online instead, and Juliet's Web site had been the first to come up. I wasn't surprised. It was sometimes the first to come up when your search string was "Chinese restaurants" or "plumbers." I was pretty sure she'd done something to Google that was both illegal and supernatural.

The site listed Juliet's church accreditations—Anglican and Catholic—as pending. Susan thought that was good enough, and called her.

"And now here you are," she finished, brightly. "Two for the price of one." She smiled her tentative smile at us both, turning her head left and right to do it. It was the first time she'd acknowledged my presence since she started to tell her story.

"Here we are," I agreed. I stood up. "And I guess we'd better confer about the case. Could you excuse us for a moment?"

"Of course," said Susan, blushing a hectic red. "I have to lock up again, anyway."

She got up and bustled away, keys jangling. We retreated up the hill to the Rybandt vault, with full night coming on.

"So you think it's a demon, rather than a human soul?" I said, when I was sure we couldn't be overheard.

Juliet didn't answer for a moment. When she did, I got the sense that she was measuring her words. "The scions of hell," she said. "I know by their habits and by their spoor. It's not likely that any of them could be this close to me without me knowing it. But it would take one of the older powers to do that on hallowed ground. Just as it takes all of my strength to enter a place like that and not be hurt by it. I have to prepare myself, put a guard up—and not stay there very long."

"Then what? What do you reckon it is?"

She turned to face me, and I could see that she was troubled. Which meant that she was letting me see, because Juliet can control her body language in the same way that a fly-fisher can place a lure. "If it wasn't for the cold," she said, "and for the other signs, I'd swear that there was nothing here. Whatever it is, it has no smell. No body. No focus." She sought for words, grimaced as if she didn't like the ones she'd found. "Weight without presence."

"What have you tried?" I asked her, keeping it businesslike.

"A number of things. A number of askings and tellings, any one of which ought to have made whatever is in those stones show its face to me. They all came up blank. I'm grabbing at smoke."

I remembered the roiling shadows I'd seen reflected in the bowl of water, and nodded. It was barely a metaphor.

"And yet—" Juliet murmured, and hesitated. I'd never seen her be tentative about anything before: it was, to be honest, a bit unnerving, like seeing an avalanche swerve.

"What?"

"Occasionally I feel a very faint presence. Not in the stones themselves but close. Close, and moving, moving against itself, in fragments, like a cloud of gnats. Whatever it is, I think it's linked to what's inside the church—but as soon as I look toward it, it hides itself from me."

I remembered what I'd felt as I stood waiting by the church's front door. "Yeah," I agreed, "I think maybe I got that, too. A scent, I mean, but not strong enough to pin down."

I glanced over at the lych-gate: Susan Book was waiting for us there, her pale face visible through the gathering gloom.

"You want me to try?" I asked. The stuff Juliet was talking about was probably necromancy—black magic—most of which I tend to regard as a mountain of quackery and bullshit surrounding a few grains of truth. What I do is different: the expression of a talent that's inside me, with no recitations or rituals and no steganographic mysteries. It was a sincere offer, but Juliet was shaking her head: she wasn't asking me to do her job for her.

"I want you to tell me if I'm missing anything," she said. "You've been doing this a lot longer than I have."

That was true, as far as it went. Juliet was a good few millennia old, from what she'd told me, but she'd only been living on earth for a year and a half. There were things about the way the living, the dead, and the undead interacted on the mortal plane that she didn't know or hadn't thought about.

But if this *was* a demon, then her experience counted for a fuck of a lot more than mine. What could I tell her about the hell-kin, when for her hell was the old neighborhood?

I chewed it over. I liked it that she called on me when she was baffled—I liked it a lot—and I didn't want to just turn my pockets out and show they were empty. But this wasn't like anything I'd ever seen before.

"Let me think about it," I temporized. "Ask a couple of friends. Right now I can't think of any angle you've missed."

"Thank you, Castor. I'll share the fee, of course—if this turns out to need our combined efforts."

"The twinkle in your eye is reward enough. Although actually, since I'm here, you can do me a favor in return."

"Go ahead."

"In your—um—professional capacity—"

"*This* is my professional capacity now."

"Well, yeah. Obviously. But in the old days, when you were—hunting, hunting someone specific, I mean, and they knew you were coming and tried to hide. Did you—how did you—?" It was hard to find a delicate way of putting it, but Juliet was smiling, really amused. Demons have an odd sense of humor.

"You mean, when I was raised from hell to feed on a human soul—yours, for example—how did I find you?"

I nodded. "In a nutshell."

"I hunt by scent."

"I knew that. What I was trying to ask was *which* scent? Was it the soul or the body that you tracked?"

"Both."

Now we were getting somewhere. "Okay," I said. "So did you ever come across a situation where your—"

"Prey?"

"I was going to go with 'target,' but yeah. Where your prey knew you were coming, and managed to brush over his trail in some way. So you couldn't smell him anymore?"

She thought about this for a moment or two, visibly turning it over in her mind.

"There are things that disguise the body's scent," she said. "Lots of things. For the soul—a few. Running water would hide both."

I nodded. That much I did know. "But did you ever have a situation where you were following a trail, and the scent was strong, and then suddenly it just went cold. Completely died on you."

She shook her head without a moment's hesitation. "No. That couldn't happen."

"Somebody did it to me earlier on today."

"No," she said again. "That may have been how it felt to you, but it was something else that was happening."

Good enough. And food for thought. "Thanks," I said. "I'll stop by again tomorrow, see how you're getting on."

"Come in the evening," she suggested. "We can have dinner."

That was a very appealing prospect. "On you?"

"On me."

"You're on. Where do you want to meet?"

"Here, I suppose. We'll find somewhere close by—perhaps around White City. I'll see you at eight thirty."

I turned to leave, but then I remembered something that had slipped my mind. That twin-peaked sound: surge and fall, surge and die, like waves of some curdled liquid crawling up an unimaginable shore. I turned back.

"It didn't come to me," I said.

"What?"

"The noise in there. You said it would come to me, but it didn't. You think you know what it is?"

"Oh." Juliet gave me a slightly disappointed look, as if I were asking her for the answers on a test that was too easy to need thinking about. I shrugged, partly in mock apology, mainly just asking that she cut to the chase.

"It's a heartbeat," she said. "Beating about once a minute."

Chapter Five

I went back to the car, which I'd parked in the back lot of a wine ware-house that closed early on Mondays. It was Pen's Mondeo, which she lets me use whenever she doesn't need it herself. With Dylan's Lexus currently handling most of her transport needs, I had it on semiper-manent loan.

I let myself in, locked the doors behind me just in case because my attention was going to be elsewhere for a few minutes. In a Sainsbury's bag in the front passenger seat of the car was Abbie's doll. I took it out, held it in both hands, and closed my eyes.

And shuddered. There it was again: the fathomless ache of Abbie's long-ago and long-sustained unhappiness, brimming behind the frail ramparts of rag-stuffed muslin. Got you, you bastard, I thought with cold satisfaction. You can throw me off the trail, but only when you know I'm on it. You can't be on silent running all the goddamn time.

Laying the doll down on the steering wheel like a tiny Ixion, I took out my whistle and launched into the opening notes of the Abbie tune, which was still fresh in my mind.

Within seconds I got the same response as before; the same sense of something touching the music from outside, as though it was a physical skein that I was throwing over West London. Except that it was stronger this time. I was barely a quarter of a mile to the west of my office in Harlesden, but I was a good mile and a half farther south. And yes, the orientation was different—the faint tug on the web of sound coming not from over my left shoulder now but from straight ahead, from where the sun had set not long before. That made it easier to shift my attention, my focus, into that one quarter. The touch was faint, vanishingly faint, but I opened myself up to it, shutting out all distractions, tautly listening in on that one channel even as I was creating it, sustaining it, with the soft, drawn-out complaint of the tin whistle. She seemed to recede. I held a single note, almost too low to hear, the barest breath into the mouthpiece, and slowly, by infinitesimal degrees—

Suddenly a shrieking discord bit into my mind like a deftly wielded Black & Decker power drill. It came out of nowhere, slicing through my nerves, sundering thought and feeling and music so that their writhing, severed ends leaked chaos and agony. I screamed aloud, my back arcing so that my head slammed back into the headrest of the driver's seat and my feet jammed down on the pedals as if I were trying to bring the already stationary car to a dead halt.

It only lasted for a second: less than that, maybe. Even while I was screaming, the pain was subsiding from its lunatic peak and I was slumping forward again, a puppet with its strings cut, my forehead thumping against the body of the doll that was still lying on the steering wheel in front of me.

I lay there weak and dazed for a few seconds, static fizzing and stinging through my nervous system, trying to remember where I was and why I was drooling bloody spittle onto a stuffed toy. My tongue throbbed in time to my heart, seeming too big for my mouth: I'd bitten deeply into it, and that bitter tang was my own blood. I wiped it away with the back of my hand, pulled myself together; a job that I had to tackle in easy stages.

I fished out my flask of I-can't-believe-it's-not cognac and unscrewed the lid with shaking hands. The first sip was medicinal: I swilled it around my bitten tongue, trying not to wince, rolled down the window, and spat out the blood. The second sip was for my jangled nerves. So were the third and fourth.

I suddenly realized that as I stared down between my feet, my gaze had met another pair of eyes gazing back up into mine. With a queasy jolt, I picked up the head of Abbie's doll from the floor of the car: it must have parted company from the body when my head crashed forward into it, and it was pretty amazing that it hadn't shattered as it fell. I slid it into the pocket of my coat, automatically. The decapitated body I dropped back into the Sainsbury's bag, like any tidy-minded serial killer.

I think it became official right about then, for me at least. I was in a duel of wits, and I was three-nil down. The man was good, no doubt about it. But there's more than one way to skin a cat, as you'll know if cat-skinning is your thing.

I was looking forward to meeting him.

And punching his teeth down his throat.

Still shaky, I got the car moving and threaded through the side alleys back into Du Cane Road. I passed the church, heading east, and almost immediately I saw a familiar figure walking ahead of me. It was Susan Book, now wearing a long fawn-colored duffel coat but still recognizable because the hood was down and she was still looking around her every so often as if she'd heard someone call her name.

I brought the car to a halt a few yards ahead of her and wound the window down. She began to skirt warily around it, then saw that it was me.

"Do you need a lift?" I asked.

She seemed surprised and a little flustered. "Well, I only live about a mile or so away," she said. "In Royal Oak. The bus goes straight there."

"So do I," I said. "Through it, anyway. It's no trouble to drop you off."

She fought a brief, almost comical struggle with herself. I could see she didn't like the idea of accepting a lift from a stranger, which was fair enough; also that she didn't relish the wait at the bus stop with the dark coming on.

"All right," she said at last. "Thank you."

I opened the door and she climbed in. We drove in silence for a while—a sort of charged silence. She was so tense it was like a static hum in the car.

"Have you known Miss Salazar long?" she asked at last, in a very quiet voice that I found hard to catch under the noise of the engine.

"Juliet? No," I admitted. "She . . . hasn't been living around these parts very long. I've known her less than a year."

She nodded briskly, understandingly. "And you're . . . sort of partners," she said, and then added quickly, "in the professional sense? You work together?"

"Not really," I said, feeling as though I was falling in Susan's estimation with every answer. "We did, briefly, but only while Juliet was learning the ropes. She worked alongside me for a while so she could see how the job pans out on a day-to-day basis. She's in business for herself now, so tonight was . . . more in the nature of a consultation."

"Yes. I see," said Susan, nodding again. "That must be very reassuring. Being able to call in favors from one another, I mean. Knowing that someone's . . . ." She tailed off, as though groping for the right words.

"Got your back?" I offered.

"Yes. Exactly. Got your back."

We were already at Royal Oak, and I'd pulled off the Westway onto the bottom end of the Harrow Road, seemingly without her noticing.

"Whereabouts do you live?" I asked.

She started, looked around her in mild surprise.

"Bourne Terrace," she said, pointing. "That way. First left, and then first left again."

I followed her directions, and we stopped in front of a tiny terraced house that was in darkness except for a single light upstairs. A garden the size of a bath mat separated it from the street. The gate was painted hospital green and had a NO HAWKERS notice on it.

"I'd invite you in for tea," Susan said, so stiffly that she sounded almost terrified. "Or coffee. But I live with my mother and she'd think it wasn't proper. She has very old-fashioned ideas about things like that. She wouldn't even be happy that I'd accepted a lift from you."

"Then it'll be our secret," I said, waiting for her to get out. She didn't. She just sat there, staring straight ahead, her eyes wide. Then, very abruptly, she brought her hands up to her face and gave a ragged wail that held, held, and then shattered into inconsolable sobbing.

It was so completely unexpected that for a second or so all I could do was stare. Then I started in with some vague, consoling noises, and even ventured a pat on the back: but she was lost in some private hinterland of misery where I didn't exist. After a minute or so, I began to make out words, heaved out breathlessly in the midst of the tears.

"I'm—I'm not—I'm not—"

"Not what, Susan?" I asked, as mildly as I could. I didn't know her well enough even to risk a guess at what was eating at her, but whatever it was it seemed to have bitten deep.

"Not a—not like that. I'm not, I'm not. I'm not a les—a lesb—" The words melted again into the formless quagmire of her sobbing, but that brief flash of light had told me all I needed to know.

"No," I said, "you're not." I reached past her to hook the glove compartment open, found a pack of tissues in there, and handed one to her. "It's not like that. Juliet just . . . does that to people. You can't help yourself. You just fall in love with her, whether you like it or not."

Susan buried her face in the tissue, shaking her head violently from side to side. "Not love," she sobbed. "Not love. I'm having c . . . carnal . . . I'm imagining . . . Oh God, what's happening? What's happening to me?"

"Whatever you want to call it," I said matter-of-factly, "looking at Juliet makes you catch it like people catch the flu. I feel it, too. Most people who ever get close to her feel it. Whatever it is, it's not a sin."

I couldn't think of anything to add to that. Maybe she was the kind of Christian who thought that gay love was always a sin, in which case she'd just have to work it through for herself. Bur straight, gay, or agnostic, what Juliet did to you came as a shock to anyone's system. I could tell her what Miss Salazar really was—by way of a prophylactic—but it wasn't my secret to tell and under the circumstances it might make things worse rather than better. Carnal thoughts about a same-sex demon? Susan probably wasn't in any state to take the knock.

I did the best I could to talk her down, and eventually she got out of the car, leaving the soggy tissue on the passenger seat. She mumbled something by way of thanks for the lift, to which she added, "Don't tell her! Please, please don't tell her!" Then she fled into the house.

There probably wasn't anything I could have said to her that would have helped. Love is a drug, like the man said. But the harshest truth of all is in the gospel of Steppenwolf rather than Roxy Music: the pusher doesn't care whether you live or die.

———

I called the Torringtons from the car as I was driving back east across the city. Hands-free, of course; I wouldn't want you to think I don't put safety first. Steve picked up on the first ring, which made me wonder if he'd been sitting with his phone in his hands.

"Mr. Castor," he said, sounding just a touch breathless. "What news?"

"Good news as far as it goes," I said. "You were right, and I was wrong."

"Meaning—?"

"Abbie's not in heaven. She's in London."

He exhaled, long and loud. I waited for him to speak.

"Can you please give me a moment?"

"Of course."

Maybe he covered the phone, or maybe the voices were too low to hear over the sound of the car's engine. There was about half a minute's silence. Then he came back on. The pitch of his voice was unsteady—like the voice of a man fighting back tears.

"We can't thank you enough, Mr. Castor. Do you think you can find her?"

"I'm prepared to try."

He gave a relieved laugh, harsh and emphatic and broken off short by some kind of psychological wind-shear. "That's excellent news! Excellent! We've got every confidence in you."

"Mr. Torrington—"

"Steve."

"Steve. I don't want to raise your hopes. This still isn't going to be easy, assuming I can do it at all. And I'm going to need to have some money to spread around. If you can front me two or three hundred quid to be going on with, then I can make a start on—"

He cut me off. "Mr. Castor, my wife and I count as affluent by any standards. You're over-finessing, if I can use a bridge metaphor. Whatever you need, we can afford it. Possibly you feel as though you're taking advantage of our grief. From our point of view, it's not like that at all. We've heard that you're the best, and we're grateful that you're prepared to help us." There was a rustle, and then the *scratch-scratch-scratch* of a fountain pen nib on paper. "I'm writing out a check," he said, "for a thousand pounds. I'll put it in the post tonight. No, better—I'll go over to your office and drop it off myself. I'll add some cash, too, to tide you over until this clears. If it's more than you were planning to charge, and if that makes you uncomfortable, then please just give the rest to the charity of your choice."

Good enough. I should have more clients who are that respectful of my sensitivities. I asked him for Peace's address, which turned out to be in East Sheen: not a part of the city I knew all that well, and a lot farther south than I was expecting.

"I'll be in touch," I said, and hung up.

Driving on automatic pilot, I'd already caught the Westway and driven on through Marylebone past Madame Tussauds and the planetarium—which now has commerce only with stars of the daytime TV variety. I was just about to swing off north onto Albany Street. But I had another call to make, and it was in the east of the city rather than the north. So I kept on going—east all the way, heading for the distant fastnesses of Walthamstow.

I was tired, and I still had a headache from that psychic mind-blast, but there was nothing to gain by putting this off until tomorrow. Night was always the best time to see Nicky if you wanted to get any sense out of him.

I parked the car at the top of Hoe Street. It was a fair walk from there, but the car was likely to be there when I got back, possibly with engine and wheels still attached. That was worth a little additional effort.

A couple of minutes' walk past the station there's a building with a Cecil Masey frontage that still looks beautiful through all the shit and peeling paintwork and graffiti. Aggressively Moorish, like all his best stuff: the centerpiece is a massive window in that elongated, round-topped, vaguely phallic shape, flanked by two smaller versions of itself. The same shapes appear up on top of the walls like crenellations, or like waves frozen in brick. The interiors are all marble and mirrors and gilded angels, courtesy of Sidney Bernstein or one of his underpaid assistants.

It opened in 1931 as a Gaumont, had its heyday and its slow decline like all the other prewar super-cinemas, and gently expired exactly three decades later. But then some ghoul exhumed it in 1963, and reinvented it as a members only establishment with some grandiose name like the Majestic or the Regal. For the next twenty-three years it screened softcore porn to jaded bank managers at prices set high enough to keep the riffraff out. Now it was dead again, its second demise mourned by nobody, and Nicky had bought it for a song—probably the "Death March from Saul."

It was the perfect home for him: he was also on his second time around.

I went in around the back, up the drainpipe, and through an unlocked window, the front being boarded up solid. The council nailed the boards up in the first place, but Nicky has added some additional barricades of his own. You can buy Nicky's services if you know his price, but he doesn't have much use for the passing trade.

Inside it was dark and cold, heat being another thing that Nicky has no truck with. As I walked along the broad, bare corridor to the projection booth, past peeling posters from two decades before, a draft of arctic provenance played around my ankles. I rapped on the door, and after a few seconds the security camera up top swiveled to get a better look at me. I'd passed three other cameras on the way up, of course, so he knew damn well it was me, but Nicky likes to remind you that Big Brother is watching. It's not so much a matter of security—although he takes his security more seriously than Imelda Marcos takes her footwear; it's more the statement of a philosophical position.

The door opened, without a creak but with the faintest suggestion of roiling vapor at floor level, like the effect you'd get from a dry ice machine set on low: either a side effect of Nicky's spectacularly customized air-conditioning, or something that he does on purpose.

I pushed the door open carefully, but I didn't step inside right away. I don't like to barge in without a direct invitation, because this is the keep of Nicky's little castle—and he really does think in those terms. He's installed all kinds of deadfalls and ambushes to stop people from intruding on his privacy. Some of them were ingenious, bordering on sadistic. In my experience, there's nobody who can think of more varied and interesting ways to abuse living flesh than a zombie.

"Nicky?" I called, opening the door a little farther with the toe of my shoe.

No answer. Well, someone had to have unlocked the door, and someone had to be operating the cameras. Taking my life—or at least the integrity of my balls—in my hand, I stepped inside, into a chill that you could reasonably say was tomblike.

I looked around, but saw no sign of Nicky. The booth is larger than that word makes it sound: a sort of first-floor hangar, with a very high ceiling which apparently helps the whole heat-exchange thing. Nicky keeps his computers up here, and anything else that's close to his cold, cold heart at any given moment. Right now, that included a hydroponics garden, which seemed to be doing nicely despite the blisteringly cold temperature. There was a screen across one half of the room, made up out of a row of malnourished, canelike plants rooted in buckets of evil-looking brown swill. The tallest of the plants were stretching to the ceiling and spreading their leaves out across it—reaching for the sky just to surrender, as Leonard Cohen sang somewhere or other. They'd grown as far as they could without bending their backs and shooting out horizontally, and as it was they looked to be balanced pretty precariously on the inadequate foundations of the plastic buckets.

Normally Nicky would have been at the computer terminal on the other side of the room—or maybe leaning on his elbows at the plan chest off to my far right, poring over maps and charts of London, England, and the world scribbled over and over with his own hermetic symbols. Both of those spots were currently empty.

"Hey, Nicky," I called, a little irritably. "Whenever you're ready, mate. Meter's running."

"Open your coat, Castor." Nicky's voice doesn't carry all that much, so it wasn't a shout—just an insinuating murmur that didn't seem to come from any particular direction, but crept along the ground with the sparse tendrils of water vapor. I finally placed him, though: he was standing behind the row of spindly cane trees looking like Davy Crockett at the Alamo—except that the pistol he was holding in his hands was no museum piece: it was a chunky service automatic with a lot of miles on the clock but a very convincing, businesslike look about it. Nicky was looking pretty serious, too; ordinarily the fake tan he insists on wearing gives him a slightly clownish look, but a gun adds a whole big helping of gravitas.

"Have you lost your fucking mind?" I asked him.

"Nope. There's some fucking weird shit going down in the big city right now, and I'm not planning to be a part of it. Just open your coat up. I want to see if you're carrying a weapon."

"Only the usual, Nicky. Unless that's some kind of coy euphemism for—"

"Do it, Castor. Last time of asking." The volume was turned up a little bit this time, which meant he'd taken a big breath just for the occasion; when he's not talking, he forgets to do that.

Swallowing some very bad words, I unbuttoned my paletot and

shrugged it open to left and right. "There you go," I said. "No shoulder holsters. No bandoliers. Not even a machete in my belt. Sorry to disappoint you."

"If you'd disappointed me, you'd know it. Turn out your pockets."

"Christ Jesus, Nicky!"

"I told you—this isn't anything personal. We're friends, as far as that goes. If I trusted anybody, it'd be you. But we're in uncharted territory tonight, and I'm honest to God not taking any risks." His hand made a pass-repass over the gun, and I heard a sound that I recognized from countless movies and maybe twice in real life: the sound of the slide release on an automatic pistol being racked back and then forward again.

I stopped arguing. There wasn't that much in my outside pockets in the first place; what there was—keys, wallet, Swiss army penknife with things for getting stones out of horses' hooves—I hauled out and dropped to the floor. There was a second set of pockets sewn into the lining of the coat, though, and with the things that were stored in there I took a fair bit more care: an antique knife with an inlaid handle, a small goblet in stained and heavily oxidized silver, the porcelain head of Abbie's doll. These I laid down on the floor with care, one at a time. Last of all came the tin whistle. "Just one hand," Nicky warned as I slid the whistle out and held it up. As far as he was concerned, this *was* a weapon—and it had his name on it.

I'd had just about as much of this as I could take by this time, and I was in the mood to do something rash. Slowly, with elaborate and exaggeratedly unthreatening gestures, I bent from the waist and laid the whistle down on the bare cement floor. I gave it a little flick with my thumb as I did it, so that it rolled. I knew Nicky's eyes would follow it, the way your eyes would follow a grenade without a pin. Then I knelt down a little lower. The bucket that held the cane tree at the end of the line nearest to me was just within the reach of my left hand at full stretch. I grabbed it right below the rim.

I stood up in one smooth movement, and the bucket toppled: the tree that was rooted in it went over, too, toppling its neighbor and starting a chain reaction that sounded like the swish of a thousand canes. And Nicky was standing in line like he was waiting for a spanking. Without a gasp or a whoof or a yell—because again he hadn't laid in any spare breath for it—he went sprawling. His head hit the wall with a dull thud, but that wouldn't slow him down much. From off to my right, though, there came a different sound: a metal-on-stone clatter, quickly swallowed. That seemed like the better bet, so I made a lunge even before I saw where the gun had ended up, in the spreading pool of sludge from the overturned buckets. Nicky had managed to disentangle himself from the undergrowth and he was scrambling on all fours in the same direction. Being at ground level already he got there first, but my foot came down on his wrist just as his fingers closed on the gun.

"I'm not putting my full weight down," I pointed out. "If I do, something's going to break."

Nicky has a morbid fear of physical trauma: being dead already, he doesn't have any way of repairing it. All the systems that in a living body would reknit flesh and bone and channel away infection are nonstarters in a walking cadaver. He dropped the gun in great haste and I scooped it up. It was old and heavy—but someone had been looking after it and I had no doubt at all that it would work, even covered in thick brown slurry. Not knowing how to put the safety back on or eject the clip, I aimed it at Nicky instead. He threw his hands up, desperately scrambling back across the floor on his backside.

"Easy! Easy, Castor! I won't heal! I won't heal!"

"Easy? You fucking bushwhacked me, you maniac!"

"I wanted to make sure you weren't going to kill me."

"What?" I lowered the gun, pained and exasperated. "Nicky, you're already dead. Did you forget that? Killing you would be fucking futile."

"To damage me, then." He was trying to get his legs under him and stand up without using his hands, which were still high in the air.

"Damage you. Right." I crossed to the window and tried to open it. Nothing doing: the sash was nailed down solid. I smashed it instead, raising a wail of indignation from Nicky, and dropped the gun out of the window onto the weed-choked sprawl of asphalt that used to be the cinema's car park—a party favor for the next courting couple who decided to take a walk through the long grass.

Then I turned to face him again. He lowered his hands and came across to look out of the window, then favored me with a resentful scowl. I noticed for the first time that he was wearing a butcher's apron over his usual Zegna suit. It was an odd and unsettling combination, even though the stains on it were mulch-green and mud-brown rather than bloodred.

You know what you're getting with Nicky, most of the time. He was paranoid even before he died, and if anything, that event had only reinforced his conviction that the universe was out to get him. So I wasn't really surprised by any of this: just morbidly curious as to what exactly had triggered it.

"Why the fuck would I want to damage you?" I asked him. "No, let me rephrase that. I want to damage you all the time—but why would I choose today to de-repress?"

He was sullen and defensive. "Why does anybody choose a particular time to freak out? All I know is that a lot of people are choosing now. Did that get by you somehow? I thought you had this big umbilical thing going with London. Tuned in to the . . . zeitgeist. City geist. Whatever. So if a whole lot of Londoners eat poison and lose their minds, I thought there was a chance you might get brainsick, too. But I guess today you were receiving on other wavelengths." He could see that none of this meant anything to me—and also that I was starting to look a little pissed off—so he came in again from a slightly less oblique angle. "You know how many murders there are in London in the average year, Castor?"

"Nope. I don't. I know we're behind New York but trying harder."

Out of nowhere he put on a smug look that I instantly recognized— the look he gets when he's dealing out arcane knowledge from undisclosed sources. "About a hundred and fifty. Worst year on record, a hundred and ninety-three. There was a big spike last year, but generally the rate stands nice and steady at two point four per annum per hundred thousand head of population. Say, one every couple of days, or just over. Know how many there were last night?"

"Again, no."

"Seven. Plus two arguables, and six old-school tries. And that's not counting in the rapes, the mutilations, the aggravated assaults. Sick shit for all the family, in a dozen different flavors. I'm telling you, Castor, we're way, way over to the right of the bell-shaped curve." He glanced off across the room, nodded toward the computer workstation. "Take a look."

I shot him a wary glance, but at least he wasn't armed now, and we seemed to be back on comfortable territory—wild conspiracy theories and tortured statistics. I walked over to the computer and glanced at the two monitors that he's got set up kitty-corner-wise in the corner of the room. A whole lot of files were open on the desktop, and most of them were stories from Internet news feeds.

UXBRIDGE MAN SLAIN WITH OWN TIE
WOMAN IN REGENT'S CANAL WAS MURDERED,
POLICE SAY
HUSBAND AND WIFE SLAIN, EXECUTION STYLE
SHOOT-OUT AT TESCO METRO

It did seem to have been a bad day—especially given that it was a Sunday, when most people in London are traditionally sleeping off hangovers or washing their cars. I took hold of the mouse and minimized some of the windows: there were more stories behind them, stacked one on top of another in an infinite regression of atrocities.

"You see?" said Nicky. "A sensible man takes precautions."

"How would you know?" I countered. "So what, you think London lost its collective mind last night?"

"Well, it certainly looked into the abyss. And the abyss gazes also, know what I mean?"

"Right. So you get yourself a gun. How do you know you're part of the solution rather than part of the problem, Nicky?"

He frowned, stopped in his tracks. "What?"

"There's an outbreak of murder and mayhem. You get scared, decide to make sure you don't end up on the wrong end of it, and the next thing you know, you're waving automatic weapons at close friends. There's such a thing as friendly fire, you moron."

"Friendly—?" He thought this over, looking like he'd sucked on a lemon and discovered that he still had some functional taste buds. He got sullen and defensive. "Hey, don't you fuck with my head, Castor—it's not funny. Whatever the hell happened, these killings were geographically clustered, okay? So we're talking a chemical or bacteriological agent, or something like that—something dispersed in either air or water. I don't drink water. I don't metabolize oxygen. There's no logical way I could be infected."

I nodded understandingly, mainly to make him shut up. "Nicky, seven murders in one night is one for the record books—but only until some industrious soul takes it up to eight. It's like every other summer is the hottest summer on record."

"That's just because of global warming."

"Right. And this is because of global rabies. That's how records work, Nicky: they keep going up because they can't go down. Anyway, leaving all this bullshit aside for a moment, I'm going to need a favor."

He didn't unbend: clearly it hurt his pride that I'd out-paranoided him with my "part of the problem" remark. "I'm not in the mood to do you any favors, Castor. You stamped on my wrist. You realize what I'd have to go through to repair a bone? I got no antibodies. I got no fucking white cells. I've just got my own two hands."

"I brought you a present."

"Like I care." I was going to count the seconds, but the pause was too short. "What is it?"

My relationship with Nicky is based on several distinct layers of ruthless pragmatism. Being dead, and risen again in the flesh (I'm avoiding the contentious term "zombie," which these days the government is calling hate-speech) Nicky doesn't get about as much as he used to. He prefers to keep his body chilled to a level where the processes of organic decay can be slowed to a manageable minimum. He still has a subtle aroma of formaldehyde and foie gras, but he takes the edge off it with Old Spice aftershave, and since most other dead-alive people I've met smell like a freezer full of spoiled meat, that's quite impressive.

But his limited mobility means that in some respects now he has to rely on the kindness of strangers—those comparatively rare strangers who don't find the company of the dead uncongenial. So whenever I want something from him, I bring him a little gift to sweeten the deal. He likes fine French reds of hard-to-find vintages (he just inhales the aroma, like one of Yeats's ghosts) and hen's-tooth-rare early jazz recordings: getting hold of that stuff without bankrupting myself in the process is an ongoing challenge. Tonight, though, I had a winner. I handed it over without a word—a vulcanite disc in a stiff cardboard sleeve, one side of the label marked up with postage stamps to the value of three cents. Nicky turned it over in his hands, read the recto side of the label, and said nothing for a while. Then he said, "Fuck, Castor. How big a favor are you looking for?"

It was something a fair bit rarer than a hen's tooth: a recording of Buddy Bolden, the tragically unhinged trumpeter who—by some accounts, anyway—single-handedly turned New Orleans ragtime into jazz. The A side was "Make Me a Pallet." There wasn't any B side, which under the circumstances didn't really matter. Bolden is popularly supposed to have left no recordings of his work, but I've got sources who don't take no for an answer.

"It's two favors."

"Go on."

"Number one is easy. I want you to get me some background on an accidental death. A girl named Abigail Torrington—time frame somewhere over the summer of last year. She drowned on a school trip. Some other kids died at the same time."

He sat down at the desk and typed a few of the details down in a notepad program.

"Okay. So far, that's a Ronco Twenty Golden Greats favor. What makes it a Buddy Bolden favor? Shit, I think you did crack one of my wrist bones, you jumpy bastard."

"Number two is a bit more open-ended. I'm looking for someone who doesn't want to be found. A man named Dennis Peace."

"How are you spelling 'Peace'?"

"Like the kind you've got to give a chance to. Guy's an exorcist, and from what I know already he's pretty damn good at it. Anything you can get me will trim the odds a bit more in my favor—and believe me when I say I'm taking all the help I can get here."

"Anything else you can give me? Last known address? Social security number? Known associates?"

I gave him the East Sheen address that Steve Torrington had given me over the phone. "That's pretty much all I've got. Except that he was in a malpractice case a few years back—on the receiving end." I hesitated, wondering if I should tell him about what had happened when I tried to locate Peace through Abbie's toys. But that would have entailed a hell of a lot more explanation than I wanted to get into right then.

"I'll stop by tomorrow," I said. "You can either give me a progress report or stick an assault rifle up my nose. If you get anything juicy before then, call me, okay?"

"Sure. I'll call you."

"Oh, and one more thing, since we're on the subject. Where did that crummy retread of the Oriflamme open up?"

"The exorcist bar?" Nicky sneered. "Like I'd be caught dead there." It was a weak joke, and I didn't do anything to encourage it. "Over in the West End," Nicky said, when he saw I wasn't rising to the bait. "Soho Square." He scribbled the address for me on a piece of printout paper, put it into my hand. "Didn't you once describe the Oriflamme as a busman's holiday?"

"Yeah, I did. And now I'm trying to catch a bus conductor."

I left him to it. Under the circumstances, I felt I was ahead of the game just coming away without any freshly minted holes in me.

I went back to Pen's, where I found a note from Pen on my bed telling me that Coldwood had called again and asking me to feed the animals again: she was going to visit Rafi, she said, and then head on out to Dylan's flat afterward to help him unwind after another late shift. Well, I thought resignedly, if you're going to play doctors and nurses you were onto a winner with an orthopedic surgeon.

Doling out liver to the ravens and pellets to the rats took up about half an hour. When I was done, and cleaned up again, I called Coldwood on the mobile number he'd given me—a much better option than going through the station switchboard.

He picked up immediately, and he didn't bother with small talk. "I've been trying to reach you all fucking day," he said. "Brondesbury Auto Parts: there was blood all over the shop, and it was a match with Sheehan's."

Brondesbury Auto Parts? Sheehan? It took me a moment or two to work out what he was talking about, then I remembered the bleak, empty warehouse out on the Edgware Road, and the pathetic ghost with half its head missing.

"Oh," I said. "Right. Well, congratulations."

"Premature. We arrested Pauley, but he made bail. That's why I called. Your name hasn't been mentioned anywhere, but your statement was what bought us the warrant: Pauley's got very big ears, and friends in a lot of fucking unlikely places. So watch your back, okay?"

"Seriously?" I was surprised and not pleasantly. It's been tried on a few times, but evidence from spiritual conversations has never been accepted in a court case. Not in England, anyway. I never dreamed this druglord might have anything to gain by topping me.

"Seriously. If he can get the warrant invalidated, he can stop the case coming to court. One way of doing that is to put you out of action and then allege conspiracy."

"Conspiracy?"

"To pervert the course of justice. It's just a form of words. He says you were in our pocket, a judge looks at the warrant submission, they get a verdict. If it goes their way he's got a get-out-of-jail-free card, because all our sodding evidence is inadmissible."

"This is great. You gonna lend me some bodyguards, then?"

"Yeah sure, Castor. Out of the same budget that I use for your company car and your health benefits. Look, I'm not saying it's going to happen. I'm just saying watch yourself. It's just about possible he'll try to put the frighteners on you. Are you around tomorrow?"

"Depends. What for?"

"At some point I'm gonna want you back at that warehouse. I want to set up a walk-through of how we think Sheehan died, and see if the ghost reacts in any way."

"How time sensitive is it?" I asked.

"Right now? Probably not very. We're still waiting on some of the forensics results. Why? You thinking of staying in and washing your hair?"

"I'm on another job."

Coldwood's laugh was short and explosive. "Then we're truly living in the last days. What case is this?"

"I'm looking for a girl."

"You're doing missing persons now?"

"No, she's a dead girl. Name of Abigail Torrington. It's a long story."

"Then keep it. I hate long stories. Call me when you're free, okay?"

He cut me off as abruptly as he'd picked up. I fished out Pen's old *London A–Z* from the back of a cupboard and opened it up on the kitchen table. I also found a highlighter pen, which was exactly what I needed. I flicked through to the page that had Harlesden on it, cracking the spine ruthlessly so it would lie flat on the table. It was about five years out of date in any case: I'd buy her a new one when I picked up Steve Torrington's friendly envelope full of cash and checks.

I drew a cross in Craven Park Road, roughly where my office was. That was where I first picked up Abbie's doll, and I'd been facing the window, which was sort of . . . north. Or so. The trace—the sense of something responding when I played my little tune—had come from behind me, to the left. I drew a broad, ragged line with the highlighter that took in Park Royal, a long stretch of Western Avenue, Hanger

Hill, and Ealing . . . I had to stop somewhere, so I decided to make the M4 elevated section my rough-and-ready boundary marker.

Then I found Du Cane Road, and the little cross that marked St. Michael's. The car park where I'd made my second attempt, earlier this evening, was about a hundred yards farther up the road. I'd been facing into the setting sun, and that was where the response had come from—until I was hit with that little psychic cluster bomb that left me with a hole in my tongue and a ringing in my ears like a peal of bells in Hades.

Due west. I drew in the second line, out through Acton, Ealing, and Drayton Green to the rolling hills of the Brent Valley Golf Course. No way Peace would be hiding Abbie there, though: the green fees were astronomical.

The two lines intersected over a huge swathe of West Acton and North Ealing. I'd drawn them wide on purpose, of course, because this wasn't rocket science or any other damn science worthy of the name: it was just me, extrapolating hopefully from a messy and inadequate data set.

And that metaphor made me think of Nicky again.

Which made me remember the crumpled piece of printout paper in my pocket, with his handwriting on it.

The Oriflamme.

I looked at my watch. Only eleven, so the joint would still be hopping. And maybe Peace would think he'd hurt me worse than he had with his little psychic overload ambush. There was nothing like stealing a march on the opposition.

Chapter Six

There was a broad flight of stone steps up from the street, the stairwell separated off from the pavement by wrought-iron railings with the arms of the borough of Camden worked into them—complete with the pious motto *Non sibi sed toti*, usually translated as "I hope you brought enough for everyone." I guess at some time in its recent past this place had been a government building of some kind.

Not anymore, though, clearly. The two bruisers who checked me at the top of the steps didn't have the look or the dress sense of any civil servants I'd ever seen, and probably didn't have much of a future in local government unless Camden one day decided to open up a gorilla-wrangling department.

They weren't checking me for weapons or concealed booze, although there was a perfunctory frisking of my pockets and linings: mainly they were verifying that I was alive, and more or less human by the yard-sticks they were using. First they made me clench a silver coin tightly in my hand for a few seconds and looked to see if I showed any reaction to the metal, then they took my pulse in a rough-and-ready way at throat and wrist. There's something a bit off-putting about having a guy who's three inches taller than you, with the build of a wrestler, pressing his thumb against your windpipe. It's one reason why I don't drink at exorcist hangouts more often.

Another reason is that I'm an unsociable bastard who hates shoptalk worse than dental surgery.

The Oriflamme is the exorcists' hangout par excellence, in case you hadn't guessed that already: or at least it was in its first incarnation. Back then, it stood in the center of a roundabout on Castlebar Hill, in a building that was formerly a museum and then went through various changes of ownership before settling into the hands of the famous Peckham Steiner—a father figure for all London exorcists, so long as you had a drunk, abusive father who was only on nodding terms with sanity.

Steiner then made a gift of the place to his good friend Bill Bryant, better known by the semi-affectionate nickname of Bourbon. It was a very long way from anywhere, but it had a kind of dank, heavy atmosphere of its own and a reputation as the place to be seen if you were looking to make a name for yourself in the trade, so it limped along from year to year in spite of the lousy location. But then about three years ago, somebody burned it to the ground. It was a firebomb attack, mercifully when the place was closed, and it did the job nicely. The barman's cat survived, but apart from that they didn't save so much as an ashtray.

Nicky has a whole bunch of theories about who did it and why, and every so often he tries to tell me some of them. I usually manage to get clear before he reaches the part where satanists are taking over the government, but sometimes it's a close call.

Meanwhile, in one of those ironies that dog our profession, the Oriflamme rose from the dead—or at least the name did. A guy named McPhail, who as far as I know had never had anything to do with the place on Castlebar Hill, had his own vision of a place that would sort of be the exorcists' version of a gentlemen's club—with a bar, a lounge, poste restante facilities, a place where you could crash if you were just in the city for a couple of days, baths, the whole works.

He didn't have any premises—or collateral—but he did have the kind of can-do attitude that you usually associate with serial killers and corrupt politicians. He stole the name from Bourbon Bryant (who threatened to sue but didn't have the money for a cab to the court-house, let alone a lawyer) and set up shop in Soho Square. The rumor was that he was squatting rather than paying for a lease, and I could believe it: rents are so high in Soho these days, even the homeless guys sleeping in doorways are paying a grand a month.

I walked on up the steps, having passed muster as a warm body with no passengers, and went in through a door that was as thickly decorated with wards and sigils as a wedding car is with ribbons and old tin cans. That took me straight into a large bar area that had prob-ably had more atmosphere back when it was a rent office or whatever. Lighting was provided by a dozen or so bounce spotlights at floor level around the edges of the room, pointed up at the ceiling: a nice idea, but spoiled by the fact that most of the people in the room were stand-ing or sitting close to the spots and blocking off most of the light. Huge shadows came and went on the ceiling, and light levels rose and fell from one second to the next as people shifted in their seats or stood up to get the next round in.

The bar itself was a rough barricade of packing cases with tarpau-lins over them, off in one corner of the room. They were serving beer by the bottle, wine and spirits by the unmeasured slug—enough in itself to get the place closed down if anyone from Customs and Excise stopped in for a quick one. Of course, most revenue men have a very faint pulse in the first place, so they probably wouldn't get past the bouncers.

The clientele were colorfully mixed. I spotted half a dozen people I vaguely knew in the seething mass at the bar, and a few more sitting in quiet corners in intense tête-à-têtes with strangers who could have been clients, partners, or paid informers. I was looking for someone specific, though, and I saw him at last, leaning against a pillar on the far side of the room, all on his lonesome. Bourbon Bill himself, the owner of the original Oriflamme that had died in the flames and been reborn as this un-phoenixlike shithole. He was wearing a leather jacket over a red shirt and black denims that looked as though they might date from the American Civil War; Doc Martens of a similar vintage graced his feet. He was nursing a nearly empty shot glass while taking occasional slugs from a hip flask in his inside pocket. I swung around by way of the bar, picked up two large shots of whisky, and came up on him from behind.

I pushed one of the glasses into his free hand, clinked the other one against it. "Cheers, Bill," I said, as he looked around.

"Felix Castor." He sounded surprised. "Unexpected privilege. You don't seem to get out much these days." He raised the glass and downed it in one. He drank whisky like other men drink water, and as far as I know he only used water for brushing his teeth. He could have gone through a half bottle tonight already, depending on how early he started, but there was no indication at all in his voice or in the way he was standing. His fondness for booze wasn't a great asset in a bar owner—former bar owner, I should say—but his incomparable ability to deal with it definitely was. More than one man who'd tried to drink him under the table had been carried away on top of it.

"I get out as much as I ever did, Bourbon," I said. "I just don't like to get drunk in the company of ghost-hunters. It feels like I'm still on the clock, somehow."

"That's your rep, Fix." He grinned, but it didn't last. His face settled back down into its habitual dour lines: he was someone whom life had kicked in the balls, and he still wore the expression that comes after the initial pain of impact has subsided. He'd always had a basset hound kind of face, now it was more deeply seamed than ever, and his complexion matched his crest of wood-ash hair. "You used to come out to the *real* Oriflamme, though, time was. Couple of nights a week, if I remember rightly."

I nodded. "Then I got myself an office. Biggest mistake I ever made."

"I hear you, brother." He laughed ruefully, shook his head. "Biggest mistake for me was going up to Scotland for my brother's wedding. Came back to a pile of cinders and a bill from the fire brigade. Three years on and I still don't have a blind clue who did it."

"Any progress on that front?"

"Not recently. Had a lead a couple of months back, might come to something. Most likely not. I'm patient. Got a sort of a Zen mentality, these days. You know, flowing with the water."

"That's not Zen. That's Tao."

"Whatever. I don't let stuff get to me. But when I find those mother-less bastards, I'm going to take their effing teeth out with pliers." His expression changed, became suddenly more animated in a slightly un-healthy way. "Why are you asking, anyway? Did you hear something? I'm offering a reward for information, you know."

"If I hear anything, I'll pass it on," I assured him hastily. "Bugger the reward. No, I came down here looking for someone else. Maybe you can point him out to me, if he's here."

"Shoot."

"Dennis Peace."

"Yeah, I know Peace." That was why I'd gone straight over to Bour-bon when I saw he was here: he knew everybody. "Seems like he's fla-vor of the month all of a sudden. You want to do some business with him?"

"Not exactly, no."

"Then what?"

"I need to contact him on behalf of a client. He may have taken something that doesn't belong to him."

"Hah." Bourbon didn't look altogether surprised about this mis-sion statement. "Well, maybe so. Wouldn't be the first time, I've got to admit. He was always a bit of a wild boy. I remember him coming into the bar one night and talking about knife fights. I called him on one story because it sounded like he was talking shite. So he rolled up his shirt and showed me his scars. Jesus fucking wept! He looked like Boris Karloff had chopped him up and stitched him back together again."

"Did he pick a fight with someone and lose?" I asked, trying to pin down that echo.

"He picked a fight with Stig Matthews. They both lost. Both ended up in hospital."

Yeah, that was what I'd heard. Two men trading punches until they both fell down, with broken noses and half-pulped faces: the sort of thing that gives even machismo a bad name.

"I thought he was trying to be good just lately, though," Bourbon said reflectively. "Starting to quiet down a bit. That's what people tell me, anyway. He came back from America a changed man, they say. But I can't help you anyway, Fix. He's not here."

"You sound pretty sure."

"Well, I saw him walk out about half an hour back. Looking a bit rough, I have to say—like he hadn't slept in a while. He bought some FFs from Carla, and popped a couple right there. Then he was off again. Didn't even stay for a drink."

Damn. I'd been that close. But a miss is as good as a mile. "Is Carla still here?" I asked. Bourbon looked around the room for a few seconds, then pointed to a formidable-looking redhead sitting close to the bar, in intense conversation with a bare-armed bald guy so heavily tattooed that it was hard to make out his facial expression. In other company, he might have made you feel a little nervous: next to Carla he sort of faded into the background.

"Thanks, Bourbon. So Peace used to be a regular at the old place. You know anything else about him?"

"There's a difference between what I hear and what I know, Fix. Peace is the sort of man that people like to tell stories about—but you know how it is. A lot of those stories used to be told about other people before and they'll be told about someone else after. All I know—know for sure—is that he used to be a rubber duck a while back. He was part of the collective. Not anymore, though; he got fed up with all the arguments. And I think he told me he's a friend of Rosie Crucis, although as far as I know he wasn't part of the team that raised her."

"You're right. He wasn't."

"Oh yeah, that was you and Jenna-Jane Mulbridge, wasn't it? The Sussex Gardens Resurrectionists. That's all I can think of. Never saw him in anyone's company except his own. He's almost as antisocial as you."

"Tell me some of the stories, then."

He grimaced. "I'd just as soon not, Fix, if it's all the same to you. Not my style."

"Sorry I asked, then. Thanks, Bourbon. I owe you one."

"You bought me one. Just don't go in half-cocked, okay? Peace is a nasty piece of work, in some respects, but in my experience he plays straight with people who play straight with him. On the other hand, if you piss him off he can be a right bastard."

"Shit, he really is like me. Have a good one, Bourbon."

"You, too, Fix."

I strolled over toward Carla's end of the bar, watching her out of the corner of my eye while I ordered another drink. I don't like hitting people up if I don't already know them: the law of unintended consequences applies with big, spiky knobs on. I could have asked Bourbon to make an introduction, but why the hell should I drag him into my shit when he's got shit enough of his own?

Biding my time, I ordered another drink. By the time it came, Carla had finished her conversation with the illustrated man. Money had changed hands, and so had a little brown paper bag that had been folded many times and taped shut. The guy took off for the street door looking happy and excited—at least, as far as I could tell under all the paintwork.

FFs, Bourbon had said, by which I presumed he meant *fast-forwards*, rather than, say, back issues of the Fantastic Four comic book. So Peace had an amphetamine habit. Well, he wouldn't be the first exorcist to keep his pencils sharp with chemical assistance—or the last. Interesting that he'd looked so wiped, though: could be that was an after-effect of fielding all my various attempts to raise Abbie's spirit, as well as hitting that screamer back my way earlier in the day. Maybe if I kept up the pressure there, I'd get through his guard.

Or maybe the next ricochet I caught would mulch my brains until they leaked out of my ears.

I crossed to Carla's table and sat down in the just-vacated chair. She was just getting up: she looked at me with a certain amount of surprise and not much pleasure. Close up, she was an even more impressive lady than she had been from across the bar. Not tall, but very solid; at a distance you could tell yourself that some of her bulk was fat, but from this range, I could see that she was made of something harder and less yielding. She looked to be about forty, and her slablike face under its layers of foundation makeup looked like a redbrick wall. Her incongruously soft brown eyes were cordoned off like a crime scene with lines of mascara; the rest of her features had disowned them. She was altogether the wrong shape for a belly shirt, but that was what she was wearing nonetheless: the pixie skirt was another red herring, but I felt that the wrestler's boots were an honest statement of intent.

"I'm closed," was all she said.

I shrugged as if I was easy either way. "I'm not buying," I said.

"Then fuck off." No rancor; nothing personal. But no give, either.

"I'm just looking for someone you know. Dennis—"

"I said fuck off." She put a warning finger in my face. "I don't know you."

"Well, that's true. My name's Castor. Felix Castor. My friends call me Fix." I held out a hand, which she didn't even look at. Instead she just got up and made to walk around the table, past me toward the bar. Having a good deal more tenacity than sense, I jumped up, too, and stepped into her way. She really wasn't tall, her head was only on a level with my fourth rib.

She stopped. There was a silence, which started with her and then moved on out across the bar. Without turning around, I knew we'd just become a local center of attention.

"Sport," she said, in the same cold tone, "you really don't want to do that."

"Maybe not," I conceded. "I really do want to meet Dennis Peace, though. Maybe you could tell him I'm looking for him. Felix Castor. He can get my number from Bourbon Bryant, or leave a message for me here."

"You'd better move aside now," was all Carla said.

I moved aside. She glanced up at me once: a hard, unreadable look.

Then she went on past me to the bar, and there was a collective breathing out in a number of different keys.

Okay, so my intended charm offensive had fallen a little flat. Well, in terms of charm, anyway: I'd managed the offensive part well enough Never mind. Bourbon had given me some food for thought, and some leads to follow, enough to be going on with for now.

———

The rain was coming down again heavily, and the slick black asphalt of Soho Square reflected the fragmented glitter of a few car headlights like shooting stars in a clear sky. It wasn't cold, though: in fact it felt good after the canned air of the cryptlike bar. I didn't even turn up my coat collar as I walked.

It was well after midnight now, and there weren't many people around. Two heavyset guys—one of them very, very tall—were talking in murmurs at the edge of the pavement. They stepped to either side to let me pass in between them, one of them flicking a cigarette away over his shoulder.

I'd left the car on the other side of the square, so the quickest way was right through the cramped little park area in the middle. I rounded the Tudor folly that used to be an ice cream stand and the farther gate came into view: it was closed, which wasn't a good sign. A few more steps brought me level with it, and I gave it a tug. Nothing doing, they'd locked it for the night.

I turned around, to find the two men I'd walked past moments before now heading straight toward me. "Gate's locked," I said mildly. I wasn't looking for trouble, and I didn't automatically assume that they were: true, they were still heading toward me even though they knew now that there was no through road. But maybe they were hard of hearing; there's an innocent explanation for most things if you keep an open mind.

"Good," said the guy on the left, speaking from way back in his throat. He drew a knife from his belt in a smooth, practiced motion. The one on the right, the bigger of the two, who had eyebrows so thick they looked like bottle brushes, smacked his fist into his palm. Oh well, I only said *most* things: I guess this was the exception that proved the rule.

They kept on coming. Over their shoulders I could see the street, which was empty in both directions: no help there. I braced myself to give them as much of a fight as I could—but they were both faster and slicker than I expected. They left the path and peeled off to either side of me, so that I couldn't keep both of them in view at once. I backed away to avoid being sandwiched, but the locked gate was right behind me, and two steps was all the backing-up room I had. I kept darting my eyes back to the taller guy whenever he moved, because he looked like the business end of the partnership even though he hadn't produced a weapon. That was all the opening the other guy needed: he did a standing jump, slamming into me hard, and knocking my feet from under me.

I hit the gate with his shoulder still wedged against my chest, and he put all of his weight into it so that the breath hiccupped agonizingly out of my lungs. I slithered down onto the crazy paving in a dead slump, and they were both on me before I could get up. I twisted wildly, in the hope that the knife would get tangled up in the thick fabric of my coat or go in obliquely and miss all the many vital organs that nature sprinkles so liberally through our body cavities—but for some reason the blow didn't come. I carried on thrashing, and the knife man almost fell over his colleague as we bucked and writhed together on the cold, wet stones.

The knife man cursed, and some stuff that must have fallen out of his pockets or maybe out of mine clanged against the fence, then clattered away across the rain-slick stone. I jabbed an elbow into his throat, but without much force—and there was enough muscle there to stop the blow from being anything more than a minor irritant. He punched me in the mouth a couple of times just to get my attention, then once more for the sheer fun of the thing. After which the one with the eyebrows hauled me to my feet, unresisting, his massive fist clamped on my throat. As I came up, though, my hand closed on a stubby metal cylinder that had fallen between my arm and my body. I brought it with me.

The big guy was even bigger than I'd realized. He lifted me clear off the ground, so that my own weight began to choke me even more effectively than his constricting fingers. His heavy-featured face leered into mine. He had a very wide mouth, with too many teeth in it.

"Knock it off, Po. You're killing him," the knife man snapped. His voice was so deep and harsh, it sounded like he was spitting up razor blades.

"I thought that was the idea," the big guy rumbled. With my throat clamped shut, I couldn't inhale: as the tall man's breath passed over me in a hot, fetid wave, I was able to appreciate the upside of that position.

"Bring him down here. I'll tell you when to fucking kill him."

With a snarl, the taller man dropped his forearm an inch or so, letting my toes touch the ground.

Frowning in concentration, the knife man judiciously adjusted the height of his colleague's extended arm—a millimeter this way, a touch that—so that I'd be able to avoid choking myself so long as I didn't actually try to move. It reminded me of a dentist adjusting his chair: I wished it hadn't.

I'm not one to judge a book by its cover, but he was an ugly son of a bitch. He didn't exude the sheer, physical menace his heavily eyebrowed friend did, but there was something wrong with his face, with the proportions of it. The jaw was subtly too long, the eyes set too low. It was like a face that someone had gotten tired of halfway, screwed up, and thrown away. And then this guy had fished it out of the basket and reused it.

"So now we talk," he said at last, his voice the same broken-edged growl.

"You . . . first . . . ," I mumbled thickly. The bastard had split my lip.

"Yeah," he agreed. "Me first. My name's Zucker. My friend here is

Po. And I've got sad news for you, Castor. My friend is not your friend. My friend wants to bite your throat out."

"Sorry . . . to hear it," I managed.

"I'll bet," he hissed, his mouth up close to my ear. His breath had a sour stink to it, too. Why couldn't I be intimidated by people with good personal hygiene?

"You know why Po wants to hurt you?" Zucker asked me.

"No idea . . . ," I wheezed.

"No," he agreed. "You have no idea. Which is why I'm going to tell you. You've been hanging around with the wrong people. Whoring yourself out to any fucker that asks. Storing up trouble for yourself."

Ironically enough, it was around about then that I came to the conclusion that I had a chance. For some reason this fruitcake didn't want to kill me—or at least, not until after he'd given me a stern lecture and maybe a spanking. If that reluctance made him hesitate at some point when he and his burly friend had the drop on me, then there was an outside chance that I might one day be in a position to look back on this and laugh.

Either way, though, I couldn't answer the charge in any detail while the hand of the taller man—Po?—was still crimping my windpipe. Zucker seemed to realize this: he tapped imperiously on Po's wrist, and Po slackened his grip a little.

"Well," I said, swallowing with a wince of discomfort, "you tell me who the wrong people are, and maybe I can avoid them in the future." I slurred the words more than my already-thickening lip required, and I let some bloody drool come out with them; it was probably good if they thought I was more damaged than I was.

"There's something in your tone that sounds like sarcasm." Zucker brandished the knife in front of my eyes. The edge of the blade had a two-tone sheen to it, suggesting hours of loving work with a strop and a wad of Scotch-Brite. I probably wouldn't even feel it going in. "You can't imagine how unhealthy sarcasm could be for you right now. You should be thinking in terms of humility, contrition, and open cooperation. We're looking for nothing less."

I threw up my hands, palms out. "I'm just doing a job—like you," I said. "Okay? No need for heavy threats."

"Like me?" The comparison seemed to sit badly with Zucker. "Like me? Say that again, and I'll cut your tongue out." I thought the anger might be a sadist's window dressing, but the glint in his eyes was real enough. I'd touched a nerve, and he was ready to touch back. Good. That was another point in my favor: if he was angry, he was likely to be stupid and hasty and misread my move when I made it. Unfortunately, he was also likely to make good on his promise and cut my tongue out. I was treading a fine line.

"Sorry," I said, making my voice a servile mumble. "Sorry, mate. No offense."

By now, that additional sensory channel I've got that is more like hearing than anything else was jammed with deafening discords. These guys looked human enough, the eyebrows aside, but they were loup-garous: dead human souls that had invaded, possessed, and shaped animal bodies to the point where you couldn't tell any longer what they'd originally been. Not until the dark of the moon, anyway—then all bets were off. When I realized that this was what I was dealing with, I dropped my eyes to the ground: some were-men respond to direct eye contact in the same way male silverback gorillas do. Come to think of it, Po could have been a gorilla at some point in his post mortem history. Maybe that was a touch exotic for central London, though: the risen dead tend to do their shopping locally.

"Well, maybe you'd like to show us exactly how sorry you are," Zucker suggested sardonically. "Maybe you'd be interested in switching sides. How does that sound?"

"Love to. Love to. Whose side am I on now, then? I mean, whose side *was* I on before I switched to yours? Because I jumped across as soon as you suggested it. Straight up. You tell me whose back you want me to stab, and I'm there. Just give it a name, okay?"

Zucker hesitated. I knew why, too: when you're the one with the other guy's balls in your hand, so to speak, it goes against the grain to answer a direct question. It's almost as though you're giving away the advantage. He couldn't quite bring himself to do it. "Examine your conscience," he suggested, baring his teeth. "Who's been asking you for favors lately?"

Who indeed? Juliet. The Torringtons. The London Met. If this was what an embarrassment of riches felt like, I decided I could live without it: it was too sharp and pointy by half. But it would really help to know who I had to thank for this special attention, so I decided to push the issue just an inch or so further.

"I'm hugely in demand," I said. Po had unconsciously relaxed his grip by a fraction, so I was getting some of my breath back now. "You'll have to give me a clue. You're not working for a drug pusher, are you? Gent by the name of Pauley? No? Because my mate in Serious Crimes reckons I might be in line for what he called 'the frighteners.' Do you gents qualify as frighteners, or are you more in the line of softeners-up for the frighteners still to come? Sort of a John the Baptist deal, if you take my meaning?"

They were looking at me in bewilderment. But then they gave it up and got down to business again. The edge of the knife touched my cheek in a way that was unpleasantly suggestive. While this was going on, though, I was turning over in my hand the object I'd palmed when they dragged me to my feet. Metallic, certainly, rounded, basically cylindrical but hollow at one end and with a tapering extension at the other. The goblet. I'd picked up the goblet I carry around with me for the very rare occasions when I'm tempted to try my hand at black magic.

"We need information," said Zucker. "And you need to convince us that we shouldn't cut all sorts of pieces off you. So listen to me, okay? Just listen. We know how far they got, and we know why they stopped. Someone didn't close the circle, right? A little bird flew the nest? But if there was even a partial breach, we could be knee-deep in each other's entrails before the fucking day is out. Did they promise you immunity? If they did, they didn't mean it. You're not stupid enough to fall for that line, are you?"

All of which made about as much sense to me as the Dead Sea Scrolls.

"Maybe I'm more naive than you think," I said. It seemed safely noncommittal.

It was at this point that Po reentered the conversation. "Let me eat one of his eyes," he suggested.

Zucker ignored this suggestion. "You think it might be possible to squeeze some advantage out of the situation," he said. "Your sort always do. I can promise you, Castor, there's no profit here for anyone. Just death, and then after that the things that are worse than death."

"You're going to kill me and *then* rape me?"

Po lifted his free hand over my head and balled it into a fist, but Zucker shook his head just once and the move stopped dead.

"They'll close the circle," he growled, bringing his face up very close to mine, "and do the whole thing again from scratch. Things will get bad, then. Very bad, very quickly. And they won't need you anymore. Do you think any assurances they've given you will still hold after that? Do you think they'll keep you as a pet?"

He put out a hand and pressed his index finger against my temple. His nail was as sharp and tapered as a claw, but he didn't break the skin. With Po still gripping my throat I couldn't pull away as the nail traced a path across my face until it rested on my left cheek, a millimeter away from my eye.

"If you'll work for us," he said, with an absolute calm that was a lot more chilling than Po's slightly crazed anger, "then there's a point in keeping you alive. If you won't, we're wasting our time."

I put a pensive expression on. And underneath it, I really was thinking hard. What I was thinking was this: since I didn't have the slightest idea what these two escaped lunatics were talking about, the likelihood that I could talk them into not ripping my head off and sucking out the juices with a straw was small. So the time had come to play my ace in the hole.

"All right," I muttered, dropping my gaze again. "All right. I admit it, they made me a good offer. Fuck, what would you have done?" As

I said it, I threw out my hands in a mute appeal—and brought my right hand around on the rebound, jamming what was in it directly into Po's face.

I'd rather have had the dagger, to be honest—but the chalice was made of silver, too, and the base had a sharp rim. I drove it into the guy's cheekbone hard enough to draw blood, because that was the whole point. Seeing that white metal gleam in my hand, the other were-man took a hasty step back and brought up his hands to protect his face and chest even before he saw what it was he was protecting them from.

Loup-garous don't like silver: it's some kind of an allergic reaction that comes with the package—with being a pirate soul and flying the colors of someone else's flesh. Po shrieked in agony the instant his spilled blood made contact with the virgin metal, and as he slapped both his hands to his face he let me drop.

I ducked out from under his outstretched arms, and as I came up I landed an almighty punch on the point of Zucker's jaw. Not the punch I would have chosen—you can break your wrist on a jawbone very easily, and nine times out of ten a jab to the stomach will give you a better return—but it made the most of the angle and the fact that I was already moving. The knife fell out of his hands as he staggered backward, and I snatched it up on the fly. Luckily enough, I caught it by the hilt: if I'd closed my fist around the blade I'd have left behind a few fingers.

Then I was off and running, Po's outraged bellowing fading at my back. I was heading for the open gate I'd come in through, but once I rounded the folly and put it between me and the two loup-garous, I swerved off the path into the undergrowth, uttering a fervent prayer to the God I don't believe in that I didn't trip over a root or a pothole in the dark.

The fence loomed ahead of me. I threw the knife over, planted my hands on top of the fence, in between the decorative flat-metal spearheads, and vaulted up. More by luck than judgment, I was able to get one foot up on the top of the fence, and then the other.

While I balanced there, indecisive, looking for a way to shinny over without impaling myself on the spikes, something thumped into my left shoulder, hard and cold. That settled the matter: I lost my balance and went sprawling down into the street, my coat catching long enough to jerk me sideways before it tore and dumped me onto the ground on my face.

Pain was spreading out from my shoulder in hot filaments, but my arm still seemed to work, so I had to ignore it for now. I scrambled to my feet, snatching up the knife again, and glanced around. This was the next hurdle: I didn't have a bloody clue where I was in relation to the car. I took a look behind me and wished I hadn't. The two dark figures on the other side of the fence were loping through the undergrowth on all fours, covering the distance at twice my speed. One of them—Po, I assumed, since he was about the size of a rhino—tensed for the jump, and I knew damn well he'd clear the fence like a Grand National winner.

I ran without thinking, got my bearings as I was running, and realized that the car was up ahead of me, maybe fifty yards or so, and on this side of the street. There was a sound at my back of something touching down heavily, and nails or claws or something of that general nature scraped on the wet pavement as Po checked his fall and took off after me.

I fished in my pocket for the car keys, pressed and pressed and pressed the stud on the key ring until a cheerful *bingly-beep* sound from up ahead told me that the car had unlocked itself. At the same time, the sidelights flashed three times: a feature that I'd never even noticed until my life depended on it.

I got the door open and crammed myself inside, pulling it closed behind me. Something slammed against the door at the same time as I palmed the other button on the right of the key fob, locking it again: it didn't give. The knife, which I'd forgotten I was holding, clattered onto the floor of the car. I left it there; trying to fight my way out of this was going to get me killed in very short order.

Shaking like a bead of sweat in a bellydancer's cleavage, I somehow managed to get the key into the ignition, but then I slammed it into gear as I was turning it and stalled dead. Something smashed hard into the driver side window and it starred right across. Involuntarily, I turned my head to look.

It was Po. At least, that was my best guess. Right now it was something out of a nightmare, crawling flesh half-congealed into a shape midway between human and something vaguely feline. I was judging mainly by the teeth, you understand, because for some reason it was to the gaping mouth that my eyes were drawn.

The car started up just as the thing outside drew back its clawed fist for a second blow that would probably have punched through the glass and ended up embedded in my face. The car leaped away, clipping the back bumper of the BMW in front with a sickening crunch before lurching out across the full width of the road. I plowed into the pavement, but fortunately missed the wall of the Bank of Scotland by the width of a nun's chuff. Po was bounding across the street behind me, but I floored the gas and left him standing.

Thank you, nonexistent God. One I owe you.

Chapter Seven

In Pen's bathroom mirror, glimpsed out of the corner of my eye because I was having to twist my head around to an angle that would have challenged Linda Blair, the ragged gash in my left shoulder looked really ugly.

"What in the name of God have you been doing to yourself," Pen asked, with a certain degree of awe.

"I had some help," I muttered, teeth gritted. Pain always makes me irritable: I'm sure as shit not the stuff that martyrs are made out of.

My arm had started to stiffen up as I was driving, with occasional lightning strikes of pain shooting from shoulder to fingertips. After a while, I was driving just with my right hand and only using my left—when I couldn't avoid it—to change gear. And getting my coat off, when I'd finally managed to park the car, find my door keys in the wrong pocket, and let myself in, had been a whole heap of fun. Luckily Pen had turned out to be home, since Dylan was on another late shift. With her help, I was able to peel the coat away from the wound, yelping in anguish as it opened again. My shirt we just cut away and dumped in the waste bin: even Persil wasn't going to bring it up white again. Then I sat on the edge of the bath, a large whisky clutched tightly in my hand, occasionally biting back colorful expletives as Pen cleaned out the edges of the cut.

Now, examining the results in all their reflected glory, I had to admit that the wound was impressive, in a grim and grisly way. It was a broad slash about three inches long on the very top of my shoulder, exactly midway between arm and throat. Small streamers of ribboned flesh hung down on either side of it, testifying to a serrated blade or a shape that had a lot of separate points and edges to it. A throwing star, maybe, although those two loup-garous hadn't exactly struck me as being the ninja type. That involves stealth, just to go for the obvious point.

On the whole, though, this didn't look too bad. The fact that it was a ragged cut meant it would knit together that much quicker, and Pen had done a thorough job of cleaning it out. All it needed now was a dressing strip and the home team was back in the game.

Pen wasn't quite so convinced. "You should let Dylan look at it," she said. "If this festers, Fix, it'll be bad news."

"It wasn't exactly 'Your annuity matures' to start with," I grumbled back gracelessly. Then, remembering my manners, "Thanks for patching me up. But let's not bring Dylan into this. He might draw the wrong kind of conclusion about the circles you move in."

"Was it this that cut you?" Pen asked, holding up the knife. I'd put it down on the side of the bath earlier, well out of the way. I really didn't like to see it in her hands: that edge was just too damn perfect, and Pen was too emphatic with her gestures when she got worked up. I took it from her, quickly but gently.

"No," I said. "This would have made a clean cut. A really clean cut. Have you seen the edge on it?" I turned the blade edge-on to her so she could see it in all its scary beauty. That meant I was looking at the flat of the blade, and I noticed now that it had a floral motif on it: leaves in pairs, etched directly into the steel, ran from the hilt to within an inch of the point.

Pen gave the knife an ill-favored look as I put it down again on the sink top. Then I had a better idea: I took a used toilet roll tube that looked to be about the right width and slid the knife inside it. The broad tang stretched the cylinder enough to hold the blade rigidly in place. I was a lot less likely to lose a finger on it now.

"I hate it when this stuff happens," Pen muttered, dropping blood-encrusted swabs of cotton wool into the waste bin. "Why do you take jobs that get you beaten up and cut open and thrown off roofs and all that macho rubbish? Aren't there enough of the other kind?"

"The other kind?"

"You know what I mean. 'Get that bogey man out of my closet. Bring Granny back so she can tell us where she put the rent book. Tell my Sidney I've remarried and there's no room in my bed for him anymore.'"

She turned her back on me to wash her hands. It looked unnervingly symbolic.

"I can't always tell which kind of job is which," I said, defensively. "I don't get any special kind of pleasure out of this stuff."

"No," she agreed glumly. "I suppose not."

"How's Rafi?" I asked, to change the subject.

"Still asleep." She turned to face me again, wet arms folded, face set. "I'm serious, Fix. You should just walk out of this one while walking is still an option."

This was a disturbing development: normally when I bring up Rafi it derails the conversation at least long enough for me to get to the door. Obviously we were starting to know each other too well.

"The problem is, Pen, I'm working on a lot of different things right now. I can't walk out on all of them." It was the plain truth for once: I really didn't know which job Puss and Boots had been sent to frighten me away from. The answer could be right there in what they'd said to me, but I was buggered if I could dig it out. "Someone didn't close the circle, and a little bird flew the nest." That didn't sound like Coldwood's drug barons. It might refer to the thing in the church, but there was nothing birdlike—or little, for that matter—in the presence I'd sensed there. Abigail Torrington? Maybe. But she hadn't flown anywhere: she'd been flat-out stolen.

What it came down to was that I didn't have enough information just then even to guess who wanted shot of me, still less why. But it didn't matter in any case, because the part of me that's stubborn and intractable and bloody-minded—which is not a small part, by any means—was determined to stay with this until I knew what it was about. Pen read that conclusion in my face and shrugged, giving it up in disgust.

"Just remember I told you so," she said. "So I don't have to say it later on when something ten times worse happens to you."

"I'll sleep on it," I said. Then I gave her a hug and retreated to my room at the top of the house, which normally gives me a bit more perspective on the world.

Tonight I was too bone weary to think. But before I surrendered to gravity and sleep, I called Nicky. He didn't sound very happy to hear from me.

"Christ, Castor. What is it, three hours? Even Buddy Bolden doesn't give you the right to ask for fucking miracles."

"I'm not looking for a progress report, Nicky. I was just wondering if you happen to know where the *Collective* is moored right now."

"Thamesmead," he said, without a pause. "Thamesmead West. Pier Seventeen, just down from the Artillery Museum." Yeah, that would be the sort of information a paranoid zombie would have at his well-preserved fingertips.

"Who's on board?"

"No, Who's on first."

"Ha ha ha."

"I'm not the society pages, Castor. Last I heard, Reggie Tang was over there. Couple of guys from South London I don't know from fucking Adam. It's nine-tenths empty, like always."

"Thanks, Nicky."

"Yeah, you're very welcome. We live to serve. Since you're here, though, there are a couple of things I can tell you about your man Peace."

I pricked up my ears. "Go on."

"When I'm trying to get a handle on someone I don't know, I go on the principle of *cherchez le dirt*. In Peace's case, I'm telling you, you could open up a pig farm."

"Go on."

"Well, just for starters, he's done time."

"Oh yeah?" I was a little disappointed, but it was something. At least it was something if it was recent: ex-cons have got their own networks in the real world, and you can crash them sometimes if you know where to start from. "So how long was he pleasuring Her Majesty for, then?"

"Uh-uh. Wrong time. Or rather, wrong place. This was in Burkina Faso—French West Africa. He got himself hauled in for drugs possession, pissed off the magistrate, and ended up being sent down for two years. Then he managed to grease the right palms, which he could have done for half the price before the conviction, and walked out on a procedural pardon. He was only inside for a week or so."

"And this was—?"

"Nineteen ninety-two. The year that *Unforgiven* got the Best Picture Oscar—but that son of a bitch Pacino scooped Best Actor, and for what? *Scent of a Woman*, for Christ's sake!"

"Thanks, Nicky." I cut him off before he could run through the list of top-grossing movies—which would be bound to lead in to some conspiracy theory he was currently shaping. None of this stuff was any good to me: it was all too long ago. Even if Peace had made some good friends in Ouagadougou State Prison, and they'd all moved to London when they'd gotten out, I couldn't pick up a trail that was well over a decade cold. It was a dead end. "You got anything else?"

"I've got plenty." Nicky sounded hurt—as though I was impugning the quality of his intel. "The West Africa thing, that's just the tip of the iceberg. This guy was a real hell-raiser in his youth—into all kinds of shit, invariably up to his eyeballs. Did a stint in the army—royal artillery—then bought himself out about a day or so ahead of a dishonorable discharge and did the usual street shit for a while. Added a few column inches to his charge sheet along the way—breaking and entering, public affray, felonious assault. Sometimes it stuck, sometimes it didn't."

"No more spells in jail, though?"

"Nope. He moved around too much. Jet-setting lifestyle, you know? The world was his fucking playground. He was in the States for a while and he got mixed up with Anton Fanke's crowd."

"Anton Fanke? Who's that?"

"What, you never heard of the Satanist Church of the Americas?" Nicky sounded incredulous.

"Obviously not," I said.

"Fanke's one of these religious boot boys, like the Bhagwan or Sun Myung Moon. Only, his religion happens to be devil worship. You know the type—gets a million grunts to sell flowers at major airports so he can run a fleet of limos and live in a mansion in upstate New York."

"Got it. So Peace is a satanist?"

"Dunno. Maybe. I'm just saying his name was linked with Fanke's. There was some court case they were both involved in, way back. I haven't managed to shag the details yet."

It was a disturbing thought. If the Torringtons were right, Peace was mainly concerned with using Abbie's ghost as leverage to restart a dead relationship. But if he was into necromancy, all bets were off.

"Thanks, Nicky," I said. "Keep up the good work."

"Yeah, well, you bought a lot of goodwill. Makes a change."

He hung up.

I really didn't want to think right then about the implications of what he'd told me, or about the weird, circuitous threats and warnings that the werewolves had been doling out. Truth to tell, this had been about as stressful a Monday as I could remember. I tumbled into bed, already half-unconscious, and slept it all away.

I had some really nasty dreams, involving men who mewed like cats and jumped out at me from a variety of unexpected angles, and a little girl who was walking through a maze of gray stone with church bells ringing up ahead of her. Mercifully, the details didn't stay with me when I woke up.

The headache did, though. It felt like a really bad hangover, but casting my mind back over the night before, it didn't seem to me like I'd overindulged. I could only remember the whisky I'd swallowed to dull the edge of the pain while Pen scrubbed my wound out with TCP and lavender soap.

The wound. It felt uncomfortably hot, but not particularly painful. I prodded it gingerly, and flexed my arm in various directions to see how much traverse it had. There was a little bit of stiffness, but all things considered it didn't feel nearly as bad as it had the night before. If I were a concert pianist, I'd probably be worried; being the human wreck I am, I figured it would all come out in the wash.

It was about six in the morning, and Pen was still asleep: at least, there was no sound from the basement except for the occasional creaking and rattling as Edgar or Arthur stirred on his perch and shrugged his bony shoulders. Like rust, ravens never sleep. I went through into the kitchen and made some coffee, then drank three cups of it while I flicked through Pen's *A–Z* and worked out a route to Thamesmead. There was no sense driving—I'd have to go through the Blackwall Tunnel or take the Woolwich Ferry, both hassles that I can do without at the best of times. The smart option was to go to Waterloo and then take an overground train to Woolwich Dockyard. From there I could walk it.

A brisk wind had come up in the night and swept the thunderheads away to someplace else, so it was sunny but fresh as I walked to Turnpike Lane tube station, and my head started to feel a little clearer. I was glad of the change in the weather for another reason, too: shredded at seam and shoulder, and crusted brown with blood on the left-hand side of the collar, my paletot was hors de combat for the time being. I was wearing the only other coat I owned that had enough pockets for all my paraphernalia: a fawn trenchcoat with a button-down yoke that makes me feel like an exhibit in some museum installation about the evolution of the private detective.

Since I'd gotten such an early start on the day, I couldn't get a Travelcard, so I just took a single. I didn't know where I'd be going after

Mike Carey

I left the *Collective*. Maybe Paddington and Rosie Crucis: it depended on whether I found any leads I could actually use.

Bourbon said that Dennis Peace used to be a rubber duck. In trade jargon, that meant only one thing: an exorcist who chose for professional reasons to live on water rather than on dry land. It's something we all try out, at some point, if only to get a decent night's sleep: no ghosts can cross running water, and the morbid sensitivities that keep us in business are all anesthetized for once. Takes a certain kind of personality to live with it long term, though: I always end up feeling like I'm trussed up inside of a plastic bag, my own breath condensing on me as cold sweat.

The *Collective* is a floater community on the Thames. Everybody in my world knows it, everybody's been there, but that doesn't mean you can necessarily find it when you want to: like the Oriflamme, the *Collective* is a movable feast. Come to think of it, there's another link between the two, although it's an accidental and tendentious one along the lines of "how many degrees of separation are you away from Kevin Bacon?" Only, for Kevin Bacon it read "Peckham Steiner."

Steiner is one of the few flamboyant legends of our reclusive and insular profession. He was an exorcist before the fashion really got going: by which I mean before the huge upsurge of apparitions and manifestations in the last decade of the old millennium turned people like me into a key industry. Specializing in spiritual eradications for the rich and famous, he garnered a certain amount of fame (or at least notoriety) for himself along the way—along with a shedload of money. An American heiress was in it somewhere, if I remember rightly. Her dead ex-husbands had been giving her all kinds of grief until Steiner sent them on to their last judgment, and out of gratitude she left him the bulk of her fortune when she died. Her kids from all three marriages sued, and the case dragged on for years, but as far as I know none of them ever managed to lay a legal finger on him. By that time, anyway, he had three books out, a movie deal for his life story, and a controlling share in ENSURE, a company that made ghost-breaking equipment and consumables. He retired at forty-six, richer than God.

Unfortunately, he was also crazier than a shithouse rat. Maybe the instability had always been there, or maybe it was the pressures of the job and then the explosive de-repression of having enough money to remake yourself and the world closer to your expectations. I mean, look what that did to Michael Jackson.

I met him once—Steiner, I mean, not Jacko—and it was a scary thing to see. By that time I'd already read a couple of his books, and I'd come to respect (although not actually to like) the cold, clever mind that was on show in them. But when I got to talk to him, it was as though that mind had deliquesced and then solidified again in a different, largely nonfunctional shape.

It was at some weird party or other in a London hotel that was hosting a conference on Perspectives on the After-Life. Jenna-Jane Mulbridge, an exorcist-turned-academic who'd taught me a lot of the tricks of the trade when I was still very wet behind the ears, had blagged a ticket for me and insisted that I come along: the chance of meeting Steiner had swung it.

From what I can still recall of that conversation, he was already well on the way to becoming the surly, crazed recluse that everybody now remembers him as. He talked about the dead and the living as though they were two armies in the field, with himself as some kind of commander marshaling the forces of the warm-blooded. He looked the part, too, I have to admit: spirit-level straight, unyielding as stone, his gray hair cropped close to his scalp. And if he were a general, he seemed to feel that the exorcists were his crack troops: an elite commando unit trained to take anything the enemy could throw at us. The enemy? I hedged at first, sure that there was some subtlety I was missing, but there wasn't. "The dead," he said. "And the undead. The ones that want to supplant us, and take the world away from us."

Even back then, when I was blasting unquiet spirits without qualm or question, I still couldn't see the situation quite like that. Apart from anything else, it only seemed to lead in one direction, to a door marked "abandon hope." Out of some halfhearted attempt to keep my half of the conversation up, I asked him how it was possible to fight a war where any casualty in your own forces became a recruit for the other side.

"What do you mean?" he demanded, frowning at me over a glass of champagne, which he was clutching tightly enough to make me nervous.

I made the best fist of it that I could, which wasn't all that good because most of my concentration was tied up in looking round for an escape route: this was as big a disillusionment as finding out that the reason Father Christmas smells like Johnnie Walker is because he's your dad in a fake beard and a red mac. "I mean we're all going to die, Mr. Steiner. If the dead do hate the living, they don't have to fight us: they only have to wait. In the end, everyone goes the same way, right? If life is an army, everyone deserts sooner or . . ."

His glare made me falter into silence. I knew damn well, looking into those mad, uncompromising baby blues, that if we *had* been in a war zone he'd have had me shot right there and then for bringing aid and comfort to the enemy. Since we were at a party, he didn't have that option: he was visibly weighing up alternatives.

"Fuck off and kill yourself, then," he growled at last. Then he turned and walked away, shouldering aside some of the great and good who'd gathered around so that they could be seen and photographed with him.

After that, the stages of his decline were charted with endless fascination by the ghost-hunting community. From seeing himself as general and commander in chief, he came more and more to see himself as a prominent target. If the ghosts—and their servants and satraps, the were-kin, the demons, and the zombies—were engaged in a war against the living, then sooner or later they were bound to try to strike at the people who were leading the campaign on the other side: the exorcists. He started to take elaborate precautions for his own safety, and the first—highly publicized—step he took was to buy a yacht. Since the dead can't usually cross running water, Steiner had decided that he'd make sure he was surrounded by running water most of the time, and only step onto dry land when there was no way of avoiding it. He suggested in a couple of interviews that this might be the lifestyle of the future. He imagined itinerant populations, floating cities built on decommissioned aircraft carriers and oil tankers.

But crazy though he was, I guess he realized somewhere along the way that the idea of relocating whole urban populations onto house-boats would be a hard sell. Something else—some other measure, achievable but effective—was going to be needed, so that when the inevitable assault came and the evil dead overran the land the living would have somewhere to retreat to. A visionary to the last, he pro-posed a series of safe houses, ingeniously designed, which would stand "with hallowed ground to all four sides, behind elemental ramparts of earth and air and water." Houses built on this design, he said, would blind the eyes and blunt the forces of the dead. The first design used actual moats: the later ones had double walls with the water flowing between them invisibly in plumbed-in metal tanks. The earth and air and fire parts I'm not so sure about. He sent the designs to the housing departments of all the London boroughs, and offered his services free as an adviser if they'd commit themselves to a building program.

As far as I know, none of the boroughs ever responded—not even with a po-faced "your letter has been received and taken under advise-ment." Steiner raged impotently; even with his millions, there was no way he could do this on his own.

There was an upside to his madness, though: he still saw the exorcists—especially the London exorcists—as his boys, his special charges. He gave Bourbon Bryant the premises that became the Ori-flamme, because he loved the idea of ghostbusters meeting up and sharing ideas (he was probably also working on the principle that there's strength in numbers). And when he died, he left his yacht to a trust with Bryant as the first president, changing its name in his will to the *Thames Collective*. Money from his estate would be diverted to keeping it seaworthy and in a reasonable state of repair, and any Lon-don exorcist would have the right to live there at need for as long as they liked, with berths being strictly rotated if too many people took up the offer at the same time.

To begin with, it looked like that might actually be a problem: a whole lot of people liked the idea of living for free in a luxury yacht. But the *Collective* wasn't as luxurious as all that: to increase the number of berths, Steiner had the big staterooms subdivided with plasterboard partitions, so living space was cramped and somewhat rough-and-ready. There'd been problems with the administration of the trust, too: the idea was that London-based exorcists would volunteer for one- or two-year stretches so that the burden wouldn't fall too heavily on a small group. But not many, even of the people who wanted to live on the *Collective*, were enthused by the idea of devoting any of their time to running it. It was also hard to define who was eligible, because anyone could say they were an exorcist with no more proof than a letterhead or a shingle. In a welter of resentment, recrimination, and mutual backstabbing, the trust more or less imploded. The *Collective* still existed, but the money that should have kept it in good repair was legally frozen and it was falling apart in melancholy slow motion. It went from berth to berth along the Thames, bringing down the tone wherever it stopped and so always unwelcome even though it could pay its way. The people who lived on it now tended to be people who were only staying in the city for a short while, or who had no other options.

What did I know about Reggie Tang? Just barely north of nothing. He was a rising star of the kind that old dogs like me watch suspiciously and from a distance: rumored to be a very quick study, a bit on the quick-tempered side and very handy in a fight. His dad had been some sort of broker in Hong Kong before the handover; he was a Buddhist, or so I'd heard; and he was active on the gay scene. That was pretty much it. I'd only ever met him once, and the bulk of that had been a frank exchange of views: a shouting match, in other words, on the theme of how far any of the medieval grimoires could be said to be worth a rat's arse when it came to defining the names and natures of demons. Reggie thought the *Liber Juratus Honorii* was the dog's bollocks: I thought it was the most feeble-minded piece of crap I'd ever set eyes on. We didn't get much further than the is-isn't-is stage of the discussion, though, because we were both passing-out drunk. I was hoping he'd remember that evening fondly, or at least still have a vague idea of who I was. Otherwise the best I could hope for here was the cold shoulder.

I found the *Collective* exactly where Nicky had said it would be, at the end of a pier just down from the Artillery Museum—but getting on board turned out to be a bit more problematic because the only way to get onto the pier was through a locked gate with a nasty tangle of razor wire on top of it. I took a look at the lock. The keyhole was a very distinctive shape: an asterisk, more or less, with seven radiating lines that were all the same length and thickness except for the one going vertically downward from the center, which was both longer and slightly wider than the rest. It was a French design, and I was never likely to forget it once I'd met it because the company that made it was named Pollux—and Castor and Pollux are the twins that make up the constellation Gemini. More to the point, I could crack the thing in a minute flat.

But when I rummaged through the pockets of the trenchcoat, I came up empty. I'd transferred my whistle, obviously, and a couple of other bits and pieces that had survived my close encounter with the two loup-garous the night before, but I hadn't remembered to take any of my lockpicks.

So all I could do was hammer on the gate and shout, and then wait until somebody heard me. It was a harsh blow to my professional pride.

Eventually, though, I got a response. There were approaching footsteps, and then the gate rattled as someone unlocked it from the far side. It swung open, and a face I didn't know appeared in the gap.

It was a face you couldn't do much about, like it or not, except maybe commiserate with the owner. It was pale and flat and had the slight grayness of unbaked dough. The messiest tangle of spiky light-brown hair I'd ever seen stood up on top of it like couch grass on a sand dune. You couldn't tell whether the body attached to a face like that would be young, old, or somewhere in between. The furthest you'd want to go would be to say that it was—on the balance of probabilities—male.

"Morning," I said, with a winning smile. "Is Reggie in?"

The face just stared. I considered the possibility that it was on the end of a pole rather than a neck. But then the guy opened the door a fraction more and I could see for myself that he was alive and intact. He was the same height as me but skinny as a rake. He was dressed in ragged jeans and an op-art T-shirt, and on his feet he wore novelty slippers in the shape of Gromit the dog. "Reggie?" he said, sounding slightly baffled, as if he was hearing the name for the first time. There was an Essex lilt to his voice.

"Yeah, Reggie Tang. You're from the *Collective*, right? I heard he was living there right now."

The guy didn't concede the point by so much as a nod. After a loaded pause, he said, "Who are you?"

"I'm Felix Castor." I stuck out my hand. He shook it without much interest, but the momentary emotional flash I got while our hands were touching had some odd harmonics in it: unease, resentment, and something like alarm.

There was no trace of any of that in his voice, which was disengaged if not downright lugubrious. "Greg Lockyear," he said. "So you're Castor? Heard your name, here and there. Lot of people seem to reckon you." His gaze went down to my feet as he said this, as if he were checking my shoes against health and safety standards, and then back up to meet mine.

"Reggie's inside," he said, sounding resigned now. "Come on in."

He turned and led the way along the pier to the *Collective*'s gangplank. The ship had been a floating mansion once: now she was a wreck. I hadn't seen her in six years, and I could see there were at least that many years' worth of dirt on her sides. Lower down there was a slimy ring of algae, and below that, winking redly up at me as the water slopped against the hull, a little rust. At this rate the *Collective* wasn't going to last out too many more winters.

Lockyear went on board, and I followed him—along a short companionway and then sharp left into a stairwell that led down to the lower level of the deckhouse. "Mind the steps," he called out, without looking back. "One of them's loose." The warning came a fraction of a second too late: a plank turned under my heel and I just about managed to avoid going over on my face. I was starting to feel a little bit like an Egyptian tomb robber.

The deckhouse was about the only space on board the *Collective* that was still the same size and shape as it had started out. It was on two levels, connected by a spiral staircase in carefully matched dark woods, and it still had a sort of faded elegance about it. Very faded: the original leather and built-in tables and couches were sort of overwhelmed now by bootlockers and cupboard units from the provisional wing of MFI—and there was a smell of stale grease in the air from the galley in the corner, which had an arc of smoke-blackened ceiling above it like the hovering spirit of fried meals long since past. The only other door out of the room was there, and it was half off its hinges. The balcony rails edging the deckhouse's upper level, about eight feet above us, were missing in places, so that a casual promenade could become a life-or-death affair if you didn't look where you were going.

There was a kind of breakfast bar in the galley area, with a counter bolted to the wall and a few high stools scattered along its length. The same tastefully blended cherry and walnut paneling decorated the area around the bar, showing up the rest of the room for the tip it now was. The guy sitting there, tucking into a sausage and egg breakfast, was Reggie Tang. Actually he wasn't so much tucking into it as playing with it. He looked up as I came in, and he gave me a cold nod as he shoved the plate away from him decisively. He did cold very well, being the spitting image of Bruce Lee circa *Enter the Dragon*. He was ten years my junior. Since he was wearing only an undershirt and a pair of boxers, I could see that he was in taut, wiry good shape.

"Sorry," he said, standing up. "I know the face, so I'm assuming we've met somewhere. But I can't remember your name." I'd forgotten his voice until I heard it again now: it was deep and vibrant, with an almost musical lilt to it.

"No reason why you should," I said. "We only met the once. I'm Felix Castor. I'm sorry if I disturbed your breakfast."

He shrugged easily. "Place is meant to be open to our kind all the time. Part of the deal. Castor, yeah, it's starting to come back to me now. You're a Liverpudlian, aren't you? Part of the north-south brain drain. Good to see you again."

He took the hand I offered and gave it a firm, brief shake. Nothing readable there, but I hadn't expected there to be; he looked like the sort of guy who kept his emotions pretty tightly locked down. He nodded me toward a couch that was stacked with old newspapers, magazines, and unopened mail. "Grab a seat. You looking to sign in?"

I sat down, shoving some of the old letters aside. Behind me, Lockyear crossed to the galley. I watched him out of the corner of my eye as he picked up a still-smoking cigarette from an ashtray there, half-raised it to his lips, but then seemed to change his mind and stubbed it out without taking a drag. "Not right now," I said. "Actually, I was hoping to get a little free advice."

"Advice?"

"Yeah. You know, tap the whisper line."

Reggie smiled at my coy phrasing. "Well, go for it. We're happy to help if we can, aren't we, Greg?"

"Sure. Happy to," Lockyear echoed. He sat down at the breakfast bar, a long way from Reggie's unfinished breakfast.

"Thanks. The fact is, I'm looking for someone."

"Someone I know?"

I nodded. "Could be, yeah. Someone who used to live here, anyway, but maybe not during your time. Guy name of Dennis Peace."

Reggie frowned in thought, as if he was running that name through his memory banks. "Peace. No, doesn't ring any bells. You know a Dennis Peace, Greg?"

Lockyear looked round at the sound of his name, his expression the same mildly astonished double-take I'd seen him use outside. I was reminded of Stan Laurel, although maybe that was just the hair. He stubbed the cigarette out again, absently, in spite of the fact that it was already dead. "Yeah," he said. "I know Peace. Well, I used to know him. He lived here for about six months of last year. Bastard never cooked once. Why? What's he done?"

This was addressed to Reggie, but Reggie turned to me because obviously that was my question to answer if it was anybody's.

I decided to tell the truth, as far as I could. It's not like exorcism as a profession generates a whole huge heap of fellow feeling, but I didn't want to try to extort any information out of these guys by selling them some tired line about Peace owing me money or whatever. That sort of thing will inevitably turn around and bite you in the ass sooner or later. "Someone hired me to find him," I said. "He's meant to have a kid with him. A little girl, who—well, who isn't his. She was abducted from her parents' house. Peace was there the day it happened, or at least that's what I've been told. So her parents think maybe he took her. I want to see if that's what happened. And if it is, I'm being paid to get the kid back."

Reggie said nothing, just kept looking at me with a gambler's deadpan.

"Well, I never met the man," I conceded, responding to the skepticism in that look. "This is just a job, and it could all be bullshit as far as I know. Sooner I find him, sooner I find out."

"Sounds like a job for the police," Reggie observed. He was standing over me, watching me more closely than the occasion seemed to call for. Having offered me a seat, he made no move to sit down himself.

"Yeah, I guess it would be, if the girl was alive. But she's dead."

"All the more reason—"

"I mean, she was already dead when he took her."

Reggie gave the kind of slanted nod that means "hell of a story." "There are some very nasty people out there," he observed. "A lady takes a terrible risk."

I recognized the quote, let it pass. "Does anyone make a note of forwarding addresses, when someone leaves here?" I asked, giving a tottering pile of envelopes a meditative tap.

"The Trust does. But we're not the Trust."

There was definitely an edge in Reggie's voice now. I could see that we were heading for a point at which he was going to give up the unequal struggle between mood and manners and tell me to sod off. But I was feeling a little bloody-minded myself, now—maybe because of the headache, which was back worse than ever—and I wasn't quite ready to back off. I looked across at Greg Lockyear, who was now leaning forward with his elbows on the counter and looking out across the Thames toward the Gallions Point marina as if it were the most riveting thing he'd ever seen. A conviction started to grow in me.

"Greg," I said, leaning out past Reggie to get a better line of sight. "You keep in touch with Peace at all, after he left here?"

Reggie didn't like the fact that I'd just done an end-play around him, and Greg—when he turned his dazed-rabbit eyes my way—didn't look all that happy to be back in the conversation. This was making friends and influencing people the Felix Castor way. "No," Greg said, shaking his head emphatically. "No, I never really got on with him all that well. Glad to see the back of him, to be honest."

"Any clues as to where he was going? Or did anyone ever visit him while he was here? Anyone who might have put him up afterwards, I mean?"

He looked out of the window again, as if checking an Autocue, then back at me. "No."

I turned my attention back to Tang. "Who else is staying here, Reggie?" I asked. "I mean, besides you two?"

Reggie folded his arms. "Nobody."

"And you've been staying here since—?"

"Castor, you said you came here looking for advice. You really think acting like a cop is going to get you any?"

"Well, you said you were happy to help. I'm just taking you at your word."

"Okay. I think we helped you enough now. So my new word is sod off out of it."

"That's more of a phrase," I pointed out, reasonably. "I'm not a cop, Reggie."

"You think I'm simple? I said you were acting like one."

"Not even that. A cop would be picking up on all your bullshit and shoving it back in your face to see if you blink."

There was a moment's—or maybe just half a moment's—tense silence. "What bullshit?" Reggie demanded.

"Well, let's see. You're a Buddhist, but when I come in you're sitting in front of a plate full of sausage, eggs, and bacon. You can't bring yourself to actually touch the stuff, but you do your best to pretend it's yours. And Mr. Potato Face over there had the same problem with the fag, so it's fair to assume that somewhere nearby there's a chain-smoking, carnivorous mate of yours who doesn't want to be introduced to me for some inexplicable—"

It was just as well that Reggie's eyes flicked upward. Like an idiot, I'd been watching the door at the back of the galley, but seeing that telltale glance I rolled off the couch a split second before a burly form crashed down feetfirst from above, and two size-ten boots thumped into the space where I'd just been sitting.

I hit the floor and rolled, fetching up against Reggie's feet. He jumped back hastily, proving that his Bruce Lee looks were all window dressing, but the guy with the roomy footwear was a bit more aggressive. He strode across to me, lifted me up by my lapels with surprisingly little effort, and slammed me into the wall.

"Hold on to him!" he bellowed.

Reggie and Greg rushed to comply, taking an arm each. I could have fought back, but only at the expense of a few more hard knocks. I figured the time for that would come.

The man standing in front of me, rubbing right fist into left palm, looked like hard knocks were a daily fact of life for him. He was big enough to be covered by building regulations, and his hard, craggy face bore a couple of days' growth of stubble. His hair was sand-blond, his complexion sandpaper-rough. There were deep shadows under his eyes, as dark as bruises. He must have been fairly handsome once, in a weather-beaten, roughly chiseled out, oversize kind of way. Now, in middle age, he looked like someone who was just starting to feel the pull of gravity and letting it get to him—psychologically, if not physically. He was wearing one of those shades-of-gray urban combat jackets over a green turtleneck sweater and olive-drab trousers tucked into those intimidating *Dixon of Dock Green* boots. An incongruous flash of gold from his wrist caught my eye: he was wearing a bracelet. But before I could take in the details he reached out and grasped my cheeks in his hand, tilting my head up so our eyes met.

He glared at me—a warning glare.

"I got your message," he said. "That was you, yeah? At the Oriflamme? So you wanted to talk to me. Well, here I am. What do you want to talk about?"

"Abbie Torrington," I suggested.

That was meant to be an opening gambit, but it got a more spectacular reaction than I was expecting. Peace gave a wordless roar and punched me in the stomach. I saw the punch coming and threw myself backward as far as I could into Reggie and Greg, trying to ride with it. Even so, it was like standing in the path of a cannonball. The pain was incredible, and I folded up with a feeble hiccup of displaced air. I sagged, but Reggie and Greg held on so I didn't actually fall.

"You don't—you don't even talk about her!" Peace bellowed. "You don't even—you bastard, you think I'm going to let you—? Who's paying you? Who fucking sent you here?"

He grabbed a handful of my hair and jerked my head up again—but not before I took a closer look at that bracelet and saw it for what it was: a heart-shaped locket on a golden chain, wrapped twice around his muscular wrist.

"Who sent you?" he asked again.

"Her—her mother," I wheezed.

"Well, you tell that bitch she's never seeing Abbie again in this world or any fucking other. That's over. It's over! I would've—I would've—I'll kill before I let that coldhearted bastard—"

He ran out of words, his face flushed so deep a red it looked like he was about to bust a major artery. He brandished his fist at me again, but didn't go for a second punch. He took a long, shuddering breath, visibly struggling to get himself back under some kind of control. I remembered that he was popping speed; that's not generally conducive to moments of calm reflection.

Then things took a turn for the worse. Peace flicked his jacket away from his body on the left-hand side and pulled a handgun out of his belt. He shoved it hard up against my cheek.

"Take it easy, Den," Reggie Tang murmured anxiously.

"Shut up, Reggie," Peace growled. He looked at me with a sort of agonized hatred. He seemed to be working himself up to something, and I opened my mouth to try to head it off. Before I could speak, his free hand shot forward, balled into a fist. I didn't have time to move—just to close my eyes. A splintering, rending sound came from just to my left. Opening my eyes, I turned my head a fraction and saw the gaping hole that Peace had just punched in the decorative fascia above the breakfast bar. He curled and unfolded his fingers three times: as far as I could see, he hadn't even broken any skin.

"If I ever see you again," he said to me, a fraction calmer now, "I'll kill you. I mean it. I'll kill you. Don't come looking for me unless you're ready to cut my throat while I'm asleep, because that's the only way you're getting her. And don't assume I'm asleep just because I've got my fucking—eyes—closed."

He punctuated these last three words with three sharp jabs of the gun barrel into my face. He flicked a glance at Reggie, and then at Greg. "Give me five minutes," he said, "and then let him go."

Reggie nodded. Greg just blinked. Peace was already heading for the wide open spaces in any case, tucking the gun back into his belt, and he didn't look back as he ducked to clear the low door.

Well now. I liked these odds better.

I drooped a little in Reggie and Greg's grip, making them take a little more of my weight. Irritably they hauled me upright, which meant that they were off balance when I came up with them and shoved backward. We all lurched against the bulkhead together. I dragged my arm clear of Greg's grip and punched Reggie hard in the throat. He gave a choking gurgle and staggered sideways into the breakfast bar, letting go his hold on my other arm as both of his hands flew to his neck. I didn't need the arm, though, because I was already taking Greg out with a sharp butt to the bridge of the nose.

I was out through the door before either of them could recover enough to mount a counterattack, but by the time I got up the stairs and out into the companionway, Peace was already legging it down the gangplank. He turned on the quayside and looked back at me.

He kicked the gangplank away just as I got to it, and it tumbled end over end into the Thames, hitting the *Collective*'s hull with a series of hollow metallic booms like a clock chiming the hour inside a coffin. The distance to the shore was only ten feet or so, but I had to back a few steps to get a run-up, and meanwhile the guy was already having it away on his toes.

I made the jump, and I landed with both feet under me—but then a moment's dizziness, coming out of nowhere, made me stagger and almost fall backward into the river. I pulled myself together and took off after my quarry, who'd reached the pier's gate by now and was hauling it open.

To my horror I saw him take the key out of the near side of the lock and throw it toward the water. Then he was through and slamming the gate shut behind him a second before I reached it. I dragged down on the handle but the damn thing didn't budge.

Damn damn damn damn damn! No lockpicks, no time, and the razor wire on top of the gate looked like the most serious kind of bad news. I cast around for some object I could use to smash the lock, and saw the key: it had landed on the edge of the pier, a couple of inches short of the water.

I snatched it up, put it in the lock, and turned. Running out onto the street, I looked left just in time to see Peace's burly figure disappear around a corner fifty yards away. As I started in pursuit, a car roared past me, heading in the same direction and accelerating: it was a battered-looking Grand Cherokee, sheathed in dried mud and looking faintly military. With a jolt of alarm, I saw that there were two men in the front seats, the passenger a man so tall that he was folded over on himself, his raised knees showing in the window. Even from a single high-speed glimpse, Po was unmistakeable.

I put on a fresh spurt of speed, but they still reached the corner well before me and disappeared around it with a *whump-chunk* sound as the car rocked and yawed on its wheelbase. When I got there, I saw Peace running hell for leather along a narrow stretch of road where the pavement all but vanished. Faceless low-rise office blocks hemmed him in on both sides, with no alleys or breaks that he could duck into. Up ahead of him, though, the street opened out on one side onto the broad, asphalted plain of a car park. It was laid out as a mazelike grid of two-foot-high concrete bollards, some of which were linked by chains.

The Jeep was only a few feet behind Peace when he reached the first of the bollards. He jumped right over it like a hurdler and kept on going: the Jeep was forced to swerve wide, back out onto the street, first of all keeping pace with him and then accelerating past him. When it got to the far end of the open space it swerved to a pinwheeling halt and the passenger door was thrown open.

Po clambered out, at first human but unfolding as he moved into something that looked like it never had a mother. His arms elongated and thickened and he bent from the waist to lay them on the ground. His mouth gaped, and kept on gaping, deforming into a fang-ringed muzzle like the maw of a shark. I'd been right after all about him being an exotic, but he was no gorilla. He was a hyena, or something that had been a hyena once, and even on all fours like this he was as high at the shoulder as a man.

Peace saw that he'd been outflanked, stopped at a skid, turned, and went into full reverse, his arms and legs pumping. Po loped after him, slow at first but gathering speed. Meanwhile the Jeep heeled around, passenger door still flapping and banging, and headed back down the street toward me. Again it came alongside Peace and then accelerated past him. If it hadn't been for the bollards it could have just moved in and cut him off. As it was, the driver had to brake again and jump out himself. It was the other man I'd met last night—Zucker, the one with the deep, growly voice and the fondness for sharp edges. I was barely twenty yards away now, and running toward him, but he only had eyes for his quarry. He jogged forward to meet Peace, completing the pincer movement.

But Peace turned in a wide arc, heading for the back of the car park where a high wooden fence separated it from the watersports dealership it presumably served. The fence looked too high to climb, but Peace's two pursuers saw the danger that he might somehow slip away from them and pushed themselves harder, narrowing his lead.

I reached the Jeep, and saw from the slight vibration of the bonnet that the engine was still running. Without even thinking about what I was doing, I jumped in and backed it out onto the street.

Peace was almost at the fence, the two were-kin were only a few yards behind him. I gunned the engine, slammed it into second, and roared forward. The two bollards directly in front of me were linked by one of the chains: I hit it full-on and it parted with a crunch, the loose ends snapping away like steel whips to either side. I kept on going, swerving to avoid the barriers where I could, smashing straight through them when I had to. Something caught in one of the front wheels and the Jeep started to lean to the right; I turned the wheel frantically to compensate.

Up ahead of me, Peace had reached the fence, and he tensed for a leap that would take him some of the way up the side of it. Before he could, Po closed the last few yards and was on him in a frenzy of claws. They both went down. There were two gunshots, so close together that the second sounded like the echo of the first. Peace kicked Po away from him—a pretty amazing feat in itself—and scrambled up again. The were-thing was hurt, blood on its face seeming to blind it so that although it swiped out with one obscenely long, clawed forelimb, it missed Peace by a good few inches.

Zucker was closing fast. Seeing how bad the odds were about to get, Peace turned and made a powerful leap, hitting the fence about four feet off the ground and hauling himself up with his hands. Close behind, Po gathered himself on his haunches to do the same thing—but his leap would bring Peace off the wall in the way a cat would claw down a low-flying bird. At the same time, Zucker was groping in his pocket, probably for his knife. One way or another, Peace didn't have a chance in hell of making it to the top.

I clamped my hand down on the horn. The harsh, diminuendo *blat* of sound made the loup-garous turn, and they saw their own car bearing down on them: four thousand pounds of metal, give or take, tearing out its engine as I pushed it up to fifty in second gear.

It was too late now for Po to tackle Peace. Instead, he and Zucker grabbed tarmac on either side as I accelerated past them. At the last moment, I pulled the wheel hard over. I hit the fence full-on, about ten feet to the left of where Peace was still scrambling up: hit it, and went straight through it onto a paved forecourt where the remains of the fence rained down around me as splintered flotsam.

The front tires blew and the Jeep settled like a broken steer, its front bumper hitting the ground in a shower of sparks. That took care of a lot of my speed, which was good as far as it went, but a second later the air bag inflated, slamming me backward in my seat and pinning my arms. A secondary impact after that told me I'd smashed into something else that I hadn't even seen.

I lay there dazed. There was a wailing sound in my ears, and for a chilling moment I thought I must have hit someone—but then I realized it was an alarm of some kind going off.

Forcing myself to move despite the aches and the shock of impact, I managed to get my hand into my pocket and groped around until I found my penknife. On the third try, I succeeded in puncturing the air bag: then I had to wait until it had deflated far enough for me to slide out from under it.

Staggering out of the remains of the Jeep, I saw that I'd actually slammed into another car on the forecourt of the sports shop. It had been a very nice electric blue BMW: it still was, except for the front third, which was twisted scrap.

Amazingly, nobody was coming to see what the noise was. The shop hadn't opened yet, and neither had any of the offices on the street behind me.

There was no sign of Peace, or of the two loup-garous. I took that as a good sign, because if they'd brought him down they'd still be right there questioning him or beating him up or eating his remains.

There was nothing I could do except make myself scarce before someone came along to investigate the noise and the shattered fence. I headed back toward the *Collective*. I was in the right mood now to have another round with Reggie bastard Tang and his gormless little friend, and see if I couldn't shake some more information out of them.

But when I got back to Pier 17, all my well-chosen phrases died on my lips as I stared, nonplussed, across a widening swathe of water toward the *Collective*'s receding stern rail. The gap was a good ten yards already, and the ship was heading out into the river at a slow, shuddering two knots.

Reggie was standing up on deck, a black silk jacket thrown on over his undershirt and pants, his hands thrust deep into the pockets. He favored me with an unfriendly, appraising stare.

"Go on home, man," he said, sounding stern and sad. "Have some fucking self-respect and go on home."

For one crazy moment I actually contemplated trying to make that jump. I'd have ended up trapped in the viscous Thames sludge until sometime in August, when the heat turned it back into dust again. Instead, I stood and watched the ship out of sight around the next bend. Reggie stayed up on deck the whole time, watching me as though he wanted to be sure I didn't try anything. After a while, Greg Lockyear came and stood next to him, a hand on his shoulder. Then the graceless curve of Ferry Approach intervened, the *Collective* slid out of sight, and I was left alone on the pier, looking—if I can get technical for just a moment—like a complete fuckwit.

Chapter Eight

I headed back west. Switching onto the Jubilee Line, I passed within a stone's throw of Paddington. At some point I'd probably have to drop in there for a word or two with Rosie Crucis. But now wouldn't be a good time. I was still feeling a bit seedy and hungover, and you need a full set of options to stand a chance against Jenna-Jane Mulbridge; anyhow, Rosie is more nocturnal even than Nicky.

Yeah, maybe I was just putting off the inevitable, but right now that worked for me.

So I dropped in at the office instead, and dug out some emergency supplies from the bottom drawer of the filing cabinet. It was just a foil-backed bubble sheet with eight slightly odd-looking pills on it—white squares with rounded edges, marked with a cursive "D." There'd been space for twelve pills originally, but four had already gone. The nurse who'd given them to me in the course of a brief, tempestuous relation-ship had said the "D" stood for "Diclofenac," although the tablets had a couple of other active ingredients as well. "They're magic," she said, sliding them into my breast pocket with a wicked grin. "Strongest painkillers you'll ever take, but they leave you as sharp as if you'd just popped a handful of dex. Only don't drink too much booze with them. Or . . . um . . . go out in direct sunlight, because with this stuff in your system you'll burn like a sausage on a grill."

It was probably the most thoughtful present anyone had ever given me—as I'd had cause to find out when I took the other four. I swallowed two now, and the pain and stiffness in my shoulder receded almost immediately. I was back in the game.

With Nicky still fresh in my mind, I checked the answerphone in the office as well as the messages on my cell phone: nothing doing on either one, so I was still on my own as far as that went. The good news, though, was that in among all the bills and other love letters from local government and national utilities, there was a heartwarmingly fat envelope with no stamp on it and just my name written in a flowing hand.

I opened it up and found a short note from Stephen Torrington, along with a check for a thousand pounds and a further five hundred in cash. The note just said that this was to be considered as a payment on account, and that I could send along a receipt whenever it was convenient. It occurred to me that that was going to be fairly difficult to do, because all I had by way of contact details for the Torringtons was Steve's mobile number. I dialed it now, and he picked up on the first ring. Either he had spectacularly good reflexes or he lived with the thing in his ear.

"Torrington."

"Castor," I said, answering in kind. "I got the money. Thanks."

"Mr. Castor. No problem: as I said, we've got more money than we need, and nothing could possibly be better than this to spend it on."

"You asked for a receipt. But I don't have your address."

He laughed self-deprecatingly. "The ordinary niceties break down at a time like this. I'm sorry, I should have given you my card. And Mel's, of course, in case I'm in a meeting or something. Send it to the house. We live on Bishop's Avenue. Number sixty-two."

Nice address. London's first gated community, in fact if not in name: millionaires and former government ministers only, and if you play the stereo too loud nobody will care because you've got at least two hundred yards of garden and so have they. The downside is that it's a three-day expedition to nip next door and borrow a cup of sugar. "I'll slip it in the post today," I said.

"No hurry. Is there anything new to report?"

I considered lying, but again it went against the grain: if this guy was paying my wages, the least I could give him by way of value for money was the truth. "I think I met our Mr. Peace this morning," I admitted.

"Met him? But—"

"It was a brief encounter. He was running like a bat out of hell and I couldn't quite keep up."

Torrington blew out what sounded like a deep lungful of breath. "My God. So close! Where? Where was he hiding?"

"The *Thames Collective*. It's a houseboat on the river where London-based exorcists sometimes stay. I don't think Peace was in residence, though: it's a bit too public. Most likely he was just visiting. Borrowing money, maybe, I don't know. He was seen at another exorcist haunt in Soho, too, so I guess he's shaking the tree for something—something that's worth the risk of being seen. Anyway, the bottom line is that even if he was staying at the *Collective*, the *Collective* just up and left. Until it comes into another mooring and I can find out where, I can't check it out again."

"But you actually walked in on him? You saw him?"

"Almost felt him, too—the tip of his boot, anyway. I'm really sorry. Next time I'll be more—"

"No, no." Torrington's tone was sharp. "You're as good as we were told you'd be, Mr. Castor. You actually found your man within forty-eight hours, with little more than his name to go on—that's nothing short of incredible. I don't think it'll be too long before you find him again, and I know you won't let him take you by surprise this time. Thank you. Thank you for everything you're doing for us. And if there's anything else that I can provide that will make the job easier, just call me. Any time of the day or night."

After a few more awkward pleasantries, we hung up. I wished I could live up to the Torringtons' touching faith in me, but right then I felt like one of those poor guys in Plato's cave, trying to make sense out of things I couldn't see directly, just by squinting at the shadows that the fire cast on the cave wall. And to make things worse, I was standing in the goddamn fire.

I thought of Reggie Tang's parting words, and the implication behind them. Peace was a bad lad, Bourbon Bryant had said—a bit wild and unpredictable—but all the same he seemed to have more friends in the London ghost-hunter community than I did right now: enough so that a lot of avenues I might normally have used seemed like bad ideas right then. Nicky still hadn't gotten me anything beside stirring tales of the guy's criminal past, and Rosie wouldn't be open for business until midnight. I was meant to be having dinner with Juliet, of course, but that was more than eight hours away, so I was looking down the barrel of a wasted day unless there was something I could follow up by myself in the meantime.

And there was. It might not be directly relevant to the Torringtons' case but it was pretty damn important to me and now was as good a time as any.

I took the tube to Kensington and went looking for a knife man.

"It's not as old as it looks," said Caldessa, in a quavery voice ridged with tempered steel. On the whole she made that bland comment sound pretty scathing. But then in her business, old is good, and new things trying to look like they're old are beneath contempt: lamb dressed as mutton. When I reached out my hand to take the knife back, though, she didn't give it to me. She turned it over in her hands again and sighted along the blade in a way that was downright unsettling for such a respectable, tweed-wearing senior citizen.

My knife man had turned out to be a woman. That was fine by me: when I'd turned up in Kensington Church Street, I'd only had the vaguest notion of what I was looking for—but I was fairly sure that this was the best place to find it. You just walk down Knightsbridge past Kensington Gardens and hang a left, and you find yourself (predictably, maybe, given the price and provenance of the surrounding real estate) in the densest concentration of antique shops in the civilized world. Okay, some of these places are mainly dedicated to the painless extraction of the tourist dollar, which means they sell Victorian milking churns at a thousand quid a pop, but in among the purveyors of overpriced, elegant tat there's a sprinkling of people who are well worth getting to know: fanatics with insanely narrow areas of specialization like Belgian tea cozies of the Merovingian dynasty or left-handed field altars from the Spanish Civil War.

One of the biggest shops is Antik Ost, run by a distant relation of Pen's whose name I have to look up and memorize again every time because it's so damn long: Haviland Burgerman. He was my first port of call, and he cheerfully admitted that his knowledge of knives was more or less limited to which end you use to cut your cigar. But he pointed me across the street to Evelyn Caldessa's, and Caldessa had the goods.

She was something of an antique herself. Her skin had that faint, pearly-white translucency of the very old, her features were finely sculpted, and her build was thinner than a stick. Looking at her, you felt reasonably sure she'd ring like bone china if you flicked her with your thumb. The scarf she wore tied over her long gray hair, peasant-style, gave her an Eastern European look, but her accent was pure prep school.

I intimated that I had something to sell, and that it fell within her area of expertise. "A knife. I found it among some things that belonged to my uncle."

"Belonged?"

"He passed away."

"Oh you poor thing." Space of a single heartbeat. "Let's see it."

I took out the cardboard tube, carefully slid the knife out into my palm, and handed it across to her hilt-first. She exclaimed under her breath when she saw it, then held it a long way away from her to get a better look. That blade didn't look any nicer in daylight than it had in Soho Square after midnight. It was very much a weapon that was made for actual incision and slicing, in a context far from the Sunday roast.

"The blade is hollow-ground," she said. "That's why it's so thin and sharp—and also one of the reasons why it looks older than it is. A full hollow sacrifices everything to the one concern of getting the best edge. So it wears down fast, assuming it doesn't break. The other reason it looks old is because it doesn't have a bolster—most modern knives do."

"A bolster?"

"The thickened part just above the handle."

"It wasn't machine-milled, though," I pointed out.

She looked up and gave me a dry, quizzical stare. "What makes you think that?" she asked.

I pointed. "When you turn it into the light, the reflections let you see the grind marks on the steel. They're not evenly spaced."

She nodded like a schoolmistress, satisfied that I'd done as well as I could with my limited understanding. "That's true," she said. "Although some machine-milled blades are hand-finished afterwards, for a variety of reasons."

"Such as?"

"Such as persuading the buyer that he's getting a handcrafted item." I slapped my hand to my forehead, Homer Simpson style, and she smiled drily. "Yes, it's a dirty business. Stay out of it, dear heart, if you want to keep any illusions about human nature." She ran her thumb along the edge of the blade, very carefully. "This could have been hand-milled, just about, although if it was then it was done by someone with a very good eye. Thickness, you see: not the slightest variation along the whole blade. Possible to achieve by hand, but a lot easier with an electric mill.

"Now the wood . . ." She rubbed the handle appreciatively. "That's nice. Very nice. Amboyna burl. Southeast Asian. You'd never guess to look at the living tree that the heartwood would have that red luster to it. The bark is as gray as I am.

"But here's the giveaway." She tapped the design at the tang end of the blade—the delicate floral motif, which was the thing I was most interested in. "Machine-etched," she said. "The electrolyte solution leaves a minute amount of staining on the steel, which gets worse over the course of a few years and then stabilizes unless there's a fault in the steel itself or it wasn't properly neutralized in the first place. In this case there's a green sheen at the base of the major lines in the design—here. This was done with an industrial-standard etch-a-matic using copper and bronze electrolyte and a sodium-based neutralizer. It's letting the side down, really, because overall this is a nice piece. But"—she laid it down on the counter, reversed it, and slid it across to me—"no more than fifty years old, in my opinion. And not worth as much now as it was when it was new."

I tapped the heel of the blade. "Have you ever seen this design before?" I asked her.

She frowned. Possibly she registered that as being an unusual question to come from a tragically bereaved nephew. "No," she admitted. "Not on a knife blade, in any event. I recognize the actual plant, of course."

"You do?" I was impressed. "Why?"

"Because I deal in antiques, dear. There's always at least some degree of stylization in floral motifs, so they're easy to memorize. And they're very useful in identification, so it's worth the effort. This is belladonna—deadly nightshade, to give it its more poetic name. You can tell by the asymmetrical leaf pairs."

"Right, of course. Asymmetrical leaf pairs."

"With the flower coming out of the larger leaf. Look."

It *was* quite distinctive, now that she mentioned it. Pretty, too. "But does it mean anything?" I demanded, looking her in the face.

She looked back at me, world-weary and a little disapproving. "You're not a policeman, are you, young man? I positively despise policemen. Rabid little rodents, the lot of them."

"I'm not a policeman, Mrs. Caldessa."

"Just Caldessa will do, thank you very much. Very well. I'll get my book."

The book was called *Identifying Marks in Cutlery and Metalware*, by Jackman and Pollard, it was dated 1976, and it was thicker than a telephone directory. Caldessa leafed through it with one hand, holding the knife in the other, and muttering to herself under her breath the whole time. There didn't seem to be an index of any kind, although there were headings at the top of each page that consisted mainly of words like "inflorescence" and "lanceolate," and numbers that might have been ranges of dates.

Finally she tapped a particular design, glanced from the page to the knife and back again a great many times, and looked up to fix me with a gaze of frank puzzlement.

"Tell me a little more about your uncle," she suggested.

I shrugged apologetically. "There is no uncle," I admitted, telling her what she must already know. "I swiped that knife from a couple of guys who were trying to perform amateur surgery on me with it. Now I'd love to know who they were."

"Anathemata Curialis."

"Not deadly nightshade? I thought you said—"

"No, no. The organization that uses this design. It's called Anathemata Curialis. Did you get a good look at the men who were trying to kill you?"

"They weren't men," I said, remembering the feline shape that had chased me across Soho Square and shuddering involuntarily.

"That's a very harsh judgment," said Caldessa sternly. "I'm not a believer myself, but I respect the opinions of others. Most of the time. Unless they're ridiculous, like female circumcision."

"Whoa. Wait a second. What are you telling me? That this is . . . ?"

"A religious symbol. In effect, yes. If this knife actually belonged to the two men you mentioned, then they were Catholics. Jackman and Pollard, on whose opinion I have many times staked my reputation, identify the Anathemata Curialis as a wing of the Catholic Church."

She beckoned me around the counter so that she could show me the relevant entry in the book, but seeing it in black-and-white didn't really help much. I couldn't make any sense out of this no matter whether I was reading it across, down, or diagonally. The Catholic Church hated and feared the undead with the same passion and enthusiasm they'd once reserved for people who said the world was round. Among the very few things I could tell you for certain about those two loup-garous was that they weren't faithful and committed adherents to the Roman communion.

But pictures don't lie. Or if they do, they don't do it with such a straight face. I ran my eyes down the list. In among the names of Oxford colleges, regiments of defunct colonial armies, and arriviste aristos whose forebears had puckered up and gone down on long-dead kings, there was a single entry in italic type: "*Anathemata Curialis, Catholic Order, disc. 1882.*"

"Disc?" I queried aloud.

"Discontinued," said Caldessa. "Nobody has made knives with that livery since 1882."

"Well, now we know something that Jackman and Pollard don't know," I mused grimly. Caldessa raised an eyebrow and nodded, conceding the point.

Remembering my manners, I thanked her and asked her if I could pay her for her time, but she waved the suggestion away summarily. "I honestly doubt you could pitch your price high enough to avoid an implied insult, dear. I'm a luxury commodity. If you ever have anything of real value to sell, you know where I am. And in the meantime, you can take this tawdry little gewgaw out of my sight."

I put the knife back into its tube and went back out onto the street. It was the middle of the afternoon now, and the tourist crowd was thicker than it had been. Walking up toward Notting Hill Gate, I considered the logical next step—my older brother, Matthew—and tried to find reasons not to take it. If anyone could give me a labeled diagram of the innards of the Catholic hierarchy, it was him: he's a priest, after all, and he loves his work. He's a lot less fond of mine, though, and our conversations have a habit of disintegrating into name-calling before we even get past the small talk.

Because I was thinking about Matthew, and because thinking about Matthew tends to trigger a whole lot of other, darker thoughts, I was more or less oblivious of my surroundings. So it was a while before I noticed I was being followed. I wasn't even sure where the realization came from: I just caught sight of a movement in my peripheral vision, and on some level almost below consciousness I turned up a pattern match. I had to fight the urge to turn around. Instead I crossed to a shop window and used it as a mirror—a hoary-whiskered trick that works one time out of three, tops.

This time it half-worked: I saw a tall man in a heavy black over-coat about twenty yards behind me, there for a second as the crowds parted and then gone again. He had his shoulders hunched and his head down, so I couldn't tell who he was, and the steep reverse angle of the window meant that in that split second he'd already moved outside of my field of vision.

I stepped into the shop and took a quick look around. More or less the same range of goods as all the other shops I'd passed, at least to my untutored eye: horse brasses abounded, along with heavy wooden furniture that it would be generous to describe as distressed, old pub signs, and wrought-iron boot-scrapers. No other customers in there; the shop assistant, a guy in his twenties with the odd combination of a street-legal razor cut and a silk Nehru jacket, was reading *Miller's Price Guide* for light relief. There was a smell of must and silence and churchlike tranquillity. Time for hoary dodge number two. I went up to the counter, and the assistant glanced up at me with a professional smile, friendly but brisk.

"Is there a back door out of this place?" I asked.

The smile faded to an affronted deadpan. "The workrooms aren't open to customers, I'm afraid."

"I'm being followed." I decided to elaborate, and I reached for a story that would press the right buttons for an upmarket rag-and-bone man. "Loan shark muscle. They want to beat the shit out of me. I'd rather they didn't do it at all, and you'd probably rather they didn't do it in here. Please yourself, though."

The assistant looked both shaken and disgusted. Fixing me with a hard stare, he picked up his cell phone from behind the counter and gripped it tight as though it were the cure for all the world's ills. "Yeah,"

I agreed, "you could call the police. And while we're waiting you can tell me what not to bleed on."

The workrooms were impressive, and they had a potent smell compounded of beeswax and shellac, but I didn't have time to take the guided tour. The assistant led the way, glancing back at me every other step to make sure I was still there. We went along a corridor lined with wooden crates into a room dominated by a single massive workbench, chairs, and occasional tables hanging on racks above it like some torture chamber for sinful furniture. Then through there into a storeroom stacked with cans of varnish, bales of wire wool, plate-size tubs of Brasso.

At the far end of the storeroom there was a door that he had to unlock with a key from his pocket, and then unbolt at top and bottom. He threw it open and held it for me, glaring at me as though this might still be some kind of fiendish trick. I examined the pass-not ward on the lintel of the back door as I stepped through it: hazel. "This is out of date," I told him, flicking it with the tip of my index finger. "It's almost June. If you don't want poltergeists, get a sprig of myrtle."

He didn't answer. The door slammed shut behind me and I was alone in an alley wide enough to take a delivery van. Not much cover, and it obviously opened right back out onto the street again. Still, we'd see what we'd see.

I went cautiously to the corner and looked out. There were enough people walking past in both directions so that unless anyone was looking for me to emerge at exactly that point they'd take a while to notice me. So I had the luxury of being able to look up and down the length of the street without having to watch my back at the same time.

Nobody lurking around the doorway of the shop I'd gone into. Nobody browsing the windows of the shops to either side of it. I looked across to the other side of the street, bearing in mind that if this guy was any good he'd have chosen a place where a casual glance wouldn't pick him out.

A casual glance didn't, but on the second sweep, bingo, there he was. Just opposite the shop I'd gone into, there was a stand selling roasted nuts—the kind of thing that American tourists get their picture taken with, mistaking it for part of London's rich cultural heritage because it involves both bland food and a cheeky, cheerful Cockney. The man in the black coat had positioned himself close to the back of the stand where he'd be hidden from two sides, and from the other two would most likely look like someone patiently waiting to have his nuts roasted. He was a quarter onto me, so I was mostly seeing the back of his neck and I still couldn't tell whether I'd ever met him before.

Just then, as I was staring at him and willing him to turn around, my phone started to squirm in my pocket like a living thing. There was no noise: I'd set it on vibrate a while ago when for some reason silence had been an issue, and now I kept losing my way in the menus when I tried to turn it back. But noise or no, it came out of nowhere and it made me start. And it was as though that minute movement alerted my stalker even though his eyes were elsewhere. His head jerked up and around, abruptly, triangulating on some cue that beat the hell out of me, and then his body swiveled, too, so that he was facing in my exact direction.

It was eerie and unsettling. So was the face, now that I got a good look at it, because it was Zucker.

Son of a bitch. These guys were tailing me around London with insolent ease. I could understand it if I were wearing a sandwich board like the deranged vegetarian who used to hang out at Oxford Circus (LESS LUST THROUGH LESS PROTEIN) but inconspicuous is my middle name and I pride myself on the hair-trigger accuracy of my professional radar. Did they have the office staked out? Or the *Collective*? Where had I picked them up, and how had they gotten this close to me twice—or three times, counting the Oriflamme—without me spotting them?

It was a conundrum for a quieter moment. Right now, Zucker was staring directly at me across the width of the street, and even with the surging throng turning this into a game of peep-o there was no way he hadn't seen me. I turned my back on him and fled.

When you're playing follow-the-leader in what the military would call a broken ground situation, the leader has all the advantages so long as he keeps his nerve. Weaving in and out of the crowd with my head down, I kept moving fast until I reached another alley, then broke free and sprinted the full length of it, coming out in Brunswick Gardens. The crowds were thicker here if anything, because there was a street market on and the road had been closed to traffic. Tinny music from someone's wooferless boom box scraped along the air along with scents of almond essence and vanilla pods. The stalls, selling mainly antiques and collectibles but also T-shirts, sweets, spices, and bootleg DVDs, crowded the curbs on either side and gave passersby a lose-lose choice between the narrow, obstacle-strewn pavement and the heaving, shop-or-drop chaos in the center of the road.

Perfect.

I threaded my way between two stalls, crossed the street, and continued on the other side. Then fifty yards farther on I crossed back, legs bent at the knee to keep my head down, squeezing myself skillfully through the mob wherever a gap presented itself, and carried on down to the corner, where Kensington Church Street picks up again after the dogleg. Here I inserted myself back into the more orderly crowd of antique-hunters. Okay, I'd gotten turned around 180 degrees, and I'd have to go home by a different route, but I reckoned that no one on God's earth could have kept me in sight through that maneuver.

So it was kind of a bitter blow when I got onto an eastbound train at High Street Ken and saw, walking down the steps on the other side of the barriers, that now familiar black coat and slouching, head-down gait. The train was idling, doors open, waiting for a signal to change or for some other, more arcane London Underground augury. Packed in between a whole bunch of other straphangers and their interesting collection of armpits, all I could do was stand and watch. The man slid his ticket through the machine and the barriers opened. He walked on past me without looking up, and without any sense of urgency that I could see. Then, just like on the street, he looked up—first left and then right, finally locking eyes with me just as the doors hissed shut.

Our eyes met. He might have been angry, or embarrassed, or

nonplussed, but he wasn't any of those things. He just smiled, baring teeth that seemed to include a few too many canines. I smiled back, sardonically: then the doors slid open again and the smile slid off my face like lumpy custard.

Zucker took a single step toward me. He didn't take a second one, because with the strength of panic I grabbed the guy standing next to me—a young Turk from the city, to judge by his splendid suit—by the shoulders and pushed him off the train. He collided with Zucker, who tried to step around him and then, as he staggered and flailed, just flicked him out of the way, one-handed. They were only entangled for a second: then that gorgeous Alfieri homespun was down in the dirt and Zucker was stepping toward me, unencumbered.

But that second had been worth buying. The doors slammed shut again in his face and the train pulled out. A second later the tunnel's arch slid like a magician's cloak across the scene, magicking it away.

I was hunter, and I was hunted. I was missing something. And if these guys were Catholics, I'd eat my tin whistle and fart the Hallelujah Chorus. To tell you the truth, the whole thing was starting to sour my mood.

So did standing on the train all the way to Turnpike Lane. I felt bone weary by this time, and there was a sort of itchy heat behind my eyes that I usually associate with the start of a fever. My left shoulder was aching again, too, so that I had to grip the handrail with my right arm the whole way. By Caledonian Road it had started to cramp up on me. No doubt about it, I was a mess. I needed to go and lie down in a darkened room until my body decided to let me off the hook for the abuse I'd subjected it to over the past couple of days.

Instead of which I was looking at a dinner date with Juliet followed by tea and biscuits with Rosie Crucis. I didn't feel up to either one of them.

As it turned out, though, I was worrying unnecessarily, because the evening was about to take a different turn in any case. I went back to

Pen's, found it empty, which was no surprise—she was probably out somewhere having a life. I took a shower to get rid of the sweat and aches, and to put on some clothes that were better suited to a social engagement with the sexiest, most debonaire hell-spawn in town. I went with a plain white shirt, a burgundy tie, and a pair of black cargo pants. Oh, and a new dressing on my shoulder wound, which had been weeping slightly: pus yellow with burgundy was a combination I didn't think I could carry off.

Then I finally remembered the phone call I'd gotten earlier on and checked my messages. There weren't any, but the missed call alert gave me Pen's mobile number. I called her back, got no answer, so I left her a message just saying that I'd called and that I was around for the next hour or so. Then the phone rang again about ten seconds later.

"Fix, it's me." Pen's voice, sounding just a whisker away from hysterical. "I'm at the Stanger. You've got to get over here. It's Rafi, Fix. It's Rafi!"

"What's wrong with Rafi?" I asked, my heart plummeting into my shoes.

"Nothing!" she said. "Nothing!" And then tears choked out her words for a good couple of minutes.

Chapter Nine

Rafi cried for a good long time, and that was painful to watch—but his present calm was worse in a way. It had a flavor of shellshock to it.

"Two years! Two fucking years! No, that's not—that's not even funny." He shook his head, hitting that solid wall of incomprehension again—unable to make himself believe.

Pen was beside him on the faded sofa: beside him, and entwined with him, and clinging to him as if he were a life jacket and she was adrift in stormy seas. She was crying, too, and repeating his name whenever she could get her breath in between the racking sobs. He looked at me over her head, a look of mute terror and appeal.

"It feels like I just went to sleep, and then woke up," he muttered. "I was in that sod-awful flat down Seven Sisters Road. You were there, Fix. I was talking to you, and for some reason I was . . . I guess, lying down, or something. Anyway, you were above me looking down. Then I closed my eyes, and . . . I had really bad dreams. The kind where if it was a movie you'd wake up screaming, but you try that and you find out you can't." A new thought occurred to him. "Ginny. Did Ginny see all this? Where is she? Is she outside?"

"Was that the girl?" I asked, and he nodded. I remembered the white-blond, stick-thin apparition who'd worked beside me through the hours of that night, shoveling off-license ice packs into the bath where Rafi lay sprawled to stop the water that was keeping his temperature down from boiling away. Rafi was right, it had been a bit like a dream—and she was one of the things that faded with the daybreak. I'd never seen her again, and it turned out the flat was only in Rafi's name so there was no way of contacting her. "I lost touch with her," I murmured, which had the merit of being accurate without hitting him in the face with how quickly his lady had bailed out on him.

He knew how to read between the lines, though, and two years of being Asmodeus's finger puppet had left him a little deficient in the putting-a-brave-face-on-it department. I had to look away from the naked pain in his eyes.

I was fervently grateful that this scene wasn't being played out in Rafi's cell. Dr. Webb—despite the lingering unpleasantness of Saturday's punch-up—had allowed us to use one of the interview suites, only insisting that a male nurse stay in attendance and that we should all be locked in until we signaled that the visit was over. The nurse—a humorless Welshman named Kenneth, about the size and heft of a bulldozer—stood in the corner of the room watching *Coronation Street* without sound on the wall-mounted TV. It was as close to privacy as the Stanger offered.

"I was possessed," said Rafi, sounding as though he were once again trying the concept on for size and finding that it didn't even go over his shoulders. "Asmodeus took me over. Lived inside my body."

"Rafi, love," said Pen, wiping her bleary eyes, "you shouldn't keep going over this. You want to get well first. Then later on, when you're . . ."

She tailed off into silence because Rafi was shaking his head with slow, stern emphasis. "No," he said. "I need to know where I've been. You can't just sit up in bed, yawn, and stretch and get on with your life. Not after two years."

"It won't be that easy in any case," I said, feeling it my duty as bastard in residence to shoot his hopes down before they flew high enough to hurt themselves. "Getting on with your life, I mean. You're not here on your own recognizance, Rafi. You were sectioned. Getting you out is going to take time. You'll have to convince a whole lot of people you're sane again."

Pen glared at me as if it was my decision to make. "He was never mad, Fix," she said, her voice betraying her because all the crying had left it shaky and high. "You know that."

"Yeah," I agreed. "I do. But it doesn't matter a good goddamn what I know, Pen. Rafi isn't in here because anyone ever really thought he had a mental illness: he's here because demonic possession isn't legally definable—and because Asmodeus couldn't be let out on the streets to amuse himself with the traditional demonic pastimes of torture, mutilation, and murder. We did what we had to do. And unfortunately, once it's done, it's not quick or easy to undo."

Pen stood up, her fists clenched, and faced me down. Just for that moment, it seemed, I was the enemy—the voice of all the unreason and all the hypocritical hedging that had put Rafi here in the first place and was happy now to leave him here until he rotted.

"I think we'd like to be alone for a while," she said pointedly. I threw out my hands in a placating gesture and headed for the door.

"Wait, Fix."

When I turned, Rafi was looking at the ground—or maybe he had his eyes on the ground while he looked within himself for a script for what he was going to say next. That search seemed to absorb every ounce and inch of his attention.

"What?" I asked, a little brusquely. I was with Pen on this one: I wanted out. Wanted to leave them alone to match velocities again after two years in which Pen had had a life and Rafi had had a padded room. And I particularly, fervently, needed to be somewhere else when the conversation got as far as Dylan.

"It's not . . . undone," he said. There was a long, terrible silence. Then just as I opened my mouth to ask for a translation, he looked up and stared at me with an intensity that shoved the words back down my throat. "I mean, Asmodeus is still here. A piece of him. It's not like he just up and left. It's more like"—his mouth moved for a moment in silence—"like he took his weight off me so that he could lean over sideways and do something else. But I can still feel him, and he can still feel me. We're still joined."

"No," Pen protested, in a tone that was almost a moan. Neither Rafi nor I responded to that poor, orphaned little syllable.

"Maybe that gives you a window," I offered, uneasily. "Maybe someone could do a full demon-ectomy on you now. If he's loosened his hold . . ."

"Someone," said Rafi. "Not you?"

"You don't remember," I told him, bleakly. "If you did, you wouldn't ask me. I tried once, Rafi, and I fucked up—badly. That's why his soul and yours are wrapped around each other in a lovers' knot."

"That's not the only reason. I invited him in to start with."

In spite of myself I felt a quickening of queasy interest. I'd always wondered what the hell Rafi had thought he was doing that night. "So it was Asmodeus you were fishing for?" I asked. "It wasn't an accident?"

Rafi laughed—a laugh with a crazed edge to it. "An accident? It was an accident that I let my guard down. But you can't say it's an accident if you light your cigarette with a blowtorch and you lose your eyebrows. Asmodeus was the one I was after, Fix. The books said he was one of the mightiest demons in hell. And one of the oldest. I didn't see any sense in working my way up from the bottom: I wanted the goods, and I wanted them fast. So I don't blame you for what happened, Fix. I blame myself. And I'll take any help I can get right now."

I shook my head. "No. You need someone with a lighter touch. Or a steadier hand." Call it cowardice or scruple or whatever the hell you like, but I wanted that cup to pass away from me. I'd ruined Rafi once: I didn't think I could live with myself if I did it again.

"You got someone in mind?"

I thought of Juliet. "Maybe. I know someone who could come in and give us an opinion, anyway."

He smiled the most unconvincing smile I've ever seen. "Thanks, Fix. You're a brick."

"One letter out," I riposted, more feebly still.

Pen was still looking daggers, flails, and chainsaws at me: the two of them still had a lot of ground to cover, so my turn would have to come later. I let myself out into the corridor, where Webb was hovering expressly to catch me as I exited. Another male nurse waited in the background—presumably in case I turned violent and had to be sedated.

"You're looking a little tense," I told Webb. "Is something on your mind?"

"I need to know what I'm dealing with here, Castor," he snapped back, my solicitous tone doing nothing to improve his mood.

"A miraculous recovery?"

"Is that what you think it is?"

"I don't know," I hedged. "Why, what do you think?"

"I think Ditko—or the thing inside him—is playing a new game. It wouldn't be the first time. I've called Professor Mulbridge."

Those words affected me like intravenous ice cubes. "You had no right—" I began, but Webb wasn't about to be stopped when he'd barely started.

"I have every right to consult with a colleague," he interrupted. "Professor Mulbridge is an acknowledged expert in the field."

"What field?" I demanded, pinning him to it.

He hesitated, trying to sniff out the trap before he fell into it.

"What field?" I repeated. "Metamorphic ontology? Because your diagnosis of Rafi is schizophrenia. Are you saying you've changed that assessment?"

"We both know—"

"What we both know," I said, shouting over his already raised voice, "is that you're so desperate to get rid of Rafi, you'll try anything. And right now, saying that he needs specialized facilities elsewhere looks like a much quicker option than going through MHA screening and getting him independently assessed."

"He does need specialized facilities," Webb yelled back. "He's a danger to everyone he comes into contact with."

"That was last week," I said, in a tone that was just barely short of a snarl. "And believe me, Webb—if you start flirting with Jenna-Jane, you're going to be explaining in court exactly when your professional opinion of Rafi Ditko's condition changed—and why you didn't see fit to tell any of his friends or family about it."

Webb flushed a very fetching shade of brick red that set off his pale yellow shirt nicely. "Castor, you're chopping logic," he hissed, "and I won't be intimidated by you. I have to do what's best for the whole of this therapeutic community, and I believe my actions will stand the scrutiny of—"

I walked away, leaving him yelling apoplectically after me. I needed to get clear of him before I hit him, handing him the moral and legal high ground on a plate.

Also I needed answers, and I wasn't in the mood to wait until I knew what the questions were.

———

"It's good to see you again, Felix," my brother Matt said, as I squeezed into the booth opposite him. "You're in my prayers a lot."

"I'd feel happier about that if I knew what you were praying for," I countered with a cold smile. Letting him get away with a line like that would get the conversation off to a bad start.

We were in a little coffeehouse just off Muswell Hill Broadway, with questionable decor in the general neighborhood of art nouveau—or maybe a few blocks down. Figure paintings by Mucha and Hodler lined the walls, and square-edged Tiffany-style lampshades hung down dangerously low over each table. Upbeat twenties jazz was playing softly in the background to make the point that this was all a period quote—but incongruously there was also a TV playing in the background with the volume turned all the way down. Currently, it showed a reporter standing in front of a row of shops, talking soundlessly to the camera with an earnest face. From where I was sitting, the reporter stood on Matt's right-hand shoulder like his conscience.

He'd already ordered, which was fine with me: what I felt like drinking right then wasn't on the menu here. When I passed this way, I preferred to drink at the O'Neill's pub on the Broadway, which is built into the shell of a deconsecrated church. But Matty doesn't share my sense of humor and I wanted to establish a convivial atmosphere, so we'd settled on the coffeehouse.

I'd called Matt from the Stanger and asked him to meet me. When he asked why, I said it was for the good of my soul and hung up. He knew I was most likely kidding, but he never quite allows himself to despair of me seeing the light. Pretty much any light will do.

He was in civvies, by which I mean he wasn't wearing his collar. Looking at him, you'd just see a slim-built, slightly bookish man on the cusp of forty, in a dark sweater and jeans that looked old without being shabby, with thinning mid-brown hair and very hard blue-gray eyes. Everything about Matty is hard: he's got a weakness for moral certainties. He's also got a good eye for detail, and he looked me up and down searchingly.

"You don't look well," he said. "There's something hectic about your complexion. And your lip is swollen. Did you have an accident?"

"I was mugged," I said.

"In the line of duty?" His lips pursed. He really doesn't approve of how I earn my living.

"You could say that. How's Mum?"

"She's well. She had a bad chest infection a few weeks back, but they gave her antibiotics and she's fine now. They've put her on an inhaler, too." He frowned. "She won't stop smoking, in spite of the emphysema, so keeping her airways open is the main priority. I thought you said you were going to go up and visit?"

"I am," I said. "I've got a couple of things to clear first, that's all."

"Right."

He took a sip of his coffee, eyes cast down, looking like a man who was trying hard not to say anything.

To fill the gap, I dug in my pocket for Zucker's knife and put it down on the table between us.

"You ever see anything like that before?" I asked him.

Matt stared at the knife, and his eyes widened slightly. "That object belongs in your life, not in mine," he said softly. Too softly; he never did learn to lie with his face as well as his voice.

"Funny you should say that," I mused. "Because the guy who tried to use it on me was definitely one of your crowd."

"A priest?" Matt's tone was disdainful.

"Yeah, in a way. Maybe. A functionary of your church."

"My church doesn't employ armed men."

"It doesn't? I suppose the crusaders were using your registered trademark without permission, then?"

Matt sighed heavily. "The last crusade ended in the thirteenth century, Felix. I used the present tense."

I tapped the hilt of the knife. "This thing is present, Matty. And it makes me tense enough for both of us. Tell me about the Anathemata."

He was silent.

"They're trying to kill me," I said. "It would help a lot if I knew why."

Another silence, but this time I went with instinct and let it stretch.

"They don't—kill—indiscriminately," Matt said at last. "And they're not agents of the church."

"Then why are they listed as a church organization?"

"They're not. Unless you were using an old book."

Again, I waited, and eventually, reluctantly, Matty filled the silence.

"They're a very old sect," he said. "But their history is patchy. Under some popes they barely existed. At other times they were as powerful in their way as the Society of Jesus or the Inquisition. Their brief was to deal with those things that mother church considers abominations—*anathema*, in the Greek word. Anathemata is just the plural form. In recent times . . . over the past ten years or so . . . that had come to mean the risen dead."

A murky light, like bioluminesence in a bloated corpse, was starting to dawn.

"What exactly does 'deal with' mean in this context?" I asked.

"I don't know," Matty admitted. "I was never a member, though as a student of church history I was aware of their existence."

"Are you telling me there wasn't any loose talk behind the confessionals on a Saturday night?"

He frowned. "There were rumors, obviously. Contradictory, and based on nothing more than hearsay. Felix, the Catholic Church isn't a vast, secret conspiracy, whatever you happen to think—in terms of freedom of information, it compares favorably to most governments."

"Set your bar a little higher," I suggested sourly. "Matty, I'm not talking about the Little Sisters of Maria Assumpta—I'm talking about a group within your church that's using werewolves to run their errands. Are they reaching out to our hairier brethren? Is 'deal with' a polite way of saying 'recruit'? And they have daggers made to their own design, for fuck's sake. You think they open a lot of mail? Cut a lot of cakes, what?"

"I don't know what they do," Matty repeated patiently, refusing as always to lose his temper with me. "I will tell you, though, if you're interested, why an up-to-date listing of church groups would leave the Anathemata out."

"Go on," I said. I was distracted by the TV images over his shoulder. Broken windows, and policemen in riot gear charging forward in a solid line.

"Because they were disbanded," Matt said, with just an edge of smugness. "The new pope questioned their methods and their usefulness. He ordered the seniors of the order to stand down, after first reallocating their members to other groups and tasks. This was all quite recent—only a year ago."

"And did it take?" I asked pointedly. I glanced down at the knife. "Because that thing on the table was even more recent."

That reluctance came back. "The prelates of the order took issue with His Holiness. I gather that they argued . . ." He hesitated, and then didn't seem to know how to start up again.

"They argued . . . ?" I prompted.

Matty nodded curtly. "Don't try to browbeat me, Felix, please. I'm trying to word this in a way that doesn't make it sound too sensational. They argued that the rising of the dead, and the appearance of infernal creatures as the shepherds of the dead, were an indication that the Last Days had begun. They felt—many of them felt—that their own dissolution would leave the field open to hell, and that they would be remiss in their spiritual duty if they accepted it."

He'd been looking at the knife. Now he looked up and met my gaze. He'd clearly reached the thing that he hadn't wanted to say, and I was impressed by how well he swallowed the pill.

"So they refused. En masse. And they were excommunicated."

I whistled, long and low. "That's strong stuff," I said.

"Yes, Felix, that's strong stuff. It put their souls and their bodies outside of the church's communion and comfort. It denied them the possibility of a place in heaven."

"It left them with nothing to lose," I summed up.

Matty opened his mouth to speak, but I stopped him with a raised hand. "Matty, do you know where these people operate out of?"

"No."

I considered that bare monosyllable. It seemed to me to be concealing at least a moderately sized multitude of sins.

"Would you know how to contact them, if you had to?" I asked.

Matt breathed out, long and hard, through his nose. "The Anathemata are historically linked to the Douglas Ignatieff Biblical Research Trust in Woolwich," he said. "I say historically, because it's been a long time since anyone in the movement published any papers or took part in religious debate. I doubt very much that the connection is an extant one."

"But would there be someone there who—?"

I stopped dead, my brain finally catching up with my eyes, and leaned over to the right to get a better look at the TV on the wall behind him. It was showing a scene of chaos on the nighted streets of a city: running people, a yellowish flare of distant flames, and in the foreground the corner of some building, one wall of red brick, the other of glass with a huge hole in the middle of it like a jag-toothed mouth. The camera was handheld and the light wasn't good, but it looked like an office block of some kind—low-rise, only three stories above a street of shopfronts.

"Wait." I got up and crossed to the set. "Can you turn up the volume?" I called out to the waiter. The resolution was still as clear as mud, but I could read the strap line at the bottom of the screen well enough: it said WHITE CITY SIEGE.

The waiter looked a little indignant. "We keep it low so it doesn't disturb the other diners."

"Yeah, I know. Just for a moment. It's important."

He held out for a moment longer, but I kept staring at him implacably and he folded. He found a remote from somewhere and aimed it at the set: the whisper of sound became a just about audible mumble. "—are feared to be dead, although it's obviously the hostages who are the immediate concern right now. The police have surrounded the Whiteleaf shopping precinct, and they've closed off Bloemfonten Road at both the north and south ends. Now they're waiting to see if there are any demands. But since they don't even know who they're dealing with, or whether the motive is political or something else entirely, it's far too early to say whether we can expect—"

I lost the rest of the sentence, because I suddenly caught another glimpse of what I thought I'd seen before: a pale, familiar face in the ragged-edged hole in the glass—leaning out from some anonymous strip-lighted space, with two male faces behind her, one of them holding what looked to be a kitchen knife.

It was Susan Book, the verger at St. Michael's Church.

I turned to Matty.

"I need a car," I said. "Did you drive here?"

To my surprise, he reached into his pocket and handed me the keys. He'd seen my face as I was staring at the screen, and I guess it didn't leave him with any questions.

"It's a Honda Civic," he said. "Dark blue. On Prince's Avenue."

"Thanks." I gave him a nod, grateful that he wasn't wasting my time by asking for explanations. "For the loan, and for the information. Shall I bring the car back here or—?"

"There's a Carmelite convent over in Hadley Wood. You can leave it there. The sisters know me."

A predictable joke about the Biblical sense of that word died on my lips as I stared into his solemn, concerned face.

"Or leave it somewhere else, if you have to," he said. "Explain to me later, Felix. If there's something important hanging on this, you'd better go."

I went.

Chapter Ten

I drove back up Colney Hatch Lane like a bat out of some part of hell where life was particularly cheap, took a hair-raising left onto the North Circular, and accelerated to eighty. That took me past the Stanger, and I thought fleetingly of the incredible change that Rafi had undergone.

Why now? What had happened to trigger it? Were the forces that seemed to have driven so many Londoners over the edge into murderous insanity only one half of some cosmic seesaw that had also tipped Rafi back into his right mind? And was either end of the seesaw connected with the sudden interest that the Anathemata were taking in me? The link there was Peace. I was looking for him, and they were, too. So were they only following me to get to him, or was there some other reason why I couldn't spit without hitting them? And given what Matty had said about their attitude to the undead, what were they doing handing out stake-out jobs to the likes of Po and Zucker in the first place?

I pulled my attention back to the job at hand. Whatever was going down in White City, I needed some more information before I walked into it, that was for damned sure; otherwise what I didn't know could end up hurting me quite a lot. I didn't even know what I was going to do when I got there. I just had a feeling, maybe activated by seeing Susan Book in the middle of all the bad craziness, that this was somehow connected to what Nicky had described: the wave of murder and mayhem that had swept through West London on Saturday night. That part of the city was the epicenter of something very nasty, something subterranean, that broke the surface as a murder here and a rape there—and now as a riot. I couldn't believe there wasn't a link.

I turned on the radio, one-handed, and after a few wild stabs in the dark found the channel search button. Samples of pop, reggae, advertising jingles, and the occasional solemn BBC voice washed around my ears as I realized that I didn't even know exactly where I was headed. Bloemfonten Road. I didn't know at all, but the announcer on the TV news had said it had a north and a south end, so we were probably talking about either a turning off the Westway or one of the maze of streets around the stadium. I just had to hope that once I got close enough I could find my way by following the flames and the sirens.

The road was reasonably clear at first, and I made good time—but the traffic was bound to start piling up once I got to Hanger Lane, and in any case there was a quicker route down through Willesden to Scrubs Lane. I realized as I turned off onto the Harrow Road that I was going to drive within a hundred yards or so of my office. Well, Pen was always telling me I should spend more time there.

"—in what has rapidly turned into a siege situation." Finally! The tone as much as the words told me that I'd found what I was looking for. I stopped the channel search, again with a fair bit of fumbling, and turned up the volume. I also switched on the back wipers and the hazard lights along the way, but this was no time to worry about fine details. A man's voice, solemn but with an undertone of excitement, blared out of the speakers, the car's crummy sound system giving him a tinny echo. "It's thought that there could be as many as twenty people still inside the shopping center, but we don't have any idea as yet how many of them are being held against their will, or even who their attackers are. The fires are mostly out now, and the immediate danger is passed, but these armed men and women have issued no demands and given no indication of what their agenda is. The earlier destruction seemed almost random, and from the sounds we can hear it's still going on inside the center. Only five minutes ago, an exercise machine came flying through a window on the upper level and fell onto a police car parked on the street below. Thankfully, nobody was hurt, but it's a very tense situation here and there's little prospect of it being resolved anytime soon."

A sudden absence of street sounds in the background made it clear that we'd gone back to the studio, as a second voice, female this time but with the same titillated solemnity, took up the story—or rather, hijacked it away into rarefied realms of speculation about terrorist cells and soft economic targets. I tuned it out. This wasn't about terrorism, I felt that in my guts: it was about Nicky's bell-shaped curve. And send not to ask for whom the fucking bell tolls, because you're not going to like the answer.

My phone went off and I took it in case it was Pen wanting to know where the hell I'd scooted off to in such a hurry. But it wasn't.

"Hey," said Nicky. "Catch you at a bad moment?"

The Civic was an automatic: I could manage with just the one hand, but I had enough to concentrate on without shooting the breeze with Nicky on top of it all.

"Yeah," I said. "Can I call you back?"

"Sure. You watching TV?"

"I was. Now I'm listening to the radio."

"Interesting times, eh? Call me when you've got a moment. But make it quick. This shit you need to hear. Actually don't call me, because I'm going out to the Ice-Maker's. You can meet me down there."

"Peckham? Nicky, it's been a long day—"

"Fine. Wait until tomorrow. It's your call. But if I were you, I'd want this particular dish served hot."

"I'll see what I can do."

I tossed the phone onto the seat beside me. I'd almost reached the Westway, which meant I had to be getting close to the action now. I slowed just a little as I came around the underpass, in case I ran into any of those police roadblocks. Nothing to see, but as I passed White

City Stadium I caught sight of the flashing lights of the black-and-whites a couple of hundred yards up the road. Okay, "X" presumably marked the spot. I took the first left, then a right—past a closed-up nursery school whose deserted swings and climbing frames leaped into the bleaching glow of my headlights: in the harsh light they were divorced from their functions in a way that was frankly sinister, looking more or less like the contents of a torture chamber.

I was counting off the distance roughly in my head, but long before I got to the next intersection I could see exactly what I was aiming for. Up ahead of me was a wall of red brick that was already familiar from the TV news bulletin: the giveaway, though, was the wide strip-sign hanging out over the road, which proclaimed WHITELEAF SHOPPING CENTRE in an italic font with plenty of scrolling. Heavy coils of smoke hung above and around it, wearing out their welcome in the damp, still spring air.

I turned off the lights and pulled over. Up ahead of me the street was packed with people: cops in uniform, ambulance crews, passersby who'd stopped to watch the drama play itself out. I walked up, skirting the edges of the crowd as I looked for a way to move in a little closer without drawing unwelcome attention to myself. I didn't have any definite plans past that point, except that I wanted to get inside the building and take a look for myself at what was going down in there. And that I wanted Susan the verger to get out of this intact, with all her doubts and hesitations. A modest enough goal, I thought. The police could sort out the rest of it: that was what they were paid for.

But the crowd was a solid wedge, and even if I could get past them there was a police cordon all around this face of the building. To the right that cordon stretched all the way up the street back as far as I could see—probably all the way to the roadblock on the Westway. On the other side the houses came right up to the wall of the shopping center, the last one facing it at an oblique angle like a dinghy that had collided with an ocean liner and been knocked spinning. I was going to have to try elsewhere.

That last house offered a possibility, though. It had a strip of garden to the side, bordering right up against the wall of the shopping center. I slipped in through the gate, trying to look like I owned the place, and trotted around to the side. There was a fence at the back that was low enough to vault over; then another strip of garden, helpfully shielded from the house it belonged to by a clothesline full of washing. Unfortunately there was a stout, hatchet-faced brunette in the midst of the washing, presumably evacuating it to the safety of the house. She had two or three clothes pegs in her mouth, but she gaped when she saw me and they fell out. Her shriek of surprise and protest pursued me across the narrow lawn to the higher brick wall on the far side. I took a flying jump and scrambled up using elbows and feet.

I found I was looking down into a delivery bay where a dozen or so lorries in red and silver livery were parked. No sign of any police cars, or any rioters for that matter. Straight ahead of me there was a loading bay, and its corrugated steel rolling door was only three-quarters shut. That's an open invitation to a thief. I jumped down lightly on the farther side, hearing a woman's voice behind me yell, "There was a man, Arthur! There was a man in the yard!" and a male voice truculently reply, "What effing man? I can't see a man."

I glanced around to make sure there was nobody in sight, then crossed quickly to the loading bay. There was a lorry drawn up there, its back doors wide open and its loading ramp lowered. An overturned pallet nearby had spilled brown cardboard boxes across the concrete apron in front of the rolling door. Whoever had been working here had downed tools pretty abruptly; hopefully that meant they'd fled when the riot started, but it was also possible that they were among the hostages inside. I wondered belatedly what the hell I was getting myself into here, but it seemed a little late to start having second thoughts. Probably the trick is to rule out stunts like this at the first-thoughts stage.

The rolling door would probably lift if I got my hands underneath it and pulled, but there was no way of telling how much noise it would make. Instead, I went down on hands and knees and went under it.

If someone had been waiting on the other side of the door, I'd have been an easy target as I crawled through on all fours and scrambled to my feet again on the far side: this wasn't exactly covert infiltration. But the room I found myself in, long and narrow, stacked from floor to ceiling on either side with boxes and crates, was thankfully devoid of bloodthirsty maniacs armed with broken pieces of furniture. I stood still for a moment or two, listening, but the silence was absolute. All the action was clearly happening somewhere else.

But as I moved forward into the room, I started to become aware of a whole range of sounds almost at the limits of my hearing: dull thumps and muffled shouts, softened by the distance, so that if you closed your eyes you could almost convince yourself you were listening to a cricket match on the village green.

There was no door at the farther end of the room—just a square arch that led out into a larger warehouse space. I threaded my way cautiously through this, the back of my neck prickling every time I passed a darkened aisle. I came across an elevator shaft big enough to take me and the Civic I'd rode in on, but the elevator itself was elsewhere: the gaping doors opened onto a vertical corridor of gray cinder blocks whose bottom I couldn't see. I kept on going, until finally a pair of black rubberized swing doors let me out into a tiled corridor. The posters on the wall here, advertising designer jeans at less than half price and three hundred top-up minutes with every new phone, told me that I wasn't backstage anymore: I was in the mall itself.

I expected the corridor to bring me out into the central arcade, but I'd got myself turned around somehow and I ended up in a blunt cul-de-sac facing the toilets and an "I speak your weight" machine. The noises were fainter here, but as I turned around to go back the way I'd come my other sense—the one I use in my professional capacity—went haywire. Something was coming down the corridor toward me, and I didn't need any pricking in my thumbs to tell me that it was wicked. It was dead, or it was undead, or it was something worse, and whatever it was, it was heading straight toward me. Another second would bring it around the bend in the corridor and right into my line of sight.

Since there was nowhere else to go, I took a silent step backward, pushed open the door of the ladies' toilet, and slid inside. If the thing was already on my trail, then it would certainly follow me inside—but at least now I had a few seconds to prepare a suitable reception.

My own silver dagger is barely more than a fruit parer: I keep it, like the chalice, mainly for ritual occasions. But the knife that the loup-garou had dropped the night before was still in my outside pocket. I took it out and slid the cardboard sleeve off the wickedly sharp blade. Then I took up position behind the door and waited.

Footsteps echoed hollowly on the tiling outside, coming toward me, and then stopped. There was a silence, which stretched agonizingly: I imagined the thing, whatever it was, standing in the corridor just on the other side of the door, its own senses straining as it tried to decide whether I'd gone for the gents or the distaff side.

Then the door opened, and I tensed to lunge at whatever came into view when it swung closed again. The only thing that stopped me was a sigh, which sounded both long-suffering and a little disappointed.

"Castor."

False-footed, I let the knife fall to my side. Juliet pulled the door back toward the closed position a little way, and stared at me around the edge of it. Under a floor-length coat of black leather she was dressed in bloodred silk: a rose in a gloved fist. In the medieval *Romance of the Rose*, floral metaphors were used as a way of smuggling smut past the vigilant eyes of the church. I thought of roses opening, and had to wrench my mind back brutally from pathways that would take up too much time, and leave me too far off balance.

"I thought so," Juliet said.

As always when I feel like an idiot, I went on the offensive. "You thought so? What about that infallible sense of smell of yours? You should have seen me coming a mile off."

"Too many other smells about," muttered Juliet, closing her eyes and inhaling deeply, as if to make the point. "There's something else walking around in this building, and it's a lot bigger and ranker than you are."

"I suppose I should take that as a compliment."

"Take it however you like." I suddenly realized that she was rigidly tense: the muscles in her neck standing proud of her alabaster flesh like filigreed ropes, and her posture stiff with readiness. The last time I'd seen her like this, she was hunting me; whatever she was hunting now, I felt sorry both for it and for anyone else who got in the way.

"So where are they?" I asked her. She shot a glance at me as if she was surprised to find that I was still there. "The hostages," I clarified. "And the rioters?"

Juliet glanced up at the ceiling. "Up there," she said. "Almost directly above us."

"How do you want to play this? And what are you even doing here in the first place? Did you see Susan Book on the TV news?"

She shook her head, frowning momentarily as if I'd accused her of something faintly indecent. "No," she said tersely. "But if I had, it would have been that much clearer a confirmation. This is all connected to what happened at St. Michael's. I'm certain of it. I'm getting the same sense here that I got there—the scent that faded when I tried to focus on it. This thing has broken cover. If I can get close to it, I'll be able to see it for what it is."

I digested that statement with some difficulty, but I wasn't going to argue with her. Having important conversations in the toilet is very much a girl thing.

"Look," I said, "we don't really have the faintest idea what's going on here." She seemed about to interrupt, but I plowed on. "All we know is that there are some people up on the mezzanine tearing the place apart, and some other people who got in the way of that. You could be right: maybe there is something making that happen, and maybe it's the same something that's setting up house over at the church. Doesn't really matter in any case. Now that we're here, the best thing we can do is pull our little playmate out of the line of fire and then get the hell out before the police start to lob in the tear gas."

Juliet shook her head irritably. "I'm only interested in finding the thing that brought me here. The thing I'm smelling. By all means rescue Book, if you want to. I can't see how she's relevant."

"She's in love with you," I told her.

"What?"

"Well, in lust, I mean. She's got a bad dose of that stuff you dish out, anyway, and being as how she's both devout and straight she doesn't have any idea how to handle it. You mean to say you didn't notice how she looks at you?"

"I tune that information out," Juliet said, but she looked a little disconcerted. "You're not asking me to feel—whatever it's called—guilt about this, are you?"

"No." It was my turn to be impatient. "But think about it. She might not have gotten herself into this if she hadn't been wandering around in a moon-eyed daydream thinking improper thoughts about you. I just didn't feel happy about leaving her in there."

"Her emotions are no business of yours—or of mine."

"Fine. I'm not asking you to feel guilty. I'm just saying that I feel a little bit responsible for her myself."

Juliet didn't say anything to this, which was a pretty fair indication that I'd given her some food for thought. She's taking this business of trying to be human very seriously. She still finds an awful lot of it completely unfathomable, but she is keen to get the details right and she does have the whole of eternity to work in.

"Look," I said, "I've got an idea that might get the both of us what we want. Let me show you something."

I stepped past her, pulled the door open, and went back out into the corridor. She followed me as I retraced my steps to the warehouse, and I showed her the open elevator shaft.

"No use to me," I said. "But I thought maybe you could . . ."

"Yes," said Juliet. "I could. But why should I?"

"You want to look for your demon, and you don't want to be watching your back all the time in case these nutcases stick a knife in it—especially not when the siege might turn into a firefight at any moment. So it makes sense if we clean up first and look around afterwards."

"Just tell me what you want me to do, Castor."

"You take the high road, and I'll take the low road. While they're watching me, you sneak up behind them and take them out with your usual mixture of elegance and brutality. Then we'll look around and see what we can see."

I was really impressed with my own performance: my voice didn't shake in the slightest. You'd have thought I waded into the middle of riots every day of the week—whereas, in fact, since my student days ended I've more or less kicked the habit.

I'd expected more opposition from Juliet, but she made a one-handed gesture that suggested she was sick of the subject. She shucked her coat and let it fall to the ground. Roses opening. "All right," she said. "I'll climb the lift shaft. And you'll—?"

"I'll use the escalator. I want to stop in at Top Man."

I walked away before she could change her mind, still trying not to think about roses.

The other end of the corridor opened directly onto the main concourse, which was looking as though a hurricane had hit it while it was pulling itself together after an earthquake. The floor was a carpet of broken glass from storefront windows, in which display dummies lay sprawled like placeholders for the dead. Someone had trodden down hard on the head of one of them, shattering it into powdery shards. For some reason I thought of Abbie's porcelain doll, and shuddered in a kind of premonitory unease. Dress rails that had been used as battering rams lay half-in and half-out of the window frames they'd shattered, and up against one wall a gutted till leaked copper coins like congealed blood. This didn't look like looting, though. Not that looters have any higher standards of respect for the retail environment, but the crunching debris under my feet included wristwatches and shiny gold bracelets from a jeweler's carousel that I'd already had to step over. At some point, the sheer fun of destruction had taken over from any purely mercenary considerations here. That told me a little bit more about what I was dealing with—in fact, at that precise moment, more than I wanted to know.

The escalators were right out in the center of the lower piazza, which meant that as I approached them I had plenty of time to look up at the galleries on the second and third floors. The second floor seemed to be deserted, but up on the top level three men were struggling with a fourth in what I took at first to be a good-natured scrum. Then I realized that I'd misread the situation: it only seemed friendly because three of the men were laughing. The fourth wasn't making any sound at all, because they'd gagged him before slipping the noose around his neck. Now they were tying the other end of the rope around the railings; it wasn't hard to guess what the next item on the agenda was.

Okay, it was definitely time to make an entrance. I stepped onto the escalator, which wasn't moving, and put my whistle to my lips. Walking slowly up the steps, and almost stumbling because of their uneven height, I played a shrieking, nasal blast like the scream of a lovesick bagpipe. The mall had pretty good acoustics, at least when it was relatively empty like this. Up above me the crazies paused in their recreations to look around and find out who was killing the cat.

They separated and stood up, allowing me to get a better look at them. They looked scarily ordinary: one in late middle age, bespectacled and balding, dressed in shirtsleeves and suit trousers; the other two much younger—one of them maybe no more than a student—and in casuals. You couldn't imagine them carrying out a murder together. You couldn't even imagine them standing in the same bus queue.

But this wasn't the time to speculate about how they'd met and discovered a common interest in death by hanging. No, this was show time. Theater was going to be all important here. I wanted them to keep watching me rather than getting back to the business at hand. I started to scuff my feet on each step, Riverdance style, to get a rhythm going in counterpoint to the skirling notes I was pushing out of the whistle. Left foot and then right, raising my knees high and swaying my upper body from side to side like some kind of deranged snake charmer trying to go it alone after his cobra had left him.

All of which combined to produce the desired effect. The three men abandoned their hog-tied victim and crowded to the railings to watch me walking up toward them. Then a whole lot of other faces appeared behind theirs, men and women both, clustering at the railings to peer past them with varying expressions of alarm, eagerness, and incomprehension. I hadn't seen these people before because they'd been standing away at the back of the upper gallery, presumably in a tight, attentive cluster.

My skin crawled. Somehow the intended execution was made infinitely worse by the fact that it would have had an audience. If I'd had any doubts before as to whether I was in Kansas or the merry, merry land of Oz, I ditched them now: whatever was going on here, it wasn't natural.

I stepped off the first escalator, turned, and crossed the short expanse of tiling that separated it from the second. That meant presenting my back to the crazies, which I didn't welcome at all, but on the credit side it meant the escalator was going to bring me out on the opposite side of the upper gallery from where they were. Something big and heavy crashed to the floor right in front of me, showering me with shards of glass and plastic. It had been a sound system of some kind, speakers not included, and one of the fragments close to my foot bore the OLU of a BANG & OLUFSEN logo: not a missile you see used all that often. I stepped over it, and kept on going.

There were howls and jeers now from the gallery above me, followed by a rain of smaller objects that I didn't bother to acknowledge. One of them thumped me in the back, but it wasn't sharp, or heavy enough to break bone. Maybe I hiccupped on a note, but it's not like I was playing Beethoven's Ninth to start with. It was just noise, loud and discordant and impossible to ignore.

As I climbed step by step up toward the top level, the crazies ran around the gallery to meet me. That was good insofar as it took them away from the man they'd been about to kill, but bad because I still couldn't see any sign of Juliet and I honestly didn't think they were running to get my autograph. I got to the top of the escalator just as they rounded the last corner and came running toward me in a solid wall. I tried to swallow, but found that my mouth was dry. This was the moment of truth, and I normally prefer elegant prevarications. I cast one last forlorn glance around the gallery in the hope that my curvaceous, demonic cavalry might appear in the nick of time: no such luck. With a muttered curse, I slipped my whistle back into my inside pocket, out of harm's way, clinched my fists, and braced for impact.

The first of the rioters to reach me was a woman, dressed for the office in a pastel-colored two-piece and sensible heels. The only thing that spoiled the ensemble effect was the claw hammer she was waving over her head. I jumped awkwardly back out of its way as it came down. Then, since she followed through with her entire body, bending from the hip to get more of her weight behind the blow, I was able to hit her on the back of the head with a roundhouse punch. She went down heavily, the hammer skidding away across the tiles. I didn't feel particularly good about it, but this was no time for chivalry.

In fact it was probably a time for running away, but I wasn't thrilled by the prospect of being run down from behind and trampled. As two burly men lunged for me at the same time, I ducked and crouched low to the ground, and their momentum carried one of them on past me, the other over my head in a graceless somersault.

That was it for tactics. A great many arms were clutching at me all at once, a great many fists pummeling at my shoulders and the back of my neck. I was hauled to my feet, then knocked sprawling again as the crazies got in each other's way in their eagerness to claim a piece of me.

At that moment the shop window behind them, one of the few that was still intact, exploded outward in a rapidly expanding flower of glass splinters that somehow, miraculously, gave birth to Juliet. She dived through the window headfirst, but rolled in the air and landed on her feet with a barely perceptible flexing of the knees. Then, having made her entrance and her point she strode forward with perfect poise, glass splinters pouring off her like water.

The crazies had turned at the sound, their assault on me slackening for a moment as they took in what was happening—and then for another moment, as they stared at Juliet and came to terms with her scarily perfect beauty.

Then the nearest guy swung a metal bar at her head. It wasn't much of a bar; it looked as though it had been torn from a clothes rail of some kind, and it was probably hollow, so the chances are that it wouldn't have done that much harm to Juliet in any case. But we never got the chance to find out: she ducked gracefully around it, took the guy's arm at wrist and elbow, and flung him backward over her shoulder through the window she'd just smashed. Another man did manage to land a blow, with his bare fist, on the point of her jaw. She took it without comment and kicked him in the stomach, making him fold with an unpleasantly liquescent gurgle.

Without breaking stride she walked into the midst of the rioters, a cat among seriously unbalanced pigeons. They closed around her, hands and weapons raised, which only went to prove that they hadn't really been watching when she came through the plate-glass window. It takes a lot to hurt Juliet, and then a lot more on top of that to slow her down. There were sounds of organic impact, truncated gasps and grunts, then the dull thunder of collapsing bodies as people fell like wheat around her.

There was a hypnotic fascination to it that made it hard to look away. But since the heat was off me, I reckoned I'd better put my time to some productive use. Turning my back on the scene of rapidly diminishing mayhem, I sprinted along the gallery to the section of railing that had been turned into an impromptu gallows. The man they'd been looking to hang was lying on his stomach on the floor, his hands and feet tied tightly and then an additional length of rope lashed between them so that his legs were bent back, his feet sticking up into the air. I used the loup-garou's knife to cut this last rope, but the blade was too sharp for me to risk using it close to his wrists and ankles. I rolled him over on his back and hooked the gag away from his mouth. He was pale and sweating, his dark hair lank and his eyes exopthalmically huge. The fact that he was wearing a tie struck me as a piquant little grotesquerie: who goes to a riot wearing a tie?

"The hostages," I said. "Where are they?"

He spat in my face. "You fucking piece of shit," he screamed. "Satan will ream your throat out, you degenerate bastard motherfucker! He'll shove his fist up your—"

A little of that kind of thing goes a long way. I stuffed the gag back in his mouth and wiped away the spittle while he glared and grunted at me. "Not on a first date, pal," I murmured.

Hostage, hostage, who's got the hostage? I looked around for inspiration. The news footage had been shot from the front of the building, out in the street, and that was where I'd caught sight of Susan Book's face peering out through the smashed window. I tried to orientate myself, remembering which way I'd come in and which way the main concourse underneath me ran. It seemed that the front ought to be over to my left, where foot-high red capitals shouted T.K.Maxx to the world.

"Where now?" said Juliet, appearing silently and alarmingly at my elbow.

I got to my feet and pointed. She walked across the gallery without a sound and entered the store. I shot a single glance back to the scene of the earlier engagement: bodies littered the ground, and none of them were standing.

I ran to catch up with her. "Did you kill anyone?" I demanded.

"No. There's one who could die from her wounds—one of her comrades slashed her neck and shoulder with a knife, trying to get through to me. The rest will live."

"Thank God for that," I said drily. "I was thinking you'd just turn up the heat under their libidos and melt their brains into slush. This was a little more . . . direct than I expected."

"I tried," Juliet snapped. "They should have been incapable of any aggression as soon as they saw me. They should have been incapable of anything except involuntary orgasm."

"Oh. So what went wrong?"

"Perhaps I'm losing my touch."

It wasn't that. Even without looking at her, I could feel her sexuality washing over me like a warm, caressing tide. And I knew from terrifying experience how strong the undertow was in those waters. But I think we both knew the answer: The demonic miasma was all around us now, and it had been ever since we got up onto this top level. These poor sods were possessed.

Without having to discuss tactics we both shut up at this point. We were walking through the shop, which was eerily silent apart from the mournful echoes of police bullhorns from the street outside. Our own footsteps were very effectively muffled by the clothes spilled from the racks and strewn on the ground. The rails and shelf units were none of them higher than about four feet off the ground, so we had a good view of the big open-plan area we'd moved into, but up ahead of us the store curved around in an L-shape, which we couldn't see until we got to the end of the aisle. We weren't trying for stealth, exactly—Juliet didn't have much use for stealth—but we didn't want the sound of our conversation to drown out any warning we might get of a possible ambush.

Rounding the corner, we found ourselves right in the thick of the party. The wall ahead of us now was the front face of the shopping center—windows from floor to ceiling, with the night pouring in through that ragged hole in the center pane that I'd seen from the other side in the news broadcast. To either side of it, maybe three or four men knelt low or flattened themselves against the wall, peering out at the cordon in the street below as if they'd never heard of police snipers. Farther away from us still there was a circular display area ringed with floor-level mirrors, which seemed to have been intended for trying on shoes. In this cramped amphitheater, two more men, one armed with a baseball bat, kept watch over a small, terrified huddle of presumably innocent shoppers. That was all—and it looked like good odds except that one of the men at the window had a rifle. Long-haired and thickly bearded, he looked, as he swung back the bolt and put the first bullet into the chamber, like someone who'd accidentally wandered off from the set of *Deliverance* and found himself in an episode of *Eastenders*.

All heads turned toward us, and I glimpsed Susan Book in among the hostages. I also saw a man lying full-length on the ground, a bloody hole where his face ought to have been. Susan was sitting right next to this poor bastard. Her eyes widened when she saw me, and she opened her mouth as if to speak.

I spoke first. "Hey, guys," I said. "Saw you on the nine o'clock news. Where do we sign up?"

We were walking forward all this time, but now the man with the rifle swung it around to cover us. "You don't," he snapped, coldly. "You get with those dumb fucks over there, and you shut up."

We kept on coming. "What kind of weapon is that?" Juliet murmured to me under her breath.

"Sports rifle," I growled back, sounding a lot more definite about it than I actually was. "Semiautomatic—which means one bullet at a time." The truth is, I know sod all about weapons, despite having once lived for a year with a sweet girl who subscribed to *Arms and Ammo*; but this thing was all dark red wood and elegant curves. No gun that dolls itself up as pretty as that ever gets asked out to an actual battle. Plus it had a dinky little magazine about the size of a mobile phone. If it was ever set on auto, it would run out of bullets in the time it takes to scream, "Die, mother—." On the other hand, and assuming the guy had a steady hand, that would be plenty long enough to see me and Juliet thoroughly ventilated. She'd probably survive that, unless the bullets were silver: the odds on me were a little longer.

Fortunately, these guys weren't all singing from the same hymn book. The other three men, wielding various makeshift clubs and cudgels, chose that moment to charge us, helpfully blindsiding their friend. Juliet accelerated so that they'd reach her first, taking out two of them with strikes that I'd be happy to call surgical because most surgery leaves you unable to walk for a while and maybe a body part or so short.

The third man I managed to drop with a flying tackle, which was probably the best result he could hope for under the circumstances. We went down together, but with me on top, and though he swiped at me with the jagged metal shard he was using as a knife, my elbow in his face threw off his aim and slammed his head hard against the floor. He was still moving, though, and a lucky slash with that thing would leave me bleeding out on the floor, so I brought my knee up between his legs, introducing him to the concept of planned parenthood with immediate and devastating effect. Leaving him curled around his pain, I scrambled to my feet just as the rifle went off.

It wasn't aimed at me, of course. These guys might be crazy, but it would be a special kind of crazy who pointed the gun somewhere else when Juliet was bearing down on him with her killing face on. The back of her jacket opened up at chest height as the bullet tore through, and a fine red spray showered my face and upper body.

The rifle was semiauto: it had to be, because the man got a second shot off even as Juliet kicked him backward through the window. He fell with a scream that sounded more enraged than afraid, and that was all he got in the way of famous last words. I heard the dull *thump* as he hit the street.

"Juliet!" I shouted. "For fuck's sake, they're possessed. There's something riding them!"

She didn't seem to hear me. She turned, a little bent over, her movements too slow, just as the two guys who'd been guarding the hostages charged her from the side.

One of them had a knife, and he slashed at her stomach. The other swung his baseball bat and hit her full in the face. She reeled with the blow, then stabbed out with her left hand, putting her thumb and middle finger through the second man's eyes.

That left the knife man, and as he brought his hand back for a second thrust I finally, belatedly, forced myself to move. I went directly for his knife hand, grabbing hold of it in both of mine and twisting it up behind his back with brutal, desperate force. He dropped the knife, and Juliet, glancing over her shoulder and seeming to notice him for the first time, swept her fist up in an uppercut that almost took his head off his shoulders. He slithered to the ground between us, already unconscious.

"Are you all right?" I asked her, my chest heaving both with the effort to catch a breath and with the nausea that was beginning to hit as the adrenaline turned sour in my stomach.

"I'm fine," she muttered, but there was a breathy gurgle behind the words that scared the shit out of me. Her shoulders were bowed: she was inspecting the bloody mess in the center of her shirt front, and her feet shifted a little as if she was having a hard time keeping her balance.

I jumped to a conclusion. A whole generation of entrepreneurs were making their first fortunes by trading on the fears that the living felt for the living dead: silver-coated ammunition was just one of the fads that had come in as a result. "Juliet, was the bullet—?"

I could only just hear her answer. "Silvered. Yes. But it only went through my lung. I think I can . . . deal . . . with the . . ."

Her voice trailed off, but she didn't fall. All her attention was turned inward, and wherever she was right then I knew she wasn't going to be aware of her surroundings for a while. From the street outside came shouted orders and the wail of a single siren. The police weren't going to wait much longer before storming the place: not with bodies flying out of the windows.

I turned to look over at the hostages. Susan Book was already heading toward me, but the others were all still in a huddle against the base of the wall, some of the kids sobbing and keening, nobody daring to move. I opened my mouth to say something—probably something along the lines of "you're safe now." Susan's hand lashed out, and as I reflexively parried, something red shot from her fingers to bounce off my chest and hit the floor at my feet. I didn't even see her other hand come up: her nails raked my cheek, savagely deep, and I staggered back in numb surprise. She followed up, punching and clawing at me as she screamed obscenities into my face. The same obscenities I'd heard from the almost-hanged man outside, mostly, focusing on my sexual relationship with my parents and the cocks I'd suck in hell. It was like some kind of virus.

I fended Susan off, using my height and reach to block her wild, uncoordinated attack. I didn't want to hurt her, though, so I was backing away across the floor, calling out her name as I gave ground in an effort to wake her out of whatever trance she was in. Then a shelf unit bumped against my back and I had to stop, which meant that she was finally able to close with me: out of options, I knocked aside her clutching hands and punched her hard on the point of the jaw. She went over backward, and there was an alarming crack as the back of her head hit the tiles.

It was followed a moment later by the crump of a detonation, and another window blew out as something hard and metallic shot through it to arc end over end through the air, trailing a plume of feathery smoke. As it landed and bounced, another and then another window burst, and the screams of the hostages drowned out all other sounds—even the hiss of the tear gas grenades releasing their indiscriminate loads.

I staggered back to where Juliet had been standing, almost slipping as my foot came down on something smooth and hard. I glanced down: it was a Victorinox Swiss army penknife, multifunctional blades extended at both ends. Susan's weapon: I'd been within an inch of being corkscrewed to death.

Juliet was kneeling over the body of one of the fallen rioters, her hand on his chest. I thought she was checking him for a pulse, but then I realized that she was searching his pockets. I grabbed hold of her arm and her head snapped up: her dark eyes locked on mine. My eyes were starting to water as filaments of CS gas drifted across the store.

"We've got to get out of here," I shouted over the shrill screams. "This is to soften up the opposition. Any moment now they're gonna storm the place."

Juliet stood, with some difficulty. "I'll have to lean on you," she rasped, and she almost fell into my arms as I led her back the way we'd come. The hostages would be okay, I told myself. They'd suffer from the effects of the gas, but the cops would be all over the place within the next couple of minutes so the riot was over. There was nothing we could do for them now that the paramedics couldn't do a whole lot better.

All the same, I felt more hollow than heroic as I staggered back down the stalled escalators, Juliet leaning heavily against my chest, the harsh gurgle of her breath in my ears. She'd been right: something *was* loose in here, and it had our number, turning victims into aggressors with a magical wave of its invisible hands, wrapped around and around us like some kind of spiritual smallpox blanket, infecting where it touched.

Skirting the debris in the ground-floor arcade was a lot harder now that I was steering for two. As we headed for the corridor where the toilets were, I heard the loud slam of the main doors off to our left and the crunch of running, booted feet on the shattered glass. I went a little faster, risking a misstep that would send us both sprawling on our faces. We got into the corridor and the echoing steps ran straight on past. I was expecting a voice from behind us to shout, "Stop where you are. Put down the succubus—slowly!" But it didn't happen.

The loading bay was still empty. I got Juliet to the edge of the platform, set her down, then jumped to the ground myself and hauled her after me. Amazingly, exasperatingly, in spite of everything that had just happened and the sick horror that was throbbing inside my head, I was still responding physically to her closeness—still breathing hard and heavy, and feeling my prick stir inside my pants, as I inhaled her primal perfume.

She couldn't climb the wall: she could barely walk. But there was a gate at the far end of the yard, and it was only bolted rather than locked. I slid the bolts and we limped through, both of us torn and exhausted and blood-boltered, like the last contestants in a dance marathon in hell.

I had to slow down once we got out onto the street. It was dark, so if we stayed away from the streetlights nobody would be likely to see our various wounds and blemishes, but the way we were staggering would draw attention anywhere. I pulled Juliet close to me and tried to pretend that we were lovers drunk on our own hormones—and, yeah, before you ask, that was an easy part to play. Every inch where our bodies touched was an inch I was painfully, achingly aware of.

The road we were in led back around to the street where I'd parked, bringing us out again behind the rubbernecking crowd. There was a whole lot more going on now, and nobody had time to notice us. Police were pushing the lollygaggers back while officers with riot shields and impact armor ran across the road toward the mall's front entrance. White-shirted ambulance crews brought up the rear. The assault had begun in earnest now, and we'd gotten clear with seconds to spare.

I propped Juliet up against the car and got the passenger door open. She was starting to pull out of it now, or at least to recover some degree of control over her own movements, and she was able to lower herself into the seat without much help from me. I shut the door without slamming it, went around to the driver's side, slid in, and started the engine.

Since the road ahead was blocked I had to make a three-point turn in the road. Fortunately there was enough street theater going on that nobody spared us a glance. We drove back toward White City Stadium, where I pulled over because my hands were shaking so much that I wasn't really safe to drive.

Juliet's breathing was shallow now, but even, and she was looking at me with something of her old, cold arrogance in her eyes.

That stare made a lot of possible words die in my throat. Finally I said, "I'm sorry I dragged you into that."

"It's all right," she answered, her voice still a harsh rasp. "It was . . . interesting."

"No, I mean I'm really sorry you were there. You killed a man, and probably blinded another. If I'd known you were going to let out your inner demon—"

She cut across me, remorseless. "One man was dead already. How many more do you think would have died if I hadn't acted?"

"We can't know that."

"No," she agreed, sounding almost contemptuous. "We can't."

"Was it worth it?" I asked, still shellshocked. "Did you get any kind of a handle on what we're dealing with here?"

"Oh yes. Didn't you?"

"No," I admitted. "Although—" I fell silent. There *had* been something familiar in the way that formless evil had presented itself to my sixth sense, but it had been mixed up with a lot that was purely alien. The gestalt effect hadn't been something I'd been able to focus my mind on for very long—like trying to join the dots when they were spinning separately in a whirlpool. I didn't finish the sentence: there didn't seem to be any good way of explaining what I'd felt. "Go ahead," I said. "Give me the starting prices."

"Soon," said Juliet. "Not yet. And not here." There was a long silence. Then she turned and stared at me. "Castor—" Her voice had a breathy echo to it that suggested she still hadn't finished repairing the damage to her lung.

"What?"

"Is that how you dress for dinner?"

Chapter Eleven

There's a Thai restaurant up by Old Oak Common where I'd eaten a few times before. It's a perfect place for snacks and cocktails after work, or after summarily executing deranged riflemen in gutted malls—and since there's no dress code, it doesn't even matter if you've been shot through the chest and a massive exit wound has spoiled the line of your jacket.

To be fair, by the time we got there Juliet was looking almost as fresh and fragrant as if she'd just stepped out of the shower—an image I had to rein in sternly before my imagination got out of hand. The blood that had saturated her shirt front had disappeared, and the line of bruising along her jaw had faded to near invisibility. I'd seen Asmodeus do something similar to Rafi's body when it had taken some damage in one of his rampages, but this was more extreme and a whole lot quicker—I guess because Rafi's body was still made of real flesh and blood at the end of the day, while Juliet's was made of—something else. I never know how to ask.

A maître d' whose suavity was a little dented by Juliet's black-eyed gaze seated us in the window—no doubt seeing what kind of effect she was likely to have on the passing trade. As soon as he'd left, she reached into her pocket and took out a thick wad of paper, which she unfolded and put down on the table between us.

"Patterson, Alfred," she said, fanning them out. "Heffer, Laurence. Heffer, John. Jones, Kenneth. Montgomery, Lily."

It was a sheaf of photocopied pages, all in the same format. Each one had a passport-size photo in the top right-hand corner: mostly men, a few women, all ordinary to the point of banality. The faces stared up at me with the terrified solemnity you'd expect from people whose lives had just body-swerved away from them into insanity and despair.

"These are police SIR sheets," I said.

Juliet nodded, looking at the menu.

"How did you get hold of them?"

"A nice young constable at Oldfield Lane ran them off for me."

I thought very carefully about the wording of the next question. "Did you bribe him, or—?"

"I let him hold my hand."

A waiter had started to hover: he was barely more than a kid, with ginger curls and plump, freckled cheeks. He couldn't take his eyes off Juliet. Of course, better men than me have fallen at that hurdle. I looked up, tapped the table with my fingertip. After a moment he turned with a slight effort to meet my gaze, as if he was unwilling to acknowledge that I was there. "Can I get you any drinks to start with?" he asked, in an artificially bright tone.

"I'll take a whisky," I said. "A bourbon if you've got it."

"We've got Jack Daniel's and Blanton's."

"Blanton's. Thanks. On the rocks."

"Bloody Mary," said Juliet, predictably. The waiter tore himself away from us with difficulty and trotted off, looking back over his shoulder at her a couple of times before he disappeared from view.

I went back to the incident forms. Some of them I vaguely recognized from the news articles I'd seen open on Nicky's desktop last night. Alfred Patterson was charged with strangling a complete stranger with his own tie in an office off the Uxbridge Road where he used to work. The two Heffers, father and son, had apparently raped and murdered an eighty-year-old woman and then thrown her body into the Regent's Canal. Some of them were new, though. Lily Montgomery had been arrested and remanded after police were called to a loud domestic: they found her sitting on the sofa quietly knitting next to her dead husband, who had choked to death on his own blood after his throat was perforated with two sharp objects entering from different sides. Her knitting needles were oozing half-congealed blood all over the baby booties she was making for her niece, Samantha, aged eleven months, but she didn't seem to have noticed.

There were more. A couple of dozen, at least. After a while I just skimmed them, noting place and time while avoiding the noxious, heartbreaking details in the summary box.

The waiter came back with our drinks. He almost spilled my bourbon in my lap because of the problem he was having with his eyes, which still kept being wrenched back to Juliet's face and body whenever he let his concentration slip for more than half a second. We made our food orders, but it was kind of a triumph of hope over experience. The kid wasn't writing anything down, and nothing was going to stick in his mind except the curve of Juliet's breast where it showed through the ragged tear in her shirt.

He hobbled away again, and I shook my head at her. "Can't you let him off the hook?" I asked.

She arched an eyebrow, mildly affronted. "He's eighteen," she said. "I'm not doing anything—that's all natural."

"Oh. Well, could you maybe go into reverse or something? Pour some psychic ice water over him? It'll only improve the service."

" 'Go into reverse.' " Juliet's tone dripped with scorn. "You mean, suppress desire instead of arousing it?"

"That's exactly what I mean."

"I'll leave that to you."

"Ow." I mimed a gun with my right hand, shot myself through the heart. That brutal directness, so easily mistaken for sadism, is one of the things I like best about Juliet. She's a good corrective to my own natural sentimentality and trusting good nature.

I turned my attention back to the SIR sheets, going through them a little more carefully this time.

"Okay," I said. "I get the point. They're all local, and the odds against this many violent incidents in such a small—"

I stopped because she was shaking her head very firmly.

"Well what?"

"This." She tapped the bottom sheet, which I'd somehow managed to miss because it was in a different format and seemed to be just a list of names. I'd vaguely assumed it was an index of some kind, since some of the names were the same as the ones on the incident forms. Now I looked again, and the penny dropped. If the bourbon hadn't already been exquisitely sour, it would have curdled in my stomach.

The list, which had been produced on a manual typewriter with the help of a small lake of Tipp-Ex, was headed with the single word "Congregants."

"Holy shit," I murmured.

"No, Castor. Unholy shit. That's the point."

"These people all go to church at St. Michael's?"

Juliet nodded.

"And now they've all turned into homicidal maniacs."

"That's a question of semantics."

"Is it?"

"If you call it insanity, you assume they've lost the ability to make moral judgments."

"Raping pensioners? Knit one, purl one, puncture windpipe? What do *you* think they've lost?"

"Their conscience. Whatever evil was inside them already has been given free rein. Whatever desires they feel, they satisfy by the simplest and most direct means they can find. If it's lust, they rape; if it's anger, they murder; if it's greed, they pillage a shopping mall."

"So you think those people at the Whiteleaf—?"

"I don't think. I checked."

She reached into the same bottomless pocket, brought out a small clutch of wallets and billfolds and let them fall onto the table. I suddenly remembered her on her knees next to one of the men she'd felled: I thought she was checking him for a pulse, but obviously she was frisking him.

"Jason Mills," she said. "Howard Loughbridge. Ellen Roederer."

I checked the list, but I already knew what I'd find there.

"And Susan Book," I added, just to show that I was keeping up.

"And Susan Book. Of course."

Our food arrived. The waiter drew the process out as long as he could, his eyes all over Juliet from every angle he could decently manage. I sat on my impatience until he'd gone.

"So what are you saying?" I asked. "All of these people were in church on Saturday, when . . . whatever it was that happened, happened? And it somehow turned off all of their inhibitions? All of their civilized scruples? Made them into puppets that can only respond to their own desires?"

Helping herself to some *mee goreng* that she hadn't ordered, Juliet nodded curtly. "They're possessed," she said.

"What, all of them?"

"All of them. Do you read the Bible much, Castor?"

"Not when there's anything good on the TV."

"Commentaries and concordances? Textual exegesis?"

"To date, never."

"So do you know what the Jewish position on Christ is?"

I shrugged impatiently, really not wanting to sit through what looked like it might be a very circuitous analogy. "I dunno," I said. "They probably think he got in with the wrong crowd."

"I mean, what exactly do they think he was? What *kind* of being?"

"I give up. Tell me."

"They think he was a prophet. Like Elijah, or Moses. No more, no less. One in a long line. Someone who'd been touched by God, and could speak with God's authority, but not God's son."

"So?"

"But Christians think that the indwelling of God in Christ was different in kind from his indwelling in the prophets."

I took a long slug on the whisky, as an alternative to playing straight man. Presumably she'd get to the point without any prompting from me.

"As in heaven, so in hell," she said. "When demons enter human souls, they can do it in a lot of different ways." There was a pause while she ate, which she did with single-minded, almost feral enthusiasm. Then she fastidiously licked the corner of her mouth with a long, lithe, double-tipped tongue. That had made me shit a brick the first time I'd seen it. Nowadays I just wondered what else she could do with it besides personal grooming.

She held up an elegant hand, counted off on her fingers. Her finger-nails shone with copper-colored varnish; or, possibly, just happened to be made of copper tonight. "First, and easiest, there's full possession, in which the human host soul is overwhelmed and devoured, and the body becomes merely a vessel for the demon as long as it chooses to use it. That's commoner than you'd think, but usually it can only be done with consent."

"You mean people ask to have their souls swallowed?"

"Essentially, yes. They agree to a bargain of some kind. They accept the terms, and the terms include forfeiting their soul. Obviously they may have an imperfect understanding of what that means. An eternity of suffering in hell, or separation from God, or whatever the current orthodoxy is. But for us, it only ever means the one thing. It's open season. We can eat them."

Strong-stomached though I am, I was in danger of losing my appetite. She was enjoying this too damn much for my comfort.

"Who lays down the rules?" I demanded. "Open season implies someone dealing out the hunting licenses. Is that—?"

"There are some things I'm not prepared to tell you," Juliet interrupted, making a pass through the air with her hand like someone waving away a paparazzo's camera. "That's one of them. But if you were going to say 'Is that God?' then the answer is no. It's more . . . involved than that."

"'Involved'?"

"Complicated. Things fall out in a certain way, and accidents of the terrain give birth to rules of engagement. But in any case, that's one form that possession can take—the most extreme form. The demon devours the human host and lives in its shell."

"Okay," I conceded. "Go on."

"Number two is house arrest. It's possible for a demon to overwhelm a soul without its consent and hold it captive. Again, that would allow it to use the host body as if it were its own, but the human soul would still be inside, witnessing its own actions and even experiencing them, but as a passenger rather than a driver."

"Fuck." I let my laden chopsticks fall back into my pad thai. That was what Asmodeus did to Rafi: hijacked the bus and made him watch while he went on a joyride that was still going on two years later.

"One and two have a lot in common," Juliet said, ignoring my discomfort. "They both involve the demon literally invading the human host. But there are other ways in which human and demon can be grafted together. Other degrees and gradations, I suppose you could say. At the opposite extreme, a demon can *gift* a man or woman with a tiny part of its own essence."

"Gift?"

"Infect, if you prefer. Impart. Impose. Don't argue semantics with me, Castor. You can't expect me to have the same moral perspective on this that you have."

"I guess not," I acknowledged. "And yet, here you are."

Juliet shrugged with her eyebrows. "It's a job."

"Right. Like if bubonic plague was a woman, and she signed on as a charge nurse in a hospital."

She actually laughed at that. "Yes. Exactly. Anyway, the point about gifting is that we can do it as many times as we like. It diminishes us a little, and that imposes a limit. A strong demon could gift a couple of hundred people at once, but it would be severely weakened afterwards. To get its full strength back, it would have to call all those pieces home eventually."

"But in the meantime—?"

"In the meantime it would be as if each of those people had a tiny demon of their own, inside them—not controlling them, but encouraging them to see things from a more infernal perspective. And again, the stronger the demon, the more intense the persuasion. You might experience it just as a slight change in perceptions—so you'd suddenly be aware that if that traffic cop flags you down you could swerve just a little, hit him with your near-side wing, and give him something else to worry about. Or that if your girlfriend doesn't want to kiss on a first date, drugging her and raping her is still an option."

"Can I get you anything else?" The waiter had appeared again, assiduous as ever, like a dog who has to have a stick thrown for him every so often to stop him from humping your leg. I asked him to bring me another whisky; Juliet passed.

"Okay," I said after he'd gone, "you've made your case. St. Michael's was visited by a demon, and little pieces of this demon rained down on all the people who were there at the time. But the demon didn't possess them fully: he's still there, inside the church, in some form or other, which explains the cold and the slo-mo heartbeat and all of the rest of that shit."

"I didn't say that," said Juliet.

"Just joining the dots. Isn't that what you meant?"

Juliet downed her Bloody Mary in a single swallow. "It's a possibility," she said. "But I was giving you an example, not an explanation. Something possessed the St. Michael congregation, yes. Something strong enough to leave a piece of itself in each and every one of them. That could be a demon, but it wouldn't have to be. Human ghosts can possess living things, after all—you've met the *were*."

I nodded reluctantly, but I wasn't sold on that explanation. "Yeah," I agreed, "I have. And if there's one thing I know about loup-garous, it's that they go for animal hosts for a reason. Human minds are too hard—way too hard. You hear stories about that kind of possession, but I never came across a case yet where it's been proved to have happened."

"Then I might be about to make history."

Her tone worried me. "I thought we were here to discuss strategy," I said. "Looks like you've come up with a plan all by yourself."

"I'm going to go in," she said.

A whisky appeared at my elbow. I took it without even looking: right then, the sight of the waiter's eager puppy face would just have screwed up my mood even further.

"Go in where, exactly?" I asked, although I had a pretty good inkling already.

"I'm going to treat St. Michael's Church as if it were a living thing," Juliet said, "and try to possess it. If there's an invading spirit there, whether it's a ghost or a demon, then it ought to be driven out by my arrival."

"You could do that?"

"Yes. It's not the way I normally work, but I was born and raised in hell, Castor. Of course I can do it."

I mulled the prospect over, unhappily. Something about it gave me a dull twinge of foreboding, but it took me a moment or two to isolate what it was. Then I saw the flaw. "You said it would take a fairly big player to do something like this," I reminded her. "To possess so many people all at the same time. Whether it's a demon or a ghost or whatever the hell it is, what do you do if it's stronger than you? I mean, suppose you go into your trance or whatever, and you send your spirit out into the church . . . Do demons even have spirits?"

"No. Demons *are* spirit. If it's stronger than me, it will lock me out. I'll try to penetrate, and the church simply won't let me in. I'll find it solid and dense instead of porous. In any case there'll be no risk to speak of. I'll either succeed or I'll fail. And if I succeed, it might help me with that dietary problem we were discussing."

"You could feed on this thing?"

"I could absorb it. It wouldn't be like feeding for me, because I feed when I fuck. It would be more like taking nourishment through a drip."

"Which is better than starving to death," I allowed, without much enthusiasm. I tried to catch the waiter's eye, failed, managed to snag the maître d's instead. "But the same point applies. If you go head to head with this thing, and if it's bigger and stronger than you to start with, then maybe it's you that'll end up on the menu."

"Yes," agreed Juliet. "Maybe. Does that worry you, Castor?"

I measured my words out with care.

"It's a job," I reminded her. "You offered me part of the fee. If you get eaten by a church, I end up a little poorer."

She looked at me with wicked amusement. "Do you think that would be a waste?" she asked. "Me being eaten? Or do you want to volunteer for the job yourself?"

I put my chin on my fist, pretended to consider. "I took the pledge," I said at last. "I'll never let another woman pass my lips."

"A man of principle. I despise that: it's bad for business."

"When are you planning to do this?" I demanded, cutting through the banter. It was making me uncomfortable because the physical desire Juliet arouses is very real and very acute; and because, given that she is what she is, I know exactly where that desire leads. That fact makes jokes about oral sex ring a little hollowly.

"Tomorrow," she said. "Five minutes to midnight."

"Why so precise? What happens then?"

"Moonrise—except that tomorrow is the dark of the moon. It's a propitious time."

"I'd like to be there for it. As backup, in case something goes wrong."

She looked a little perplexed. "What could you do to help," she demanded, "if something went wrong?"

"Maybe nothing," I said. "But that party at the mall gave me the thin end of a scent for this thing. Maybe I could run interference for you." I half-lifted my tin whistle out of my coat pocket, let it slide back again.

Juliet's eyes narrowed slightly, which I could understand. Showing the whistle was a little bit like offering Superman a kryptonite sandwich. But her tone stayed cool, even slightly bored. "You know where I'll be," she said. "And when. If you want to come along and watch, be my guest. Don't bring the whistle, though. Or if you bring it, keep it in your pocket. Your aim isn't as good as you think it is."

It was hard for me to argue with that, with Rafi chafing at the edges of my thoughts the way he was right then. That was certainly a demonstration of how dangerous friendly fire could be. I knew I was better now than I had been then, but I could see why Juliet wasn't keen on the idea.

I stood up, leaving the cash on the table.

"My treat," I said. "I came into some money."

"'Mackie,'" Juliet quoted, "'how much did you charge?'"

"Funny. I always knew they'd play Bobby Darin in hell."

"Kurt Weill," Juliet corrected.

"Bless you," I deadpanned.

The waiter looked stricken to see us go. If Juliet ever came off that diet, she'd be sure of a good meal here.

We said good-bye on the street without much in the way of small talk, and Juliet walked away with her usual ground-eating stride, not looking back. Showing her the whistle seemed to have spoiled the mood somehow: probably because it reminded her that I was the closest thing the human race had to an antibody against her kind. I'd have to remember that another time, and be more tactful.

I was bone weary, but Nicky had said he had important news for me, and I'd agreed to meet him at the Ice-Maker's place, south of the river. That was a fair old haul, but at least the roads would be clear now. I considered leaving Matty's car where it was and taking the tube—since I didn't have the "it's an emergency" excuse to call on anymore—but that would mean getting back here somehow, probably after midnight, and then driving all the way back east again. I couldn't quite face that.

I drove south down Wood Lane, vaguely intending to cross the river at Battersea. But in the mood I was in, brooding about the various things I'd left undone or half-done, it wasn't long before my thoughts came back around in a big, ragged circle to the Torringtons and Dennis Peace. I'd almost had him at the *Collective*, I thought with grim irritation—but that was a polite gloss on what had really happened. It would be fairer to say that he'd almost had me: certainly I'd been lucky to avoid his kamikaze airborne assault. And then Itchy and Scratchy had turned up and it was a whole different ball game—with Peace's balls being the ones on the table, or so it seemed. Why? What did he have that these breakaway provisional-wing religious zealots wanted so badly that they'd hire werewolves to find it? The only thing I knew he had was Abbie Torrington's ghost; that didn't seem to fit the bill.

No, I was still seven miles from nowhere here, much as it hurt me to admit it. Okay, I had Rosie Crucis as an ace in the hole, but given her legendary flakiness, and the unappetizing prospect of having to go through Jenna-Jane Mulbridge to get to her, maybe now was a good time to go back to plan A—making contact with Abbie's spirit directly. I still had the doll's head with me, and a vivid memory of the tune that it had inspired.

What the hell, it was worth a try. I pulled the car over onto a broad ribbon of freshly laid asphalt on the steeply canted foothills of the Hammersmith overpass, and got out. It wasn't that the reception would be any better outside the car: I just felt that I needed the touch of the cool night air.

I strolled across to a crash barrier that offered a scenic view of the westbound carriageway, and leaned against it, just taking in the sights for a moment while I got myself into the mood. It had turned into a crazy day, and an even crazier evening. I ought to be curled up around a half-empty bottle of whisky right about now, but here I was with miles to go and promises to keep. The dull ache in my head and neck had come back, too, and there was a hot, itchy feeling behind my eyes. I was definitely coming down with something, and I wished I knew what the hell it was.

There was a faint smell of wood smoke on the wind, as though someone was burning a bonfire in one of the gardens nearby—kind of an odd thing to do in May, though, and just for a moment it gave me an odd, dizzying sense of rushing forward through time. Like I'd only been here five minutes and already it was autumn.

I fished the doll's head out of my pocket. Tentatively, I traced the line of the cheek with the tip of my little finger, feeling the tiny roughnesses where the glaze was starting to crack. It was a miracle it was still in one piece, given the kind of day I'd had. As soon as I touched it, Abbie's unhappiness welled up and overflowed, traveled up my hand and arm by some sort of psychic capillary action until it filled my head. That was all I needed, really: just a top-up, so I knew exactly what I was aiming for.

I stowed the doll's head again and took out my whistle. The contrapuntal lines of yellow and red headlights were a little distracting, so I closed my eyes, found the stops by feel, and let the first note unfold itself into the night.

For a long time, nothing: just the slow, sad sequence of sounds endlessly descending like a staircase in an M. C. Escher drawing that never really gets to where it's going.

Then Abbie answered me. Just like the two previous times, I felt her distant presence stir at the limits of my perceptions—a tropism, a blind turning to the music that was herself. Maybe because my eyes were closed I felt it more strongly this time; or maybe ghosts have tidal rhythms that move them like the moon moves the sea. She was there: a long way away, in the dark, but separated from me by nothing except that distance. It was as though I could reach out, pull the city aside to left and right like curtains, and bring her through.

The cutoff, when it came, was instantaneous, but I was ready for it this time, and going by some instinct I couldn't have explained I banked the music up into a crescendo the instant the contact failed. I can't say whether or not that made a difference, but it felt like throwing a spear after the fish has broken your line. The sense of direction I'd already got crystallized into something almost painfully precise. Abbie and me, hunter and hunted, caught on opposite ends of the same rigid splinter of sound.

For a long time after I stopped playing, I kept my eyes tight shut and listened to the echoes in my mind. They were still strong. I'd come very close this time, and I had no doubt at all that Abbie had not only heard me but seen me, too. Across the night, across the city, we'd stared into each other's eyes.

"I'm coming for you," I murmured. "Don't be afraid. Whatever you've been through, little girl, it's almost over now. I'm coming to find you."

"Lovely," said a man's voice right beside me. "Can I quote you on that?" My head jerked around so fast it almost came off my shoulders—or at least, that was how it felt; the ache seemed to have become both sharper and deeper.

The man leaning on the crash barrier next to me had a slender, hawk-beaked face, black hair as slick as an otter's arse, and the sour, what's-this-stink-under-my-nose expression of a hanging judge faced with a drunken football hooligan at a Saturday-night remand hearing. He had the kind of build that people call wiry—skinny, but the overall impression was of a stick that's been sharpened for a purpose, not something that's just wilting for lack of sustenance. His white raincoat was pristine, and it contrasted so boldly with the black suit underneath it that I found myself thinking of a priest's robes. Yeah, that was it: not a judge, a priest taking confession. Your sins will be taken down and may be used in evidence against you.

"Felix Castor," he said. His voice was soft and cultured, and so empty of emotion it reminded me for a moment of the programmed voice of Stephen Hawking's vocoder.

"Hey, me, too," I answered, holding out my hand. "What are the odds on that?"

He looked at my outstretched hand for a moment, then studiedly looked away. Pity. Skin contact might have told me a lot, and I could have done with some crib notes right about then.

"Playing it for laughs," he observed. "Well, why not? The gift of laughter enriches life. No, you can call me Gwillam, if you want to call me anything. And my sense of humor mostly turns on things that would make you weep."

It was hard to believe, from that bloodless face and voice, that he had a sense of humor at all, but I played along, nodding as if I understood and approved. I did approve, in a way: when a guy starts off by telling you how tough he is, in my experience he's mostly overfinessing because he's actually got the moral fiber of a blancmange and he doesn't want you to suss him right out of the gate. It gave me something to work from, at least.

"So tell me a joke," I suggested.

"Perhaps I will." His gaze flicked past my shoulder and I knew without looking that he wasn't alone. A second later, that guess was confirmed as a boot scraped on gravel a few feet behind me. "I've found out a lot about you in the last two days," Gwillam observed, almost absently. He looked away again across the river of traffic, narrowing his eyes as the smoky breeze played across his face. "You've got something of a name for yourself, and from what I'm hearing the name is *not* fool. So I'm wondering why exactly you're doing this."

His words stirred up echoes of an earlier conversation, and I suddenly got an inkling of who I might see if I turned and looked behind me.

"Why I'm doing what, exactly?" I asked, understudying sweet little Buttercup.

Gwillam frowned and breathed out deeply through his nose, but the level tone of his voice didn't change by an inch or an ounce. "I'm not a fool, either, Castor. It will do nothing good for my mood if you try to play me for one."

"Okay," I said, "I'll bear that in mind." I don't have the patience for fishing at the best of times. I could never be bothered sitting by the ice hole for hours on end when you could just chuck in a grenade and have done with it. "You want to know what I'm doing over at the church, and whose heart is beating in there. You're wondering what that heartbeat has got to do with all this shit that's going down in West London right now, including the riot tonight. Maybe you'd also like to know who Juliet Salazar is and where she figures in all this. Right so far?"

He gave me the kind of pained, wondering stare you'd give to an aged relative who'd just tried to put their underpants on over their head.

"I was talking about the girl," he said, very quietly. "The little girl you just made your heartfelt promise to. Unless that was a different little girl. Perhaps this is a hobby of yours."

Just for a second I had a sense of events accelerating away from me in a direction I wasn't braced for—like I might go sprawling on my face and lose what was left of my dignity. I really didn't feel too good now: my head was spinning, and there was a smell in my nostrils like the very faintest hint of rotten meat.

"The girl?" I repeated.

Gwillam looked just a little irritated, as if the edge was starting to wear off his patience. Compared to the robotic calm he'd shown up until now, it was almost a relief. "Abigail Torrington," he said. "Or Abigail Jeffers. Whichever you prefer."

"Oh, *that* girl." I tried to sound as if everything was falling into place now, although I felt like I was treading water in lead-soled diving boots. I filed the other name away for future reference: that was something, at least. "But that's just a missing person case. Unless you've got some other reason to be looking for Dennis Peace? Is that what this is all about? Is Abbie a means to an end?"

Gwillam frowned sternly, two straight-edged vertical lines appearing in the center of his forehead. "Peace is completely irrelevant," he said. "Obviously we appreciate what he did, but his motives being what they are, we can't trust him to follow through. No, it's Abigail we need to find. And we need to find her before anybody else does. We're not prepared to consider any other possibility. After all you've seen since Saturday, you ought to know exactly what's at stake."

I played this back at various speeds, without much luck. "It's funny," I said, giving it up. "All the words you're saying make perfect sense, but somehow when you put them all together it comes out as shite. Why should Abbie matter to anyone besides her parents? Or is this a question of the sparrow that falls in the marketplace? Do you guys look out for every lost soul that comes down the pike? I mean, that's inspiring, but it's also a little hard to—"

I stopped because a heavy hand clamped down on my shoulder, and I was twisted around about ninety degrees to the left. I found myself staring into a hostile face dominated by a massive barricade of eyebrow.

"Show respect," said the loup-garou sternly, showing me his teeth.

"Po." Gwillam's tone was mild, but very efficacious. The huge loup-garou let go of my shoulder and stood back, almost like a soldier called to attention. I could see Zucker now, standing over by the Civic as if they thought I might cut and run and they were ready for the possibility. Their own car—another off-roader, even bigger than the Jeep—was pulled up onto the curb about a hundred yards or so farther down. They'd walked the rest of the way under the cover of my playing.

Gwillam didn't look concerned, either for my well-being or about the possibility that I might abscond. I guess he just wanted to have his say more than he wanted to see me get my throat ripped out.

He nodded to the loup-garou at my side, acknowledging the swift obedience with silent approval, then turned his attention back to me.

"Pythagoras is meant to have made a clever comment about levers," he murmured. "Levers, and moving the world. I was never entirely convinced—it sounds a little too post-Enlightenment to me. But I'm sure you know the one I mean." He stared at me expectantly for a moment. Being in no mood to play straight man, I stared right back. "Well," Gwillam went on, "that's what the little dead girl is. A lever large enough to move the world. Which is a troubling thought, to me at least. Because insofar as I have a preference, I'd like the world to stay where it is."

This was still about as clear as Mississippi mud. Time for another grenade, I thought.

"Are you just speaking for yourself?" I asked him. "Or for the Catholic Church as a whole? Which, incidentally, has to be a fucking sight more catholic than I thought it was, given who it's employing."

There was a moment's silence, during which Gwillam just stared at me, nonplussed. Then he nodded, not at me but at Po. And then an explosion of pain in my left side made me crumple and fall, thudding against the crash barrier on the way down. A kidney punch, administered with finely measured force, designed to cause spectacular agony but stop short of actual rupture.

It was a long time before I tuned into my surroundings again—half a minute, maybe, but I'm not the best judge. Given that for a lot of that time I was struggling to suck in a breath without moving a single muscle on my left-hand side, it felt a fair bit longer to me.

"You were warned once," said Gwillam, his voice sounding hollow and distant. "But from what Zucker and Po said, I was afraid that you might not have taken the warning seriously enough."

I still couldn't get enough breath to answer—which might have been for the best, since the words uppermost in my mind right then were "fuck you." As I knelt there, folded up around my pain, something cold and hard was pressed against the back of my neck.

"We *are* serious," Gwillam said, quietly but with very precise, almost stilted emphasis. "We don't take life lightly, but we're empowered to do so, if the need arises. Right now, killing you seems to me to be very definitely the lesser of two evils."

"And yet . . . ," I grunted, wincing as the effort of speech tugged at muscles that weren't quite ready to move again, ". . . I can't help noticing . . . I'm still alive."

"Yes."

The pressure on my neck disappeared, and a moment later there was the unmistakable sound of a safety being pulled back, with a slight catch along the way, into the on position. The son of a bitch had had the gun cocked. If he'd sneezed at the wrong moment he could have blown my head off. I looked up, moving my head as little as possible, to find him sliding the gun back into a shoulder holster. Meeting my gaze, he shook his head.

"We were watching you at the mall," he said. "At that point, killing you was very definitely part of my night's work. But then I saw you and the woman—is she a woman?—dealing with the possessed and saving the hostages. I'll admit that wasn't what I was expecting—and it made me a little uneasy. You see, if I'm going to turn Zucker and Po loose on you, I'd rather do it with a clear conscience."

"They didn't seem to be on the leash last night," I wheezed.

"At that time, they were under orders not to kill you. Hurting you wasn't particularly discouraged. Castor, I'm going to ask you again, and probably for the last time. Whose side are you on in this?"

If I'd had more notice of that question, I might have given it some thought and come up with a cute, ambivalent answer. As it was, I didn't hesitate.

"Abbie Torrington's side."

Gwillam made a sound that was halfway between a snort and a chuckle. "That's even possible," he said. "If so, those stories about you not being a fool may just about be true. Although it's still more likely that someone is playing you the way you play that whistle."

He went quiet for long enough that I thought he'd finished.

"If I stand up," I asked, risking a very slow and very gradual glance over my shoulder, "will this asshole knock me down again?"

Gwillam went on as if I hadn't spoken. "You were ahead of us at the *Collective*," he said. "That was . . . impressive. Do you have any other leads on where Peace is hiding the girl?"

Well, I had about a half of one, and I was keeping it to myself. I got a hand up on the crash barrier and began to lever myself back up onto my feet. My teeth were clenched shut with the effort, so of course I couldn't answer Gwillam's question.

He sighed again, sounding like a man with the weight of the world on his shoulders.

"If I tell you to find your reverse gear and back out of this—say until you hit China—is there any chance that you'll do it?"

It's probably a sin to lie to a priest, and I've got enough sins on my conscience already without going out looking for new ones. I just shook my head once: more than once would have been pushing it, given that I'd only just got myself back on the vertical.

"I didn't think so," said Gwillam sadly. "But I'm telling you anyway.

It's by way of being an acknowledgment of what you did tonight. A professional courtesy, let's say. It's the last you're going to get. Good night, Castor—and good-bye."

He made the sign of the cross over me—not threateningly, or ironically, but deadpan serious. Then he signed to the two werewolves and they fell in to either side of him as he walked back to the car.

As they drove away Zucker misjudged the angle—or maybe, got it exactly right—and scraped along the passenger side of Matt's Civic with a sound like the shriek of a neutered elephant. Then he accelerated into the eastbound traffic and within a few seconds their taillights had merged with the rest of the river.

———————————

Imelda Probert, better known as the Ice-Maker, lives in a squalid little third-floor flat in Peckham, in a block whose brickwork has been painted black in some sort of abortive experiment with stealth technology. The door off the street is boarded up, so you go in around the side through a yard that's like an urban elephants' graveyard, strewn with the rusting, wheelless hulks of expired cars. It's something of a conundrum, given how much hard cash the Ice-Maker must pull down, week in and week out. After all, she offers a specialized and much sought-after service. But then again, I guess by the same token she doesn't have to worry about bringing in the passing trade: people who need her find her.

Before I went in, I checked an additional piece of equipment that I'd picked up along the way. It was a sprig of myrtle, borrowed from a graveyard. Myrtle for May: if I'd been on the ball, I should have had some already, then I wouldn't have to shinny up cemetery walls after midnight. I whispered a blessing to it, feeling like a fraud as I always do when I'm mucking about with things that laypeople would call magic.

The stairwell smelled of piss and stale beer—two stages in a conjugation that usually ends with "dead-drunk guy facedown in his own vomit." But I didn't meet anybody on the way up, and when I knocked on the door on the third floor—the only door that wasn't covered over with plywood and nailed shut—the sound echoed through the building with telling hollowness.

After a few seconds, the door was opened by a skinny black girl of about sixteen or so, whose eyes were each, individually, bigger than her whole face. I only knew she was a girl by the pigtails: the hard, hatchet face was one-size-fits-all, and the black jeans and manga-chick T-shirt were unisex.

"Yeah?" she said.

"Friend of Nicky's," I told her.

She frowned at me with truculent suspicion. "You got a pulse?"

I checked. "I do, but it's running kind of slow. Is that a deal-breaker?"

She swiveled her head and looked behind her into the flat. "Mom," she called. "There's a live man out here."

"Is he police?" a much deeper voice answered from somewhere inside. "If he's police, Lisa, you tell him to go fuck himself because I paid already."

The moppet turned her face to me again. "Mom says if you're police, you can—"

"Yeah," I said. "I got it. I'm not police. The name's Castor. If Nicky Heath is in there, I'm here to see him and give him a ride home."

She called out over her shoulder, keeping her eyes on me this time in case I tried to steal something. It would have had to be the door or one of the walls: there was nothing else on the landing, not even carpet to cover the warped floorboards. "He says he's Castor and he's gonna give Nicky a ride."

"Oh, Castor." There was edgy disapproval in the voice, and I knew exactly why. "Yeah, you show him into the parlor, Lisa. He can just hold his horses until I'm done here."

Rolling her eyes to show what she thought of these instructions, Lisa flung the door open. Showing me into the parlor meant pointing to a door off the narrow entrance hall to the left as she took off in the opposite direction herself. There was a door right at the end of the hall where I could see Imelda's back as she labored over her latest patient. She was singing to herself, a gospel song, most likely, but it was under her breath and from this distance I couldn't make out either the words or the tune.

I'd been here before, about two years back, so I knew the drill. I also knew that Imelda didn't like me very much: exorcists were bad for business. Sending me into the parlor to wait was a piece of calculated sadism, but there wasn't a hell of a lot to do about it, so I just took a deep breath, held it, and walked in.

The Ice-Maker is basically just a faith-healer with a very specialized clientele: a clientele whom no other doctor, whether alternative or vanilla, is likely to want to poach. She deals exclusively with zombies, and she claims, by laying-on of hands, to slow the processes of decay almost to a standstill. I always thought it was bullshit, but Nicky goes to her twice a month without fail—and he's been dead a long while now, so I respect his judgment on matters of physical decomposition. Her monicker—Ice-Maker—comes from her boast that her hands are as good as a deep-freeze in terms of keeping dead meat fresh.

But the smell in the parlor, I have to say, was one of sour-sweet decay, deeply ingrained. Like I said, this wasn't my first visit, so I knew what to expect, but it still hit me like a wall and almost knocked me down. I went on inside, and six or seven of the walking dead glanced up to appraise the newcomer. The sitting dead, actually, since the room was laid out like a doctor's waiting room with chairs all around three walls, and most of the chairs were taken. There were even magazines: a chalk-faced woman in the corner with a small hole in the flesh of her cheek was flicking through a vintage copy of *Cosmo*.

Zombies don't breathe, so sharp intakes of breath were out of the question; and there wasn't a stand-up piano to tinkle and plunk its way into shocked silence as I walked in. All the same, though, I could feel the tension. The zombies who'd already looked up to clock me carried on staring: the others, catching the mood, glanced up to see what was happening.

I sat down, just inside the door, and picked up a *Reader's Digest*.

Flicking through it, I found an article about a possible enhanced role for walnuts in the treatment of colonic cancer, and started to read. The great thing about the *Reader's Digest* is that it exists outside of space and time as we know them: mystics and ecstatics read it to achieve a trance state deeper than normal meditative techniques allow.

Sadly, though, I wasn't going to be allowed to attain a lower consciousness tonight. Over the top of the magazine, I saw a man's broad torso heave into view.

"You're alive," said a harsh voice, through a bellowslike soughing of breath.

"Yeah," I agreed, without looking up. "I'm working on it, though. You know how it is."

"The fuck you doing here, you blood-warm piece of shit?" This was said more vehemently, and the waft of fetid breath made me wince.

"I'm waiting for a friend," I said mildly.

There was a heavy pause, and then: "Wait outside."

I looked up. The guy must have been a real holy terror back when he was still counted among the living, and if anything he was even scarier now that he was dead. He stood about six two, and it was mostly muscle: the kind of sculpted, highly defined muscle you get from working out. And his arms were bare and his T-shirt was tight, so you got to see the muscles sliding against one another when he moved like tectonic plates. His bald head glistened—not with sweat, obviously, so I guessed it must have been with oil of some kind. He was a thanato-narcissist, in love with his own defunct flesh and keeping it polished up like a museum piece.

But I'd been pushed around enough for one night: enough, and heading inexorably toward more than enough.

"I'm fine right here," I said, and returned to the good news about walnuts.

He smacked the magazine out of my hands. "No," he growled. "You're not. 'Cause if you stay here, I'm gonna rip your tongue out."

I glanced around the room, took in the reactions from the rest of Imelda's dead clientele. They seemed a little uneasy about what was happening—but then, Imelda's services aren't cheap. Most of them looked to be a lot more well-heeled than this sad piece of worm-food, and they probably had that whole middle-class anxiety about making a scene. That was good news for me: it meant they were less likely to mob me and tear my arms and legs off if this went badly.

"Okay, sport," I murmured. I stood up and he squared off against me, waiting for me to throw the first punch. He was sure enough of his own strength to know that nothing I could swing would put him down and having allowed me an ineffectual tap at his chin, he could dismantle me at his leisure.

I had the myrtle twig wrapped twice around my hand. I just slapped it to his forehead and spat out the words "*hoc fugere.*" He shot backward as fast if I'd stuck a shotgun into his mouth and pulled the trigger.

It wasn't an exorcism—nothing like. It's just the most basic kind of nature magic, an elemental ward that has efficacy for about three weeks of the year, so long as it's been properly cut and blessed. To the dead, whether they're in the body or out of it, getting too close to a ward is like touching a main cable: it hurts a fuck of a lot.

The zombie hit the floor hard, and lay there jerking spastically with his eyes wide open. One of his arms, flailing out, hit the leg of the woman who'd been reading *Cosmo*. She jumped aside to avoid the contact.

"I really don't want any trouble," I told the room in general.

"Yeah," said Nicky from the doorway. "That's fucking plain to see."

Behind him, Imelda gave a yelp of dismay and stormed past him into the room, knocking him aside. She's a big woman, with fists like hams: it would take a lot more than a myrtle switch to take her down. "Castor!" she bellowed. "You have no right! You have no right! You get out of my house now, or I swear I'll call the police on you."

"Hey, he was the one wanted to fight," I said. "I was happy with the *Reader's Digest.*"

Kneeling down beside the still-shuddering zombie, she laid her hand on his forehead and shot me a glare of pure contempt. He quieted under her hand.

"Then you deal with him like a man," she said. "Not like a cockroach."

"I just used a—" I began.

"I know what you used," she snapped. "You swatted him with a stay-not like you'd swat a bug, because you couldn't win the fight any other way. You're just a goddamn coward. Now you get out of my house before I throw you out."

That was a much more serious threat than the one about phoning the police. Imelda would never ask the man to fight her battles for her, but she really could pick me up and throw me, and the way I felt right then I might not survive. I put up my hands in surrender and left the room, hearing Nicky behind me apologizing on my behalf and assuring her I'd never come round here again.

Little Lisa was out in the hallway, leaning against the wall. She grinned at me, wickedly amused.

"What's the joke?" I asked.

"You beat that big lych man," she said scornfully, "but you couldn't beat my mom."

"Can you?" I asked.

She shook her head vigorously. "Fuck, no."

"Well, there you go."

I waited for Nicky in the yard, but when he came out he walked right on past me. "The car's out in the street," I said, falling into step with him.

"Fuck you, Castor," he snapped, speeding up. "I'll take a frigging cab."

"Look, the guy was going to fold me into a paper plane, Nicky. I'm sorry. But I did what I had to do."

"You know what it would mean for me if Imelda decides I'm bad news? The only other guy I know who can do what she does lives in *Glasgow*. I am fucking screwed if she gets mad at me. I wish to Christ I'd told you to wait until tomorrow."

Mike Carey

"Okay," I said. "I'm sorry. I already said I was sorry. What did you have to tell me, anyway? What is it that couldn't wait?"

We were out in the street by this time. He slammed the yard door shut with a bang that resounded across the street—in this neighborhood, not a wonderful idea.

"What couldn't wait?" he echoed, sarcastically. "You've been fed a line, is what. I wanted to tell you you're running on pure bullshit. This kid Abbie Torrington—you said her parents hired you to find her?"

"Right," I agreed, a little unnerved by his savagery. "Get to the point, Nicky."

He rounded on me, thrust his face into mine.

"The point is you had me chasing my own fucking tail, looking through morgue records and autopsy reports and fuck knows what else. And it's all a waste of time because the kid's not dead."

He hit the punch line with grim satisfaction.

"The kid's only missing. It's the *parents* who are dead."

Chapter Twelve

When I was eleven years old, and coming up to my twelfth birthday, I dropped a lot of heavy hints about a bike. It was a lot to ask, even if it was a secondhand one, because my dad had just been laid off from the metal box factory on Breeze Hill and we'd reached the point where we either had to eat dirt literally or go to one of the local loan sharks and do it figuratively.

As the day approached, it became clear that there was a big secret I wasn't in on. Conversations between my mum and dad would stop when I came into the room, and there was a general air of silence and tension. When I asked my big brother Matt what was going on, and whether or not it had anything to do with me, he told me to fuck off out of it because he had homework to do. I concluded that the bike had been bought, and that it had probably added to the financial strain the family was already under. Selfish little shit that I was, I took that as good news.

Then about three days before my birthday, my mum left home. My dad, John, had finally kicked her out after finding her in bed with his work colleague, Big Terry (so named to avoid confusion with the merely medium-size Terry Seddon). She went in the middle of the night, so the first we knew was when we woke up the next morning and she wasn't there. Dad told us she'd gone back to live with Grandma

Lunt in Skelmersdale, which was a half-truth: her own mother threw her out, too, since she didn't have a job and couldn't "turn up" for her keep. She ended up going down to London looking for a job, and we didn't see her again for three years.

So I'm prepared to admit that sometimes I ignore what's right under my nose: I'm not always right in there with the intuitive connections and conclusions. It's probably not overstating things to say that—sly as I undoubtedly am—I can sometimes get lost in the wood while looking at the trees.

But this time it was the world's fault. This time reality had pitched me a spitball I couldn't have seen coming.

At first I tried to slot Nicky's nasty little revelation into what I already knew. "When?" I asked. "When did they die?"

"Last Saturday. Sixth of May. Somewhere between noon and six p.m. according to the pathologist's best guess. The guy—Stephen— was shot in the face at point-blank range, and he was kneeling at the time. No sign of a struggle: He saw it coming and he took it pretty well. A good sport, obviously. With the woman it was messier: She was tied up and beaten with the leg of a chair, then shot in the stomach. And the killer took his time, because the path team put the time of death a good three hours after the guy."

"But—" I managed. "I met them two days after that—on the Monday. That doesn't make any kind of sense. Are you telling me—?"

I tailed off. I realized that a couple of lights had come on in windows across the street. This clearly wasn't the best place to be having this conversation. I headed toward the corner. "The car's over here," I said. "You can tell me as we drive."

Nicky didn't move. "I told you, Castor, I'll take a cab. Right now the less of your company I get, the better. You want to hear this, you hear it here."

I turned to face him. "Can we at least get off the street?" I asked, throwing out my arms in a shrug.

Nicky hesitated. "I'll give you five minutes," he said after a couple of beats. "There's a bar on Troy Town. It's hot and cold, or at least it was the last time I looked. Come on."

He led the way, sullenly silent. I decided to let him simmer down before I broached the subject again: I'd get more out of him that way. But the wheels inside my head were spinning without traction, the gears squealing so loud I could almost hear them. Mel and Steve died two days before I met them. So either I met really good fakers or the dead bodies had been wrongly identified.

But it was Tuesday now—or rather, Wednesday morning. If the cops had made a bad ID on Saturday night, they'd had ample time already by Monday to have met the Torringtons, cleared up the little misunderstanding, tipped their hats, and gone on their merry way. And that would be on file. And Nicky would have seen it there.

That left the other possibility—that the people I'd met who called themselves Mel and Steve Torrington were two somebody elses entirely. In which case, why pretend? Why introduce themselves as two people who'd just died and whose murders could be the next day's front-page news?

Because there wasn't anyone else who I'd have said yes to. They needed me to look for Abbie's ghost, and that lie was the only one that was certain to do the job.

We turned the corner into Troy Town—which has nothing epic or eye-catching about it apart from its name. Nicky crossed the road, and I followed. On the other side was a short row of Georgian terraces. Every second house had a flight of steps behind wrought-iron railings, leading down to a basement level below the street. Nicky descended one of these flights of steps, and as I followed I heard voices and music from ahead of me, although everything was still dark. Then he opened a door and light flooded out. Not much of it, it has to be said, and not strong: maybe "oozed" is a better word than "flooded."

The bar was actually in the basement of a house. It was called The Level, and it was indeed hot and cold, like Nicky said. That meant that living and dead were equally welcome. You could smell the dead part of the equation as you came in off the street: a faint sour whiff like leaf mold, mixed with the surgical tang of formaldehyde. Seeing them wasn't so easy; the only lighting in the room was from candles in the necks of bottles strategically positioned on tables and on shelves around the walls. There was a good-size crowd lurking in the plentiful shadows—and a poor-size bar, wedged into a corner of the room. I ordered a whisky, Nicky passed. Introducing foreign organics into his system is something he tends to avoid. "If you're dead, your immune system is more or less closed for business," he'd told me more than once. "No blood flow, right? No transport for antibiotics, phagocytes, any of that shit. So once you start letting infective agents in, you're fucked, pure and simple." If this was a more upmarket place, he would have ordered red wine and inhaled the scent of it, but he wouldn't stoop to whatever the house red was in this place.

We sat down at the most remote table we could find—but privacy was provided by the other conversations going on all around us. Anything we said would be lost in the general noise. The wallpaper was a virulent red and looked like flock. I reached out and ran my finger down it: it was. Maybe this place had been a curry house back in the day.

"Whenever you're ready," I said, and I took a gulp of the whisky to fortify myself.

Nicky's mood had calmed somewhat. He was still as pissed with me as he had been, but he enjoys being the fountain of arcane wisdom almost as much as he enjoys jazz. "I would've spotted it sooner," he said, "only like I said, when it comes to murders we've had kind of an embarrassment of riches just lately."

Of course. The spike in the bell-shaped curve. I suddenly remembered one of the headlines I'd read over Nicky's shoulder on his computer monitor: HUSBAND AND WIFE SLAIN, EXECUTION STYLE. Son of a bitch, it had been right in front of my eyes and I'd let it slide on past.

"They were found in their own house," Nicky went on. "Somewhere out toward Maida Vale."

"Maida Vale?" I broke in. "The Steve Torrington I met gave me an address on Bishop's Avenue."

"What number Bishop's Avenue?"

I dredged it up from memory. "Sixty-something. Sixty-two."

"That's the squat, you fucking moron. And what did he give you the address *for*? Did he ask you over for cocktails?"

"It was so I could send him a receipt," I admitted.

"Right. Like he fucking cared where that ended up. Anyway, the real Stephen Torrington lived in Maida Vale—and he doesn't fucking live there anymore. I've got the address if you want it, but my advice is to stay clear.

"Place of death was the living room; some of the furniture had been moved to clear a big space—killer with a sense for the theatrical. The entire place had been ransacked. Every drawer, every cupboard, everything hauled out and strewn over the floor. Like there'd been a search, the file notes said, but they were just guessing. With the place being so messed up, they couldn't even tell if anything was missing. And they couldn't figure out what had happened to the girl."

"Abbie," I breathed.

"Yeah, her. They knew there was a kid even without going through any records on the Torringtons, because there was a room that was obviously a kid's room. That had been turned over, too, just like the rest of the house."

Of course it had. And some things had been taken. I knew because except for the doll's head in my goddamn pocket they were sitting in a big black bag in my office—a gift from the guy who called himself Steve Torrington. I imagined him raking through Abbie's things with her real parents lying murdered in the room below, and I was filled with an unreasoning rage at my own naïveté. No wonder he'd sent the woman back to the car: whoever the fuck he was, he knew his own acting skills were up to the job, but he didn't want to have to rely on hers. And he was right; he'd got the grief spot-on, mostly—except that grief isn't usually that articulate. I should have known. I should have smelled something.

But if I had, what would I have done? Refused to take the case? Abbie was dead—that much I knew, because I'd touched her spirit across the London night. And I'd felt the choking well of unhappiness that was all she knew back when she was alive.

Lies or not, I'd taken this job on because of her: so fair enough, I'd see it through because of her, too. Right then I hoped that meant that somewhere along the way I'd be running into the soi-disant Steve Torrington again, so that I could salvage some of my self-respect with the judicious application of a tire iron.

That image made me think about "Mel's" bruises. They were just there for effect, I was suddenly sure: a stage prop to engage my sympathy and maybe to explain the relative awkwardness and lack of expression in her voice. This bastard didn't miss a trick—and he didn't care who he hurt.

"So what do the cops think happened?" I asked, pulling my thoughts off that particular track with a twinge of unease.

Nicky gave a one-handed shrug. "They don't know a thing," he said. "At least, nothing that's on file as yet. They analyzed the bullets six ways from breakfast, so they'll know the gun when they find it. Guns, sorry—two different weapons. But there's nothing in their ballistics database to say either of them's ever been used in any other crimes, so that's a dead end for now. They dusted the place for prints, got nothing apart from the ones that should have been there anyway—not even virtuals. Retrieved a few footprints, which again will only help in nailing the perps once they find them."

"Statements from the neighbors?"

"Nobody saw, nobody heard. Bits of street gossip creeping in here and there, though. Some people thought it was just a matter of time. The Torringtons were lowering the tone of the place, apparently. Lots of undesirables turning up at the house all hours of the day and night. One guy in particular seen going in and out a lot: tall, well built, in a long leather coat, with two goons dancing attendance like he was God. They figured he was either a gangster or a record company producer. Maybe both. There's a complaint on file with social services. One of the neighbors was worried enough about all the coming and going to raise a query about whether the Torringtons might be pedophiles, farming Abbie out for abuse."

I froze with my glass half-raised to my mouth. That would certainly explain the misery.

"And?" I prompted, both wanting and not wanting to hear the answer.

"One follow-up visit, records appended to the file. I couldn't access everything, but I gather Abbie seemed to be a healthy, normal girl. A little solemn and preoccupied, but well fed, well looked after. Room was nice, clothes were neat and tidy, she checked out okay at interview, you know the drill. 'Did not display precocious knowledge of or concern with sexual matters.' No smoking pistol—not even any powder burn. Sorry to bother you, sign off, hit the road."

"But there was something going on there," I mused, grimly. "Lots of visitors. Some of them regulars. Turning up often enough for the neighbors to clock them and take notes. What were the Torringtons up to?"

"Selling drugs?" Nicky said. "Cosmetic surgery? I deal in data, Castor, not reading fucking fortunes. What I got, you've now had. As of now, that's the entirety of what the Met have managed to nail down since Saturday night. Abbie is officially missing, her parents are indisputably dead. I know you see a lot of ghosts in the way of business. You ever been *hired* by them before?"

For once, Nicky didn't even laugh at his own joke. He'd caught the edge of my somber mood, and of course he was still choked with me for souring his arrangement with Imelda.

I took another slug of whisky, didn't even taste it.

"What about Peace?" I asked. "You dig up anything else there?"

Nicky turned coy—the way he always does when he's got something really eye-popping to tell me. "Yeah," he admitted, "a little. I don't know how much of it is strictly relevant, though."

"Meaning—?"

"Meaning it's mostly old. Lifestyle stuff. Not the kind of intel you could use to find out where he is now."

"Tell me anyway," I suggested.

He flared up, coyness giving way to the irritation that was still slow-burning underneath. "Castor, I am not exactly in your fan club right now. It hacks me off when you talk to me like I'm some kind of skivvy you can just—"

"Please," I amended. "Pretty please. Pretty please with sugar on the top."

"Better. Well, it's a case of the more you dig, the more you find. That charge sheet I mentioned runs to more than one page—wherever Peace lays his hat, he starts some kind of trouble. After that army tour I told you about he found a way to turn his training to good account. He became a merc—signed up with some private security firm in the Middle East that had a very nasty name for itself, but then half the board got locked up for trying to trigger a coup in Libya and he was out on his ear again."

There was something in his eye that told me he was saving the best till last. Under other circumstances, I might have been short enough on patience to yell him out about that: tonight I decided I'd better humor him.

"Anything else?" I asked, playing straight man.

"Yeah. Since you ask, there is."

"Go on."

"Peace filed suit back in 1999, under the jurisdiction of the State of New York. Against Anton Fanke—you remember, the satanist guy I told you about before?—and a woman whose name appears on the affidavit as Melanie Carla Jeffers, a.k.a. Melanie Carla Silver, a.k.a. Melanie Carla Torrington."

I swore aloud, and Nicky nodded his head in agreement. "Yeah, it's a peach, isn't it? Only that's not the part that made me prick up my ears. Get this: it's a suit for custody. Plaintiff alleged that defendant was unfit to be a parent, and asked the court to award him guardianship rights over . . . well, you can see this coming, so there's no point drawing it out."

There was a roaring in my ears: I couldn't tell how much of it was the fever, how much the adrenaline surge as my mind raced ahead to where Nicky was going.

"A little girl named Abigail?" I hazarded, my voice sounding hollow and fuzzy in my own ears.

"Got it in one. Abigail Fanke, she's called at this particular juncture."

"She's Peace's daughter."

"Well, he thinks she is. And the court records agree, as far as that goes, because surname notwithstanding there's a birth certificate on record for her in Burkina Faso, thirteenth of March 1993. Mother: Melanie Carla Jeffers. Father: Dennis Peace."

"That's not long after he got out of prison," I said.

"Good to know you're listening. Yeah, it is. And armed with that little tidbit, I went back to the court records. Which was a bastard, because I don't need to tell you they were all fucking handwritten. I had to call in a favor or three, but I got there in the end. Melanie whatever-her-name-is bailed Peace out of jail, and presumably spread those bribes around. Makes more sense, I guess. Like I said before, if he had the money himself he could have bought off the judge before he was sentenced, for about half the price. But maybe he didn't have any money. Maybe he needed an angel."

"An angel. Right."

"Then they have a night of passionate celebration, and nine months later little Abbie is born. Makes sense, kind of. And now he's on the run with her—alive or dead, we don't officially know."

"I know."

"Sure you do. Only what you didn't know was that he stopped to murder her mother and the mother's current boyfriend along the way. And that someone wants him badly enough to make up all this bullshit and get you on board."

I shook my head, which was aching so badly now it felt like it might fall off. Nicky was affronted. "What, did I hurt your professional pride?"

"No. But you said they wanted Peace. It's not Peace who's the point of this, Nicky—it's Abbie."

"Well, from *his* point of view it's Abbie, obviously. I mean, it looks like he killed two people to get hold of her. But the guys who are looking for him—"

"If they're looking for Peace, why not hire a proper detective? Why come to me?"

Nicky opened his mouth to speak, blinked, shut it again.

"You see? There's a whole lot of people out there who could do a better job of tracking down a man who doesn't want to be found. But finding him wouldn't necessarily mean finding Abbie. No, to find a ghost, you need an exorcist. And that's what they went out to get."

I stood up, a little unsteadily.

"Are you drunk?" Nicky asked, with the scorn of the teetotaler.

"No. I think I'm coming down with something."

"Doesn't surprise me a bit, the shit you pour into yourself. Your body may not be a temple, Castor, but it sure as hell isn't a skip. Take it from me, if you want to live to be old, you'll—"

"Save it up and mail it, Nicky. I'm not in the mood. You serious about that cab?"

"Dead serious."

"To coin a phrase."

"Funny."

"Whatever. Thanks for your help. The fare's on me."

I dropped a couple of tenners onto the table and lurched toward the door. I must have looked right then like one of The Level's zombie customers: I sure as hell felt like one.

Approaching Matt's car from the wrong direction, I was able to see firsthand what a mess the Catholic werewolves had made of the near-side wing. I felt bad about that; it seemed like a poor exchange for his trust. He might even have trouble with his insurance, given that I wasn't a named driver. The only consolation was that—to the religious mind—adversity is good for the soul.

I got in and drove, trying to focus on the road ahead as dark filaments swam across my vision. Whatever was wrong with me, it seemed to be getting worse rather than better. On the other hand, it had been a hell of a night. I didn't need to look all that far to find reasons why I might be functioning at less than a hundred percent.

I really needed to concentrate hard on the road, but I found my mind wandering back onto what Nicky had just told me. Little Abbie may not have had much happiness in her life, but she sure had a hell of a lot of parents. Two who'd died on Saturday night, two more who'd turned up at my office on Monday morning, and a fifth, Dennis Peace, who didn't figure in either tally. And then there were the Catholics: the Anathemata wanted her, too—wanted her badly. I got the feeling of wheels turning within wheels, and little fires touching off bigger ones. Whatever was going on, Abbie was the key to something huge: I knew I was right about that. Unfortunately, I didn't seem to be any closer than before to figuring out what that something actually was. "Someone didn't close the circle," the werewolf Zucker had said, charmingly mixing his metaphors, "and a little bird flew the nest." Still sounded like garbage whichever way you played it, but I was suddenly certain that the little bird was Abbie Torrington. Whatever she'd run from, it had to be bad if even being dead didn't get you free.

It was half past one when I rolled the car into Pen's driveway. The house was dark, which didn't mean anything because the windows of Pen's basement room look onto the garden, not the street. I was hoping she might still be awake so we could make our peace, knock back a glass or two of brandy, and I could maybe try her out on some of the stuff Nicky had just dropped on me—see if her credulity was any more elastic than mine.

I never got the chance to find out. I'd taken about three steps toward the door when some headlights went on across the street, pinning me like a butterfly to a board. Some doors slammed, and footsteps sounded from my left and right simultaneously. I bunched my fists, preparing to go down fighting.

"Relax, Castor."

I did, but only a little way. It was Gary Coldwood's voice. A moment later, he loomed out of the light like some negative Nosferatu and clapped a hand on my shoulder, a little too close to my neck. I winced. My head was throbbing so badly now, even that overfriendly touch sent spikes of pain through it.

"Burning the candle at both ends," Coldwood said. "You look like shit."

"I feel like shit," I said. "It's a set."

He stared at me for a moment in silence. He seemed to want to say something, and it seemed to be something that needed a hell of a run-up.

"Something about Pauley?" I prompted him.

He looked blank. "About who?"

"Robin Pauley? Drug czar and murderer? I'm going to be a material witness at his trial, remember? You told me to look out for frighteners."

Coldwood nodded, waved the topic brusquely away.

"Pauley's dead," he said. "Three of his lieutenants, too. We hauled them out of the Thames this morning. We're thinking now that Sheehan's murder was the first move in a gang war. Sorry, Fix. I should have told you."

"Yeah," I agreed, deadpan. "You should. And now you have. But next time you could just send me an e-mail. Squad cars on the doorstep in the middle of the night get the neighbors talking."

He didn't move. He didn't really seem to be listening. "We go back a long way, Fix," he said.

"No," I told him. "We don't."

He laughed unconvincingly. "Hell, you're right. We don't, do we? But I've sort of come to trust you. I mean, up to a point. Bullshit aside—and you're a great man for bullshit—I don't think you've ever lied to me."

There was another silence. "So what," I said. "Did you come out all this way just to hug me?"

Coldwood shook his head. A woman and a man had moved in on either side of me while we spoke, and now he flicked a glance at each of them in turn. I didn't bother to look: in the glare of the headlights, I couldn't see much of them anyway. "Fix, this is Detective Sergeant Basquiat and Detective Constable Fields. They've got a crime scene, and they'd like you to look it over with them. Since I'm your designated liaison, they went through me. I said you'd be fine with it. But I also said, bearing in mind how late it was getting, we might have to ask you to come over in the morning."

Coldwood's tone had turned clipped and formal: words chosen carefully, for the record. It was that tone more than anything else that made me nod my head—also carefully, to minimize the risk of it exploding or falling off. This sounded like the kind of bad shit that has repercussions: I needed to know what it was about.

We drove west, which seemed kind of inevitable. Through Muswell Hill and Finchley, and into Hendon. There were two cars: Coldwood bundled me into the back of one, got in beside me; a uniform drove, and Fields and Basquiat followed in the second car.

"Want to tell me what this is about?" I asked, after a minute or so of stony silence.

Coldwood just looked at me. "Not yet a while," was all he said.

It wasn't a long journey, but it felt like forever. I was so tired now that my eyes kept closing by themselves, and the pain in my head had translated itself into a kind of roaring static in my ears. This must be some kind of flu, and it couldn't have come at a worse time. Pen occasionally reads the future in tea leaves, which is a tricky thing at best: a cop's body language, though, can be a very reliable indicator of which way your immediate future is going to go, and unless I was very much mistaken I was in a shitload of trouble.

We pulled up at last somewhere off Hendon Lane. Coldwood got out, and held the door open for me. I stepped out, too, only realizing how overheated the car had been when the night air touched the sweat on my face.

"In there," said Coldwood, pointing.

We were standing in front of a yellow brick building that looked like some kind of church hall. The car had actually pulled up off the road itself onto a narrow apron, also paved in brick, that was obviously intended as a car park—but police incident tape had been put up across three-quarters of it, one length of which bore a large KEEP OUT notice. The building itself was clearly closed for business, as the shuttered windows and the foot-high weeds growing at the base of the walls both proclaimed. There was a signpost off to one side, and as I looked in that direction the headlights of the second police car, rolling up off the road and coming to a halt with a muted sigh of hydraulic suspension, spotlighted it neatly: FRIENDS' MEETING HOUSE. Well, great; it's always nice to be among friends. The rest of the road was lined with factories and warehouses: all dark apart from the streetlights, and even some of them were out, no doubt smashed by kids with good aim, a reasonable supply of half bricks and too much free time.

Two constables stood to either side of the open door, and they nodded respectfully to Coldwood as he passed. He ignored them.

The hallway inside had no lights, but the bright yellow-white of mobile spots shone from some inner room. We went on through, shielding our eyes against the sudden glare. The echo of my footsteps immediately suggested a much larger space, even before I could get my eyes adjusted to the point where I could actually see it. Dark figures were walking backward and forward across an empty expanse of floor. Their footsteps crackled and rustled on thick plastic sheeting.

"Got another bullet here, Len," a voice said.

"Out of the floor?" a second voice called back. This one belonged to a guy who either smoked way too much or had the worst case of chronic bronchitis I'd ever heard.

"No, in this beam here—way out of the way. Shooter must've got a bounce before he brought the weapon into line."

"Okay. Measure the reflexive and mark it up."

The room assembled itself piecemeal in front of me, my tiredness making the normal process of visual accommodation take twice as long. It was even bigger than I'd thought, because it was only the area lit up by the spots that I was seeing at first: further volumes of shadow lurked around the edges, concealing greater depths.

It was a typical church meeting house in the modern style: short on the bullying majesty that a lot of older churches have, but pretty in its way. Large amounts of pale wood, mostly in the form of beams and window trim; a symmetrical floor plan with bays every so often, so although the general shape was square there was a sense of some complex, origamilike shape, outfolding from a wide, open central space. Suburban transcendence for the Ikea age. Only what was going on here now was kind of the opposite of all that: forensic science, the triumph of the rationalistic worldview. Men and women in white coats tracked backward and forward with swabs and tape measures, typed notes into PDAs, called out to each other in clipped, unlovely jargon.

A door slammed behind me, making me turn my head. Detectives Basquiat and Fields loomed out of the night in a gust of cold air, like bad news. I saw them clearly for the first time. Basquiat was a hard-faced blonde dressed in shades of blue—from clinical all the way through to conservative. Her hair—short and straight—was pulled up from the sides in a way that looked vaguely continental, and if anything made the lines of her face look sharper and more uncompromising. Fields was middle-aged and tending to fat, but with the sad remains of Mediterranean good looks in his dark eyes and tightly curled black hair. That he was still a detective constable at his age suggested either some monumental fuck-up in his past or an equally monumental lack of ambition.

"You gonna walk him through it, or what?" Coldwood asked.

Fields looked at Basquiat, awaiting orders. "Why don't you do it?" Basquiat said, turning to Coldwood. "He's your man."

Coldwood shook his head. "No, no, no. Your crime scene," he pointed out, deadpan. "Don't be pulling shit like that on me."

Basquiat sighed, rolled her eyes, flashed Coldwood a pained look that said plainer than words "Are we really going to have to do this all by the goddamn book?" Coldwood met her stare, not giving an inch. Okay, I could see where this was going now—or part of it, anyway.

Someone here had the jurisdictional blues. I played dumb, though: there's nothing cops hate worse than a smart-mouthed civilian.

"Over here," Basquiat said to me, with a peremptory gesture as though she were calling a dog to heel.

"Thanks for looking out for me, Gary," I murmured to Coldwood, keeping all but the trace elements of sarcasm out of my voice.

"Hey, you don't know what I did for you and what I didn't," Coldwood muttered back, looking angry. "I tried to call you earlier, but you were out all day and your mobile was busy. And I don't know if you've noticed, Fix, but it's meltdown out there. They had a fucking riot over in White City."

"I heard."

"The innocent have nothing to fear. Go ahead and surprise me."

I went across to where Basquiat was standing, more or less in the center of the room—and of the plastic sheeting. She watched me come. She really was very attractive under the strictly professional hair and outfit; and she really didn't like me at all. Glancing down, I realized that I was treading on dead people: or at least, on the numbered plastic tags that forensics teams still use as place markers for where people died. One. Two. Three. Someone had been busy here—and fairly indiscriminate.

As I drew level with her, she pointed down at her feet. Under the plastic, a circle about five feet in diameter had been drawn on the floor in thick, grainy white chalk. Within the circle was a smaller circle, and between the two, going all the way around the ring with letters very carefully spaced, were the words VERHIEL SERAGON IRDE SABAOTH REDOCTIN. The center of the circle was inscribed with a pentagram: the five-pointed star used in certain kinds of black magic because, supposedly, it merges the four elements of matter with the single defining reality of spirit. Makes nice jewelry for little Goth girls, too, but that's just a happy coincidence. There were also elaborate curlicued marks in each segment of the circle between the five legs of the pentagram: they were based on Greek letters, but with a great many additional strokes.

What I noticed about this one, though, was that in spite of the care taken in drawing it, it had been pretty comprehensively messed up. The floorboards were chewed up into splinters in a long line that cut through one segment of the circle, and something brown had spilled at the center, which then flowed out almost to the opposite edge, effacing part of the pentagram on its way. There was another plastic marker here. It was red, and bore the number "1" in spotless white.

Someone didn't close the circle.

"Saturday night," Basquiat said, from right beside me. "Sometime after eight and before, say, two in the morning. A whole bunch of people came in here. We've got tire tracks on the forecourt outside and a whole bunch of footprints. We're guessing maybe a couple of dozen people in all, but that's still in the air.

"What we do know is that they didn't just walk in off the street. Some of them had been living here for a while before that, out in the back." She pointed off into the dark. "There are six sleeping bags there, a portable latrine, a lot of canned food, and a dozen or so black bags full of various kinds of domestic garbage. So let's say we've got a core group doing caretaking duties here—keeping the place in order, watching out for any untoward attention. Then we've got a bigger group that just turns up on Saturday night for the party."

She went down on one knee, sketched out the outline of the circle with one well-manicured hand. "And we can guess what kind of a party it was. This is a pseudo-Paracelsian magic circle, based on an original in the *Archidoxis Magicae*. Necromancy. Someone was doing black magic here, and"—her fingers hovered over the dark brown stain at the center of the circle—"it involved a sacrifice."

She stood up again. "And this is where it gets interesting," she said, although her tone stayed level to the point of indifference. With a nod of the head, she indicated a part of the room I hadn't even looked at: one of the bays, dark like the other corners of the room out of the spotlights' beams. "An uninvited guest," she said, "comes in from that way—or he was there all along, waiting for the right moment. There's a window, boarded up, but someone's pried the board away and left it propped up against the wall. He was quiet, so they didn't hear him coming. Or maybe they were chanting. Either way, he gets up close without anyone turning to look at him. We know that, because the people who were standing here, here, and here"—she counted them off, frowning as though with the effort of memory, although the dark smears under the plastic marked the spots well enough—"were shot in the back."

She turned to face me, stared at me with cold appraisal for a second or so, but then she pointed past me toward the back of the room. "The rest of the magic-makers start running—not away from the man with the gun, but toward him. They're not armed themselves. Or at least, no other guns get fired as far as we can tell. All the bullets we've retrieved come from the same weapon—an IMI Tavor assault rifle, Israeli military issue. That's a weapon with both semiauto and fully automatic functions, but the magazine—so I'm told—only carries thirty rounds. Doesn't matter. This man's not wasting them, and he's not missing."

Basquiat walked past me, forced me to turn to follow her as she continued the lecture. This kind of browbeating by facts, figures, and ballroom dancing is standard cop procedure. I was listening, but on a level underneath that there was a question I kept turning over and over in my mind with a kind of sick dread, more or less in time to the throbbing in my skull: What—or who—had been standing in the center of the circle?

"But there's no way he's got time to reload," Basquiat said, like a maths lecturer saying "compute the angle." Her tone was still flat, but there was a kind of excitement or at least a kind of animation in her face. I could see she loved her job. And I wondered, briefly, whether a case like this might be a career-making deal for a young, upwardly mobile detective sergeant.

"And he's used up about six bullets just introducing himself," she went on, "so assuming he had a full clip when he came in he's now got a couple of dozen shots left. If they rush him, which is what they're doing, he's in trouble. Fully automatic fire will scatter a crowd, but he doesn't have any time to switch over and in any case anyone who doesn't go down in that first sweep will be right on top of him and he'll have nothing left to fight with except his hands."

She scanned the floor, as if she were reading the story there. "Maybe he expected them to run. Maybe he's surprised that they don't get the message. He's not scared, though, that's for sure, because he walks to meet them. One—two—three." She pointed to a scuff mark on the floor in between two of the sheets of plastic. "He stops here. And then he does something very odd."

"He fires at the floor," I said. My throat was unpleasantly dry, and it came out as a croak.

Basquiat looked at me curiously. "That's right," she said, acknowledging the point with a nod. "He does. And why does he do that, Mr. Castor?"

I shrugged unconvincingly. I knew the answer, but I was still hoping I was wrong. "Warning shot?"

"After shooting three people in the back? I don't think so."

Okay, what the fuck. If she was determined to make me dance . . . "The circle," I said, tiredly. "He blasted a hole in the circle."

"I'm still asking why," said Basquiat. "It seems a strange thing to do. Can you shed any light on the reasoning?"

"Maybe," I said, facing her stare as levelly as I could. "But maybe you'd like to tell me why I'm here first. It would help to know."

Basquiat's jaw tensed so hard that for a second I could see every muscle in her throat. "I'm surprised you have to ask." The words came out laden with something like anger, something like contempt. "You're one of DS Coldwood's regular informants—or so he says. And he uses you a lot in situations like this, isn't that right? You tell him where someone's died, and how they died, and how they've been getting along since."

"Yeah," I said. "That's about it. So do you want a reading, detective?"

"Not at this particular point in time, Mr. Castor, no. Maybe later. What I'd like right now is an answer. How did you know that Abbie Torrington was dead?"

So there it was. It opened up inside my stomach like a pit, just waiting for one more word from Basquiat to fill it.

"I'm an exorcist," I said.

"So what, it's a sparrow in the marketplace kind of deal?" she spat, unconsciously echoing my own words to Gwillam. "Everyone who dies, you get to hear about it? How's my grandad doing? Last time I checked, he was still okay, but maybe you can give me an update."

She glared at me again. I was still trying to think of something to say when DC Field lumbered up and handed her a note without so much as a glance in my direction. She took it, read it, and handed it back to him with a curt nod. He went away.

"A man and a woman came into my office two days ago," I told Basquiat, as she turned her attention back to me. "They claimed to be Abbie's parents. And they asked me to find her."

"To find her dead *body*?" The detective's tone was incredulous.

"No. To find her ghost."

It didn't sound much better. Before Basquiat could answer, I held up my hand in a kind of surrender. "Just tell me, sergeant, did Abbie Torrington die inside that circle?"

"Yes," said Basquiat coldly. "She did. Stabbed through the heart by some sick fucks playing at witches and wizards." She came right up close to me, dropping her voice so that her next words would just be between the two of us. "We've got her body down at the morgue right now, and you can bet we're going over it with a fine-toothed comb. And if I find out you were one of the people who killed her, Castor, no power on earth is going to keep me from ripping your balls off. And then reading you your rights at great length while you bleed."

The pit filled up. I thought it would fill with grief—grief for little Abbie, cut open like a side of meat as part of a satanist ritual—but it turned out to be anger.

"Let me read the scene," I told her, biting back a lot of other words that were clustering behind my teeth, trying to get out.

"You are dreaming, my friend," Basquiat snarled, shaking her head. "Whatever impression I may have given you earlier, you're a suspect here. I asked Coldwood to bring you over in case you turned out to be the type who falls apart and confesses at the scene of the crime. Might have saved us some time. But since you're not, I'll have to see how the evidence pans out. The only reason I'm not hauling you in and sweating you right now is because Gary vouches for you—or more precisely, because he's got you on the books as an informant, which means there's interoffice paperwork to be filled in before I can get Fields to kick your teeth down your throat."

"You let Fields do your dirty work?" I said. "I'm disappointed. Used to be, when you asked a cop for some strict discipline, you could at least rely on personal service."

Basquiat had been on the point of walking away, and she already had her back to me. She swiveled on her heel and dealt me a scything, sideways punch to the head. Since my head was close to meltdown and my balance was all to fuck, I went sprawling. I heard a tuneless whistle of appreciation from one side of the room, running footsteps from the other. Looking up blearily, I saw Gary Coldwood standing over me.

"Mr. Castor tripped on the protective sheeting," Basquiat said to him.

"Yeah. I saw. But I think he's got his sea legs now. I don't see him tripping anymore."

"Depends if he stays around me," said Basquiat. She knelt down, stared into my face. "I use Fields to do the softening up," she said. "All the detail work I'll do myself."

She walked away, and Coldwood helped me back onto the vertical— or something close to it.

"Let's get you some fresh air," he muttered.

We went back out through the hall onto the street. I leaned against the front of the building, feeling the world turn around me.

"She's got this thing about kids," Coldwood explained. "Takes it personally when they get hurt. There was a pedo out in Kingston—guy who'd done time for raping a little boy, and it looked like he might be getting back into old habits. Fell down some stairs at his house while Basquiat was over there to run some questions past him. Broke his arm, did some serious damage to his back that he might never recover from. She booked him for assault: said he attacked her and went down the stairs when she used a judo throw in self-defense. Story stank, but who cares? He did another six months. Happy ending for everyone."

I didn't say a word. I was taking this personally, too, but I wasn't going to start swearing any oaths of vengeance in front of a police officer. They've got a different set of rules for the general public.

"Get yourself a lawyer, Fix," Coldwood said sadly. "A good one. Sooner or later, we're going to pull you in formally, and a bad lawyer's gonna leave you with egg on your face whatever happens."

"I need—a lift home," I said, slurring the words.

Coldwood examined me critically for a few seconds, then turned to one of the uniforms standing by the door, who were pretending not to listen.

"Drive him back," he said.

"Yes, sir."

"And get the license number of that car he was driving. Just for the record."

He went back inside without saying good night. I guess he felt he'd done me enough favors to be going on with.

Chapter Thirteen

Whether I dreamed or not that night, I don't remember. Sleep was like a lead-lined box that I fell into, and the lid slammed shut over my head. It was as cold as the grave in there, and mercifully quiet.

But at some point in the night, someone must have torn away the sides of the box, because light started to filter in under my eyelids. Only a little, at first, but those first splinters broadened into crowbars, prying their way in, twisting me open to a day I didn't want to have anything to do with. There was a tapping sound, too, of chisels working their way into the cracks and crevices of my consciousness.

I tried to turn to get away from the light and the intrusive noise, but it seemed to be coming in from all sides. And movement was difficult in any case, because my muscles were cramped and screaming.

I opened my eyes, which felt as though they'd been sealed shut with a silicon gun. I was in a car—Matt's car, I realized when I saw the pine tree air freshener hanging over my head like mistletoe. What the hell was I doing there? I'd parked the car at Pen's and then Coldwood and his little friends had bushwhacked me and spirited me away to Hendon. And since I'd gotten a police escort home . . . No, the details wouldn't coalesce. The fever had been raging by then: I must have crawled back into the car under some vague impression that I still had to drive home, and then fallen asleep at the wheel instead. Good job. If I'd actually gotten the thing out onto the road, I'd be waking up in a morgue somewhere and finding out firsthand what out-of-body experiences are like.

The tapping came again, louder, from right behind my head. With difficulty, I levered myself around in the seat without turning my neck, which felt like it would snap rather than pivot. Pen was standing beside the car, looking in at me with an expression of puzzled concern on her face.

I unlocked the door and climbed out, almost losing my balance. Pen jumped in to catch me and keep me upright.

"Thanks," I mumbled. "Not feeling too clever, to be honest."

She winced as the smell of my breath hit her unsuspecting airways: judging by the taste in my mouth, I could sympathize.

"Fix," she admonished me, but a lot more gently than I'd have expected, "have you been drinking?" I could understand the question. I was trying to lock the car and failing to get the key into the lock. Pen took the keys from me and locked it with the beeper on the fob.

"No," I said. "No more than usual. This is—something else. I'm coming down with some kind of bug."

She steered me toward the house. "What did you do to the car?" she asked, sounding concerned.

"The car?" I echoed stupidly. My mind was a sprawl of flabby fingers that wouldn't make a fist. Then I remembered the sideswipe on the Hammersmith overpass. "Oh, yeah. That wasn't me. That was Catholic werewolves."

There are only five steps up to Pen's front door. Somehow, they seemed to take a long time to negotiate, and we had a near disaster at the top when I lost my balance and Pen had to shove me forward into the hall to avoid me going back down again on my arse.

"I'm calling a doctor," Pen muttered as she hauled me into the living room and dumped me without ceremony onto the sofa.

"I think," I said, "I just need to lie down. Had a hell of a day yesterday. Got into a fight at White City, then the cops hauled me in to help them with their inquiries."

"Jesus, Fix!" Pen was looking down at me with troubled eyes. "What do they think you did?"

"Murder." I stared at the ground, trying to shut out the memory of the crusted spatter of blood and the terse plastic tag—like the tag you'd get from a cloakroom attendant—that marked the place where Abbie Torrington died. Wasted effort: it wouldn't go away. "They think I murdered someone."

There was a silence, which seemed to expand like white light until it filled the room. Light-headed, I almost floated away on that white tide back into unconsciousness. I had too much still to do. I fought against my own body, and the room came back into focus. I didn't think that silent tussle had taken any time at all, but when I raised my head again, Pen was gone.

Saturday, May the sixth, I thought. Something went down on that night—something whose shape I could just barely make out through the many and disparate things it had touched. On Saturday, Stephen and Melanie Torrington are beaten and then shot in their own home. They don't struggle. They don't run. They just die. Later on, so does Abbie—sacrificial lamb in someone's satanic knees-up. Then after they've killed her someone else walks into the room and breaks up the party with an assault rifle, aiming not at the satanists—at least, not after the first few exhilarating moments—but at the magic circle where Abbie's body is still lying. Was that other someone Dennis Peace? Was this where he acquired Abbie's spirit, assuming he really had it? And if he did, was it a kidnapping or a rescue?

Meanwhile, three miles away at the Scrubs, St. Michael's Church was invaded by some entity so powerful that just being close to it poisoned the minds and souls of everyone in the goddamn building, sending them off on murderous trajectories that had sliced through the city like so many loops of piano wire through a ripe cheese.

And something else. Something I was missing.

Pen's voice, low and urgent, was coming from out in the hall. Nobody else's voice, just hers. I turned and saw her through the doorway, standing at the foot of the stairs, all by herself, talking away fifteen to the dozen. She was on her mobile, of course, but right then it seemed to me that there must be some spectral figure standing next to her, silent and invisible, as though she were reporting in to heaven, because there was a blaze of light around her head like a halo. But no, that was just the sun streaming in through the skylight over the front door. It was a beautiful day. About time. Way past time. But if the sunlight knew what the fuck it was shining on, would it bother to make the trip?

Pen came back into the room, stood over me looking irresolute. "I've got to go, Fix," she said. "Rafi's seeing a psychiatrist this morning for a preliminary status hearing. I don't want him to face that all by himself. I called Dylan and asked him to come and have a look at you, but he's on call so he can't. He's going to send someone else, though—a friend. You just—you just stay here until he comes, all right?"

"Yeah," I mumbled. "I'm not going anywhere. I'll be fine."

"Okay." She knelt down and gave me a quick, awkward hug. "Get better. I'll give Rafi your love."

And as she straightened up again, a thought was zigzagging across my brain, trying to find an intact neuron it could connect to. Pen was still talking, but I didn't hear a word over the ringing in my ears.

Something about Pen? Or about Rafi? I should be there for him. I had been there for him. That was the problem. That was why he was so fucked up now.

The door slammed, startling me out of a half doze. I tried to get up, but I didn't manage it. I opened my mouth to say "I'm coming with you," but Pen wasn't there anymore. Of course, that was why the door had slammed. She'd left already.

But that wasn't the issue, was it? Pen was fine, because she was going to visit Rafi, and Asmodeus—most of Asmodeus—was somewhere else. So what was the problem? Why did I feel like there was something I hadn't done, that I had to do right then without wasting any more time? And given that feeling of urgency, why was I still half-sitting, half-lying on the couch with my head hanging like a weight from my shoulders, staring at the floor?

This time I managed to get upright, even though the floor was lurching in every direction at once, trying to throw me down again. I groped in my pocket for Matt's car keys. Yeah, they were still there. I had to see someone. Juliet. I had to see Juliet, and tell her where to find Rafi on a Saturday night.

Out into the hall. Which way now? Had to be either left or right, because there weren't any other directions. Except I was forgetting down: there was an unreasonable prejudice against down. Down was amazing. Once you'd tried it, it was hard to get up again.

I was stretched out on the stairs, diagonally crucified on dusty carpet that didn't have a pattern anymore because the sun had bleached the threads to a uniform pale gold. It smelled of must and very faintly of tarragon: not the recipe I would have used. I couldn't even remember deciding to go upstairs, so I levered myself upright, leaned backward as far as I could, and fell down them again. You have to be decisive at times of crisis or people will walk all over you.

Lying on my back in the hallway, I saw the door open and a pair of shiny black shoes advancing toward me, apparently walking on the ceiling. A man's voice said a single word. Ship? Shit? Shirt? Then a huge face heaved itself into my field of vision like the moon rising in the middle of the day. It was a nice face, but it wasn't one I knew.

"Does anything hurt?" his lips said. A second or so later, the sound broke over me like a sluggish wave. I shook my head, infinitesimally.

"Then is there any part of you that you can't move?"

That would have made me laugh, if I could remember how laughing worked. There wasn't anything I *could* move right then. Maybe a finger, if I tried hard enough.

The guy moved on to a lot of inappropriate touching, feeling my neck and my cheeks, pulling my eyelids down so that he could peer into my eyes, finally opening my mouth and looking down my throat with the aid of a flashlight: not a doctor's flashlight, either—a Maglite about a foot and a half long that he must have found under Pen's sink or somewhere similarly insalubrious.

"Fuck you," I said. Or tried to say: maybe I didn't manage it, because he didn't react in any way or even seem to hear me. He went away and came back again, once or perhaps a couple of times. Then he put a bag down on the carpet next to me, leaned in close again.

"Do you have any recent injuries?" he asked me. "Wounds, I mean? Wounds that might still be open?"

Well, this was covered under doctor-patient privilege, so it was okay to talk. But my teeth were clenched together and they wouldn't separate. Coming through, coming through, I thought, coherent sentence coming through. But they didn't fall for the bluff, and nothing at all happened. I managed to roll my eyes in the direction of my shoulder: a minimalist clue, but he seemed to get it. He pulled my coat open, undid the top three buttons on my shirt, and peeled it back. He nodded at what he saw there.

"You've got an infection," he said, a whistling echo to his voice sounding like a cheap guitar effect. "I'm going to—"

His voice became a ribbon in the air, a flick of motion traveling from one end of it to the other like the crack of a whip seen in fascinating slow motion. When it got to the farther end, it fell off into absolute silence.

———

I half-woke with a mouth so dry it felt like it was full of panel pins. I tried to speak, and something cold and wet was pressed to my face. I was able to put my tongue to it and get some moisture. The pain faded a little, and I faded right along with it.

The next thing I was aware of was "Colonel Bogey March" playing on someone's car horn. Who invented that story about Hitler's ball? I wondered dreamily. Alternatively, who got in close enough to count?

Then memory poured in on me from all directions at once and I sat up as abruptly as if I was spring-loaded. I was in my own room, lying in my own bed, and the window was open. Alarmingly, dislocatingly, it was evening outside.

"Fuck!" I croaked. "Fuck fuck fuck fuck fuck!"

I threw off the covers, discovering in the process that I was naked and slick with cold sweat. My fever had broken while I slept, and now I felt weak but relatively clearheaded. Clearheaded enough to remember . . . something. Some revelation that had loomed out of the fog of my malfunctioning brain and caught me in its headlights just before I collapsed. But not cool enough to remember what it was.

Juliet. It was something to do with Juliet, and her plans for tonight. For some reason, I had a feeling—no, a dead, cold conviction—that it wouldn't be a good idea for her to send her spirit into the stones of St. Michael's Church. I wasn't sure why, but I had to be there and I had to stop her.

I found my clothes neatly stacked on the chest of drawers just inside the door, my coat slung over the back of a chair. My mobile was in my pocket, but when I tried to turn it on I realized that it had run out of charge. Occupational hazard for me: I came to the technology late and unconvinced. I turned out every pocket, but there was no sign of Matt's car keys.

I hauled the clothes back on in the order they came to hand. I needed a shower in the worst way, but there was no time. I stumbled down the stairs, my legs still trembling just a little.

The phone was in the kitchen, and so was a short, stocky man with a sizable beer gut. He was sitting at the kitchen table, leafing through a very old magazine, but he closed it and stood up as I came in. He was wearing a brown corduroy jacket that looked slightly frayed, and National Health glasses that did nothing for his florid, pitted face apart from magnify one of the least impressive parts of it. The top of his head was bald, but tufts of hair clung on around his ears like thin scrub on treacherous scree. I gave him a nod, but I had too much on my mind right then for small talk. I picked up the phone on the kitchen wall. The short man watched me dial.

"How are you feeling?" he asked. He had a very faint Scottish accent.

"I'm fine," I said. "Can you give me a moment?"

The communal phone at the refuge rang a couple of dozen times without anybody answering. I was about to give it up when someone finally picked up. "Hello? This is Emma, who are you?" A little girl's voice, with that awkwardly formal telephone manner that some kids pick up from grown-ups without quite knowing how it works.

"My name's Castor," I said. "Can I speak to Juliet? Is she there?"

There was a murmured conversation on the other end of the line, then, "She's gone out," Emma said. "You can leave a message if you like."

"Thanks. The message is that she should call me." I thought that through. No good: I'd be on my way west. "Actually," I said, "the message is that she shouldn't go to church. I'll explain why when I see her."

"I'll pass that message on," Emma piped.

I hung up, and turned belatedly to acknowledge the little man who was still watching me in silence. "Whatever you did to me, it worked," I said. "Thanks."

He shrugged—magnanimously, really, considering that I'd just cold-shouldered him after he'd pulled me back from the brink of—something. I had to go, but I had to know, too. "What was it?" I asked. "What was wrong with me?"

"*Clostridium tetani*, mainly," he said.

"*Clostridium*—?"

"You had a bad tetanus infection. You should have kept your booster shots up. Tell me, have you been playing with werewolves lately?"

I hesitated for a second, then nodded. "Why?" I demanded.

"Yeah, I thought so." He scratched his jaw, looking at me like he wanted to examine me some more and maybe write a monograph on me for the *Lancet*. "It's something I saw before once—and it struck me so much I tried to read up on it. The wound on your shoulder was made by some kind of caltrop or throwing star. Whoever threw it at you was a loup-garou, and he'd licked the blade first, got it nice and wet with his saliva.

"You know how the bad guys in spy novels will put a bug on the hero's car, or on the sole of his shoe or somewhere, and then use it to follow him? Well, this is a kind of no-tech version of that: they can smell the pheromones in their own saliva. For miles, according to one study. They could track you across half of London. Of course, they can also infect you with rabies—or HIV. All in all, you probably got off pretty lightly."

That explained a lot—and my feelings must have shown on my face, because the little man hastened to reassure me. "Oh, don't you be worrying about it. I shot you full of vancomycin. There's nothing living inside you now that shouldn't be there. And the povidone-iodine scrubs I used will kill every last trace of pheromone that's still on you. You won't need to be looking over your shoulder. Obviously you should have a blood test at some point to rule out any infections that have a slower progression. But as far as I can tell, you're okay."

I was more concerned with the harm that had already been done. This was how the two loup-garous, Po and Zucker, had found me at the *Thames Collective*, and then again in Kensington Church Street. And on the Hammersmith overpass, too, come to that. The bastards must have been riding on my tail for two whole days. Fortunately, for most of that time I'd been *chasing* my tail, so all they'd got for their trouble was vertigo.

"Thanks," I said again, lamely. "I appreciate it."

He waved the thanks away. "I was doing a favor for a friend," he said.

"For Dr. Forster?"

"Aye, that's right. He would have come himself, if he could. But his time's not his own."

The man's manner changed—became a little tentative and awkward. "This little girl—is there anything I can do to help? Professionally, I mean—as a doctor?"

The question caught me off balance. "What little girl?"

"When I was working on that cut, you were talking about a little girl. And a bloodstain. I couldn't make out a lot of it, but it sounded bad."

Yeah, I thought, with a sinking feeling in my stomach. And it would sound even worse in court. "No," I said brusquely. "You can't help. Whatever the hell she needs now, it isn't a doctor."

He'd come around the table, was standing only a few feet away from me, his brow furrowed with a somber thought. I could tell it wasn't the answer he'd wanted to hear. Was he asking himself if he'd just aided and abetted a child-murderer?

"Look," I said, "the girl is—kind of—a client. You know what I do for a living, right?"

"No. Sorry. I can't say that I do."

"I'm an exorcist. The girl is dead, and I was hired—this sounds crazy, but it's the truth—to find her ghost."

He nodded understandingly, as though that made perfect sense. But then he turned it over in his mind and started finding the rough edges. "Hired by who? Who steals a ghost? Who tries to get one back?"

"Who steals her? Probably her real father. Who tries to get her back, I don't know because they gave me a truckload of bullshit. Maybe some fucking lunatic satanists. But I'm still going to find her, because I think she's in trouble."

The little man gave a humorless laugh. "Worse trouble than being dead, you mean?"

"Yeah." It felt strange saying it, but I knew it was true. I realized I'd known it for a while now—even before Basquiat had shown me how Abbie died. "Worse trouble than being dead."

The doctor digested this in unhappy silence. "Well, I hope it sorts itself out," he said at last, with the look of a man trudging resolutely back into his depth. "You should take it easy with that left arm for a little while. While the muscle's all inflamed like that it's easier to tear."

"I'll do that," I said, and took Matt's car keys out of the fruit bowl where Pen had left them.

"You may still be a bit shaky," the little man said, frowning in concern. "If you feel like you're having trouble controlling the car, you should pull over and take a cab or something."

As far as solicitude went, he was getting just a little bit in my face now. I owed the man plenty, but I've never liked lectures, sermons, or public health notices. "Don't worry about it," I muttered as I headed for the door. "It's my brother's car."

The sky was darkening fast: too fast for spring. It was like a night that should have drained away a long time ago, but had clogged the sinkholes of eternity and now was backing up into the daylight. Either that, or I'd just slept for longer than I thought.

The front doors of St. Michael's were still locked and bolted, and so was the lych-gate. That slowed me down for all of twenty seconds: the gate was more of a decorative feature than an actual barrier, and—weak as I still was—it offered me plenty of handholds. My landing on the graveyard side of the wall was a little bumpy, though, and I fell forward onto my hands, skinning them slightly.

I circled round through the graveyard until I could see the back door of the vestry up ahead of me. It was standing ajar. I walked out into the open, heading toward it, but was stopped before I'd gone ten steps by a breathless chuckle. I froze, looking around for the source of it.

There was a man propped up against the cemetery's farther wall, his head lolling forward on his chest. He had long, lanky hair and he was wearing a stained mac. He looked like a drunk looking for an impromptu urinal on his way home from the boozer, but a second, slightly less cursory glance more or less ruled that out. The stains on the mac were dark, irregular spatters: the dim light didn't allow me to be certain, but they looked like blood. The side of his skull was smashed in, and one of his arms was dangling uselessly, like a pendulum, swinging slightly from left to right as he shifted his balance.

A zombie—and one who'd been taking a lot less care with his mortal remains than Nicky did.

Some suspicion that I couldn't quite explain to myself made me veer in his direction. Maybe I recognized him from somewhere. Maybe I just didn't want to have him at my back as I went into the church.

"You okay there, sport?" I said, conversationally as I approached him. I was rummaging around in my pocket for the myrtle twig, but it wasn't there. I must have left it on the floor at Imelda's, where she'd probably have treated it like a dead rat: dustpan and brush, no direct contact, sterilize afterward.

The man lifted his head to stare at me through the one eye he had left. He grinned, too, although it was difficult to see through the tangled thickets of his beard. Yeah. I had him placed now: he was the guy at the mall, who'd shot Juliet through the chest and who she'd then kicked ass-backward through a plate-glass window. Judging by appearances, it hadn't done him a bit of good.

"When will it come?" the man asked me. His voice was low, and it had a horrible, liquid undertow to it. He grinned, showing shattered teeth like a bamboo pit trap. "When will it be here?"

"Tell me what it is, I'll give you an ETA," I offered. "What is it you're waiting for?"

A shudder went through him. "The thing that ate me," he muttered, his head sagging again. After a long silence he added, as if to himself, "Got to finish . . . Got to finish the job. Can't just . . . eat me and then spit me out."

Torn between pity and nausea, I turned back toward the church door. That was when he came at me.

He was a big man, and he had the advantage over me in weight. He charged into me like a trolley car, ungainly and not even all that fast but pretty much unstoppable. As I fell he came down on top of me, clawing at me with the fingers of his one good hand, laughing deep in his throat as though the whole thing were a huge joke.

I brought my head up fast, ramming it into the bridge of his nose, and I heard the bone snap with a pulpy sound like rotten wood giving way. No blood flowed: he didn't have a heart to pump it with, and it probably wasn't liquid anymore in any case.

He got his fingers around my throat and started to squeeze. His head bowed toward me, his mouth working hard as if he wanted to devour me as well as kill me. The sour stench of his decaying flesh hit me, and my head reeled. Starting to panic now, I rolled to the side and swung a fist up into his stomach as hard as I could. He was too heavy to shift, and he didn't react at all: no functioning nerves, either.

But he only had the one arm that still worked, so my hands were both free. Feeling like a bastard, I groped my way up his face even as my vision started to blur, and put his other eye out with my thumb.

He jerked his head away from me, flailing to fend me off now that it was too late. I brought my knees up to my chest and kicked outward with both legs, sending him flying backward against a gravestone, where he fell in an untidy heap. He clawed weakly at his face, mewling like an animal. Slow spasms passed through his body, and his legs moved alternately as if he thought he was upright and walking. He reminded me of a toy robot I'd had as a kid; a clockwork one, made in Hong Kong, that kept on striding along until it wound down, even if you kicked it over onto its side, even if it wasn't going anywhere.

I got up and staggered toward him, resting my weight against the gravestone so I could lean forward and look at him. If the damage was bad enough, his ghost would let go its hold on his ruined flesh, but it might take a long time. And in the meantime he was trapped in there, blinded, terrified, his immortal spirit still shackled to his half-pulped brain and trying to make it work.

I didn't have any choice. I took out my whistle, my hands shaking, and put it to my lips. Our little tussle among the tombstones had given me a reasonably strong sense of his essence, his "this-ness": enough to get me started. The notes tumbled out into the darkening sky, feeble and tentative but enlivened by an unintentional vibrato. The dead man stared up at me with the sightless holes that had been his eyes. His mouth moved, made a string of incoherent sounds that rumbled beneath my playing as if he was trying to sing along. Then he stopped, and whatever spark was still animating him went out for good.

I went to put the whistle away, but then thought better of it. Holding it clutched in my two hands, ready to play, I crossed the grass toward the vestry door.

It was hanging on one hinge: without Susan Book to unlock it for her, Juliet must have just kicked it open. I stepped inside, the bitter chill closing over me as though I'd stepped through a hanging curtain, invisible but tangible.

The church was dark. Of course it was: light had a tough time of it in here. I hadn't brought a flashlight, but I wasn't sure how much use it would have been in any case.

The heartbeat was clearly audible now: a slowed down loop of sound, lapping insinuatingly against my ears like waves against a rock.

I went forward one step at a time: slowly, slowly, letting my feet slide across the floor rather than lifting them, so I didn't go arse over tip in the dark. The frigid air was absolutely still: the only thing that told me when I'd reached the end of the transept and stepped out into the larger gulf of the nave was a change in the timbre of the echoes my footsteps raised. My arm brushed heavily against something, and there was a reverberating din as the something fell over and unseen objects rolled away across the floor. The table where the votive candles stood. I ignored it and kept on going.

Maybe a dozen steps farther on, the tip of my foot touched something on the floor. I knelt down carefully, explored its outlines gingerly. It was a human body, completely unmoving.

I had to put the whistle away now, though I'd been clutching it like a diver clutches his lifeline. I got my hands underneath the body at shoulder and knee, and hefted it up. I suppose I'd expected Juliet to be heavy, because the impression she makes is so strong: because her physicality is denser and more vivid than anyone else's by an order of magnitude. But then again, her body is made of something other than flesh. In the event, she seemed almost weightless.

As I lifted her, I felt the presence that was living in the stones of the church turn its massive attention toward me. There was no sound; no vibration of any kind in the still air. It acknowledged me without sound, and with a vast, vindictive amusement.

I staggered back the way I'd come, Juliet cradled in my arms. But I lost my way in the dark and walked into a wall. I had to follow the wall along, bumping my shoulder against it every few yards to keep my bearings, until I found the transept going off at right angles. I trod on one of the fallen candles and my foot twisted out from under me, so that I almost fell. The building was throwing everything it had at me, trying to keep me inside while the cold worked on me. My teeth were starting to chatter, and my chest hurt as though I were breathing in icicles.

But I made it to the door and staggered back out into the gathering night. It had felt cold on the way in: now it was like stepping out on a sunny day and feeling the warm breeze on your cheek.

I still didn't feel exactly safe, though: not this close to those spirit-soaked stones. I staggered across the narrow gravel path and laid Juliet down carefully in the deep grass between two graves. I stood there, leaned against one of the gravestones with my head down, breathing raggedly, until the chill left my bones.

She looked different asleep. Still beautiful, but not dangerous. It was a kind of beauty that made me feel hollow and unmanned, as though it were a light shining on my own shabby inadequacy.

"Shit," I muttered bleakly, to the night at large.

I'd finally put it all together, now that it was too late to be of any use. Why I felt like I recognized that fugitive presence I sensed the first time I came here—and then again when I met it in the poor possessed sods at the Whiteleaf mall. The only surprising thing was that I hadn't nailed it down sooner when I was talking to Susan Book, because she was clearly as badly infected as anyone else who'd been in church last Saturday.

It was Asmodeus. This was why he'd suddenly let Rafi out from under, and this was where his other foot had come down.

Juliet had just picked a fight with one of the oldest and baddest bastards in hell. And she'd lost.

Where to now?

Chapter Fourteen

I took Juliet back to Pen's and laid her down in my own bed; I sure as hell wasn't likely to be using it myself for a while. But Pen wasn't happy: she wasn't happy at all.

She'd come back from Rafi's assessment hearing so full of good feelings that she was in danger of overflowing—practically tap-dancing, because Rafi had stayed rational all the way through and made a really good impression on both of the independent doctors. They'd even given Webb a bit of a telling off for trying to delay proceedings.

But when she saw Juliet lying on my bed, death-white like a statue stolen from a mortuary, her mood took a downward plunge.

"That's the thing that tried to kill you."

"Yeah," I admitted. I didn't think Pen had gotten a good look at Juliet's face, since at the time she'd been looking down the sights of a BB gun and firing filed-down rosary beads into her from behind—but I guess once you've seen Juliet, from any angle, the memory tends to stay etched on your brain.

"Fix, she's evil." There was a slight tremor to Pen's voice, which I could well understand. "She's so beautiful, but she . . . everything about her . . . She's like a poisonous snake, that hypnotizes you so you'll stand still while it bites."

"That's exactly what she is," I agreed. "But she doesn't bite anymore, Pen. We laid down some ground rules."

Pen wasn't reassured; it wasn't her physical safety she was mainly worrying about. "She shouldn't be here. This house is a shrine, Fix. You know that. I've worked really hard to make it into a place that chthonic powers will be attracted to. Powers of nature and light. If she stays here, they'll feel the taint. They'll leave, and I may never be able to bring them back."

She was almost in tears. "The powers seem to cope with me okay," I said, getting a little desperate now. "They can't be all that fastidious, can they?"

"They weighed you," Pen said. "You came out all right."

"Well, can they weigh Juliet?"

She hesitated. Pen hates to judge anyone harshly. I could see her fighting against her instincts, and abruptly I felt sick with myself for trying to twist her arm.

"It's okay," I said, hefting that negligible weight in my arms again. "I'll take her someplace else."

But I was pissing in the wind. Back in the car again, driving into the center of town, I racked my brains for a somewhere else that would serve. Juliet was slumped across the backseat, exuding even in her unconscious state a sweet, rank smell that was trying to insinuate itself between my hindbrain and the more refined areas of gray matter, filling my mind with indelible, carnal imagery. Asleep or awake, she was still a Venus flytrap. There was nowhere where she'd be safe.

My brain more or less on automatic as I fought against that smell and against myself, I'd swung west again: not toward Acton but into Paddington. What I had to do there shouldn't take too long; maybe if I just covered Juliet with my coat, she'd go unnoticed until I got back. I didn't have too much choice, anyway. There were so many ticking clocks around, it was getting hard to hear yourself think. The thing in St. Michael's Church was getting stronger; the parishioners were still out there in the night with heads full of poisonous shit; Basquiat was sorting through the red tape so she could arrest me for murder; and the

Anathemata had given me my final warning. The only way out of the box canyon was to keep moving forward as the walls closed in on both sides. Find Dennis Peace, find Abbie Torrington's ghost, and maybe it would all fall into place. Maybe. Otherwise we were all going to hell in an overcrowded handbasket.

I parked as close as I could to Lancaster Gate station without hitting a double yellow; I didn't want the car drawing any attention while I was gone, so it made sense to stay the right side of legal. I walked the rest of the way to Praed Street, and in through the ever-open gates of what used to be the genito-urinary clinic—the pox shop. For the past seven years, though, it had been given over to a more esoteric form of medicine: metamorphic ontology.

Jenna-Jane Mulbridge had coined the term, and then given it currency by hammering on the same drum in about two dozen monographs and three full-length studies—one on the were, one on zombies, and one on ghosts pure and simple. In the end she created the climate she needed in which to thrive, forcing university hospitals up and down the country to open their minds to a set of phenomena that hadn't seemed to be medical at all until she got her hands on them. After all, how can you cure the dead?

How can you cure the dead? Jenna-Jane echoed back. Well, you can't, of course. But if a dead soul is possessing a living host, then it becomes a condition that can be observed and treated. And if a dead soul returns to its own flesh, makes it move again and speak again and think again, then what definition of death are you using and how are you going to make it stick?

As careerist blitzkriegs go, it had paid off in spades. Most of the big hospitals had opened up MO units, and the biggest and best, at Praed Street, went to Jenna-Jane by right of conquest. She knew what to do with it, too. She pulled in all the London exorcists as consultants right from the start, got them to teach her everything they knew, then took it apart and put it together again with such ruthless, incisive intelligence that pretty soon it was us who were learning from her. That was an incredible time: a time when the baseline concepts of a new branch of science were being laid down, at a velocity that prevented anyone from questioning the route map or even from jumping down safely once it got moving.

Most of us started to have doubts about J.J. in the first year, but we stayed on board for quite a while after that. It still seemed like we were doing useful work, even if we were doing it for a self-obsessed, vainglorious fascist. Then, one by one, we began to do the moral sums and see how far they were from adding up. Whether it was for the advancement of science or just for the advancement of Jenna-Jane Mulbridge, some of the things that were being done at Praed Street fell well into the realms of the cruel and unusual, and awoke the scruples of even the most hard-bitten and determinedly unimaginative ghost-hunters.

Rosie Crucis was the straw that crippled my personal camel. It had sounded harmless enough at first. Why were all the risen dead recent? Jenna-Jane had asked. Her own researches had yielded no ghosts whose date of death was earlier than 1935. Testimony from other exorcists could push that back at most another twenty years, to the middle year of the First World War. What of the millions upon millions of ghosts from ages past, who ought to fill the streets of London like an invisible tide?

Once you get to asking questions like that, you start to feel like you need at least half an answer before you'll get a decent night's sleep again. And for Jenna-Jane, it was always a case of learning by doing. She got about a dozen of us together: me, Elaine Vincent, Nemo Praxides, and some other big names flown in from Edinburgh, Paris, Locarno, Christ knows where. She put us all together in a room with nothing except twelve chairs and a table on top of which there was a big cardboard box. When everyone had arrived, she locked the doors and opened the box.

My best guess was a severed head, but it turned out to be a lot less dramatic than that. The box contained a lot of things that were very old without being particularly beautiful: an embroidered fan, on which the colors had bleached out with age to shades of fawn and gray; a handwritten prayer book; a tinted glass bottle that must once have contained perfume; a kerchief with the letter "A" picked out in overelaborate needlepoint; a single page from a letter, without greeting or subscript.

"See what you can do," Jenna-Jane said. And we went to work.

Praxides worked by going into a trance state, so he immediately closed his eyes and dropped off the map. Elaine Vincent used automatic writing: she took out her sketchbook and started to scribble. I took out my whistle; some other guy started to tap the fingers of one hand into the palm of the other, hitting out a faint, complex rhythm. We all did what we normally did when we wanted to raise and bind a ghost.

And there was a ghost there, all right, but there was something odd about how it felt. The trace was both strong and impossibly faint at the same time. Like walking past a curry house and getting a faint whiff of fresh cardamom: you know that if you open the door your senses will be overwhelmed, and that it's only the pungency of the raw spice that's letting it reach you at all through double-skin brickwork and the olfactory static of the street.

We worked on it for a couple of hours, our professional pride very much on the line. At first we couldn't get it into focus, but then we brainstormed some tricks that we'd never have been able to try if we'd been working separately. The guy with the happy-clappy fingers worked up a counterpoint to my tune, and Elaine drew the patterns of sound that we were creating. We fed in and out of each other's talents, creating a cat's cradle of urgent, bullying concentration that opened out from the room in directions we didn't even have concepts for, let alone names.

It worked, too. The ghost rose sluggishly, aimlessly toward us, like a balloon whose string some kid wandering down in Hades had accidentally let slip. We trapped her, turned her round, nailed her down, and spread her out between us like a butterfly on a board of charged air.

She couldn't talk, at first: she learned that later. She'd been dead for so long, sleeping for so long in the gutted house of her own bones, she'd forgotten who she was. She mouthed at us, meaninglessly, terrified and angry in about equal parts. She pulled away, tightening the strings of our will around her so that every movement just tangled her up more irrevocably.

She was so tiny. A grown woman—a mature woman, scarred by disease and more generally by life itself—the size of a ten-year-old girl. It's ludicrous, I know. It was obvious already from the trigger materials J.J. had provided that we'd be dealing with a very old soul. But somehow actually seeing her brought me up against that harder and more painfully than I'd been expecting. I'm not big on religion, and never heard of a god whose company I'd be able to stomach for more than the first half of heaven's cocktail hour, but all the same this felt like blasphemy. Because she was so small and so frail, it also felt very much like torturing a child.

But I couldn't just stop playing. Stopping dead in the middle of a tune is like stepping out of a car that's moving at seventy: a wide range of unpleasant consequences can be taken as a given. So I wound down as smoothly as I could, and everyone else was doing the same thing: landing the mad, terrified, struggling fish into which we'd all dug our separate, several hooks.

Jenna-Jane was ecstatic. She hadn't expected to get such spectacular results on the first try. Before we could sort out how we felt or discuss what we'd just done, she moved in with a second team: not exorcists but psychics and sensitives trawled up just as eclectically and nonjudgmentally as our lot had been. We were elbowed out, because our part of the job was done.

I bailed out of the whole Praed Street project soon after that, and cold-shouldered J.J. when she tried to tempt me back for a repeat performance. Reading between the lines, a lot of the other exorcists who'd been there that day had the same uneasy feelings of guilt and shame afterward. She'd never been able to get that much raw talent together in the same room again, and Rosie Crucis remained a one-off.

The name was J.J.'s private joke, and it played in some way off the real identity of the ghost we'd summoned—while at the same time preventing that identity from being revealed by a casual comment.

That was important, because—to stick with the fishing metaphor—now that Rosie had been landed, J.J. had no intention of throwing her back.

The plan was to allow—or maybe induce—Rosie to possess one of the sensitives, so that her ghost would remain anchored in the living world. J.J. had laid on as expansive a buffet of psychics as she could manage: both genders, every age and race, every school and belief from classical spiritualist to lunatic-fringe millenarian to ascetic Swedenborgian and foam-flecked Blavatskian.

Rosie confounded expectation and went for J.J. herself—lived (for want of a better word) inside her for twenty days and twenty-one nights, by which time J.J. was half-dead from migraine and psychosomatic muscular aches. It was a sweet revenge, if that was what it was, but Rosie didn't know back then who she had to thank for her much-delayed and unexpected resurrection, so it was probably coincidence.

In any case, on the twenty-first day, Rosie allowed herself to be decanted into a young man from Cambridge named Donnie Collett, and that was the start of a running-on-the-spot relay race that still hasn't ended. Volunteers from MO units up and down the country, as well as from philosophy and theology courses at universities who still haven't sussed J.J. out for what she is, sign up for stints of up to a week at a time, channeling Rosie and providing her a fleshly receptacle so that the Praed Street ontologists can continue to push the envelope when it comes to our knowledge of life and death and the points where they hold hands across the wall.

And then there's an entirely different support group: the people who come in to talk to Rosie and keep her mind engaged. Being dead, she can't sleep. The person who's hosting her sleeps, and typically wakes up feeling as refreshed and energized as if they've had a week at a health spa. Rosie herself needs more or less constant mental stimulation; and since J.J. has categorically refused to allow her out of the unit, that stimulation all has to be provided on-site. She watches a lot of DVDs (there's an embargo on live TV), reads a lot of books, and talks endlessly to anyone who'll listen—with a digital recorder on permanent record in the background.

I've been part of that support group, off and on, for a good few years now. Maybe I felt like I needed to apologize for my part in bringing her back up from the dark without asking first, but I also enjoyed her company, and sometimes she made a useful sounding board. Whoever she'd been in life (she claimed not to remember) she'd had a mind like a straight-edge razor. Death had done nothing except rot away the sheath.

But I'd always timed my visits for when Jenna-Jane was away from the unit on one of her lecture tours, or scaring up funds from charities with loosely worded charters. Tonight, I knew from my moles on the inside, she was on-site; so tonight the only way to get to Rosie was to go through J.J.

And the first problem was getting to see her. The place was looking more like a fortress than ever, with an actual guard post now on the main doors where I had to state my business and then wait for authorization to come down from on high. Then as I walked along the hallways, with their familiar smell of long-departed urine, I noticed that there were alarm buttons labeled with short alphanumeric strings. A notice alongside each one reminded all passersby that a failure to observe containment protocols would result in immediate dismissal, and that in the event of a containment breach floating security staff should converge on the site where the alarm was given while all other personnel went directly to their assigned assembly points. It all sounded like the worst of my memories of holidays at Butlins. Even the razor wire was kind of in keeping.

Jenna-Jane was in the smaller of her two offices—the one that overlooked the open-plan work area of the unit the way a signalman's hut overlooks the engine sidings.

As I walked up here, I'd been mulling over how to phrase my request. Not too long ago, I'd just have been able to drop in on Rosie and say hi without any palaver: but then J.J. had caught one of the visitors carrying out messages for Rosie, and she'd tightened up the whole operation by a couple of notches. She had a lot of other prize-winning acts in her freak show now, but Rosie was the first and still the jewel in the crown: a ghost still extant on earth after more than five hundred years. So J.J. watched over all of Rosie's inputs and outputs with a jealous eye that, like Rosie's, never closed.

I knocked on the door, and J.J. looked up from a thick sheaf of papers that she was working through. She gave me a smile—a dazzling, meaningless smile that said she was beside herself with delight to see me. It said that, but it lied through its all too visible teeth.

"Felix," she said warmly, and she stood up and came around the desk. I tried to avoid the pressing of flesh but she wasn't having any of that. She kissed me on the right cheek, and then on the left for good measure, continental style. That meant I got a momentary glimpse through my sixth sense of the snake pit of her mind. It was something I could really have done without right then.

Someone had told me once that her real name was Müller rather than Mulbridge and that she'd been born in the ruins of Essen while the Third Reich was still thrashing itself to pieces in its death throes. If that was true, she had the best imitation of a tweedily harmless, upper-middle-drawer-decayed-minor-aristocracy-but-let's-not-talk-about-it English accent I'd ever heard. Like most things about Jenna-Jane, it was a feint that was designed to bring you in close enough for knife work.

She hadn't changed by a micrometer: still petite, and neat, and agelessly sweet. She had to be about sixty now, but her body seemed to have decided that midforties was a good look for her, and it had held on to it. Her hair was gray, but then it always had been: and on her it seemed less a sign of age than what you see when you scrape the paint off the side of a battleship. And like a battleship, her surface was bland and smooth and impenetrable. She affected a surgical white coat, but underneath it I saw jeans and a plaid shirt. J.J. knew how to stand on ceremony when there was something to be gained from it: the rest of the time she was just good plain folks.

"You never come to see us anymore," she went on, gently reproach-ful. "It must be two years!"

She sat me down, in a way that was impossible to resist, and then went and sat back down again herself on the other side of the desk. She handled nuance like a ninja: the greeting had been friendly and personal, but once I was sitting down this was a formal visit, too, and she could appeal to the book—regretfully, full of apologies—whenever she had to.

"I've dropped in a few times," I said, "but you're never around."

She nodded, still smiling. "Yes, I heard. I was beginning to wonder if you were avoiding me on purpose. But here you are."

Yeah. Here I was.

"So how's it all going?" I asked, on the grounds that "I need to talk to Rosie, so hello and good-bye" might have seemed a little on the abrupt side.

Jenna-Jane shrugged modestly. "The unit's still growing," she said. "We've got a fine faculty now. A lot of genuine highfliers who've gradu-ated from the European schools and come here to find out how it's really done. I don't think you'd recognize the names, because you've never been all that interested in the literature, but believe me when I say there are university proctors in Germany and America who spit when they hear my name."

"I believe you, J.J.," I assured her, meaning it.

She made a sour face.

"Please don't use that nickname, Felix," she said. "You know how I feel about it. So yes, things here are excellent. It's such a strong team now, we've got to the point where they won't be needing me anymore." Her eyes gleamed as she said this: even as a joke, she couldn't quite get that one out without an edge to it. As if she'd ever let go of her little empire without a good sprinkling of blood and hair on the walls.

"On the acquisitions side," she went on smoothly, "we've got three loup-garous—including one who's able to possess and shape insect hosts. The identical twin zombies from Edinburgh are with us now: that was quite a battle, but I was able to prove to the hospital board that we could offer them a higher standard of care. We can also chart their decay molecule by molecule with the CAT imagers, and see how far it follows a parallel course in the two different cadavers."

"Unless the dead rights bill gets through its third reading," I said. I couldn't resist; it was too pat a straight line.

J.J. didn't go for the stick, though. She passed her hand through the air in front of her face, pushing the unwelcome topic effectively to the sidelines. "I know a lot of people in Westminster, Felix," she told me. "There's no way the bill is going to pass. Not in this form, and not in this session. It would be chaos. Oh yes, eventually some measure of legal status will be accorded to the dead. There's already talk of bringing me in as a consultant on the next bill, after this one hits the rocks."

I almost laughed at that. *Could we consult you on this sheep problem, Professor Wolf?* Instead, I said, "So you think it'll be voted out?"

"*Timed* out," said J.J., with just a hint of malevolent satisfaction. "They've only set aside two days for the debate, and there are forty-seven amendments coming down from the Lords. The government won't invoke the Parliament Act for something this contentious, so they'll run out of time and shelve it until the winter session. And then the process will begin again with even less momentum. Trust me, this will run and run. And when they do finally agree on legislation, it will be drafted in a form that allows us to carry on with our work without fear of legal challenges. That, in fact, will be one of the primary desiderata of any act: the government doesn't want anything to tie their hands at this point."

"Which point would that be, Jenna-Jane?"

"The point where the dead have begun to rise in uncountable numbers, and when it's starting to look as though the demons of hell are herding them."

I shrugged. It was a theory, like any other: I'd heard them all in my time. "I thought the demons went wherever they got a whiff of fresh food."

"I know what you think, Felix. We've discussed it on several occasions. You have a dangerous tendency—in my view—to underestimate the potential threat that the dead pose. In the past, that tendency was tempered by your professionalism: your ability to ignore all irrelevant avenues while you were working on a specific task. From what I hear, though, there's been a certain . . . erosion of that quality in recent months."

She was looking at me closely, appraisingly. She paused, as if she expected me to respond to the allegation.

"It's good to know that you're still taking an interest in me," I said blandly.

"Always, Felix. Always."

"Listen, Jenna-Jane." I was trailing the field in the small-talk stakes, so I might as well cut to the chase. "I need to speak to Rosie. There's something I want to ask her about."

J.J.'s eyebrows rose. I knew they did because I saw the crease appear and then fade again on her forehead. The eyebrows themselves were gray, like the hair on her head, and pencil-sliver thin so they couldn't be seen unless you were right up close.

"I'll add you to the roster," she said, mildly.

"I meant tonight."

J.J. smiled a tight, pained smile. "That would be more difficult to arrange. We have a formal booking system now, and the time slots for tonight are entirely filled. Probably the earliest I could fit you in would be in about three or four days' time."

"I just need a couple of minutes. Couldn't you squeeze me in as someone else is clocking off?"

She shook her head with an expression on her face that was indistinguishable from genuine regret. "No, I'm afraid not, Felix," she said. "Everything goes through one of the oversight boards, and I can't preempt their decision. Even for a friend." She paused, frowned for a moment in thought, and I waited for the other shoe to drop. "For a colleague, though," she said, "it would be different. If you had an active and current attachment to the unit, I mean. I could stretch a point then, and be reasonably sure that the board wouldn't smack my hand for it afterwards."

It was a bitter pill to swallow, but then again if all she wanted was a promise I could be every bit as radiantly insincere as she could. "Well, I'm pretty busy right now," I said, "but when I've got an opening, I could maybe come over and do some chores for you."

Jenna-Jane nodded enthusiastically. "Excellent," she said. "There's one thing I'd love to have you do for us."

"What's that?" I was already standing, trying to hustle her on to the next stage in the proceedings, but when it comes to immovable objects and irresistible forces, J.J. can play both ends against the middle.

"You can persuade your friend Rafael Ditko to sign himself into our care."

My face froze, and so did I, halfway between sitting down and standing up. In the end I went for standing up, because it got me a bit of distance from her.

"Sorry," I said. "That one's not on the table."

"Isn't it?" She was all innocent inquiry. "I had a call from Dr. Webb a couple of days ago. He seemed to feel that it might be better for Mr. Ditko to be in an environment that's more directly and intentionally geared toward dealing with the kind of problem that he faces."

"J.J., no offense, but in here Rafi would *be* the problem. You don't distinguish between the carrier wave and the signal."

Jenna-Jane seemed hurt. "That's a rather opaque metaphor, Felix. And it's very far from the truth. I'm aware that Ditko and the demon inside him are two distinct entities. I'm probably more cognizant of what that means than you are, and better able to understand the mechanism by which it works. I would never confuse your friend with the passenger he has the misfortune to carry."

"No? So you wouldn't, for the sake of argument, be tempted to try stabbing Rafi with a pitchfork to see if Asmodeus bleeds?"

Jenna-Jane's disguise is close to being perfect, so there was no sign of anger or frustration on her face. She just shook her head, as if that harsh remark were the latest proof that she was never meant to live in a world as cruel and unfeeling as this.

"My first concern would be Ditko's well-being," she said, solemnly.

"It's not negotiable, Jenna-Jane."

"Then neither is Rosie, Felix. I'll add you to the roster, and you'll get a call within the next few days. Unless, of course, someone on the oversight board has any doubts about your suitability."

"And are you on the oversight board, Jenna-Jane?" I asked.

"Yes. Of course. I'm one of four faculty members, balanced by three—"

I raised my hand to stop the flow. "Thanks," I said. "I get the picture. Give my regards to any of the old gang you still see."

"Of course."

"And fall downstairs and break your neck while you're doing it. The next time I drop in, I'd love to see you in a persistently vegetative state."

"Felix!" I walked out on that tone of reproach—identical to the one I'd walked in on. I didn't want to see the expression that went with it.

What I did see, on my way back to the guard post, was one of those alarm points with its sternly worded notice. It gave me an idea that was hard to resist. I smashed the glass with my elbow and hit the button. A deep, two-tone *whoop* sounded from all sides at once. I kept moving, dredging up my memories of the unit's floor plan. There ought to be a corridor off on my right somewhere up ahead.

There was. Turning into it, I saw a whole lot of people running toward me, some of them in the dark blue uniforms of the security staff. I braced myself, but they ran on past me without giving me so much as a glance. A second wave followed a hundred yards farther on, and then I turned into a short side corridor with just the one door at the end of it.

It was locked. I hammered on it and yelled "Open up!" as loud as I could over the continued mad-cow mooing of the alarm. There was the sound of a bolt drawing back, and a surprised face appeared in the gap as the door was pulled open. It was another man in uniform, two inches taller than me and a lot heavier.

"She's got to be moved," I shouted, pointing past him into the ward.

"Moved?" He looked surprised and alarmed. He didn't budge out of my way, though: he wasn't going to buy the bridge without looking over the design sketches. "Where to? What's going on?"

"Out into the yard. There's a fire."

He looked less convinced than ever. "A fire? That's the breach alarm, not the—"

Enough is enough. I brought my knee up into his stomach, and then as he went down I spun on my heel and gave him a roundhouse punch behind the ear that laid him out on the floor. There was a fire extinguisher in a niche to the right of the door. I hooked it out and held it ready in case he got up again, but for now he was in dreamland. I felt a little bad about it, because he was only doing his job, but on the other hand, anyone who sticks around in Jenna-Jane's company on the basis of that excuse has got to be skating on ice so thin you could melt it with your breath.

I pulled him inside and closed the door, after glancing back up the corridor and finding to my relief that it was empty. It wouldn't be for long.

Rosie grinned when she saw me—a lazy, wicked grin.

"Felix Castor," she said. "I had a dream that we were married."

"I'd give you a dog's life, Rosie. I'm not domesticated."

"Ah, but in the dream, I was the man and you were the woman."

"It would still hold. I'd whore around. I know my own weaknesses."

I pulled a chair up next to her bedside. The body she was wearing right now was a new one on me, but that wasn't surprising; like I said, it had been a while. It was a young lad with dark, curly hair and a volcanic spill of acne across his left cheek. He was fully dressed, lying on top of the covers: maybe on some level he was listening in on the conversation, but Rosie was in the driving seat. She usually is.

I reversed the chair so that I could rest my arms on the back of it as I sat. "That's probably where the dream came from," I said, indicating her body with a nod of my head. "You're cross-dressing again, you dirty mare."

Rosie was still grinning: my visit seemed to have really cheered her up. Or maybe it was the bellowing alarms and what she'd seen of the fight at the door. After seven years in this place, she relished anything that was a break from routine. "I like the boys best," she confided to me. "I stroke them, sometimes, to see if I can make their manhoods stand." She sighed wistfully. "But it's like trying to tickle yourself with your own fingers: it never quite works, somehow."

"I wish I'd met you when you had a body, Rosie."

"So do I, my love, so do I. There was treasure there, and I'd have given you a charter to keep all you found."

"Rosie, I set the alarms off so I could have a quick word with you. Jenna-Jane was trying to keep me out."

"The noisome bitch!"

"Couldn't have put it better myself. And the clock is ticking: when she twigs that it was me, which will be in about half a minute, she's going to be in here with all guns blazing."

"You'd better be brief then, Felix."

"I will. I'm looking for another friend of yours—Dennis Peace."

She frowned. "Ah, Dennis," she said. "The wildest of my boys. He'll do himself a mischief someday, if he hasn't already."

"When was he here last, Rosie?"

"A few days ago. Sunday, perhaps, or Monday. He told me that it might be a long while before I saw him again, but that I wasn't to worry. He had things to do. Debts, he said, that had to be paid, and some of them were bad ones that had to be paid with blood rather than with money. But he knew what he was doing, and he was safe."

"Safe where?"

Rosie looked at me strangely, out of the young man's eyes. "What's your interest in knowing, Fix? You're not one of those he needs to pay out, are you? I'd hate for the two of you to fight."

"I'm not looking to fight him," I assured her. "But I do need to talk to him. I'm in almost as much trouble as he is, and my trouble is tied up with his in a lot of complicated ways. Maybe we can help each other. Maybe we'll just swap information and go our separate ways."

She was silent for a long time. "I don't know where he is," she said at last, and my heart sank. Then she held up a finger as if she was asking me to wait. "Not in so many words. But he said—"

There was a loud bang from behind me. Turning my head, I saw Jenna-Jane and three guards standing just inside the doorway. "Remove him," Jenna-Jane snapped, and the guards squared their shoulders as they advanced on me. There was no point in making a fight of it: they would have folded me into a paper plane.

Rosie brought her mouth up close to my ear. "He said he was staying with Mr. Steiner," she whispered quickly, just as their hands clamped down on my shoulders and hauled me backward off the chair. They spun me round to face J.J., who was staring at me with an expression of baffled sadness.

"You've really disappointed me, Felix," she told me.

"J.J.," I said, "you're only saying that to make me feel good."

One of the guards punched me in the stomach to show willing, and as I doubled up on a painful whoof of air, Jenna-Jane chided him as gently as she'd chided me. "No violence," she said. "This is a place of civilized discourse. Just show him out, and bring me the tapes from this session, when they're changed. I want to know what they were talking about. I'm sorry you were disturbed, Rosie."

"It was all rather exciting," said Rosie. "Come again soon, Fix."

"I'm afraid Mr. Castor isn't in our good books anymore. It's not likely he'll be back."

"Count on it, Rosie," I wheezed.

The guards gave me a bit more civilized discourse on the way to the front door, but nothing that would leave any marks.

As I walked, a little shakily, back to the car I played Rosie's words over in my mind. *Staying with Mr. Steiner.* Since Peckham Steiner was dead and buried, while the guy I'd briefly gotten acquainted with on board the *Collective* was definitely alive, that left one intriguing possibility, for which I'd need Nicky's help.

And maybe—you'll have to pardon the expression—I could kill two birds with one stone.

Chapter Fifteen

What do I look like?" Nicky demanded, throwing out his arms indignantly. "A fucking flophouse? Beds for all, extra blankets on
request?"

"It'll just be for a day or two, Nicky. Maybe less than that. She could
just wake up of her own accord, anytime, and walk out of here."

"Take your demon slut somewhere else, Castor. You already fucked
my life up more than enough for one week."

We were in the main auditorium of the cinema, where Nicky keeps
the pump and the generator for his air-conditioning rig. I've never
been able to work out the intricacies of his power-swapping and volt-
laundering, but somehow he manages to keep about a thousand cubic
meters at a well-chilled four degrees Celsius without making a needle
tremble anywhere in the whole national grid. I think there's a hamster
in a wheel somewhere, running its little heart out.

But tonight there was some kind of a hiccup somewhere in the
system, and Nicky was on his back underneath the pump mechanism
tending to its innards with a wrench and an oxyacetylene torch. The
torch looked like a frilled lizard, because Nicky had fitted a reflective
collar to its neck to minimize the heat splashing back against his body
as he worked. He was fresh from Imelda's healing hands, but still—a

degree or two here and there, it all added up in the end in terms of life expectancy. Life-after-death expectancy, I should say.

I tried a different tack. "Look, she can probably afford to pay you. Let's say a hundred a night. I'll get her to settle up as soon as she's awake."

"Yeah? Be cheaper to dangle me off a footbridge by my entrails, wouldn't it? You forget, I did your research for you on this: I know more about how dangerous Ajulutsikael is than you do. Pass me that masking tape."

I kicked it across the floor to within reach of his hand. He fished it up without thanks.

"A hundred and fifty a night," I suggested.

"You're not getting it, are you, Castor? I don't trust her and I don't want her around. I take my physical safety pretty seriously. You think I want some psychotic demon whore waking up grouchy in my guest bedroom?"

"Do you even have a guest bedroom, Nicky?"

"Nope. Good point."

"Maybe she could pay you in information."

"About what, Castor?"

Inspiration sailed past me like a dust mote in the frigid air, and I caught it on the fly. "About what comes next," I said. It was grotesquely manipulative, but I was getting a little tired of the way people kept saying no to me.

Nicky rolled out from under the pump to stare at me with a mixture of definite interest and deep suspicion. "What was that?"

I blew out my cheek, shrugged. "Well, I mean to say, you're good at postponing the inevitable, Nicky—nobody better—but you're gonna drop off the edge sooner or later. Wouldn't you like to know where you're likely to fetch up?"

He found a roll of paper towel, hauled off a length, and started to wipe his soot-stained fingers on it. He kept his eyes on what he was doing, knowing that his poker face isn't all that great. "I'd still be scared she'd rip my balls off and wear them as earrings," he said sourly.

"Do you have a storeroom with a good strong door and a padlock?"

"Yeah. So?"

"So she doesn't need to eat or drink, or use the bathroom. You could just lock her up until I get back."

There was a long silence as Nicky carried on with his ablutions.

"Yeah," he said eventually, sounding as casual as he could. "Okay. On that understanding. You take her down into the basement, lock her up in the film store. You collect her when you're ready. I don't have to touch her or go near her in between. Then after she wakes up we have a talk, with you riding shotgun. I get . . . let's say five questions. With straight answers. And I get to define what a straight answer is. Fair?"

I nodded. "Fair," I said. "I'll go bring her in." I turned and headed back up the aisle.

"Hey, I read where they found the kid's body," Nicky called after me. "So you were right after all—she really was dead the whole time. Should've known better than to call you on a ghost issue. One thing you maybe didn't know, though, because it's in a closed file I hacked into while I was in the neighborhood."

I stopped, stared back down the aisle at him. All the seats had been removed long ago, so neat lines of bolts stretched away from me on all sides like a field sown with scrap iron instead of seeds.

"In *which* neighborhood?" I asked.

"The neighborhood of Mapstack—the Met's internal version of the Interpol's big data exchange system. It's usually worth a look, just for laughs. These people have no idea how the world works—how the little details connect up. They try to draw links between crimes, but they only work in straight lines so they miss it. They miss everything but fucking *methodology*. Like the real criminals—I mean, the ones who are so big you never even see them—can't vary their repertoire."

"Abbie Torrington," I reminded him, derailing that particular paranoid rant before it could get a head of steam up.

Nicky peered out from under the pump, a little truculent at being interrupted. "The body was disturbed after death. Like, about a minute or so after death, when she could still bleed. Someone scraped the back of her neck hard enough to break the skin."

I tried that on for size, although my mind was full of so much shit right then that it was hard to bring it into focus. "You mean, someone drew something *across* her neck? Something with a rough surface?"

"Like that, yeah. All along the back of her neck and up the left side, stopping just under the chin."

A second pass with the knife? Take her head off after stabbing her through the heart? Could be. But then the big man with the machine gun comes stomping in, and bodies are hitting the floor on all sides. So maybe there's no time to finish the job, and all you're left with is a dotted line that says "Cut here."

I shook my head. No. Not like that. One thing you can rely on lunatic satanic cultists to do is to keep their tools sharp. If you're making a human sacrifice, you don't just take a bread knife out of the drawer and hope it's got enough of an edge on it to cut through bone. Your knives are part of a sacrament: so you kiss them and you cuddle them and you stroke them with a whetstone until the edge sings to you.

"Something was pulled *off* her neck," I told Nicky. "Something she was wearing."

"What sort of something?"

"A locket on a chain."

"Would also work. Have to be yanked off with a lot of force, though."

I remembered Dennis Peace's fist smashing through the woodwork on board the *Thames Collective,* an inch from my face.

"Yeah," I said. "It was."

I went and got Juliet from the car, chewing this over on the way. It was a sideways leap of logic—or maybe several parallel leaps—but I had a feeling that I knew at least some of what had gone down. Peace goes to the meeting house on a rescue mission. Somehow he's found out what's going to take place there, and who's going to be involved—possibly by beating it out of Melanie Torrington before he killed her. But he arrives too late. Abbie's already dead.

Too late? Or just in the nick of time?

He aims his gun at the chalk circle on the floor: chews a good third of it to matchwood. Then as the cultists scream and run, or whatever it is they're doing, he goes in and snatches the locket from around Abbie's neck.

If he can't save her body, he can at least save her spirit. But he needs something physical for it to cling to.

I must have been in this game too long, because that all sounded like it made some kind of sense. For an exorcist, used to dealing with things of the spirit as if they were cold, hard facts, there was a naked, inexorable logic to it. Most ghosts have an anchor: they can survive without one, as I'd proved when I cut loose the dead kids at the Charles Stanger clinic and set them free to roam the night. But in the white-hot panic of the moment—the moment of her death—in a strange place, surrounded by strangers, Abbie's soul would cling to something it knew. Peace was good at his job: he knew either how to identify that something or how to influence it.

The rest was just mechanics, because the decision wouldn't take a heartbeat. You wouldn't want your child's soul to stay in the company of the bastards who'd just killed her. And it was always possible that you might be saving her from something worse.

Because the satanists were still looking for Abbie, even though she was dead. Obviously something hadn't quite worked out as planned. Something that had been started needed to be finished—and whatever it was, it was a big enough issue that the Catholic Church had brought its big, excommunicated guns in.

That was as far as I could take it right then. I still felt that I was missing something that was right under my nose, and the something was probably the missing link that tied Rafi and Asmodeus and St. Michael's Church into all this, but I had more immediate fish that needed frying. I carried Juliet down into Nicky's basement under his directions, and into a cupboard the size of an aircraft hangar. It was full of all kinds of stuff that Nicky has acquired over the years: paintings and sculptures, his precious record collection, and for reasons I've never understood (because zombies don't eat) a vast amount of canned food. Maybe he had some idea of using it for barter after some future holocaust.

He spread a couple of blankets on the floor, one on top of the other, and I put her down on top of them as gently as I could. Nicky stared at her, nonplussed.

"I got no hormones anymore, Castor," he told me, in a tone that sounded a little tight and nervy. "Adrenaline, testosterone, dopamine . . . nothing. The relevant organs all stopped pumping."

"I know. So?"

"So how come when I look at her I get a hard-on?"

"Magic, I guess. That's the demonic thing she does."

He tossed me the keys, then backed away with his hands cupped protectively over his crotch. "Lock her up," he muttered, and he turned and left.

I knelt down beside Juliet and lowered my head until my mouth was close to her ear. "Hang on in there, Jules," I whispered.

I went out and closed the door. I had to lean my shoulder into it: this cupboard had been the film store, and since old film stock is only slightly less explosive than sweaty gelignite, the walls and door were flame-proof and blast-proof. It was a good place to store Juliet's physical form until the rest of her came back to it; I'd be getting to work on that as soon as I could.

I found Nicky up in the projection booth, taking a pH reading from his plants. I ignored him and crossed to the plan chest where he keeps his maps and books. Being a conspiracy addict, his reference section is better than the British Library's, and I already knew he had a set of 1:1000 maps of London in there. I took out the Ealing-Acton one and spread it out on the chest, sweeping a couple of books and a Newton's cradle desk toy onto the floor.

Nicky jumped up from his kneeling position next to the hydroponic tank and crossed the room at a run. "Hey, Castor!" he protested. "Leave my shit alone."

"I thought we could play a little game, Nicky," I said, positioning the map a little better, so that the section I needed was dead center.

"I'm not in the mood for games. I just had a physiological reaction I haven't had since I died. My prick got a fucking visitation from the other side of the grave—your side—and I'm trying to come down from it. I want you to go now."

I ignored him. I knew once I told him what we were doing, he'd be into it: I just had to sell him the concept.

"Peckham Steiner," I said, "had a big dream about a network of safe houses. Miniature, self-contained fortresses in the hearts of cities, where the living could shelter if the dead ever got their act together and tried to mount a coup."

Nicky was unimpressed. "Steiner was bat-shit crazy," he snapped. He snatched the map off the table and started to roll it up again, with slightly shaky hands. Juliet had clearly gotten to him on a level that scared him very deeply.

" 'The essential element to stop the dead from entering is water,' " I quoted. "You remember that? The letter he sent out to all the borough councils? 'But ramparts of earth and air are also useful,' de da de da, 'to blind their eyes and blunt their forces.' "

"Why are you telling me this?" Nicky shoved the map back into the drawer, slammed it shut. He was scarier now than he'd been when he had the gun pointed at me, because he was less in control of himself.

"Because it's a big joke, right? Everyone laughs about how spectacularly Steiner lost it, and the safe houses are the funniest part. Well here's the punch line: he actually built one. Right here in London."

Nicky's response was immediate and vehement. "My ass," he said, indignantly. "He fucking did not."

"How can you be sure?"

"Because I would've known about it. I know everything that happens in London. When a sparrow farts, I get to hear about it. You're telling me I could've missed something that big?"

"It was disguised as something else," I said.

Nicky glared at me for a long moment, then he opened the drawer and hauled the map out again. He rolled it out across the table with a brusque gesture, and then waved at the expanse of tight brown lines on off-white paper.

"Where?" he demanded.

I shook my head. "Uh-uh. Like I said, this is a game. You have to find it for me."

"So it's just bullshit. You don't know if there's a safe house at all?"

"Dennis Peace is holding on to Abbie Torrington's spirit—probably inside a gold locket that she was wearing when she died. And when I tried to raise Abbie with a tune, the contact died on me. First she was there, then bang, she was gone. I'd never met anything like that before. There's lots of reasons why I might not be able to find a ghost, but I've never had one slip away from me like that after I've already got the sense of it.

"Then I went to Rosie Crucis tonight, before coming out here to you, and she said that Dennis Peace told her he was 'staying with Mr. Steiner.' That reads one way for me, and only one way. He's found Steiner's safe house. Steiner said the house could blind the eyes of the dead. Maybe it can also blindside someone living who's looking for the dead."

"Sounds like a lot of maybes," said Nicky.

"Indulge me, Nicky."

He rolled his eyes, shrugged: the least convincing display of bored nonchalance I'd seen in a while. "Yeah, whatever. Go for it. It's not like I need to be anywhere else. Okay, what do we know?"

I bent over the map. "I played the whistle for Abbie three times," I said, "in three different places. I got a vague sense of direction each time. The first one was here." I found Harlesden on the map, and pointed. "From there, it felt like she was south and west of me. Somewhere out—this way. Then I tried again from Scrubs Lane, and the feeling was just westward. Almost straight out toward the setting sun."

"That's south of west," Nicky corrected me schoolmarmishly.

"And then from the Hammersmith overpass it was definitely a little north of west."

"Ealing. Ealing Broadway. Or Hanger Hill. Or Scotch Common. Or anywhere from West Acton out to fuck knows where."

"'Hallowed ground to all four sides,'" I quoted from memory.

"You know how many churches there are in London, Castor? That's about as much use as saying it's handy for the buses."

"Point taken. But then there are those ramparts of water. I'm guessing that this place will have a high water table, so that the basement at least will extend down into it."

"More likely it's just gonna have some kind of moat."

"A moat's harder to hide, Nicky."

"Maybe he built it into the middle of the Brent Reservoir."

"Maybe. But I think Steiner wanted the safe houses to look a lot like everywhere else from the outside. They were built to withstand a siege, not to invite one."

"Okay." His eyes were darting over the map now. "Gonna stand in its own grounds, anyway, though. Don't see how you could do the ramparts of earth and air on a street of semis."

"Good. And it's not going to be too far out. Steiner saw this as being like the Thames Barrier—it's a service for London, and for Londoners."

"Land rises anyway when you get out too far west," Nicky muttered. "So you'd be having to dig down further to get into the water table. Steiner was a West Londoner himself, wasn't he? From Perivale? And he always said he was gonna retire somewhere out that way."

He fell silent, his hands tracing lines across the map, his expression deepening from a frown of concentration into something more truculent and dogged.

"Think laterally, Nicky. It's going to be something right under our noses."

His right index finger came down hard on Castlebar Hill.

"You're right," he said. "It is. It's the fucking Oriflamme."

For a moment I didn't get it. "But the Oriflamme's in—" I started to say.

"Not that piece-of-shit Goth dive in Soho Square, Castor. The *original* Oriflamme. The one that burned down."

Chapter Sixteen

The Oriflamme had been intended as a museum when it was originally built, and it stood in the most unlikely location you could think of: in the middle of a roundabout on the B455, just off Castlebar Hill. So my readings when I was holding the doll had been pretty damn accurate: southwest from Harlesden, due west—give or take—from Du Cane Road.

But it had closed down as a museum because of the ineluctable laws of supply and demand. Specifically, because demand for a museum that you had to wade through three lanes of speeding London traffic to reach was negligible—the more so because it was a museum of local industry, which meant that most of the exhibits were bullshit adverts for Hoover and Hawker Siddeley in light disguises.

So Peckham Steiner got a bargain, which he passed on to Bourbon Bryant, who gave us—briefly—the Oriflamme. And then it burned to the ground. That was all the history I knew, apart from Nicky's wacky conspiracy theories. But now, walking up through Cleveland Park at two in the morning with nothing but darkness at my back, I kind of wished I'd made it my business to know more.

Dead ahead of me as I crested the top of the hill was the Oriflamme—or rather, the little island of raised ground at the center of the roundabout. The building itself was hidden from view from this angle by a small clump of trees at one edge of the island. As I got closer I could see a sign and the beginning of a path through the trees. The sign said SIR NORMAL TEBBITT MUSEUM OF LOCAL INDUSTRY. Bryant had never had it changed because he thought that was funny, although he never explained the joke to me and I never got it.

I crossed the road, which was deserted at this hour, and started along the path. It was only about ten yards long: a few steps brought me through to the clear space in the center of the island where the ruined shell of the Oriflamme stood. I hadn't been here in years, but now it all came back to me. There was a ring of earth about four feet high all around the building, created by digging out a trench on the inside of the ring. Bryant, or maybe Steiner himself, had had the bottom of the trench paved, the small artificial hill planted with flowers. It had seemed a reasonably clever and artful way of keeping the traffic noise at bay. Now I saw it for what it was: ramparts of earth and air. Nicky had called it on the money. But those ramparts hadn't saved the Oriflamme from the fourth element: like the bad fairy that never got invited to the christening, fire took the place apart.

The building was dark, as I'd expected it to be. If Peace was inside, he certainly wasn't keen to advertise the fact. I walked over to the door, which I couldn't see because the whole front of the building was in deep shadow. The streetlights were on the far side of the trees, and only a faint orange glow penetrated into the central clearing.

There was no door: just a gaping hole in the brickwork. But as I went forward, one step at a time, into the deeper darkness within, my hands touched something cold and smooth and slightly damp at chest height. I explored it gingerly, finding that it extended both up and down, and out to both sides. It was a plastic curtain, suspended over the doorway to keep out the wind. Wet with early-morning condensation, it had an unpleasant, clammy feel.

If I pushed through it, I'd be announcing my arrival to anyone who was inside. Given the way Peace had reacted to my presence on board the *Collective*, and his promise about what would happen the next time we met, that didn't seem like such a great idea.

I circled the building instead, looking for another way in. I had to watch my footing; in the aftermath of the fire, all that was left of the interior fixtures and fittings had been hauled out and dumped wherever there was room, and fly-tippers had added to the mess since, so the shell of the Oriflamme now had an additional rampart of rusting ironwork and rotting mattresses.

That worked in my favor, though, because as I went around to the back of the building I saw a possible way in. The rubbish was thickest and deepest here, piled against the wall to a height of ten feet or so—and at its apex it came to within spitting distance of an upstairs window, which like the front door had blown out and was now open to the night in a slack-jawed yawn. The only question was whether the mound of black bin bags, old fridges, and wheelless bike frames would take my weight.

I climbed onto the lower margins of the scree, carefully, wishing I'd brought a flashlight so I could see what I was stepping in. The bin bags gave and squished under me, but they didn't slide and I was able to keep my balance. Step by step, very slowly, and sideways on so that I could anchor myself on my trailing leg, I ascended the slope. There was a nasty moment halfway up when the whole mass settled a few inches under my weight and I almost slipped. But by that time I was close enough to the wall of the building to lean forward and rest the palms of my hands against it for a few seconds, until the rubbish mountain found a new point of equilibrium.

After that, I made it to the top without incident, sat on the windowsill and swung my legs over it one at a time. I was in.

I was about to step down off the sill into the pitch-black room beyond, but natural caution made me lower one leg first to test the ground. This turned out to be a wise precaution, because there wasn't any. The floor of the room must have collapsed during the blaze, so there was nothing underneath me but a twelve-foot drop back down to the ground floor and probably a broken ankle or two.

I sat on the sill and let my eyes adjust to the dark. It wasn't absolute, of course: on this higher level, more of the light from the street lamps made it through the foliage, and the interior of the room was lit up, after a minute or so, by a faint wash of orange light. It was enough to show me that the beams had survived when the floorboards gave in. I could tightrope walk along a beam to the door and see whether or not there were any stairs.

It still wasn't a pleasant prospect, but I didn't have any better ideas. Lowering my weight onto a beam that led directly across to the door, I tentatively let go of the sill with my hands and found my balance. This expedition was turning into a laugh riot.

The room wasn't big: three steps would bring me to the open doorway and the deeper darkness beyond. I took the first one okay, and the second. The third became problematic because the beam gave an audible crack under me and shifted slightly. I abandoned plan A and dived for the door, catching it in a tight embrace just as the beam sagged and parted, sending a clattering storm of sooty fragments into the void beneath.

There were no floorboards on the other side of the doorway either, so I was hugging a fat beam, charred in the middle but seemingly sound, while my legs dangled into emptiness.

"You can let go," said a gruff voice from down there. "There's a cement floor about eight feet underneath you. So long as you land on your feet, you should do okay. Throw your weight wrong and you'll bust a leg at best, but I guess that's the price you pay for breaking and entering."

"Think—you could manage—a stirrup?" I panted, slightly winded.

The voice gave a sound between a snort of laughter and a throat-clearing hack. "I think you better do as you're told," it said. "If you just dangle there like a Chinese lantern, I'm going to put some holes in you so the light shows through better."

"What light?" I ground out, still holding on tight.

The voice sighed, long and deep and slightly ragged. Then a second voice that raised the hairs on the back of my neck said, "Give him some light, Dad." It was a little girl's voice, distant and faint but perfectly clear. Abbie's voice. I craned my head sideways to see over my hunched shoulder, but it was still too dark to make out anything in the room below.

Something scratched against something else, and a neon line wrote itself across the dark, blossoming abruptly into the flare of a match. The light dipped, guttered, twinned itself momentarily into two yellow-white eyes. Then, as the candle caught and spread a meager glow across the scene, Peace flicked the match away. It died as it fell.

He was lying on the ground a few feet to my left, a blanket spread over him. And he was pointing that fucking handgun straight at me. Maybe the candle illuminated one or two other details of the room below me, but for some reason the gun was the thing that drew my attention.

"Drop," Peace suggested again. "I'm running out of patience here."

I dropped, more or less straight, and managed to keep my balance when I hit the ground. The gun stayed with me all the way: at least, I assume it did. Either way it was pointing directly at my chest when I straightened up and turned to look at Peace again.

He looked as though he'd fared badly since we met on board the *Collective.* There was a ragged wound across his face, from his left temple down across the bridge of his nose to his right cheek: a heraldic bend sinister drawn in red so deep that in this light it might as well be black. The rest of his face around that dark line was as white as milk. The hand that held the gun seemed to tremble slightly, as if it was hard work for him to keep it aimed straight.

Abbie stood behind him, almost lost in the shadows. She was little more than a shadow herself, the candlelight shining through her to highlight the rough texture of the brick wall in grainy lines of white and soot black. She stared at me with curiosity—but calmly, without any trace of fear. Given how she'd died, that was impressive: a lot of ghosts never tear themselves free from the emotions they were feeling when they crossed over. The moment of their death becomes their destiny and their eternal rest. Or lack of it.

Because I was looking for it, I saw the glint of gold on Peace's wrist.

I couldn't make out the shape with any clarity, but I knew what it was: he was wearing Abbie's gold locket as a bracelet on his right arm, just as he had been before. He wasn't taking any chances of being separated from her.

The room was a gutted shell, the walls and floor blackened. It was empty apart from the rough bivouac that Peace had set up there: a Calor gas stove, a suitcase, a bucket for a latrine. There was a sour smell in the air, redolent of old sweat and recent pain. Riding over it without hiding it at all was the sweeter scent of sandalwood incense.

I put my hands in the air, fingers spread to show that they were empty.

"You know who hired me?" I said.

"Probably better than you do," Peace answered, his voice hard. He had me on that one.

"I'm not working for them anymore."

The gun and the arm that held it still trembled almost imperceptibly, like a strong branch on a gusty day, but it still stayed pointed at my heart. "That's probably what I'd say," Peace observed, "if I was standing where you're standing. Speaking of which, I think you should sit down. On your hands. On second thought take the coat off first and fling it over by the wall. Don't want you to be pulling any surprises out of there while we're talking."

I shrugged my coat off slowly and unthreateningly; I'd heard enough about Peace's rep by now to believe he meant business. Abbie was watching all this in absolute silence—the kind of silence that only the dead can manage, since they don't breathe and they don't fidget. Her dark gaze was solemn and alert: she was a very unusual ghost. I hoped I'd live long enough to get better acquainted.

"If I was still trying to bring you in," I said, as I lowered the coat to the ground and shoved it away with my foot, "do you think I'd have come alone? That wouldn't make any sense. I'd just tell them I'd found you, claim the fee, and walk away."

"Maybe." Peace's face clenched for a moment in a spasm of pain, which he did his best to hide. "If you were sure you *had* found us. And if you were sure they'd keep their end of whatever deal you've made."

"I don't make deals with demons. Or their working partners."

Peace smiled grimly. "Sorry, friend. On the face of the evidence, that's exactly what you did. Sit down."

Again, I was punctilious about doing exactly what I was told. I was fairly sure by this time that that blanket was hiding something a lot worse than the damage to Peace's face, and I was starting to worry about what he'd do if he felt himself losing consciousness. He certainly wouldn't want to leave me hanging around as an extant threat. That added a certain urgency to the task of talking him around.

"When I asked your connection at the other Oriflamme to pass on a message for me," I said, "I meant it. All I've been looking for is a chance to talk to you."

"Carla? Yeah, that was a cute touch. But by the time she called me I already knew they had an exorcist sniffing after me. I saw you coming, remember? You tried to get a fix on Abbie and I shut you down."

"Three times," I acknowledged. "Nicely done. The second time you almost shoved my brain out of the back of my head. How'd you do that one?"

"We're not swapping recipes," Peace said, grimly. "The way I read this, you're trying to find reasons why I shouldn't kill you. Just to let you know, your score is still on zero."

"Okay," I said. "Well, let me know if any of these make the cut. One, you've been hurt really badly—probably when those two werewolves caught up with you—and you need help. On top of that, I think you've been awake since Saturday night keeping up whatever psychic defenses you've got so no one else will try to find Abbie the way I did; that's why you needed to score the uppers from Carla. Sooner or later you're going to crash, big-time: I'd put my money on sooner. If you don't trust me, you've still got to find someone you do trust—and you've got to do it fast.

"Two, after you tried to use me as a crash mat at the *Collective*, you saw me running interference with the loup-garous. That Jeep that went through the fence, and knocked the big one off his feet, that was me. So how does that square with me being the enemy? The truth is that I started to smell a whole bag of rats as soon as I took this job on: ever since then I've been trying to find out what's really going down."

I paused for breath. He'd kept his poker face on throughout the whole of that recital. I wasn't getting to him.

"Is there a three?" he asked.

"Yeah," I said, "there's a three. You've got a hell of a reputation, Dennis. Everyone says you're a hard man who's done a lot of bad things. Even Bourbon Bryant warned me not to piss you off, and he never has a harsh word to say about anyone." Peace was staring hard at me and I met that stare head-on. "But tell me this," I said, quietly. "Are you really prepared to kill an unarmed man in front of Abbie, and let her watch while he bleeds out? Because if you are, I think I'm all out of cards."

We carried on playing blink-chicken for a moment or two longer, but I had nothing else to say so I let him win: it was Peace's call now. I looked up at the black void beyond the candlelight's meager reach, and waited for him to make it. After a long silence, he lowered his arm and set the gun down on the floor. I glanced at him again. A smile spread slowly across his face: a bleak, strained smile that was painful to look at.

"You've got balls, Castor," he said.

He gave the gun a shove, and it slid across the floor toward me. It didn't get very far: the soot-streaked concrete was too rough and uneven. But it crossed the magical midway point where I'd be able to get to it before he did—assuming he could even move.

I stood up, stepped over the gun, and walked across to him. I squatted down beside him, on the opposite side of the blanket from Abbie, who continued to stare at us both in silence. I felt her solemn, calm attention like a physical pressure on the back of my neck, the light touch of cold fingertips.

Peace stared up into my face, which must have looked a bit sinister lit from below by a single candle.

"You've got a bit of a reputation yourself," he said, letting his head fall back onto the rolled-up jacket he was using as a pillow. "Let's see if you can live up to it." This close up, his face looked a lot paler and a lot more strained; or maybe he was just done with pretending now. There was a sheen of sweat on his forehead and cheek that gleamed dully in the candlelight.

"What happened to you?" I asked.

"What you said. The were-fucks caught up with me again a couple of miles further on—pardon my French, Abbie. I got one of them with a knife: clever little gadget I bought in Algiers, with a chasing of silver up the blade. He won't be doing any ballroom dancing for a while. But I had to get in close to do it, and he—" Peace gestured at his ruined face.

"Is that the worst of it?" I asked.

"No," he muttered. "This is the worst of it. Look away, Abbie."

The ghost of Abbie Torrington shook her head, but it was a protest rather than a refusal. She turned her back on us, her movements once again unaccompanied by the slightest sound. As soon as she was facing the wall, Peace pulled the blanket aside. It was hard, at first, to make out what I was looking at: it looked for a moment like a seventies tank top with a complicated pattern on it. Then I realized that it was his bare flesh; not so bare as all that, though, because his torso was rucked and rutted with half-healed cuts and flaking scabs. The predominant color was furious red, but there was yellow in there, too: some of the wounds had gone massively septic.

"Christ!" I muttered involuntarily.

"Yeah, by all means say a blessing over it. Might even help."

That was wishful thinking, though. Religious nostrums do have some degree of power over demons and the undead, but only when they're wielded by someone who actually believes in them. A prayer from me would be about as much use as one of those little stamps with Jesus on them that they used to give out at Sunday school: the royal mail doesn't accept them, so the message never gets delivered.

"You don't need a blessing," I told Peace. "You need a doctor."

Peace twisted his head away from me to stare at his daughter's ghost. "Abbie," he growled sternly, "don't you be trying to take a peek—it's not a game we're playing here."

Then he looked back at me. "No doctors," he said vehemently, trying to sit up and not quite managing it. "You don't know who you're up against. Any 999 call gets logged—any call to a GP surgery likewise. Even if you could get someone to come out here and ask no questions, he'd still get to know about it and he'd be down on me before you could fill the fucking prescription." There was a brief pause, and then he added as he let his head back down heavily onto the rolled-up jacket, "Pardon my French, Abbie."

He pulled the blanket back up to cover the horrific landscape of his wounds. "You can turn round again now, sweetheart," he muttered, but Abbie seemed not to have heard. Her insubstantial figure, barely edged in the darkness, remained staring away from us into the corner of the room where the shadows were deepest. I didn't want to speculate about what she was seeing there.

I thought about my own infection. That had come from a single cut, and it had laid me out like ten quid's worth of loose change in a sock. It was a miracle that Peace was still conscious at all. It also occurred to me to wonder how it was that the loup-garous hadn't been able to follow his scent the way they'd followed mine. Maybe the faint smell of incense had something to do with that, but I was willing to bet that Peace had ways of blindsiding them just as he'd done to me. He was a foxy bastard, no doubt about it, but now he had his leg in the trap and his options were running out.

"Peace," I said, "you're right about the call-logging, but take it from me that this is going to get worse, not better. I think you'll most likely die if you won't let anyone treat you."

He absorbed that in silence, thinking it through.

"Carla," he muttered at last. "Go and see Carla. Get me some more speed. I'll ride the bastard out." He closed his eyes, and for a moment it looked as though he was sinking into a doze, but then he bared his teeth in a grimace, letting out a long, ragged breath. "No," he said,

"I won't, will I?" The eyes snapped open again, fixed me with a fierce glare. "I can't die, Castor. I can't. If I die, then they'll . . ." He hesitated, his gaze flicking to Abbie and then back to me. "I can't leave her alone."

I nodded. "Okay," I said. "I might be able to get you what you need without going through a hospital or a practice. Can I use my mobile?"

"To call who?" I saw his fists clench: even without the gun, and even in the ravaged state he was in now, he was still a force to be reckoned with. I didn't want to have to argue with him.

"A friend," I said. "A very old friend. My landlady, in fact. Who by a very happy coincidence is currently doing the nasty with a doctor. She's also got healing hands on her own account. Holistic medicine, kind of thing. So this is a two-for-one deal." That phrase made me think of Susan Book—she'd said something similar about Juliet and me—and for a moment I felt a premonitory qualm.

Peace, on the other hand, relaxed slightly as he saw a way of squaring the circle.

"And she can be trusted?"

"Absolutely. She's not even capable of telling a lie. It's against her religion."

"God-botherer?" Peace's lip curled back in distaste, and he waved a hand over his midriff to indicate what the blanket now hid. "Those fucking Catholics did this to me."

"No, Pen's sort of a religion of one these days," I said. "Believe me, she's not going to shop you to the Anathemata."

He gave a very faint nod, surrendering the point as though he was too weak to hammer it out anymore. "All right," he said, "call her. But tell her to make sure nobody follows her. If she's that close to you, they could be watching her, too."

I called Pen at home. The phone rang six times, and then the answering machine kicked in. "Hi, this is Pamela Bruckner. I can't come to the phone right now . . ." Pen picked up as the message was still playing, to my great relief. "Hello?" she said, her voice sounding fuzzy with sleep.

"Pen, it's me. Sorry to wake you, but this is a bit of an emergency."

"Fix? Where are you? It's—"

"Two in the morning. I know, I know. Listen, you remember the state I was in when you found me on the doorstep? Well, I'm with someone else who's had a bigger dose of the same thing, and he's in a really bad way. Did that little Scottish guy leave any of those antibiotics lying around?"

"I don't think so. But I can call Dylan. Where are you?"

"Way out west. Call him now and then call me back, okay."

"Okay."

She hung up. Pen gets the point quickly, bless her, and she doesn't waste words. I turned back to Peace. "Do you want me to meet her somewhere else?" I asked. "She can pass the drugs on to me without finding out where you and Abbie are."

"You said she might be able to do some good herself," he reminded me.

"Yeah, I did say that."

"Then let her come."

He closed his eyes again, his breath coming quick and shallow now. He'd been holding on by pure willpower, and it was starting to falter now that he'd put himself in my hands. Not good: not good at all.

I felt a sensation like the epidermal prickling you get with pins and needles, and glanced up to find Abbie's wraithlike form hovering beside me.

"Will my dad be okay?" she asked, her voice touching my ear without stirring the still air.

"I don't know," I admitted. "He's in a bad way. It's not so much the wounds, it's the infection."

"Make him better," Abbie whispered, sounding younger than her fourteen years. She'd never be older now.

"I'll do my best," I said, my own voice barely louder than hers.

The phone rang, smacking me out of unpleasant thoughts. It was Pen. I turned away from Abbie and Peace to take the call.

"Dylan said he'd come himself," she told me. "He's at home—in Pinner. He says he's got some vancomycin there, but he's not giving it away without seeing the patient. So if you tell me where you are, I can tell him and he can come and meet you."

Chinese Whispers is a lousy game at the best of times. Peace had said it was okay to tell Pen: he hadn't given me permission to bring in any third parties.

I glanced around, saw that Peace still had his eyes closed.

"Peace," I called. He didn't respond. I called again, but he seemed to be sleeping. At any rate, his eyes were still closed.

I thought it through, and decided that I didn't have a choice. Without antibiotics, he wasn't going to see the night out. I put the phone back to my ear.

"Okay," I said. "Do you know Castlebar Hill?"

"No."

"Maybe Dylan does. It's almost local for him. Tell him to go to the top of the Uxbridge Road and take a right. Just before you get up to the golf course there's a roundabout. I'm on it."

"On the roundabout?"

"Yeah. It's a big one. You have to park up on one of the side streets and walk in. There's a building—the remains of a building. It burned down a few years back."

"And that's where you are? At two in the morning?"

"Don't start."

"Okay. I've told him it's an emergency. He'll get there as quick as he can."

"We're not going anywhere. Thanks, Pen."

"You can pay me back by telling me the whole story."

"If I survive it, I will."

She hung up again and I pocketed the phone. I sat down on the floor beside Peace, with nothing to do now but wait. The dead girl walked across to stand over me, her feet not quite touching the ground. For ghosts, most things come down to memory and routine. They behave as though they still have flesh but all they've really got is habits. She stared down at her father, himself more dead than alive, and the expression on her face was hard to bear.

"Help's on the way," I said.

Abbie nodded. "I don't want him to die," she whispered. "I don't want anything to hurt him."

All I could do was nod in my turn.

Peace stirred and woke from his shallow sleep, looked up at me in momentary dislocation. Almost he reached for his gun: then he seemed to remember who I was and what was going on. "There's coffee," he muttered thickly, pointing to a small stash of packets and jars up against the wall near the gas burner. "And bottled water."

I made coffee, just for something to do. While the water came slowly to the boil, I went and retrieved my coat from the floor. It wasn't a cold night, but I always prefer to have my whistle where I can get to it in a hurry. Absently, I checked the contents of the pockets, finding everything where it should be—and one anomalous item, which I didn't recognize until I pulled it out into the light: the porcelain head of Abbie's doll, slightly chipped but miraculously still in one piece. I slid it back into the pocket hastily. I didn't know what memories it might provoke for her, and I didn't want to find out right then.

The coffee was instant, of course, but I poured a slug from my hip flask into each of the mugs to sweeten the pill. I brought one over to Peace and put it down on the floor next to him. He nodded a thank-you.

"So what's the story?" I said, sitting down on the suitcase that was the closest thing to a chair I could see.

Peace sighed and shook his head. "No story. Stories make some kind of fucking sense. My life is just . . . things. Things happening. I never knew where I was going." He looked tired and old, although I guessed he only had a couple of years on me.

"I meant about Abbie," I said, bluntly. "She calls you dad. Is that just a figure of speech, or did you really have a part to play in making her?"

He gave me a bleak stare. "What do you think?" he asked, at last.

"I think there's a birth certificate on file in Burkina Faso that shows you fathered a child there. But the record shows that the girl who died last Saturday night in Hendon was the daughter of a man named Stephen Torrington."

"Yeah? Well, you should go ask Stephen Torrington about that. You'll need your whistle, though: he's likely to want a little coaxing before he talks."

"And her mother was a woman named Melanie—but after that it's pick a card any card, because she seems to change her surname the way other people change their underwear."

"When I met her it was Melanie Jeffers."

I was going to let the subject drop, but it might do him good to talk, and it would certainly do me good to listen. "Peace," I said, gently, "I've just spent three days living in a Whitehall farce where every cupboard had a cop, a Catholic, or a lunatic cultist inside it. I could get ten years just for knowing Abbie was dead when the police still thought she was alive. So could you find it in your heart to be a little less terse?"

"It's my life, Castor."

"Mine, too."

We stared at each other again: this time he broke first.

"Yeah," he muttered. "Why not? Give me another shot of that metaxa, first. I hate going back over this shit. I hate the fucker I was when I did this shit."

He seemed to have lost his reservations about swearing in front of Abbie—and she seemed not to have noticed, so maybe it wasn't the first time. I handed him the flask, thinking he was going to top up his coffee. Instead he upended it and drank it dry, then handed it back to me with an appreciative grimace.

"That was rough," he said.

"Didn't seem to slow you down much."

"Rough is what I need right now. Abbie?"

"Yes, Dad?"

"This is your story, too, and you've got a right to hear it. But not all of it. There's a bit in the middle that I'm going to send you to sleep for, because—because it's not the sort of thing a girl your age should be exposed to. Okay?"

The ghost nodded silently. Send her to sleep? I was going to watch that one with keen interest: if Peace could whistle ghosts down as well as up, and do it without risk of exorcising them altogether, he had more control of the fine-tuning than I'd ever had. I remembered the psychic smackdown he'd given me the second time I tried to get a fix on Abbie. I might learn something here—assuming he lived long enough to teach me.

"You've probably heard a lot about me by now," Peace said, "and you can take it for granted that most of it's true. There's worse, too: things that never made it into the legend because I was careful who I talked to. I'm not going into detail, but you know the sort of thing I mean. I was big for my age—bigger at fifteen than most grown men—so I came to a lot of things early and learned a lot of bad habits.

"I'm not making any excuses for myself. I did bad things because I was stupid and immature and I didn't care all that much. Saying I was too young to know any better doesn't make a gram of difference in my book and I don't see why it should in yours."

Peace hesitated, as if he was poised at the brink of a revelation he wasn't quite ready for yet. "I'm not a saint," I told him, by way of speeding things along. "And I'm not your confessor, either."

He nodded, but the silence stretched a little further before he spoke again. "It was like—I went into everything just wanting to know what I could get out of it. Screwed people over in all kinds of ways and never thought about it, because people who can't look out for themselves deserve to get taken. That's just the way the world works.

"I must have been about twelve when I found out I had the gift. For exorcism, I mean. I'd always gambled: horses, dogs, slot machines—

but my favorite game was poker and no one could beat me at it. I'd be sitting at a table with four or five other blokes, and I could look at each one of them in turn, and think—yeah, that's what you've got. You're sitting on a pair of eights, aren't you, betting on another one in the flop. He's got a king high, he's got jacks over threes, and Mr. Cool over there has got sod all, so I can win this.

"But after a while I found out I could do a lot more than that. Instead of just guessing the cards that people were holding, I started to see people as cards—as hands of cards. Live or dead, didn't matter, there was a particular hand of cards that stood for that person in my mind. That's how I bind ghosts—I deal out the right hand of cards, and then I shuffle it back into the deck. Bang. They're gone.

"Like I said, with me everything was a means to an end. I burned ghosts for money, sure—just like I gambled for money. And sometimes if I found a ghost that was still fresh and more or less together, I'd sweat it for what it had left behind when it died that might still be around for me to pick up. Like, what were the numbers on your bank accounts, and is there a little stash of money at home that you salted away against a rainy day and that your missus doesn't know about?"

He looked at me hard, which was probably how I was looking at him. "There wasn't anyone I'd have spared in those days," he said. "Man, woman, or child, I didn't give a fuck. I did it for the cash, because I went through a lot of cash, and I did it for the hell of it. Because I could."

He seemed to expect an answer—maybe outrage or accusation—but after going over this ground with Nicky there wasn't much he could say that would have surprised me. I shrugged. "Okay," I said, "you were a bad man. Maybe the worst. Let's take that as read."

Peace gave a bitter laugh, shook his head. "Give me a break, Castor. I wasn't the worst, not by a million sodding miles. Maybe I kidded myself that I was, but I was a fucking babe in arms compared to some of the people I met.

"Anyway. I went on my travels, didn't I? With the forty-five medium regiment first, and then on my tod. Wanted to see the world. Hadn't even turned twenty and Watford was too hot to hold me. I did Europe, Southeast Asia, the Middle East. Rolled on from place to place with a few bits of kit in a rucksack, living off the people I met up with and doing whatever paid. Worked as a mercenary after I left the army—not for long, though. I found I wasn't quite dirty enough for that game. Then I got in with some gangster types and ran drugs for them for a while, mostly as a mule, occasionally selling.

"That was how I ended up in Ouagadougou. I was making a delivery, and I got rolled. Guy says he's already paid, then when I refuse to hand over he gets a bunch of his mates to beat the crap out of me. So I end up on the street, penniless, and having to keep my head down because the blokes who hired me won't be interested in hearing how I lost the shit—they'll just want their money, which I can't give them because I haven't got it.

"Could've been worse, though. Burkina Faso was the edge of the bloody world in those days—the final frontier. They'd just kicked that crooked bastard Sankara out and nobody knew from one day to the next whether there was going to be another coup or a civil war or what, so people were in the mood to take stupid risks, spend their money now before it stopped being worth anything, and generally let their hair down. My kind of place, in some ways, if you leave aside the fact that everyone was shit-poor and you could get your throat cut if you flashed a dollar bill.

"Ouagadougou was the capital city, but you wouldn't know it. A few blocks of swanky buildings in the center, and then you turn a corner and you're in among the shitty little shanties again. Very strange.

"One night I was in a bar and these three drunken fucks started in on a white woman who was sitting by herself. There was something a bit odd about her: she was very fancily dressed, even for the main drag, and this was the boondocks. Cocktail dress, lots of makeup although she didn't need it. Hair up, and a necklace that was probably worth a couple of years' wages around there. These guys tried to pick her up, and she told them to sod off, so they got nasty.

"I stood up, walked over to help. They weren't nearly as tough as they thought they were, and anyone could see that this woman was very well-heeled: very easy on the eye, too: tall, built, lots of class. Eyes a little cold, maybe, and blue-eyed blondes have never been my thing when all's said and done, but still—I thought if I got in good with this piece of goods, that was another door opening. Might at least get a bed for the night and my leg over, maybe get a lot more.

"But she didn't need my help, as it transpired. Before I ever got to the table, she'd told one of these gents to keep his paws to himself, and he'd responded—being the humorous type—by grabbing hold of her breasts. His mates are roaring with laughter and he's soaking it up, loving it. For about three seconds, give or take. Then the lady took a gun out of her handbag and blew a hole in his throat."

He'd fallen into a slightly dreamy inflection, his eyes unfocused as he stared into a different darkness, a different night a decade and a half gone. Then he pulled himself together and snapped out of it, shaking his head in somber wonder.

"That was your mother, Abbie," he said, looking up at the faint shade of his daughter almost with apology. "That was Mel."

Chapter Seventeen

There was another long silence. Peace issued a shuddering breath that seemed to hurt a lot on its way out. Dead Abbie stared down at him, her eyes dark wells of sorrow and concern.

"Maybe you'd better save the rest of this story for later," I suggested.

He shook his head sharply, just once. "It's weighing on my mind," he muttered. "I think I'll feel happier once I've got it out." He was still looking at Abbie. "Sweetheart," he said, "I'm going to have to send you to sleep for the next part. There's some stuff that . . . that I wouldn't want . . ."

He tailed off into silence, but Abbie was already nodding. "Don't make it too long," she said, her voice sounding as though it was coming from a long way away. "I want to be here with you. In case anything happens."

Peace shifted his weight so he could reach under the blanket. Tension and pain crossed his face in ripples, and his movements were slow and clumsy, but when he drew his hand out again he was holding a deck of cards, tied around with an elastic band. He flicked the band off with his index finger, one-handed, and put the deck down on the floor beside his head.

"This might take a while," he muttered.

I watched him in fascination. So many exorcists use rhythm to do what they do, it's always a bit of a jolt to see someone who bases their technique on some other kind of patterning. I'd never seen anyone use playing cards before.

Peace started to sort through them, still using only his left hand. It seemed to be a regular deck, except that the cards were marked—heavily marked, with different-colored inks and even with paint in a couple of places. There were scribbled words and phrases on most of the cards, along with occasional lines and crosses striking out some of the pips. The face of the queen of hearts had just been ripped out, leaving a roughly circular hole in the card that you could have put the tip of your little finger through.

But it was the three of spades that Peace found and put at the top of the deck—faceup, at first, but then he turned it and tapped it and glared at it hard. When he turned it over again, it was the ace. And Abbie blinked out like a streetlight at sunup.

Peace pocketed the deck again, or at least put it back underneath the blanket.

"Now, Mel," he said, matter-of-factly, "Mel is really bad. Deep down, bred-in-the-bone bad. I'd never met anyone like her before. I have since, but like I said, I was still more of a kid than anything back then. I mean, I thought I was the last word until I met her." He grinned, or maybe he was just showing his teeth. "Bitch has got that whole femme fatale thing going for her. Most men love a really bad girl. At least until she's bad to *them*."

I might have argued with that once. Now it just made me think of Juliet, and I said nothing.

"These guys backed off sharpish. The man she'd shot wasn't dead, amazingly. He had his hands clutched to his throat, trying to stop the blood or at least slow it down, but he still seemed to be able to breathe, so I suppose she must have missed his trachea or whatever it's called. But his feet started to slip and slide and he was obviously about to fall down, so his two mates took a hand each and they dragged him off toward the door. They threw a couple of curses at Mel, but all the fight had gone out of them.

"That was when I noticed that the barman had a copper's nightstick in his hand: not a PC Plod effort, one of the big sidewinders that takes no fucking prisoners. He'd fished it up from some little cubbyhole under the bar, and he was walking up behind Mel with this thing under his shoulder ready to swing it up and over and crack her head open.

"I picked up a beer bottle and let fly. Caught him in the mouth and almost floored him. Then Mel turned around and saw him and she got the drop on him with the gun before he could get his feet under him again and use the stick. She stood up, pressed the gun to the side of his head, and told him to kneel down. She took the stick away from him with her left hand, still holding the gun right up against his temple.

"'You were going to hit me with this?' she said to him. 'Because your friends tried to rape me and I wouldn't play along?' He was babbling something, saying he was sorry or that he didn't want any trouble or whatever. Mel shook her head. No excuses. No mercy.

"She lifted the gun up, away from his skull, and she wagged it in his face like a schoolmistress wagging her finger. Then she brought her other arm back, just about halfway, and swung it down again. Smacked him in the mouth, really hard, with the nightstick. Crack." Peace gestured vividly. "Blood and teeth everywhere. He went down, crying like a baby, clutching his face and rolling away from her across the floor. But she'd had her fun now. She tossed the stick back behind the bar and turned to me as though she'd only just noticed me. 'We'd better get out of here,' she said. 'The police are likely to take his side.'

"But she didn't leave right away. She looked down at the barman again, moaning and whimpering at her feet. She seemed to like that. She gave him a measured kick in the balls, pivoting on her heel so that she was more sort of stamping on him with her heel. I suppose she wouldn't have got much force otherwise, with open-toed shoes.

"Then she led the way, and I followed."

"Was that the night that Abbie was conceived?" I asked, breaking another reflective silence.

Peace shook his head, pulling himself out of the vivid past into the painful present with difficulty. "No. We did spend that night together, but Abbie—that came later. That all came later.

"Mel was staying at the Independence, and she took me back there even though the doorman looked like he were sucking a mouthful of lemons when he saw how I was dressed.

"She was incredible in bed: a little bit scary, even. Not just uninhibited but totally off the fucking leash. She was into bondage—degradation, submission, slave-and-master shit—and she had some games I'd never come up with in my wildest dreams. She was into drugs, too, and we were as high as Kiliman-sodding-jaro as we fucked. I'm not likely to forget that night in a hurry. I wish I could, in a lot of ways.

"I stayed with her for a couple of weeks. Fifteen days, actually, and some odd hours. And I found out a fair bit more about the weird shit she was into. It didn't stop with sex games. In fact, I think the weird sex was a side effect of the other stuff."

"'The other stuff'?" I thought I knew what he meant, I just wanted to check, because it sounded like we might be getting to the point at last.

"Black magic. She was a necromancer. And when she found out I could do the binding and loosing stuff, she couldn't get enough of me. She used to make me raise up ghosts and bring them to watch while we were . . . you know. While we were in bed, or wherever else she chose to do it. She was a natural sensitive, so she could always see them. It used to send her right over the top—infallibly. The kind of orgasms that go into legend."

He closed his eyes for a moment, rubbed them hard with the balls of his hands. His head had fallen back onto the makeshift pillow again, and he looked even paler and more exhausted than before.

"It all got a bit intense," he sighed, with what sounded to me like exquisite understatement. "I mean, it was fun. Most of the time. But she was a bit rich for my blood, all things considered, and I didn't like some of the people she hung out with. There was this one guy especially who used to give me the creeps. Big blond bruiser with these weird violet eyes. His name was Anton, Anton Fanke . . ."

He stopped, seeing my reaction to the name. For a moment, a flicker of suspicion crossed his face. "You know him?" he demanded.

"No," I said. "But I've heard of him. Recently. A friend of mine was looking for information on you, and his name came up."

"Yeah," Peace agreed, grimly. "I'm not surprised. Fanke was something really big and special in the circles Mel moved in. Carried himself like he knew it, too. Fucking arrogant son of a bitch. Charming enough, but you know that sort of charm where it's just another way of fucking you up the arse? Like what matters is being on top the whole time, and if he can't do it one way he'll do it another. You don't want to be there when the charm offensive stops, because you know it's going to be bloody.

"But there was no way past it. Being around Mel meant being around Fanke, too. I thought she was screwing him, too, at first, but I don't think his vices were that close to normal: he was her priest, not her boyfriend, and that was a lot harder to deal with. After two weeks I'd had just about enough."

Peace looked up again and met my gaze, again inviting or defying me to judge him. "So bearing in mind what I've already told you about my MO," he said, with a sarcastic smile, "what do you think I did next?"

I shrugged, took a gulp of my coffee while I gave that one what little thought it deserved. The stuff was half-cold now, but the liquor still had a little bit of a kick to it. "You woke up before she did," I said, "and you cleaned her out. Took that necklace you mentioned, and whatever money you could get your hands on, and did a runner."

Peace nodded. "Got it in one," he acknowledged, his tone a little bleak. "She had almost two thousand dollars, and the jewelry was worth that much again even to one of the fences down on Banfora Street. I took her stash, too. Swiped the lot and scarpered, thinking what a nasty, clever little bastard I am. I get the girl and I get the money, just like James Bond.

"I went back to the scummy little flophouse where I was staying, and turned in for a bit more sleep. I'd never got much of that in Mel's bed. The next thing I know, the police are smashing the door in and I'm under arrest for drug trafficking.

"I never did figure out the ins and outs of that one. Most likely it was coincidence—or the gents I'd been working for getting their own back in a slightly subtler way than I'd have given them credit for. Maybe they'd been watching for me to go back home again, and this was a trap they would have sprung earlier if I hadn't been otherwise engaged. But at the time, it made me wonder. It was so pat: like, I burned her, and I got burned back, twice as bad.

"The cops took all the cash I had on me, so I had nothing left to bribe the judge with. They sent me down for two years. Could have been worse: if I'd been a local lad, I'd probably have been swinging on the end of a rope.

"Didn't matter much in the end, in any case. Mel came down and bought me out before I'd done a week of that time. Probably just as well, because I was already in trouble. The only white boy on the yard, and too stupid to stay out of fights. I'd taken at least one beating every day I was there, and by the time she came to get me I could barely walk."

"Everyone needs a guardian angel," I observed, downing the last of the tepid coffee.

Peace laughed. "Yeah. Everyone does. God forbid you should ever end up with mine."

"You need another drink?" I asked him, because he'd gone quiet again, his face reflecting a parade of mostly unpleasant memories.

"No more booze?"

"No."

"Then don't bother. Where was I?"

"You'd just played your get-out-of-jail-free card."

"Not free, Castor. Nothing like free. I'd already hit the eject button on Mel once, and she wasn't going to let me do it again. Or maybe it was Fanke who set it up, I don't know. Anyway, the way it worked, it wasn't exactly like I got a pardon or anything: it was more like they had me on lease, and Mel made it clear that they could send me back if I didn't mind my manners and say my prayers at bedtime.

"I said she was into slave games. She'd been the slave the first time around. Now it was my turn, and she really went to town. If ever a man was made to eat shit, that man was me."

I opened my mouth to interject a question, then shut it again, better just to assume that that was a metaphor. I looked at my watch. It had been twenty minutes since I called Pen: I reckoned another ten or fifteen before Dylan got here.

"Tell me about Abbie," I suggested to Peace. I was getting a little sick of hearing about his sex life. But I could tell from his expression that he wasn't drawing this out because of any misplaced sense of drama: there was a place in his past that he really didn't want to revisit, and we were almost there.

"I thought Mel was just a sort of weird life-form that lived on sex and pain," he murmured. "I never thought she had any agenda beyond what was happening right there, right then. But I underestimated her. I really did."

He took another tremulous breath. His voice was getting fainter, with a breathy hoarseness around the edges of it that I didn't like at all. "Fanke used to talk about something called a sacrifice farm," he said. "It was an idea he'd put together for himself by reading between the lines in the medieval grimoires. He'd read them all in translation, and then he'd gone back and read them all in the original languages—mostly Latin and high German—and if there was one thing he'd gotten hung up on, it was this idea of sacrifices. I know because I had to listen to it every time Mel had him and her other crazy friends over to play.

"If you're going to make a sacrifice to a god, Fanke said—to any god—then the sacrifice has to be earmarked well in advance and treated differently. It has a special status, and it gets special treatment. It lives apart. Until the time comes.

"He went on and on about this stuff, but I didn't listen. I didn't fucking listen."

Disconcertingly, Peace began to cry. I still couldn't see his eyes: the single candle cast deep shadows, and most of his face was in one of them. But the plane of his cheek was in the light, and I saw the tears following a single, wavering track across his pitted skin.

"So one night," he said, "Mel told me it was my turn to be on top again. And this one was going to be really special. Because this time we were going to make a baby, and we were going to do it in a brand-new way.

"She used the word 'transgressive' a lot. We were going to transgress: we were going to breach the laws of nature. That idea seemed to get her even more excited than having an audience, but when I asked her exactly what we'd be doing, she got all shy.

"There was a lot of crap: a lot of arcane paraphernalia, a lot of chanting. It built up and it built up and it built up, and it didn't seem to be going anywhere. I lost my hard-on somewhere along the way, and I almost dozed off, but she slapped me awake again. That was part of regular foreplay as far as our sex life was concerned. But then she went off-script. She stabbed herself in the stomach, with a poncy little silver dagger that had runes all up the blade, and then she got me to use the wound instead of—going in by the normal route.

"I told her she couldn't get pregnant that way. It wasn't transgressive, it was just stupid and sick. And incredibly messy. She didn't care. She wanted it. She wanted it more than she'd ever wanted anything.

"And as soon as we were finished she staggered over to the door and opened it, and Fanke walked in along with a couple of guys in surgical whites. They hustled Mel away, and he told me I could leave. Just like that. Actually it was more like on your marks, get set, go. He said he'd removed his protection from me. The cops would be looking for me as a bail defaulter, and I'd better sod off out of the country or I'd be finishing out my sentence at the *maison d'arrêt*, without remission."

Peace held up his hand, on which the golden locket glinted dully.

He checked the clasp: a nervous tic that I suddenly realized I'd seen a couple of times before while he spoke.

"So I went," he said flatly. "How are we doing for time, Castor?"

"We've still got a while. Peace, are you telling me that that was how Abbie—?"

I let the question hang. Slowly, he nodded his head.

"I didn't know anything about it then. They fired the starting pistol and I was off. I'm not kidding myself, though: I'd have run even if I'd known Mel was pregnant. I'm not the nurturing type."

There was a hectic energy in his voice now, and his face was strained like canvas on a frame. It was alarming to watch, almost as though he were coming unraveled, using himself up in this cathartic information dump so that he'd reach his own ending at the same time as he ended his story. I tried to call a halt again—for the last time.

"Peace," I said, "I can put the rest together for myself. Get some sleep now, and I'll wake you up when it's time to take your medicine."

"Don't flatter yourself, Castor," Peace muttered, with fierce heat. "You don't know shit. You listen to me, and then you can talk, okay?"

I held up my hands in surrender. "Okay. But I haven't been sitting on my hands, you know. Let me at least tell you what I've got already—you can save yourself some breath and use it elsewhere."

He rolled his eyes impatiently, but I'd already started in. "You found out somewhere along the line that you had a kid," I said. "And maybe you got curious. You tracked Melanie down to New York, and you went out there to visit her. Abbie would have been about eight years old then. You met her, got to know her, and"—I went out on a limb, but it felt like a safe one—"you gave her a gift. That locket."

Peace grunted. "Fucking amazing, Holmes. What was I wearing?"

"I'm guessing that was the first gig you ever walked into that you found it harder to walk out of," I said. "You ended up fighting for Abbie in the courts. You wanted to be her father, and not just on her birth certificate."

I stopped because he was waving his hand backward and forward in an impatient "stop right there" gesture. "I told you you didn't know shit," he said, thickly. "The court case, that was another scam. Mel was still with Fanke, and Fanke was a big wheel by this time. Fucking multimillionaire. He'd set up the First Satanist Church of the Americas—become a guru, like the Maharishi, with tax breaks and limos and all that garbage. And there's him and Mel living together like husband and wife, and bringing up Abbie like she's theirs. I bumped into an old crony somewhere in Rio and got the whole story, and I thought it had to be worth trying to shake them down for some hard cash. That's all she was to me, Castor: a fucking lottery ticket."

"Until you met her."

"Until I met her. Yeah. I didn't realize, but taking out the lawsuit let me in for all kinds of stuff that I couldn't get out of. Depositions, procedural submissions, Christ knows. If I'd seen how much time it was going to eat up I'd never have started it.

"But anyway, as part of all that there had to be meetings. Documented meetings, because you've got to go through the conciliation shit before you can go to court. And there she was, you know? Mel did all the talking, just like always, and Abbie was just sitting there, looking so sad and lost. Looking like she was waiting for a bus on a dark street, and that was where she'd been all her fucking life."

He was staring at me with haunted eyes. No wonder he'd been so flip about the sins of his youth: this was what he really had on his conscience, and it must have almost eaten him alive.

"I started talking to her. Partly because I wanted to see if I could cheer her up, partly because it seemed to piss Mel off. I bought her the locket, and a couple of other things, and I told her some bullshit stories about what I did for a living.

"And I started to wonder—if Mel was so fucking cold to her, and if she wasn't even Fanke's kid, then why did they keep her around? Was it just that whole transgression thing? That Mel had managed to turn making a baby into something obscene and sick? Was Abbie a—a trophy? It didn't make any sense.

"And there I was in a strange city, stuck there because of this stupid court case that I didn't even want to win—that I'd only sworn out in

the first place so that Fanke would pay me to make me go away. And
I had all the time in the world, and fuck all to do with it. So I started
to do some digging.

"The Satanist Church is huge over there. They've got their own Web
site, their own bookshops, sodding T-shirts, car stickers, the works.
HONK IF YOU'VE SEEN THE LIGHTBRINGER. Fucking morons. There was
a lot there, but none of it was hard to find.

"The Web site had links to articles that Fanke had written. Speeches
he'd made. It was all in public domain—he wasn't hiding it. He was
still going on about sacrifice farms, and the grimoire tradition, and
why the medieval alchemists got it all wrong. Oh sure, he said, they'd
managed to open up some lines of communication with demons, and
the demons were giving them everything they needed to turn that first
contact into serious, regular trade. Only they kept getting all the details wrong. It was a communication breakdown, according to Fanke.
Demons can speak all the languages that human beings ever spoke, or
ever will speak, but not—you know—fluently. So they were giving out
all this sales talk: you can bring the big boys up from hell, you can be
top dogs in a new world order, and all the rest of it. They were giving
fucking dictation, for God's sake. But these medieval badasses—these
Fausts—they were mostly managing to miss the point.

"They got it all wrong, Fanke said. All the stuff that really mattered,
anyway. And the thing they fucked up worst of all—the most important thing, the engine that the whole thing ran on—was the sacrifice.
Albertus Magnus raved on about rams being without blemish, and
Bruno's got a whole goddamn chapter on whether you carry the beast
in or lead it on a rope, and what color its fleece should be, and what it
should have eaten and what you do with its shit if it shits during the
ceremony, and on and on like some kind of instruction manual translated from Japanese into Latin by a fucking Dutchman. And all the
sense of it—all the meat—that just got lost in translation.

"So this is the gospel according to Fanke, which he posted on the
Internet because Mt. Ararat's a fucking long way away. To raise a major
demon, you need a sacrifice that's been dedicated from birth to the

powers of darkness. From *before* birth. It—she—it's—got to be linked
to hell even in the way it was conceived. Spiritually, and physically—
prepared—designed—" He groped for words.

"Abbie."

"What do you fucking think?" His voice rose in a snarl, but then it
turned into a cough and he folded in on himself, trying to ride out the
spasms in his throat without moving his diaphragm. "Yes, Abbie," he
said when he could speak again, glaring at me with unfocused hatred.
"The bastards brought her into the world just so they could kill her—
at the right time, in the right place, with the right fucking weapon that
Fanke and his mates had said a fucking blessing over and anointed
with holy water and horse piss." He coughed again, and this time he
had to shove his hand against his mouth to keep whatever it was from
coming up.

"Okay," I said, gently—although the anger seeping out of him like
tar from a smoker's sweat was making my skin prickle. "And then
there's another part I can fill in for myself. You lost the case." He nodded, his face still buried in his hands. "And you lost a shedload of
money, because Fanke countersued."

"Only to make me back off," Peace wheezed, wiping his mouth with
the back of his hand. A trail of spittle hung down from his chin but he
seemed not to have noticed it. His voice was a little slurred now. "He
was telling me to go away. Behind the scenes his lawyers offered me
a hundred grand if I signed a waiver saying I gave up any claim to be
considered as Abbie's father. I thought about signing it, too, and then
using some of it to have him bumped off. But multimillionaires make
hard targets. And if I toughed it out, I got one big advantage that they
couldn't take away from me without another long, hard fight.

"Visiting rights, Castor. I got visiting rights.

"It felt different now. I wanted to spend some time with her. I
wanted to make it up to her, because it was my fault she was in this
fucking mess. I'd planted the seed, and then I'd just gone riding off
into the sunset like the Lone bloody Ranger and left her to it. It was

wrong. And even if it was too late to do any good, I had to at least try. Try to put it right again as far as I could.

"I stayed in New York for nearly two years, and I saw her every other weekend courtesy of the U.S. Court of Appeals, second circuit, Judge Harmony Gilpin presiding. They couldn't stop me. They bankrupted me, not that that was hard, dragged me in and out of court on a new docket twice a fucking month, got the cops to roll me on some bullshit harassment charge and bust up my place. But they couldn't stop me.

"I got to know her, and I—she was a good kid. A really good kid. She'd grown up like an animal in a cage. Never even been to school. She was meant to be having private tutors, but it never happened except on paper. There were plenty of grade-school teachers in the Satanist Church, and they were happy to sign anything that Fanke put in front of them. 'Yes, I see this girl three times a week, and I teach her history, brain surgery, and domestic science.' 'Yes, I tutor her in beach volleyball.' I tried to get the whole outfit audited, but the lawyer I had was no good. He was the best my money could buy, but my money was chicken shit. What I could pick up doing were one-shot exorcisms on the black market.

"Fanke had so many lawyers he had to hire a bus. He could have stonewalled me forever—or just arranged with a few friends to have me turned into landfill. But I think he got unhappy about all the publicity. Anyway he just upped sticks one night and pissed off to Europe.

"There was nothing I could do to stop him. Abbie wasn't a ward of the court or anything. In theory I still had my visiting rights, but they weren't worth a whole hell of a lot when I couldn't find out where he was.

"I came back to London, stony broke. The *Thames Collective* took me in, so I had a roof over my head, and then I started building up a stake. Hired a detective to run Fanke to ground and get me his address. He was in Liechtenstein. He'd rented a castle and moved in with the limousines and the flunkies and the whole circus. I went out there, but they wouldn't let me through the door. And before I could get anything legal rolling, they moved again.

"That became a pattern. They never settled anywhere for long enough to let me get a foothold, and after a while they got better at keeping their heads down, so it was harder for me to figure out where they were. I kept the channels open, though. Kept the feelers out. And then just after the New Year—maybe four months ago now—they came to London.

"I'd been doing my homework, Castor. I knew why they hadn't killed her. And I knew why they'd come here. It was all coming together, and I was shit-scared that I wouldn't be able to stop it.

"They had to wait until she had her first period. That was part of Fanke's prescription: out of the grimoires again. 'She will be pure, she will be stained. She will be whole, she will be wounded. She will be woman, she will be child.' That was what he said it meant."

"And London?" Even as I asked the question, the answer hit me. And the only reason I hadn't seen it before was because I was sitting so close to it.

"London was where he was. The demon they wanted to raise. Except that he was half-raised already, because some other shithead had tried it two years back and gotten it wrong, the way Fanke said amateurs always do."

Asmodeus. Peace didn't even need to say it. The last few pieces fell into place as I finally made the connection that my subconscious mind had made two days ago. Yeah, something else *did* happen on Saturday night. Rafi had his episode, as Asmodeus clawed his way up out of the oubliette, yawned, and stretched.

An image came into my mind: of Rafi screaming in agony, his head thrown back, oblivious of everything except whatever it was that was tormenting him.

"You sabotaged them," I said. "You broke the ritual before they finished it."

"Only just," growled Peace, bitterly. "It took me a long time to find out where they were keeping her. And by the time I got to the house it was too late—they'd already taken her. But I caught Mel and some piece of piss who was fronting as her husband. And I got the drop on them."

"Stephen Torrington," I said. "The real Stephen Torrington. He was the guy who owned the house, right? Some English satanist who Fanke was using as a cover?"

"'Was' being the operative word," Peace spat. "I think his head will take more putting together than Humpty fucking Dumpty."

"You killed two people, Peace. It's not a joke."

He scowled at me with something like resentment. "What are you talking about? Him I killed, yeah. Mel—I hit her. I remember hitting her. Because I had to make her tell me where Abbie was. I had to stop the whole thing before it got too far. Maybe she *thought* I was going to kill her, because I must have looked like some kind of a maniac. But I didn't have the stomach for it."

"But—there was a woman's body. Tied up and beaten and then shot in the stomach . . ."

But with a different gun. I suddenly remembered that odd detail from Nicky's summary. With a different gun, and maybe as much as three hours later. That didn't make any sense. Unless . . .

"Did she tell you? What you needed to know?" I asked Peace.

"Yeah. They'd found some old Quaker meeting house in Hendon that was boarded up. It was exactly what they needed: a place where people had prayed, and sung hymns, or whatever it is that Quakers do when they let their hair down. A place where people had worshipped, anyway, because that's one of the ingredients in the shit they do. I left her tied to a chair. If I could've killed her, I would have. I fucking hated her enough to do it. I just—when it came right down to it, I couldn't pull the trigger with her looking at me. I kept thinking about Abbie. Abbie growing inside her. It made me weak."

"Don't beat yourself up," I said grimly. "Fanke finished what you started. When the cops got to the house they found two bodies, a man and a woman, and they ID'd the woman as Melanie Torrington. I think he must have figured out how you got that address, Peace—and I think he didn't like it much. So it was really handy for him that you left her hands tied: meant he didn't have to get into an unseemly scuffle or anything like that."

It also meant that the blonde he'd brought into my office, and then considerately sent away so she didn't have to relive her trauma, hadn't gotten those bruises from Peace. She was beaten up just to serve as a prop and prepare the ground so Fanke could work on my tender feelings.

Peace took the news in dazed silence. It was probably just as well: right then I was full of anger and contempt for him as well as for Fanke. He might have been protecting his daughter, but the pair of them had been dancing this slow, smoochy dance around each other for long enough, and a lot of innocent people had gotten hurt because they were caught in between.

"She deserved to die," Peace said, more to himself than to me. "After all she'd done—"

"Maybe she did," I said, wearily. "Or maybe she was just a bare-arsed bondage freak who Fanke reeled in the same way he did you—because he needed something she had. In her case it was a womb, and an open-minded attitude to sex acts that draw blood. In yours it was functional sperm. For Christ's sake, Peace, have you really gotten it that wrong? Did you think she was your enemy? Because it looks to me like you were both played by an expert." And so was I, I reminded myself. I had no reason to feel smug here: I'd fetched the stick and rolled over and played dead like the best of them.

Peace got angry, and that was a mistake because it started him coughing again and the pain closed down his lines of communication for the best part of a minute while he wheezed and hissed like an overfilled kettle. There was no steam, though: Peace's fires were burning pretty low now.

"She was a vicious, selfish bitch," he said, when he could speak again. "She got exactly what was coming to her. Don't judge me, Castor. And don't try to make me feel fucking guilty, because it won't wash. I'm only sorry I didn't manage to get Fanke."

"Fanke was at the house?"

"At the meeting hall, you moron."

Which brought us full circle, I reckoned. And since he still didn't seem to want to shut up, I might as well check that I was right about the endgame, too. "You got there late," I said. "The ceremony—ritual—whatever they were doing, it was already under way."

"It was already finished. All bar the shouting. Thirty seconds earlier—thirty bastard seconds—and I might've stopped them. If Mel had just told me where she was, instead of lying and squirming and lying some more. And you want me to feel sorry I got her killed? Fuck that. I'm only sorry I didn't top her the first night I met her.

"They were all in costume. Dressed in black, except for Fanke who was all in red and had some kind of a crown on his head. Made him a perfect target, only—only I saw her lying there, in the circle, and I lost it. I just screamed and started shooting. Walked right out into the middle of them—*blam, blam, blam.* If one of them had had sense enough to whack me on the back of the neck with a chalice, or one of their other bits of fucking paraphernalia, that would have been the end of it. But they closed up around Fanke like I was about to take a penalty and he was the goal. Protecting him: making sure I didn't muss his hair with a .45 ACP. And then another bunch came at me from the side: they must have been guarding the front door, or something. So I turned and sprayed them instead.

"I didn't expect to be walking out of there, Castor. And Abbie was dead, so I didn't care what happened so long as I did some serious damage. But right then something else happened, and it was as big a surprise for them as it was for me.

"Something started to appear inside the circle. It—didn't have any shape, at first. It was like a shadow with nothing there to cast it. Like—I dunno, like a shadow in winter, when the sun's low in the sky, because it was enormous and stretched out and sort of distorted. Then it moved and you could see that it had hands—arms. And it started to look darker. More solid.

"The satanists all went crashing down on their knees like someone had sliced through their hamstrings. Hunkered right down with their arms thrown out, shouting gibberish in Latin or Greek or it might have been the *Mickey Mouse Club* theme tune because I honest-to-God wasn't listening.

"I froze. I knew what it was that they were trying to do, but seeing it was something else. It was a demon: Asmodeus, one of the soldiers of hell. One of their fucking generals, in fact. He wasn't really there—not solid, I mean. I could actually see the angle of the wall right through him. And the air currents were moving through him, too, pulling him out of shape. But he was bending down over Abbie with this look on his face like Christmas had come early.

"I had a lightbulb moment, Castor. The words from Fanke's Web site blinked on and off in front of me like I was back in school, spelling out from flash cards. *'Spiritually and physically prepared.'* He needed her soul as well as her body. He was going to—to eat her, to consume her, right there in front of me. I had to stop it. I had to stop it.

"What I did next—I just did it because it felt right. The demon was more like smoke than anything else: you can't shoot smoke. And in any case, you're meant to aim at the base of the fire. So I switched to automatic and I shot the pentagram. I shot their fucking magic circle.

"The Tavor's a bastard on auto. It bucked in my hands and I had to lean down hard on it to keep from being thrown over backward: but I was already so close to the thing, it was like using a pointer on a whiteboard. I swung the gun round in as small an arc as I could manage, given the angle, and a couple of arms of the pentagram got chewed to pieces. I hit a couple more of their guys, too: leg shots, because I was aiming down—and before you ask, no, I don't give a fuck.

"Because it worked. All hell broke loose—no joke intended. The demon opened its mouth and it gave out with a sound I hope I never fucking hear again. Not a sound, exactly: I mean, it didn't scream. It wasn't even loud. But you could feel the pressure on your eardrums, on your goddamn skin, like when a plane hits turbulence and drops a few hundred feet when you're not expecting it. It hurt. It hurt like things were tearing inside you.

"But I was on my feet and the satanists were on their knees. And I knew what I had to do. I ran straight forward—had to jump over one guy who was lying flat on the ground right in my way, holding on to what was left of his kneecap—got to the circle and Abbie was still lying there, blood all over her chest, her eyes wide open. The demon, or the demon's shadow or whatever you want to call it, was writhing around now like a fire hose that someone's let go of, whipping this way and then another way and keeping up that silent screaming all the time.

"I didn't have my deck, and I wouldn't have had time to deal out a hand of cards in any case. All I could do was call her, and hope she came. I took hold of her locket, shouted out her name as loud as I could, shouted 'Come with me!' or something like that, and pulled. I mean, I didn't just yell: I *called* her, the way you do when you're doing it on a job. I was calling her into the locket—at least, into the lock of her hair that was inside the locket. I was making that be the anchor her ghost attached itself to."

He looked at me to make sure I understood. I nodded tersely, as though it were what I'd have done under the circumstances. The truth was, I was having a hard time believing it was even possible. Summoning a ghost into a physical object? Channeling it, as though spirit was water and you could choose which way gravity was going to run? I suppose the hair was a part of Abbie, something she already had a link to, but still . . . In other circumstances, I'd have been asking him for details and taking notes. As it was I let him go on talking, oblivious of my slightly grudging wonder.

"Without the cards, I didn't have any idea if it would work—and the frigging chain was a fair bit thicker than I thought it was: I had to wrap it around my wrist and give it a good hard yank. That did it; it snapped and I ran for the door with the locket in my fist—still holding the gun in my other hand even though it was empty now.

"Just as well I kept it, too, because one of those guys with a bit more presence of mind than his mates tried to come in from the side and shut me down. He got the stock of the Tavor in his face and I kept on going.

"My car was a long way up the street. Theirs were right outside and I didn't have time to spike them. I just ran for it, got to the car, got inside and took off like a cat with pepper up its arse.

"I didn't even know if they were chasing me, at first. Then I saw some headlights behind me, and they didn't move out of my mirror even when I took some reckless, stupid turns. So then I knew they were onto me and I had to shake them.

"The trouble was, the car kept losing power. I was flooring the accelerator and I was actually slowing down. It was as if we were pulling a trailer full of bricks. Or a dead whale, or something. I thought the engine was going to die and leave us stranded on the street for those bastards to pick off.

"I did the only thing I could think of. I turned my lights off and took every turn that came up, making it as hard as I could for them to keep me in sight.

"I was desperate, and I was driving like an idiot. I took a right at the bottom of Scrubs Lane, just by the Scrubs, you know? And it was too tight. I scraped my side against a whole row of parked cars, ripped my bumper clean off, and nearly killed some old guy who was crossing the road. The noise was incredible, and I thought we're cooked now, good and proper.

"But for some reason the engine cleared after that. I got her up to sixty and we belted off west. Got to here, which was where I was aiming for all along. No better place in London to hide a ghost, Castor. As you should know by now."

I didn't answer him. I was putting his story together with what I already knew.

Saturday evening. Bottom of Scrubs Lane. Fifty yards from the doors of St. Michael's, just as evensong was kicking into gear. It sounded like madness, but then, this whole thing was shot through with insanity from start to finish. Peace had interrupted a summoning ritual for a demon. For Asmodeus. The devil worshippers had intended to consume Abbie body and soul, but they hadn't reckoned on her dad stepping in with an assault rifle to throw into the works by way of a wrench. Body and soul: but they'd only gotten one out of two.

And Asmodeus?

Asmodeus had ended up trapped halfway between there and here. One foot in Rafi's soul, one foot in Abbie's. That was the weight that Peace had been dragging behind him as he fled for home. He didn't just have one spirit inside that piece of jewelry, he had two—one minnow and one big bastard of a killer whale. Until he turned the corner and hit the long straight of Du Cane Road. Then—what? I thought I could guess.

If some part of Asmodeus was with them as they fled—was attached to Abbie, or flying behind her through the London night like an invisible kite with no ribbons and no string—then when they shaved that corner the demon would have turned, too. Turned a little more slowly, maybe: and a little more widely. That would have taken him right across the southwestern corner of St. Michael's Church.

Peace dragged Asmodeus over hallowed ground at the exact moment that a religious service was taking place. *I will sing a new song unto the lord my God.* For a demon, it must have been like being hauled through a barbed wire entanglement. No wonder Rafi screamed. No wonder he lashed out and hurt people: he was going through what you could fairly call hell on earth.

And finally Asmodeus got wedged solid—trapped in the stones of the church and in the nets of prayer that were rising up all around him. His link to Abbie was severed, and Peace drove on through the night, picking up speed, leaving an invisible, formless monster from hell embedded in the fabric of St. Michael's like a fossilized mosquito in a lump of amber.

Except that Asmodeus was still far from defunct. His insidious will fell down on the congregation of St. Michael's like black rain, and their souls took the taint.

More innocents in the crossfire. Just like Abbie. Just like Rafi.

I pulled my mind back to the present, tried to recall what Peace had just said.

"Why?" I demanded. "Why did you come here, particularly? What makes this place so special?"

"The ramparts," said Peace, sounding just a little smug even through his pain. "Earth and air you saw, right? Outside? But it's the water that's really clever. That brickwork is double-skin, and there's a hollow space in between the two layers that's lined with lead. It's meant to be filled with water from the mains supply, with a pump to keep it circulating, but there are all sorts of holes in it now so it kept draining away again. Whenever I felt you fishing for Abbie, I turned the pumps on and put up a wall of running water between you and her. And one time I gave you a bit of salt on your tail, too, just by the way."

"I remember," I said, a touch grimly.

Peace managed a weak laugh. "'Set a thief to catch a thief,' yeah? Only it doesn't work unless you get hold of a better thief than the one you're looking for."

"And yet," I reminded him, "here I am."

"Only because someone ratted me out. You didn't find me by looking."

I let that pass. If Peace wanted to have a pissing contest, he could play both sides. In any case, I thought I'd heard a car door slam somewhere out on the road—far enough away that it was on the limit of hearing. Peace didn't seem to have noticed it, though, so maybe I was mistaken.

"I'm going to wake Abbie up," he said. "Unless there's anything else you want to ask me about?"

"No," I said. "I'm good. My bedtime story needs are met."

I turned my back on him, walked to the door, and looked out. Nothing moved in the baleful moonlight. Behind me, there were only the small sounds of Peace dealing out a hand of cards on the bare concrete floor. When I glanced his way again Abbie was back, standing at his side as if she'd never left. I had to admit, grudgingly, that he was as good as he thought he was. They were talking in low murmurs, and I felt a definite reluctance to disturb their privacy.

I stepped out into the dark instead. If I smoked, I'd have lit a cigarette. If I'd had any booze left, I'd have had a drink. As it was there was nothing I could do but wait. I must have been wrong about the car door, because nothing was stirring.

Dr. Feelgood ought to be here by now. Edgy and irritable, I fished out the phone again to call Pen and ask her to hurry him along. This time I noticed what I hadn't before: there were four missed call alerts, all from the same number: Nicky Heath's.

The first and second times, he hadn't left a message. The third time he had. I played it back.

"There's something wrong here, Castor." Nicky's voice, stiff with tension; a prolonged scraping sound in the background as he moved something heavy across the floor. "There's a whole bunch of people outside. They turned up in four cars, and now they're standing around like they're waiting for someone. I do not fucking like this. If it's anything to do with the shit you're involved with, why don't you come over here and deal with it your fucking self, okay? Call me. Fucking call me, okay? Like, now."

My throat suddenly dry, I flicked to the last message.

"This is a siege here, Castor!" Nicky's voice was a yell now, which meant he would have had to work hard to inflate his nonfunctional lungs. "They shot the cameras out. The fucking cameras! I'm blind, you understand me? They could be right outside my door, and I wouldn't—oh shit!"

There was an abrupt *click*, and then the high-pitched, single tone that means "message ends." I dialed Nicky's number with shaking hands. Nothing, for ten or twenty seconds: just silence. With a muttered curse I terminated the call and started to dial again, but before I even finished the area code I heard the sound of footsteps walking down the short path from the road.

I turned in that direction. A figure came into view a second later, stepping out of the shadows and through the narrow opening between the raised earth beds onto the driveway.

"Over here, Dr. Forster," I called, and the figure turned, came forward into the light.

When I got a look at his face, I experienced a momentary lurch of dissociation: then my heart jumped in my chest like a test pilot in crash webbing. I'd never met Dylan Forster, but I knew that face well enough. When I'd first met the guy, only three days before in my office, he'd introduced himself as Stephen Torrington. And now, in a sudden flash of elementary logic, it occurred to me that both of those names were as good as each other because his real name had to be something different again. I also knew now why he'd had to send someone else to look after me when I collapsed at Pen's house; at that point, he couldn't afford for me to see his face.

I thought of Peace's Glock, which was still inside lying on the floor of the Oriflamme. But it wouldn't have mattered even if I could have got to it. The bastard had set this up exactly the way he wanted. He already had a gun in his hand and it was pointing at my chest.

"You want to watch that thing, or it could go off," I said, because I had to say something, had to get some kind of interaction going that might buy me some time while I thought of a way to distract, disarm, and decapitate him.

He shook his head. "It won't be going off just yet," he said, in an almost languid tone. Funny that Pen had never mentioned his soft, half-elided mid-Atlantic accent. The smirk playing across his lips confirmed what I already knew.

"You're Anton Fanke."

He made a mock bow, saluting my way-past-the-eleventh-hour leap of intuitive logic. "If you'd figured that out three days ago," he said, his tone the gentlest of sneers, "I might have been impressed. Check him for weapons."

The last words weren't addressed to me, but past me into the shadows at the side of the building. Three men who must have been standing absolutely still until then stepped out of the darkness, surrounded me, and frisked me with extreme thoroughness. They didn't look like my mental image of satanists: they looked a lot more like my mental image of FBI agents. One of them was carrying a snub-nosed handgun, which he pressed to the base of my neck.

The other two, searching my left- and right-hand sides in rough synchrony, came up with my dagger and whistle respectively. They held them up for Fanke's inspection.

"Now we'll go inside," Fanke said.

I took a step toward him, but the men on either side of me moved in to block me and the gun at my neck pressed a little harder. I knew I'd never get there.

"Why Pen?" I demanded, between my teeth. "What did you need her for?"

"Rafael Ditko was the vessel," said Fanke, throwing out his arm toward the door of the Oriflamme in formal invitation. "I had to get close to him. We had our plan already in place, but if it failed—it might have been necessary to take Ditko from the Stanger clinic and kill him to release Asmodeus's spirit from him. Pamela would have been very useful in that eventuality. As things have turned out though, I think we'll be just fine as we are. Wilkes, you can lead the way. You're just marginally more expendable than Mr. Castor is at this point."

Things were coming apart fast. In desperation, I tensed to jump for Fanke as he walked toward me. He favored me with a glance of amused contempt.

"That would be a mistake," he said in a clipped tone. "I'd like you alive at this point, because you're looking like a pretty good scapegoat, but don't push me."

Caught in his sights and those of the guy behind me, I briefly considered tackling him low and seeing if they both let fly and took each other out. But that wouldn't even work in a Bugs Bunny cartoon.

Fanke was watching me closely, and he saw the moment when I stood down from the fight-or-flight precipice. "Inside," he said again. The man behind me tapped the base of my neck with his gun barrel, and I obediently followed the man he'd called Wilkes back into the Oriflamme. I'd half-hoped that Peace might have caught something of the commotion outside and scraped together some kind of an ambush. No such luck. His head snapped around as he registered the multiple sets of footsteps. As Wilkes stepped to one side of me and the goon with the gun stepped to the other to get a clear line of sight, Peace's

gaze darted to one, then the other, then back to me. By some reflex
he couldn't control, his hand shot up to grasp hold of Abbie's—and
went right through her insubstantial form. Abbie didn't even notice.
She was staring in wordless, silent terror at the strange faces. Or maybe
not so strange to her: she might be recognizing them from five nights
before. She might remember Fanke as the man who'd put a knife into
her heart.

"You bastard, Castor," Peace said, his voice a dead whisper. His second thoughts were better. He reached down and scattered the deck of
cards across the floor. Abbie flickered and then disappeared, her mouth
open to call out to him.

"Don't make this worse than it has to be," I said, and before anyone
could stop me I stepped forward.

My eyes hadn't had any more time to readjust to the deeper darkness inside the Oriflamme than theirs had, but I knew roughly where
Peace's Glock was. I didn't even have to break step: just flick my foot
out a little to the left as if I were intercepting a pass inside the penalty
box, and touch the toe of my shoe to the trigger guard.

I flicked the gun end-over-end through the air, and my aim was
good: wasted afternoons in the old gym at Alsop's Comprehensive
School for Boys, kicking and heading a ball endlessly against the wall,
brought belated and unexpected dividends.

Peace reached up, took the Glock out of the air, and fired without
seeming to aim. The thunder roared directly in my ear, and a body
slammed against a wall just to my right. As it slid to the floor the
thunder sounded again, deafening in this shell of a room with no soft
surfaces to catch and filter the sound. On my left, Fanke jerked as if
stung, then brought his own gun up to return fire. I knocked it out of
his hands with a scything, two-fisted swipe.

Then just as things seemed to be going great, something hard and
heavy and sickeningly solid slammed into the side of my head and my
feet went out from under me.

I tried to get up, only to catch a second glancing blow on the back of
my neck that took what was left of the fight out of me. More exchanges

of thunder, and a shrill, prolonged scream that didn't go in through my deadened ears but took a more direct route to my brain, or maybe to my soul if exorcists have one of those.

It sounded like "Daddy." The word that Abbie had tried to say as she faded out. The world of the dead has very peculiar acoustics.

———

I raged against the dying of the light: flailed in the dark looking for purchase, something for my fuddled wits to cling to.

I came up slowly. Came together, rather, because it felt like my mind was creeping timidly in from front, back, and sides to coalesce as best it could in my skull, which had obviously been dented right out of shape.

I tried to stand up and was hauled up onto my knees without ceremony, even before my eyes had kicked in properly. Blearily I saw a woman's face cross my field of vision, flick a contemptuous glance down at me, keep on going.

A moment later, as I rediscovered the miracle of depth perception, I saw Gary Coldwood heave into view. I opened my mouth to speak, closed it again with a grunt as my forehead and spine lit up with seven shades of agony. I sagged, but was held.

"There's"—I tried again, waving a vague, ineffectual hand toward where Peace ought to be—"injured—needs a doctor."

"You worried about the other guy, Fix?" Coldwood sounded tired and disgusted. A constable appeared beside him with a pair of handcuffs dangling in his hand, which Coldwood took with a nod. "You don't have to be. Looks like you won. The other guy's dead."

Chapter Eighteen

They took me to the Whittington Hospital on Highgate Hill, where I could look out of the window and see the sun setting over Karl Marx's tomb if I wanted to depress myself even more. There's a secure wing there that the Met use for terrorists they shoot up in the course of arrest: bars on the windows, plods on the door, and all the lumpy custard you can eat.

They thought I was in a worse way than I was, because the whack I'd taken to the side of my head had laid it open spectacularly—and the scalp being full of shallow-lying blood vessels, I'd bled like a stuck pig. But when they put me in a wheelchair and took me for a spin down to the radiology department, it turned out there was no concussion worth talking about and no intracranial bleeding. Some people are just born lucky, I guess.

Back up on the secure ward, they wheeled me right past the door to my private room and parked me in the corridor a little farther on, where I was given into the custody of two uniformed cops. I didn't bother to try to get a conversation started: they'd be under orders not to fraternize, and I wouldn't pick up anything worth knowing from them anyway.

Sitting there in one of those hospital gowns that leaves your arse hanging out, I replayed the events of the last few days with bleak self-hatred. Fanke had played me like a fiddle. Obviously he was already in place—having sidled into Pen's comfort zone to keep an eye on Rafi, not on me. But when the shit hit the fan and the second installment of their human sacrifice floated away with the sweet morning dew, he improvised brilliantly.

Or was it more than just an accident that I'd never met him as Dylan Forster? Was he playing the angles even then, keeping me in reserve in case he needed a fall guy at a later stage in the proceedings?

Either way, he'd hired me on to find Peace for two reasons, not one. The first was that he needed someone who knew London, and there was nobody on his squad who'd fit the bill. They might be hard as nails, but they couldn't read the ground: they might take weeks to find Peace, and he needed the job done a whole lot quicker than that.

And the second reason was that he already had enough dead bodies on his hands to constitute a logistical problem. There were the satanists who Peace had gunned down at the sacrifice, which was bad enough, but there were also the Torringtons, stone-cold dead in suburbia, which was worse. Whether he'd killed Melanie himself, as I suspected, or she'd met her demise in some other way, the whole operation must have been starting to look both leakier and more high profile than he would have liked. Why not bring in a third party—someone he could keep discreet tabs on, through Pen, without ever making direct contact himself—to carry the can if things got any worse than they already were?

Stitching me up was on the agenda right from the start: right from before I ever met him.

A clatter of footsteps from farther down the corridor roused me from these painful ruminations on the past into an even more painful present. DS Basquiat, and her cheerful boy sidekick DC Fields, were walking briskly up the corridor toward me. Basquiat had a handbag slung over her shoulder that looked like Prada, and she was carrying a manila file with a white file label that I couldn't read. She nodded to the nearer of the two uniforms, who unlocked the door and held it open while the other one wheeled me inside.

The room was small and bare: just a table, a few chairs, and a wall-mounted shelf on which there was a battered-looking tape recorder. I recognized the setup at once: I've been in police interview rooms before. Never one that's been designed as part of a hospital ward, but it made sense in the context.

Basquiat threw the file she was carrying down onto the table, hung her jacket—black, short-cut, very stylish—on the back of the chair, and sat down. From her bag she took a pen, which she put down next to the file. Fields leaned against the wall, a few feet away from me. The plods withdrew, closing the door behind them.

"Come on," Basquiat said to Fields, a little impatiently. "Lights, camera, action."

He reached out and pressed the button on the tape recorder. "Whittington's secure unit. Interview with Felix Castor," he said, in a declamatory voice. "Conducted by Detective Sergeant Basquiat with Detective Constable Fields in attendance." He glanced down at his watch and added the date and time.

"I want a lawyer," I said. "I won't be saying anything worth hearing until I get one."

Basquiat raised an eyebrow. "You haven't even been charged with anything yet," she said. "Wouldn't you say that's jumping the gun?"

"*Am* I being charged with anything?" I asked her.

"Of course you are, Castor. You're being charged with murder."

"Whose murder?" It was a stupid question, but right then my need to know outweighed my sense of self-preservation.

"Why?" Fields sneered. "Are you losing count?"

Basquiat looked at him, not an angry look, but one that was prolonged until he looked away. The meaning was unambiguous: it was her interview, and his contributions weren't welcome.

"You were found in a burned-out building," she said, her gaze flicking back to me, "in the same room as a dead body. This turned out to be a man known as Dennis Peace—a man whose profession appears to have been the same as yours. Exorcism. He'd been shot in the chest and abdomen. He also bore injuries from an earlier assault of some kind, but it was the chest shot that killed him, even before the stomach wound had a chance to. He choked to death on his own blood."

I bowed my head. I'd hoped Peace might have made it somehow, but it had never seemed very likely. I felt a sour, attenuated grief for him, but the real gut-punch was Abbie. What had Fanke done with her? Had he found the locket? Of course he fucking had. He hadn't crossed half of London and murdered a man in cold blood just to walk away with the real job half-done. He had her. He had her soul. Thanks to me, he had everything he needed now to finish what he'd started.

"We've talked to a few people since then," Basquiat went on briskly. "Former associates and known contacts. Reginald Tang and Gregory Lockyear, also exorcists, who used to share lodgings with Peace, were only too happy to confirm that you'd been looking for the man for the past several days. And that you'd been involved in a fight with him on board a houseboat—the *Thames Collective*. A woman named Carla Rees further claims that you tried to arrange a meeting with Peace, using her as a go-between." She was getting the names out of the file on the table, but now she pushed it away from her slightly and leaned back in her seat. She obviously didn't need cue cards for the next part.

"Of course," she said, "that's all circumstantial. It helps to build up the case, that's all. The main thing is that we've got your fingerprints on the gun and on a lot of other things that were in the room. A kettle. Some mugs. An empty brandy flask. It looks to me like you went in there with some story, got him pissed and off his guard, and then killed him. Is that what happened, Castor? You were looking for a chance at that easy shot in the back, but then you ran out of patience and did him face-to-face like a mensch, yes?"

There was no way I should have answered that question. I've been in the same situation before—although not on a murder charge, admittedly—and I know how the game is played. Basquiat wanted to get some kind of a response out of me, and the more she could needle me the better the odds would be that I'd say something stupid and incriminate myself. But my first instinct—play safe and say nothing—ran aground on one simple, terrible fact. Time was against me. I needed

Basquiat to believe me, or at least to take me seriously. I couldn't afford the luxury of stonewalling her.

"No," I said. "That wasn't what happened. Basquiat, how does your version account for the hits that I took? Someone gave me a couple of good hard smacks from behind, right? While I was shooting Peace in the chest? From in front? What's wrong with this picture?"

Basquiat looked me over cursorily, as if she'd only just noticed the bruising to my face. She shrugged. "Nothing, as far as I can see," she said coldly. "I didn't say you got Peace on the first pass. I assume you fought, you both did some damage, you shot him. He was a big man. He could easily have given you those colors you're wearing."

"Look at them," I invited her, trying to keep the urgency out of my voice. If I started to think about Abbie, and what might be happening right now only a few miles away, I wasn't going to be able to think straight: and then I wasn't going to be able to get out of this. "Those marks weren't made in any barehand fight: I was clubbed with a pistol butt."

"So?"

"So whoever took me down was armed, too. I didn't ambush Peace. There were other people there. I'm betting you must have found tracks outside the Oriflamme too. You know there were other people there."

Basquiat sat back in her seat, turning her pen with the tip of her middle finger for a second or two. Then she clicked the nib out and wrote something terse on the case sheet.

"Peace's prints were on the weapon, too," Basquiat conceded, putting the pen down again. "Come to that, we think we know where and when he bought it. Recently, if you're interested. At the same time as he bought the Tavor that was used at the Hendon Quaker Hall. I've been busy since the last time I saw your ugly face. Busy building a case.

"Bottom line? We think the two of you were neck-deep in whatever was going on in that meeting house. Whether it was a satanic ritual or some kind of a scam doesn't interest me: with your background, and his, it could equally well have been either. But it didn't go down the way it was meant to, and a whole lot of people ended up dead. Including Abbie Torrington, who we now believe was Peace's daughter.

"Peace ran one way and you ran another. You lost touch with him, anyway, and you spent the next few days trying to track him down. You were stupid enough to ask a lot of people a lot of questions, and to use your own name while you were doing it. You couldn't have given us a clearer evidence trail if you'd been trying to—so thanks for that. But if you're asking me whether it worries me that you shot Peace with his own gun, no, it doesn't. Not at all. We found a knife on you, so we're assuming that you went in with the intention of using that—but then a better opportunity presented itself and you took it."

She quirked an eyebrow. "Or did he draw on you first? Was it self-defense? Maybe we can haggle about motive."

I slammed my hand down on the table, making Field move in and loom over me with unspoken but unmistakeable threat. "Fuck!" I said, louder than I intended. "Didn't Reggie Tang tell you that I waded in to help Peace when he was attacked at Thamesmead pier? I wanted to talk to him, not to kill him!"

For the first time, a flicker of something like interest—nothing so strong as doubt, not yet—passed across Basquiat's face. She looked up at Fields.

"Did Tang say anything about that?" she asked him.

"Not a word," said Fields, scornfully.

"Listen to me," I said. "I was approached by a couple who claimed to be Abbie Torrington's parents. They wanted me to—"

"When was this?" Basquiat interrupted.

"Monday. Three days ago. They wanted me to find Abbie. They told me she was already dead, but they said Peace had somehow taken her ghost—her spirit—away from them, and they wanted her back. There are other witnesses to this. A man named Grambas: he runs a kebab house on Craven Park Road. He saw these two even before I did. He gave me their phone number."

"By Monday the Torringtons were dead. They'd been murdered two days before, on the same evening that Abbie died."

"I know that. I think these two were the killers."

"That's funny. I had you and Peace down for that, as well."

"For the love of Christ, Basquiat!" I was starting to lose it now. "Are you going to put me down for Keith Blakelock and Suzie Lamplugh, while you're at it? I didn't have any reason to kill the Torringtons, and you can't even place me there!"

"We're working on that," Basquiat said equably. "We can place Peace, by the way. We've got his prints now. On the bodies themselves, and also on a lot of the stuff that was torn up or thrown around."

"He was looking for Abbie," I said, through my clenched teeth. I had to make Basquiat believe me, and I didn't know how. "But he found out that she was already gone. She'd been taken, I mean—to that meeting house, where she was going to be sacrificed. Peace got the address of the meeting house from Melanie Torrington and he went tearing off there. Either he already had the assault rifle with him or he picked it up on the way."

"Why would he do that?" Fields threw in from over my shoulder, just to show that he was still listening.

"Why do you think?" I snapped back, without sparing him a glance. "Because he knew he was going to be outnumbered about thirty to fucking one, is why. And he left Melanie Torrington alive," I added, groping for nuggets of fact that might make Basquiat at least consider another possible scenario. "She was killed later, right? Later than Steve, I mean. She was murdered by a man named Fanke. Anton Fanke. He killed her because she caved in and told Peace where to find Abbie. He's the one that's really behind all this."

Basquiat blew out her cheek. "And it's this Fanke who killed Abbie?"

"Yes."

"And Peace?"

"Yes!"

"And Suzie Lamplugh?"

I opened my mouth to speak, gave it up. I suddenly saw the hopelessness of the situation. It wasn't even just regulation police-issue blinkers: Basquiat was on a moral crusade. She wanted someone to pay for the murder of Abbie Torrington, and she'd already decided that that somebody was going to be me.

But maybe that was where I needed to insert the lever. If I could make her consider the possibility, just for an instant, that someone else might have killed Abbie, then maybe I could put that same ruthless zeal to work on something positive.

"The second gun," I said, pointing a finger at Basquiat. She didn't like the finger and she nodded to Fields, who took my hand and placed it firmly—a little too firmly, maybe—down on the table. "The gun that killed Melanie Torrington," I repeated, leaning past Fields's unattractive bulk to maintain eye contact with the sergeant.

"What about it?"

"You must have the forensics on it by now. So check it. Check it against the bullets that were sprayed around at the Oriflamme."

"What will that prove?" Basquiat asked, coolly.

"It won't prove a damn thing. But Peace's gun will be a match for the weapon that killed Steve Torrington. I'm betting that the second gun was present at the Oriflamme, and that you'll find bullets on the wall behind Peace. Or maybe in the floor. I just want you to—think about it. That's all. Think about my version of what happened. Okay, you're going to charge me whatever I say. But check the ballistics, and if they pan out ask yourself this: Was I blazing away at Peace with two guns, like some fucking cowboy? Or was someone else involved, both at the Torrington house and when Peace was killed?

"Then if you're in the mood, look up Anton Fanke. Find out if he's in the country on a U.S. passport. He's got Abbie Torrington's ghost, and if you don't do your job, he's going to kill her again—only more so. He's going to kill her soul. That's what's at stake, detective sergeant. So just—think about it."

Basquiat stared at me in silence for a moment or two. I waited. There was nothing else I could do.

"Detective Constable Fields?" she said at last.

"Yes, sergeant?"

"I'm formally charging this man—Felix Castor—with the murder of Dennis Peace. Please read him his rights."

"Yes, sergeant."

Well, it had been a long shot. I wasn't really surprised: just filled with a sick sense of absolute failure and helplessness. Basquiat stood up, busied herself with collecting her things and putting the pen back in her handbag.

"What about my phone call?" I demanded, talking to her back view.

She glanced around, momentarily. "This is a hospital, Castor. They just have one of those payphones on wheels that they trundle around the wards. I'll tell one of the duty constables to watch out for it when it comes this way. You'll get your statutory phone call."

"Think about it," I said again.

That was a bridge too far. She dropped the file, which she'd only just picked up, and spun round to grab a double fistful of the thin fabric of my hospital gown. Her face came up to within a half an inch of mine—which might have been pleasant in some circumstances but was downright threatening right then.

"You don't get to tell me what to do, you son of a bitch," she spat out. "In a perfect world, you'd already be dead. Or there'd be prisons in England like the ones in the States, where you'd get fucked up the arse a couple of dozen times on your first day. There isn't anything that can happen to you that you haven't deserved. Anything. So do not—do not frigging push me any further than you've pushed me already. Or I'll get Fields to hold your head down on the ground while I kick your teeth down your throat."

She walked out before I could think of a snappy comeback. As a matter of fact, I'm still working on it.

———

Back on the secure ward, I counted up my options and got as far as zero.

I was three floors up, and the windows were all barred. The lock on the door was a trifle light as air, if I could improvise a lockpick, but the two boys in blue standing right outside were a different proposition. And even if I could figure a way to get past them, it wasn't going to help me much once the APB went out. I'd be running for my life in a white hospital gown: no shoes, no underwear, no money, and nobody I could turn to for help even if I could get to them on foot.

There had to be another way. And I had to find it fast.

Sometime in the afternoon I hammered on the door and demanded my phone call again. The cop who I was demanding it from looked so bored and vacant it was a mystery what was keeping him awake. He said he'd see what he could do. Half an hour later I repeated the performance, with similar results.

Half an hour after that, Basquiat came back. Without Fields. One of the uniforms unlocked the door and held it open for her and she stepped in, giving him a curt nod. He closed it and locked it again behind her.

I was sitting in the one chair in the room, reading a two-year-old copy of *What Car?* I closed it and threw it on the bed. "Ford are bringing back the Escort," I commented. "That's good news for families with exactly two point four kids."

"Shut up," said Basquiat. "Okay, you were right about the other gun, and I admit that's an odd detail. This guy Fanke? He's meant to be in Belgium, but we can't raise him there. All we get is the runaround from a whole lot of nice-sounding people who say he just left or he's just about to arrive.

"We've also verified that there were at least four other men inside that burnt-out club last night. I'm still working on the assumption that they were all friends of yours—but for the sake of argument, tell me about Anton Fanke. In fifty words or less."

"He's a satanist," I said. "He founded a satanist church over in America. He raised Abbie Torrington to be a human sacrifice, but Peace was the father and when he found out what was going down he objected. Everything else that's happened comes from that."

"Fanke was at the—whatever you called it? The place where we found you?"

"Yeah."

"You and Peace agreed to meet him there?"

"No. He was using me as a sniffer dog." She looked blank, so I dropped the metaphor. "My landlady Pen Bruckner sent him. I called her to ask if she could bring some antibiotics for Peace's wounds. She called Fanke because he was posing as a doctor. Or maybe he is a doctor. Certainly some of his friends seem to be able to lay their hands on prescription drugs without too much trouble. Anyway, he told Pen he'd come along and help, and she bought it. She led Fanke right to us. Or right to Peace, which was what he wanted all along."

"Peace's wounds."

"What?"

"You said you needed medicine for Peace's wounds. How did he get hurt?"

I hesitated. I had her taking me seriously now, at least enough to walk it through, and I didn't want to put too much of a strain on her credulity by talking about Catholic werewolves.

"Some guys set on him outside the *Thames Collective*," I said, evading the issue of who and why and with what implements. "You can ask Reggie Tang about that. He must have seen at least some of what happened from up on the deck."

"Okay. Say I swallow any of this, even for a moment. Where is Fanke now?"

I threw my arms wide. "I don't know," I admitted. "Get some exorcists onto it, Basquiat. Not me, obviously: whoever else the Met calls in on murder cases. Get hold of something that belonged to Abbie and put them on her trail. Peace was blindsiding me because the Oriflamme had built-in camouflage. But she's not in the Oriflamme anymore, so she ought to be easier to find now, unless—"

I didn't finish that sentence. Unless it was already too late, was what I meant. Unless Abbie had been used up in a repetition of last Saturday's ritual.

Basquiat was talking again. I had to wrench my mind off that train of thought and try to stay focused. "Do you know where we could lay our hands on anything that belonged to Abbie?" she was asking me.

"Yeah," I admitted. "I do. And bear in mind, if I was guilty, I wouldn't be telling you this—because it makes me look even guiltier."

"Go on."

"At my office, in Craven Park Road—next to that kebab house I told you about. There's a black plastic bag, full of toys and clothes. They all—"

"We already checked your office," Basquiat interrupted, waving me silent. "The door had been smashed in, and you'd been turned over pretty thoroughly. There was nothing there."

Damn. I groped around for inspiration. "My coat," I said. "There was a doll's head in the pocket—" Basquiat was shaking her head. It looked as though Fanke had outthought me all along the line.

Or maybe not. I remembered the golden chain wrapped around Peace's wrist. Wrapped tightly, and clenched firmly in that meaty fist. Clenched tightly because it had already broken when Peace tore it from around the dead girl's neck at the meeting house.

"When your men turned over the Oriflamme," I said, "did they find any links from a gold chain?"

Basquiat's eyes narrowed very slightly. She shook her head.

"Check again. They'd have to be small enough to miss. And maybe they could have fallen into a crack in the floor, or gotten into the seams of Peace's clothes. That chain was hers. Abbie's. She wore it every day for years. And it was broken, so it could have shed a link or two during the fight . . ."

The detective sergeant stood, briskly, crossed to the door and hammered on it. "I'm not saying I believe you," she said over her shoulder. "I am saying I'll check it."

"Fast," I told her. "Do it fast. I know Abbie already counts as dead in your book. But what Fanke has in mind for her is worse."

"I said I'll check it."

The door opened and she stepped through without a word.

"Get me my phone call!" I shouted after her. "Basquiat, get me my fucking phone call!"

The door slammed shut.

But this time she'd listened—and relented. Barely ten minutes later the door opened again, and an orderly in a white coat wheeled in a payphone on a trolley. He walked right out again, and the cop who'd opened the door looked at me expectantly.

"I don't have any money," I reminded him.

He looked truculent. "Nothing in the rules says I've got to sub you, you cheeky fucker," he grunted.

"Detective Sergeant Basquiat will pay you back," I assured him. "And contrariwise, she'll probably twist your bollocks off if her collar goes tits-up because you didn't give me my statutory rights."

He dug in his pocket and came up with a handful of silver, which he flung down on the floor. "There you go," he sneered, and stalked out. The key turned in the lock.

There was a yellow pages on a wire shelf underneath the trolley. I looked under "Roman Catholic church," found nothing, but under "Religious organizations" there were a number of places that looked vaguely promising. I eventually settled on a seminary in Vauxhall. I dialed the number, and a man's voice said, "Father Braithewaite," in slightly plummy tones.

"Good evening, Father," I said. "I wonder if you can help me. I need a number for a Biblical research organization, which I believe is located in Woolwich. Does that ring any bells with you?"

"Yes indeed," said Father Braithewaite immediately. "The Ignatieff Trust. I should be able to obtain their number—I've several publications of theirs on my shelves. Just a moment."

There was a *clunk* as the phone was put down, followed by a variety of other bangs, rustles, and scrapes which seemed to go on for a hell of a long time. Finally, just as I was about to hang up and try somewhere else, the priest came back on the line.

"Here it is," he said, and recited a number to me. Since I didn't have any way to write it down, I asked him to repeat it and committed it to memory.

Thanking him for his help, I hung up and dialed the new number. It was the right place, but all I got was a recorded voice and an invitation to leave a message on the answerphone.

Well, in for a penny. "This is Castor," I said, "and my message is for Father Gwillam of the Anathemata Curialis. Ask him to call me on this number. As quick as he can, because the clock's ticking. If he's still looking for Dennis Peace, you can tell him that the trail's gone dead. Literally. The only way he's going to get to Abbie Torrington now is through me."

I hung up, and settled down to sweat out the wait, hoping that they wouldn't come and take the phone away from me before I got my answer. Also, that this wasn't one of those cleverly doctored payphones that block incoming calls.

It wasn't. The phone rang after about fifteen minutes and I scooped it up on the first bounce. If the cops outside the door heard the sound, they didn't respond to it.

"Hello?" I said.

"Mr. Castor?"

I remembered the dry voice. I'd forgotten the inhuman, puritanical calm.

"Yeah."

"Gwillam here. What can I do for you?"

I told him, and he laughed without any trace of humor. It was like hearing a corpse laugh.

"And is there anything else you'd like?" he asked, the irony in the words not making it through to the remorselessly level voice. "Any dead relatives of yours we can intercede for? Or we could stop along the way and pick you up some pizza . . ."

"We'll talk terms later, Gwillam," I told him, in no mood for light banter. "For now, just you go ahead and let the dogs out."

I hung up, hard enough to split the plastic of the receiver.

Chapter Nineteen

I'm not good at waiting. I never have been. I've met people who can switch into Zen mode when there's nothing going on and just mentally hibernate until the toast pops up. I tend to be punching the walls after a while—or in the absence of walls, other people.

Basquiat had left me my watch, which was either a rare sign of humanity or the most insidious and refined torture. I looked at it often enough over the next few hours to wear a hole in the glass.

The day dragged on, like a glacier fingernailing its way down a mountain. I couldn't settle to the car reviews again, so I found myself leaning on the windowsill looking out across Highgate Hill, where the sun, shot down in terrible slo-mo, made the sky over Marx's tomb flare a deep enough red to have satisfied even him.

Maybe that red sky was an omen of some kind—happy shepherds notwithstanding. Just before the sun touched the horizon there was a sound like the clapping of God's hands, followed by an endlessly prolonged scream-cough-scream of breaking glass.

The fire alarms went off all over the building, including one just outside my door that drowned out any sounds from farther away. I felt the vibrations of running footsteps, though; then immediately afterward there were shouts in the corridor outside. I heard some kind of bellowed challenge or warning, cut short as something hit the door with enough force to pop the top hinge.

The door leaned inward an inch or so, and then a second impact made it topple forward into the room, crashing down a few inches from my startled face. One of the uniformed constables came down with it, obviously unconscious even though his glazed eyes were still half-open. Even though it was the one who'd tossed his small change onto the floor so I had to grovel for it, I still felt a twinge of compassion for him. But it passed.

The werewolves, Zucker and Po, stepped over the body. Zucker was in human form—or what passed for human form with him. Po was a monstrous tower of flesh, the remains of a torn shirt still clinging to his barrel-like torso in strips here and there. An unfeasible array of yellow-white fangs bristled in his face, drawing my gaze so completely that the other features became a sliding blur as he lumbered past me to check that the unfortunate cop wasn't likely to get up again soon.

Zucker flashed me a scary smile.

"We were in the neighborhood," he said. "Thought we'd drop in."

"And me without a cake," I mourned.

"We don't eat cake. You got anything you need to pick up on the way?"

I shook my head. I'd have dearly loved to get my own clothes back, but I had no idea where Basquiat would have stashed them. I was just going to have to get by.

Po loomed over me, and Zucker flicked him an appraising glance. "You know that Olympic event where people walk really fast?" he asked me.

"I've heard of it."

"Well, that's what you've got to do. If you run, my friend here is apt to knock you down, step on your head, and rip your guts out. It's his way. But we *are* in a hurry. So—as fast as you can without running."

He turned and led the way out of the room. I followed, and Po brought up the rear like a walking wall. Except that walls mostly have graffiti rather than spines, fangs, and slavering jaws.

The other cop was slumped out in the corridor, the scattered pages of a pink racing paper bearing silent witness against him. Not that he'd have had a much better chance if he'd seen the loup-garous coming: I had a suspicion that you'd need something on the scale of a howitzer even to slow Po down.

The alarms were still screaming, filling the air to the exclusion of everything else. I was sort of assuming that they were a default distress signal, but I realized as we reached the short flight of steps at the end of the corridor that the building was actually on fire. At least, the level below us was full of smoke that hung heavily in the air in visible layers, and there was an acrid, chemical smell that took a lot of the fun out of breathing.

We came down into an open space lined with chairs—a waiting area of some kind for one of the Whittington's specialist units. Zucker hesitated, then pointed to the far side of the room and headed off in that direction. I followed, at a constrained jog-trot. I didn't want Po trampling me under from behind, and I wanted still less for him to get a mental image of me as a rubber bone.

There were three sets of lift doors in a row. Zucker pressed the down buttons on all three, and the middle one slid open immediately. Po pushed me forward and I staggered in. Zucker glanced off to the left and right, then backed in himself and hit the ground-floor button.

"If the power goes, we'll fry in here," I told him, the thought genuinely making my stomach turn over slightly. I've got just a touch of claustrophobia that surfaces every now and again when I'm in enclosed spaces with semihuman monsters that smell like old, damp carpets.

"Not a problem," Zucker said tersely. "Trust me."

The doors slid open again and we came out fast into a wide corridor, Zucker still taking point. The ground floor was like some kind of vision of hell. The smoke was thicker here, shutting my line of sight down to my own arm's length, and the chemical stench was worse. There were a whole lot of other sounds now beneath the wail of the alarm: screams, shouted orders, the scrape and thud of booted feet. No footsteps from behind me, though. I looked round and saw that Po's feet were as bare as mine. The last vestiges of his clothes had sloughed away now, and with them whatever laughably slim chance there'd been of him passing for human. Even if he got his errant flesh under control, he'd be stark bollock naked.

I collided with a wheelchair that was just sitting in the corridor, almost went over on my face. Po snarled warningly: he clearly took my breaking stride as a provocative act. "How are we getting out of here?" I called out to Zucker, who was a good few yards ahead of us on account of not having to worry about losing major limbs and organs.

"Trust in God," he suggested. I looked at him curiously, but he was forging on down the broad corridor without looking behind, so that all I could see was the back of his head. There was no trace of irony in his tone.

"Not usually an option for me."

"But now you're in His hands."

A pair of large doors were in front of us. Zucker kicked them open and went on through, into an atrium of some kind. The higher ceiling made the fumes dance in hypnotic convection currents like curdled milk in coffee. My head was spinning, my stomach heaving. Neither of the loup-garous seemed to be affected at all.

I lost sight of Zucker almost at once, but he hadn't gone far. When I stepped through after him his hand shot out of the fug and gripped my wrist. His voice sounded close to my ear.

"Stay close to me," he muttered. "If we have to leave you behind, we've been told it's okay to kill you. Po is hoping it pans out that way, but I prefer to stick to the script as far as possible."

It occurred to me to wonder what Zucker looked like when he made the change into his animal form. He obviously had a lot more self-control than his partner. I decided that I didn't want to be around when that self-control snapped.

He hauled me after him into the thunder-gray semidark. I presumed that Po was still with us, but I couldn't see him anymore. I couldn't see anything. It seemed like the whole place was ablaze, although I suddenly realized I hadn't seen any flames, felt any heat.

Suddenly a face loomed out of the smoke: a security guard, in full uniform, wielding a futile torch that did nothing but reflect off the churning billows. The guard saw us as we saw him, and opened his mouth to yell.

Po leapt more or less directly over my head, landing full on the guy's chest. He went down hard. Then Zucker was on top of Po, grappling with him. "Leave him!" he snapped. "Leave him, brother! Let God find him out! Let God judge!" There were grunts, and scuffling, and then a full-throated roar from Po.

For a moment I thought I could give them the slip. That would make life a lot simpler. But stepping sideways in the stinking gloom, with the shrilling of the alarm still jangling my thoughts, I bumped straight into a wall. Then the alarm stopped, abruptly, leaving the appalling vacuum of silence to rush in and claim the space where it had been. After-echoes died away and were swallowed in the deadening fog.

Zucker's arm clamped down on my shoulder, whatever altercation he'd had with Po presumably settled.

"It's this way," he said again, with an undertone of warning.

We moved forward. There was something cold and granular underfoot: for a moment I wasn't sure what it was, then I heard the crunch from under Zucker's boots and realized that I was walking on broken glass. "Fuck!" I protested. Zucker hissed me silent. My voice sounded indecently loud in the sudden hush.

Two eyes opened in the fog ahead of us: gleaming yellow eyes, about seven feet apart. An engine revved. Zucker waved, and the eyes flashed: headlights, on full beam. But we were still inside the building.

More indistinct figures were staggering through the gloom off to our right. Someone shouted, and I saw the flash of another flashlight beam. Zucker snapped his fingers, and before I even figured out that it was a signal, Po scooped me off my feet. He ran behind Zucker, around to the left, past the lights. The side of a vehicle slid by us, dull white, and two metallic *clangs* sounded one after the other. Then I was thrown down, not onto the glass-strewn floor of the atrium but into the back of some kind of van. The two loup-garous piled in after me and we backed at reckless speed, Zucker pulling the doors closed with a deafening crash, then swung around with a squeal of tires.

"Mach two," Zucker bellowed, pounding twice on the roof with the heel of his hand.

And we tore away so fast that I was thrown over onto my face again just as I'd finally managed to get up on my hands and knees. A siren gave a mournful, oddly truncated *whoop-whoop-whoop* as the driver shoved down hard on the accelerator, making the speed limit a distant memory.

I twisted my head around; took in the gurney with its wheel locks, the medical kit on the wall, the oxygen cylinder strapped down solid in its recess. We were in an ambulance. The sneaky bastards had hijacked an ambulance.

There was a third man lounging in a fold-down seat next to the gurney. He was stocky, with a pugnacious, peeled-red face and the kind of hair that—although long and even luxuriant—starts a good couple of inches below the crown of the head, leaving a shiny circular landing area for mosquitoes. He was wearing a biker's jacket and a pair of torn jeans that looked as though the rips had all happened by accident rather than being installed at the factory, and he was holding a gun with a silencer so long it suggested desperate overcompensation. It was pointing at my head.

"I'm Sallis," he said, in a voice as raw as his face. "I'll be your stewardess for this evening, and if you so much as fucking move I'll be putting a really slow .22 hollow-point into your skull. They'll have to pour what's left of your brain out through your nose."

"What's the movie?" I asked him, and he prodded my cheek with the end of the silencer barrel as if to say that he didn't appreciate my trying to move in on his stand-up act.

"You just lie there," Zucker elaborated, sounding a little more relaxed now that the hard part—for him, anyway—was over. The ambulance was lurching from side to side as we banked and turned in the narrow streets, so the loup-garou had to grip a handrail to keep from being bounced off his feet: it made him seem more human, somehow. "You don't say a word to anyone in here, including me. The next words you speak will be when you're asked a direct question. Okay? Just nod."

I shrugged. It felt fairly quaint to be threatened with a gun when Po was squatting beside me like a bag full of muscles with a decorative motif of teeth.

"That wasn't a nod," said Zucker sternly.

"You didn't say Simon says," I pointed out.

Sallis kicked me in the ribs, but for all the tough talk they were clearly under orders not to bring me in either dead or too badly creased. I was banking on that—on the fact that Gwillam would want to debrief me before he made any last judgments about my disposal. Otherwise I might have minded my manners a little more, and tried to leave a better impression.

I had plenty of time, as we drove on at breakneck speed through the gathering dark, to figure it out. There'd never been any fire, of course. Just a lot of smoke grenades that the loup-garous had chucked out of the ambulance's doors as they'd crashed through the large picture windows that fronted the A&E block. The chemical smell was a cocktail of formaldehyde, carbon monoxide, and maybe launch gases if they'd actually fired the fucking things from a mortar.

It figured, of course. The Anathemata wouldn't do anything so indiscriminate as to set fire to a hospital—but the judicious application of panic was well within their remit. If anyone actually died in the resulting stampede, I'm sure Gwillam would fill in the appropriate form and a mass would be said. One thing you can't fault about Catholics is their organizational skills.

But of course these were *ex*-Catholics: they'd been outlawed as an organization and excommunicated as individuals. What did that make them? The papacy's equivalent of the Mission Impossible team, maybe. Fanatics, certainly; so convinced they were fighting the good fight that they'd ignored their own leaders' orders to stop.

That made what I was doing here more dangerous, and more uncertain. Fanatics are unpredictable, zigging when you think they're going to zag; they don't connect to the world at the same angle as the rest of us do, and you have to bear that in mind when you try to reason with them. Better yet, cut your losses and don't bother to try.

I'd only called Gwillam because I was out of other options, and because I didn't know Basquiat well enough to trust her yet. Maybe she'd have enough sense to see the truth when it reared up and smacked her in the face, but maybe not. In any case, I wasn't going to bet Pen's life on it, or Abbie's soul. Or my own arse, for that matter. A smart cop is still a cop, with all that that implies.

We slowed down, abruptly, then speeded up again. That process was repeated several times over the next few minutes: even with the siren, and the emergency lights presumably flashing to beat the band, we could only push so far against the press of London traffic. At one point, as we were crawling along in some jam we couldn't shift with our borrowed moral authority, Zucker suddenly tensed and Po emitted a sound that was halfway between a snarled curse and a cat's yowl. I knew what that meant, and it gave me a rough indicator of how far we'd come. It also left me a little awestruck at how much punishment the two loup-garous were prepared to take in the line of duty. We were crossing the river. They had to be in agony: running water is like an intravenous acid bath to the were-kin, and they took it in their stride.

Well, not quite in their stride: I noticed that Po's claws were gouging into the plastic anti-slip slats on the floor, reducing them to ribboned ruin. His head was bowed, his breath coming in quick, barking grunts. Zucker was leaning against the gurney, his eyes clenched shut, a sheen of sweat on his pale face.

This would have been a good time to launch a daring escape, but the guy who'd introduced himself as Sallis was just as aware of that as I was. He jabbed the gun in between my shoulder blades and held it there until Zucker got his groove back. Like it or not, I was along for the whole ride.

A few moments later we dipped very sharply, with a harsh shudder as the suspension didn't quite manage to take the strain, bumped over a series of badly fitted steel grids that shrieked under our wheels like a cageful of rats, and rolled to a halt. Zucker threw the doors open. He stepped down first, and the solid *thud* as his feet hit the ground outside had a strange echo to it. The darkness was impenetrable. Po gathered himself up and rolled out into the night with eerie, silent grace, then swiveled to stare back in at me. Sallis waved the gun, indicating that it was my turn next.

I climbed down from the back of the ambulance, and looked around. I still didn't have enough night vision to see what kind of somewhere I was standing in, but again there was that echo, from somewhere close at hand. Every scrape of foot on concrete, every *pop* and *twang* from the ambulance's engine, cooling rapidly in the night chill, had its attentive twin rushing out of the dark to join it.

A rectangle of grimy yellow light opened in front of us, and with its help I saw what I'd already guessed: we were inside, in a sepulchral space that was enormous in extent but as low-ceilinged as a church vault. White lines on the ground, parallel and evenly spaced, gave the game away still further; not a church, but an underground car park. "Get him inside," said a cold voice, which was so dead and flat that it scarcely stirred the echoes at all. A hand—Sallis's, presumably—gripped my shoulder from behind and I was pushed brusquely forward, Zucker and Po falling in on either side of me.

We stepped through the doorway into a concrete stairwell. Father Gwillam closed the door, which was a fire door, and pushed the bar back into place with a small grunt of effort. Then he turned to me.

"Good to see you again, Castor," he murmured. "On the side of the angels at last."

"Color me undecided," I suggested.

He smiled—a brief flicker of expression that couldn't take root in the affectless terrain of his face—and nodded. "Everything's set up upstairs," he said, to the company in general. It wasn't a comment I liked very much, but my personal honor guard closed in on me as Gwillam led the way up the stairs, so I didn't have much choice about whether or not I followed.

I was looking for clues as to where we were. Close to the Thames, I knew, but where had we crossed? Not as far east as Rotherhithe, surely? In any case, I was pretty sure I'd have heard the engine noise change if we'd come through the tunnel. But maybe we'd gone west. There was no way to be sure: at a rough guess, we could be anywhere between Wapping and Kew.

But as we came out of the stairwell onto a wide blue-carpeted corridor with a gentle incline, bells began to chime. I'd been here before, some time in the long-ago. I experienced a flash of déjà vu that included the insanely staring eyes of Nosferatu, and I almost had it. A cinema? Had the Anathemata found one of London's decommissioned dream houses and moved in, as Nicky had done over in Walthamstow? That would be a pretty sick irony.

But no. As it turned out, they'd gone one better than that. Gwillam threw a door open and flicked a light switch. Strip lights flickered in sequence along a wall as long as a football field. A black wall, black floor, too, scarred with the scuff marks of innumerable feet. Up ahead of me, something that looked a little like a *Tyrannosaurus rex* made of glass and black steel reared itself up to about twice my height. But it wasn't a T. rex: it was a Zeiss projector.

"Son of a bitch!" I said, impressed in spite of myself as the penny dropped.

"That's the sort of language Po doesn't appreciate all that much," Gwillam murmured, raising the disturbing possibility that he might actually have a sense of humor.

He walked around the Zeiss projector, and I followed: or rather, I was herded. The vast expanse of floor on the far side was mostly empty, except for a ghost pattern of unbleached areas on the carpet where other objects had once stood: display stands, partition walls, ancient cine cameras, life-size dioramas from great movies. The Anathemata had colonized one small area; there were a couple of guys working on laptop terminals at desks that were surrounded by thick, overlaid loops of electric cable like barbed wire entanglements. Another couple of guys were talking on cell phones, one of them tracing a line with his finger on an ops board—a huge map of London pinned to the wall, like I'd only ever seen in seventies cop shows. That was pretty much it: that, and a whole lot of empty space stretching away into the middle distance.

"You should move somewhere smaller, now that the kids have grown up," I commented, trying for a nonchalant tone that I think I missed by a mile or so. "You're probably paying more rent than you need to."

Gwillam smiled thinly. He was watching my face, taking a clinical interest in my reaction. "Who mentioned rent? They left the key under the mat, and we let ourselves in. I'm assuming you know what this used to be, before it died?"

"Sure," I said. "I know."

But Gwillam wanted to give me the punch line, and he wasn't going to be deterred. "It was the Museum of the Moving Image."

Just the words conjured up a little squall of memories. The museum was part of the South Bank complex, like the National Theatre and the Festival Hall—but it was added on after all the rest were built, because film was the scruffy little Johnny-come-lately of the art world and had to make space for itself at the table with its elbows. I'd only been here once before in my life—on a school outing when I was thirteen. All the way up from Liverpool on the train, with four stuffed pork roll sandwiches and a can of Vimto to see me through the day. I'd pretended to think it was shit, because that was what all my mates were saying, but secretly I reckoned the low-tech horror of the magic lantern shows was the dog's bollocks, and I sneaked back to watch the X-wings versus TIE fighters battle sequence from *Star Wars* twice over.

Now it was just an empty warehouse.

"They closed the place down sometime in the late nineties," said Gwillam, absently. "Took the exhibition on the road. It's meant to be opening again in three years or so. In the meantime . . . it's really handy for the West End. Sit down, Castor."

I hadn't even seen the chair. It was sitting in a patch of shadow just on the hither side of the ops board where two of the strip lights had failed to come on. A coil of rope and a doctor's little black bag lay on the floor beside it. There was a table, too: a small, round coffee table with a stained Formica top that looked as though it had wandered in here from somewhere else. Gwillam swiveled the chair around to face me.

"Please," he said, in the same deadpan tone.

"I'd rather stand."

Gwillam sighed, pursed his lips in a way that suggested he got a lot of this selfish and hurtful behavior but never quite got used to it.

"If you're standing," he pointed out patiently, "Zucker and Sallis can't tie you to the chair."

"My point exactly," I agreed.

"And I want you to be tied to the chair because it makes some of the things I'm about to do to you that much easier."

"Look," I began, "as a concerned citizen, I'm really happy to co-operate with any—" But Gwillam must have given some kind of signal to his team that I didn't catch. Po's massive, clawed hand closed around my throat and he hauled me unceremoniously over to the chair, slammed me down, and held me in position. Zucker and Sallis made busy with the ropes. They were enthusiastic amateurs where knots were concerned, but they made up in quantity what they lacked in real finesse.

While they worked, Gwillam brought up another chair and placed it opposite me. Then, when they stood back respectfully from the finished job, he nodded them a curt acknowledgment. "Sallis," he said, "you're with me. Mr. Zucker, after your recent exertions you and Mr. Po might wish to avail yourselves of the chapel."

"Thank you, Father," Zucker said, and the two of them turned on their heel and walked away into the darkness. Po looked over his shoulder at me: bared way, way too many teeth. Sallis went over to the wall and sat down with his back to it, the gun not exactly pointed at me but still ready in his hand.

"Is that a euphemism of some kind?" I asked Gwillam.

He shot me a look of genuine surprise.

"No," he said. "We have a field chapel wherever we set up, Castor. Our faith is very important to us."

"Your former faith."

Gwillam quirked one eyebrow. He didn't look upset, though; the barb didn't have quite as much sting as I'd expected it to.

"Do you know how many Catholics there are in the world, Castor?" he asked me.

"Before you and your pals got their marching orders, or afterward?"

"There are more than a billion. Seventeen percent of the world's population. Five hundred million in the Americas alone.

"So the Holy Father must of necessity be a statesman as well as a religious leader. He has to play the games of men, and of nations. And sometimes that means he has to balance small injustices against larger gains."

"Meaning?"

"The Anathemata Curialis was given a massive appropriation of funds just before the death of John Paul II. Then his successor, Benedict XVI, ordered us to disband or face excommunication. The two actions are best seen as the diastolic and systolic beats of a heart. The church has disowned us, but it has not ceased to wish us well."

"Even though you use werewolves as field agents? How broad *is* your brief, Gwillam? I'm just curious."

He knelt down, picked up the black bag and put it up on the coffee table. He snapped it open and rummaged inside. I hadn't forgotten the bag: in fact, it was fair to say that it was preying on my mind a little.

"Our brief," Gwillam said, "is narrow and exact. We fight the last war. We're heaven's skirmishers, sent into the enemy's heartlands to gauge his strength and harry his forces as he attempts to deploy them."

"The enemy being . . . ?"

"Hell, of course."

He took from the bag, one by one, a disposable hypodermic, a bubble pack with a small vial of some straw-yellow substance, a larger bottle of clear liquid, and an unopened pack of surgical swabs. "The rising of the dead," he said, looking me full in the eyes with the deadly calm of the fanatic, "was the opening of hostilities. Hell is on the move against heaven, in every sphere, in every nation of earth. It was foretold, and it was foreseen. We were not taken by surprise. But there were those in the church who wouldn't accept the evidence of their own eyes."

He smiled bleakly. I got the impression that he was remembering specific conversations; specific clashes of will and words. "They forgot their duty of stewardship," he said gently. "They became too ensconced in the comforts of the world, and forgot that the world must always and ever be a forge. You do not sit comfortably by God's fire: you are plunged into it, and shaped and made by it.

"You seem to think, Castor, that there's some contradiction between the battle we wage and the tools we use. There isn't. We fight against the demons who are Satan's generals in the field—and we avail ourselves of whatever weapons God places in our hands. If faithful Catholics return from the dead not because they conspired with the Adversary but because the rules of engagement have changed, then we will not turn our backs on them. Po and Zucker have suffered much, and they have turned their suffering to good account. I number them among my most trusted officers."

He counted off the items on the chair, pointing at each with his index finger, as if to satisfy himself that he had everything he needed. Then he nodded, satisfied, and stared at me again.

"Where is Abbie Torrington?" he asked me.

"In a police morgue in Hendon."

Gwillam blinked, once, twice. "I don't mean her shell," he said, with the closest thing to heat I'd ever seen from him. "I mean her true self. Her spirit. As you of all people must appreciate."

Me of all people? I let that one pass.

"Her soul is in a locket," I said. "Made of gold. Shaped like a heart. Her father took it from her neck just after she died. I think it has a lock of her hair inside it, and I think that that's what she's clinging to. And

Fanke has it now: he took it from Peace's body after he killed him at the Oriflamme on Castlebar Hill."

"And where is Fanke?"

"I don't know. Gwillam, if you can see that Abbie's ghost is the same thing as her soul, then how in fuck's name can you talk about destroying it?"

He raised his eyebrows. "Isn't that what we do?" he asked. "Isn't that exactly the power that was given to us?"

"'We'?" I don't know why that came as a shock: it was pretty much on the cards, given that he was the one the Anathemata had chosen to head up this mission. "You're an exorcist?"

He nodded curtly. "That was how I knew that God had chosen me to fight in His cause."

"Funny," I said. "That was how I knew I'd never have to work on a building site. What do you use? A fragment of the true cross?"

Gwillam looked at me reflectively. His hand slid into his breast pocket, and it came out holding a small book bound in black leather.

"The Bible," he said. "This Bible. I read aloud—words and phrases taken at random from different verses. The words of God make a cage for the souls of sinners—as you would expect." He put the book away. "I told you, Castor. I'm a soldier. If I could save the child, then I would save her, but I can't and won't allow her soul to become the mechanism through which hell's mightiest general is unleashed upon the world. The ritual that was used here requires the sacrifice of body and soul; therefore without the girl's soul, it can't be completed. Now, I ask you again, for the second time: Where is Fanke?"

"I don't have the faintest idea," I said. It was true, as far as it went: I didn't know where Fanke was right then. I was pretty sure I knew where he was going to turn up at some point in the very near future, but I was keeping that little nugget to myself. Maybe Gwillam was the best chance I had of dropping a wrench into Fanke's good works, but at the expense of Abbie's soul? It couldn't be done that way. Not if I was going to be able to look in the mirror afterward.

Gwillam nodded to Sallis, who stepped up beside me. He tucked his gun into a holster strapped across his chest under his jacket and took a double handful of my hair, pulling my head back as far as he could. I tensed against him, but standing over me like that he could exert a lot more leverage than I could. Unhurriedly, Gwillam uncorked the large bottle and poured some of its contents onto one of the surgical swabs. The pungent smell of some strong disinfectant filled the air. Gwillam carefully swabbed the area where my shoulder and throat met, then threw the used swab down on the chair.

"I'm telling you all I know," I snarled, finding it hard to talk with my head tilted back so sharply.

"We'll see," said Gwillam tersely. He tore the bubble wrap open, loaded the syringe with the snap-in ampoule, and pumped it lightly, sending a thin jet of fluid spraying from its tip. "Hold him steady," he warned Sallis, bending back over the doctor bag for a moment so that I lost sight of him. "If this goes into his carotid artery, it will probably kill him."

That was bad news, whichever way you looked at it. But even if I survived this, it was obvious that Gwillam was about to shoot me full of some thiopental derivative to ensure a fuller and franker discussion. Was there anything I could do to stop him? I couldn't think of a damn thing.

What did I know about truth serums? Only what I'd picked up from reading cheap spy thrillers, but that was enough to know that they didn't work. They were just disinhibitors, cutting the brake cables of your subconscious so that you freewheeled endlessly, gabbling on about whatever came into your head. People injected with propofol or pentathol couldn't consciously lie, but they could and did talk a load of free-associative shite. That was why truth drugs didn't turn up much anymore even in cheap spy thrillers.

On the other hand, did I want to free-associate in front of Gwillam about Asmodeus and Abbie and Juliet and St. Michael's Church? No, I didn't. This was definitely a good time to be keeping my thoughts to myself.

And just then, another bit of trivia that I didn't even know I knew popped up out of nowhere. I suddenly remembered what class of drugs the truth serums belonged to—and it gave me the bare bones of an idea; thin and pathetic but marginally better than nothing. No harm in trying, anyway: the only downside was that if it didn't work, I might never wake up. I started to breathe fast and deep, forcing air into my lungs.

"Would it be better if he was unconscious?" Sallis asked, with what from my point of view sounded like an indecent amount of enthusiasm.

"Hardly," Gwillam snapped. "How will he be able to answer any questions if you've put your fist through his skull?"

He loomed back into my field of vision, the needle raised in his hand.

"Gwillam!" I growled, still breathing in fast, forced gasps. I must have looked like I was starting a full-fledged panic attack.

Gwillam hesitated. "What?" he asked.

"I'm allergic."

"Allergic to what, exactly?" Gwillam asked, his tone dangerously mild.

There could be any of twenty different drugs in the syringe. All I could do was guess.

"Propofol," I said.

Gwillam shrugged. "Then you can relax," he said. "This is something different."

The needle came down toward my neck. I twisted suddenly in Sallis's hands, and Gwillam stopped: he didn't want to kill me—or at least, not until he'd asked the rest of his questions. "Hold him steady," he rasped, and Sallis threw one arm around my neck, leaned in hard against me to restrict my movement as much as he could.

All of this was just playing for time while I drew as many breaths as I could, working my lungs like bellows until the actual moment when the tip of the needle slid into my skin and Gwillam's thumb pushed home the plunger.

A red curtain fell across my mind. A black one followed, half a second later. But they weren't curtains at all, they were solid walls, and I crashed into unconsciousness so fast and hard that I actually felt the impact.

———————

I woke up slowly and painfully; bleeding fragments of thought running together like mercury, pooling like ultra-cold lakes in the fractal wastelands of my cerebellum.

The "I" came first, but there was nothing to join it to. Just I. What I? Where I? Who the fuck cared? It couldn't matter. Whoever he was, let the bastard wait. There was pain going on somewhere nearby and I wanted to lie low so that it didn't find me.

A minute or an hour later, an "am" trickled down from somewhere and attached itself to the "I." I am. I therefore think.

It was me, again, bubbling up from under the chemical sludge of anaesthesia whether I liked it or not; being harshly, achingly reborn in a dark, cold room that seemed to be hanging at an angle. But no, that was me. I was lying skewed, my cheek pressed against the floor, my legs canted up into the air. I couldn't figure it out so I let it go.

I was still alive, anyway. And I was still thinking. Any brain damage? How would I tell? If you've lost enough of your brain function to make a difference, you've probably lost the ability to see it as a problem. Maybe the terrific throbbing inside my skull was a good sign: there had to be a lot of nerves in there still doing their jobs.

Truth serums are general anaesthetics. They're the primary inducers that you're given to kick your conscious mind away into the long grass so that your body can be cut and spliced and sewn without any kickback from your cerebellum. By hyperventilating, I'd made sure that I got as big and fast a hit as the dose in Gwillam's syringe could provide. I was hoping that I'd go straight past the rambling stage into full unconsciousness. It might even have worked: I didn't have any memory of talking, anyway. But maybe a hole in your memory was normal with these things.

I opened my eyes, but there was nothing to see. Either I'd been struck with hysterical blindness or I was in an absolutely dark space. I tried to move, and couldn't. I could lift my head, just, but that turned out to be a mistake because it made the throbbing worse. I opened my mouth to swear and discovered that my tongue was glued to my dry palate.

Belatedly I remembered that I'd been tied to a chair. It seemed that I still was, but that the chair was now lying on its side on the ground. That explained the weird position I was in and the fact that I couldn't move.

Son of a bitch! Didn't the Vatican ever sign the Geneva Convention? They'd just wheeled or dragged the chair, with me in it, over to some cupboard and pushed it inside so hard or so clumsily that it had fallen over. That was no way to treat a prisoner.

As the pain gradually subsided, I worked at the ropes. They felt pretty loose: the original intention had just been to stop me moving while Gwillam interrogated me, not to keep me a prisoner forever. Consequently Sallis and Zucker hadn't bothered to check whether the knots fell within reach of my fingers.

All the same, it took me a long time—I guessed more than an hour—to get my hands free. By that time, my fingers were so sore and abraded from the stiff sisal fibers that I had to rest up for a while before I started on my legs. Getting them free was much faster, but it took a good ten minutes of massaging life back into them before I could stand.

Okay, so I was free. But where the hell was I? I set out from the chair in tiny, inching steps, my arms out straight ahead of me, until I found a wall. Then I worked my way along it to the corner. This was no cupboard, obviously: it was a fair-size room, although the roughcast feel of the walls still suggested a storage area of some kind rather than a public space.

I was intending to circumnavigate the room, but a little way along the second wall I found a door—and then its very welcome neighbor, a light switch. I turned it on with a silent prayer, and three strip lights flickered into life over my head, leaving me blinking in a harsh, white radiance.

I'd guessed right: this was a storeroom, high-ceilinged, with deep shelves running the entire length of the far wall. They were all empty, though, except for a few circular drums about a foot and a half in diameter, which were presumably old movie reels. When the standing exhibition went walkabout, they must have taken pretty much everything that wasn't nailed down. Either that or Gwillam had ordered the room cleared to make sure I didn't find anything that might help me escape.

But nobody's perfect. As my gaze came full circle and I looked across at the far side of the door from where I stood, a grim smile spread across my face. Because screwed to the wall, hiding in plain sight, was a small white box with a red cross stenciled on its face. A first aid kit.

My ticket out of here.

Chapter Twenty

The contents of a first aid kit vary a lot from place to place, but the core is always the same—bandages and sticking plasters in a million different shapes and sizes. There's usually a bottle of disinfectant and some cotton buds; this one even had a few exotics like Savlon spray and vinegar for stings. None of that mattered a damn. I was looking for items that had either a point or an edge.

I got lucky. There was a tiny pair of scissors, a pair of splinter forceps, and a half-dozen safety pins.

The door had a simple mortice deadlock with no lockmaker's name on the plate. I dropped the forceps back into the box: probably too wide, and certainly not strong enough. I bent back one of the safety pins into a nearly straight line, then using the scissors as a makeshift pair of pliers, I twisted the sharp end up and back into a hook. After a hairpin, it's my favorite kind of improvised lockpick, and it was easily up to a job as straightforward as this.

Five minutes were all it took to work the lock's three levers around into the release position, the third one falling into place with a very satisfying click. Before I tried the door, I turned the light out and let my eyes adjust to the dark again. There was no light coming from under the door: if there had been, I'd have noticed it before, when the room was still in darkness. Under the circumstances, the goal was to see before I was seen. Otherwise I'd be back to square one.

After about a minute, I eased the door open as silently as I could. Peering out, I waited until the wider darkness outside had started to resolve itself into shapes before I stepped out. I was in another part of the massive main exhibition area, as sepulchral and empty as the part where Gwillam had interrogated me. There should be any number of ways out onto the street from here, or into other parts of the South Bank complex that were still open to the public. All I had to do was to make sure I didn't bump into any of Gwillam's merry little band on the way. In the case of Po, though, that meant not just avoiding being seen but also not letting him get my scent.

The level I was on seemed to be entirely deserted, so from that point of view I was doing fine. I thought about resting up for a few minutes here before I moved on; but time was pressing: I didn't know what I might have said while I was under the drug, or how much Gwillam now knew. There was also the fact that since I was still dressed only in a hospital gown I'd probably get hypothermia if I hung around too long in this frigid air.

After a minute or so of tacking backward and forward across the huge space I found a staircase and headed down, taking it slow in the pitch dark to avoid going arse over tip all the way to the bottom. I was reasoning that at the very least I'd probably hit a door to the car park—which in turn had to connect with the street. Even if there was a security grille and it was locked shut, I was reasonably sure that I'd be able to jimmix it and get out.

But the door at the bottom of the stairwell was a fire door, with a padlock and chain hung over the bar in defiance of law and logic. I retraced my steps to the floor above, tried the door there. It opened when I pushed, so I stopped when the crack was about an inch wide and peered in.

Not quite dark here: there were lights on somewhere ahead—a dull, slightly bluish glow coming around the edge of what looked like a movable partition wall up ahead of me and slightly to my left. I listened: no sound at all, except for the very faint hum of some kind of machinery.

I stepped out and eased the door closed behind me. Sooner or later I had to come out of the stairwell, and the closer to the ground I was the better I'd like it. The South Bank Centre is a spectacular vertical maze even with the lights on. I could waste a quarter of an hour or more just shuffling up and down in the dark.

A few steps brought me to the edge of the partition wall. Moving as slowly and silently as I could, I leaned around it and looked in at the source of the light.

A man was sitting in a cheap plastic bucket chair at a computer terminal. His back was to me, but I recognized the bald spot: it was Sallis. He was scrolling slowly through endless screens of double-columned text, and he seemed absolutely intent. The gun, with the silencer now removed, sat beside him on the desk where the computer had been set up, in between a Republic of Coffee cup and a Styrofoam burger box. The Anathemata might be tooled up for war but they were living like cops on a stakeout.

I considered my options. No one else in sight, and no other islands of light in the immense room. Sallis was deep into something that seemed to have completely cut him off from the world around him. I could sneak on past him, and maybe make it to another exit without him clocking me on the way.

On the other hand, there was the gun. And the clothes. And whatever money he might have in his pockets. Needs must when the devil drives.

I took a step back, then another; and one sideways. Working from memory, that was the best I could do. I charged the partition shoulder first, taking a flying leap at the last moment so that I hit it high and had all my weight on its upper half as it came down and I came down with it.

Sallis didn't even yell. He did make some kind of a sound, but it's not one I could do justice to without specialized equipment. His head slammed forward into the desk with a solid smack as he fell, forced down by the weight of the partition and my body; then the legs of the desk gave way and he just vanished from sight under the general wreckage.

I rolled over twice and came up quickly, spinning to face him in case he was still conscious and going for the gun, but I needn't have worried. He was sprawled on the ground, absolutely still, his head and upper body under the fallen partition. I snatched the gun up myself, tried to work out which end was which, and eventually found the safety catch. With that matter sorted, I levered the near end of the partition wall aside with my foot. Sallis was out cold, a trickle of blood wending its way down his forehead from a shallow cut. He was still breathing, though, and the cut was the only wound I could see. He'd probably get out of this with nothing worse than a headache.

I stripped him quickly, shrugged into his jeans, shirt, and jacket. They fitted me pretty well, all things considered, and the slight stink of his stale sweat was a price I was willing to pay. I searched his pockets. Bingo: a small wad of notes, a card wallet, even a set of car keys on a fancy fob that bore the Mitsubishi logo. I took the gun, too, since there was no way of getting back my weapon of choice.

I was done, and I had places to be, but I hesitated because an idea had struck me. Another one came hard on its heels, way above average, and annoying because it meant going back the way I'd come. I wasn't sure whether the gain in matériel would offset the loss of time, but either way I didn't have the luxury of standing here agonizing about it.

First things first. Rooting amid the wreckage of the desk, I found a few sheets of paper and a black pen. I rested the paper against Sallis's back and scribbled a brief note. It probably wouldn't help, but it couldn't hurt so what the hell. I folded the note and tucked it into the waistband of his underpants, like a fiver into a Chippendale's jockstrap.

Then I retraced my steps to the storeroom and collected up about half a dozen of those old film canisters, shaking them first to make sure that they were full. They might be blank stock, useless now because the cameras that would take them had gone to rust and scrap decades ago; or alternatively they could be lost masterpieces from the silent era. I purposely didn't read the labels in any case, because whatever they'd been before, the only attraction they had for me now was because the blast-proof doors over at Nicky's gaff were still fresh in my mind: film burns like petrol burns.

Time to hit the road, and more than. This time around I wasn't deterred by the padlock at the bottom of the stairs, because this time around I had Sallis's gun. I missed with the first shot, blew the chain very effectively with the second, and kicked the doors open.

I was back in the car park, and it was empty. In case the indecently loud noise of the gunshots brought werewolves or security guards running to see what was what, I quickened my steps as I climbed the shallow ramp that led toward what I hoped was the exit. Halfway up there was a motorbike, leaning drunkenly against the wall in a way that suggested a broken kickstand. At the top there was a closed security grille. On the far side of the grille were light and sound and life: theatergoers and late-night revelers walked past, happily oblivious of the dark worlds that glided past theirs on sly, crazy tangents. The same night, or the next? How long had I been out after Gwillam slipped me the truth drug? The answer came pat: if I'd been unconscious for twenty-four hours I'd be a hell of a lot more seriously dehydrated than I was. It was still Thursday, and I was still in with a chance.

For a moment, I almost resented the people filtering past in the unrelenting slipstream of normality—not just for their happy or indifferent faces and their carefree conversations but because their presence right there, right then, meant I couldn't use the gun again. I tried the grille. It wasn't locked; it slid up with a stuck-pig squeal as I hauled on it.

Then I did a double take that in other circumstances might have been comic. I went back down to where the bike was parked, and took a closer look at it. The logo above the front headlight was the three-diamonds-making-a-triangle of the Mitsubishi company. The bike also had a pair of panniers at the back like a courier's bike.

I experienced a momentary qualm of near panic as I fished Sallis's keys out of the pocket of Sallis's jacket. If this worked I had to be using up someone else's luck, because this sure as hell didn't feel like mine.

Trying to look casual for the benefit of anyone who might glance in from the street, I slid the film canisters into the panniers, three to each side, and climbed on board. There were running footsteps coming up the ramp now, and I heard a shout from behind me. I didn't turn around; turning around at the sound of a shout just makes you look guilty.

The key fitted, and the engine roared into noisy, overemphatic life on the first turn. Now I did look back, and was on the whole relieved to find that the pursuit was wearing uniform—and flesh that was entirely human.

They were still fifty feet behind, giving me just about enough time to slip the helmet that was dangling from the handlebars—dark red, like the bike, and emblazoned with a winged skull motif—over my head. Safety first. Then I burned rubber, leaving the three yelling security guards to share my exhaust between them.

I wasn't sure how to go in at the Stanger Care Home. Was I a wanted felon now? The ram raid on a North London hospital had to have made the news. The question was whether they'd sorted through the debris yet and ascertained that I wasn't in it—and if so, whether they'd put out any kind of a public warning alongside the inevitable APB.

If they had, walking into the Stanger like it was all business as usual might mean walking straight back into police custody. On the other hand, there was something inside that I needed, and I couldn't see any other way of getting it.

But while I was still sitting astride the bike in the darkened car park, irresolute, providence reached out to me in the shape of Paul. He came lumbering out through the main doors, leaned against the side of the ambulance where we'd had our talk a few days before, and lit up. He blew a plume of smoke out through his nostrils, and it hung in faint lines in the still air like a runic inscription carved into the flesh of the night.

As I got off the bike and walked toward him, he glanced in my direction and then took a longer, harder look. Because of the bike he'd had me pegged as a stranger, but I saw the doubt appear in his face and I saw him tense. By that time I was close enough for him to hear me without me having to raise my voice too much. I took the helmet off and kept on walking.

"Hey, Paul," I offered.

He thrust out his lower lip in a look of truculent puzzlement. "Hey, Castor. I thought you were meant to be on the run from the police."

I nodded easily, strolling up beside him and resting one shoulder against the ambulance, the helmet tucked casually under my arm and my free hand thrust into the pocket of Sallis's leather jacket. "That's right," I said, flicking the helmet with the tip of my thumb. "Hence the cunning disguise."

"Armed and dangerous, is what I heard."

"Armed, yes." I showed him the handgun, put it away again fast. "I'd only be dangerous if I was organized. How's Rafi?"

Paul took a drag on his cigarette, blew out some more smoke. The gun had brought a pained look to his face, but he wasn't surprised or intimidated by it. "He's good," he said. "Rafael is good. Best he's ever been. You want to know the truth, I can hardly believe he's the fucking same person."

"You want to know the truth, he isn't. Paul, I need to get in and see him."

He chuckled softly and shook his head, grinning as if in appreciation of a good joke. "Not gonna happen, man," he said. "They got your face on the TV—everyone inside is talking about it. The ones who reckon you always had shifty eyes are kind of winning right now."

"They don't have to see my face." I held up the motorcycle helmet. "Just get me inside, Paul. It's important. And afterward you can say I had a gun on you."

"Have you, Castor?"

"Have I what?"

He looked me in the eye, calm and cold. "Got a gun on me?"

I winced. "Fuck, no. I didn't kill anyone, Paul, and I'm not planning to start now. But I need to speak to Rafi, and I thought you could help. If you don't want to, then I guess all I can ask you to do is to hold off on raising the alarm for a while."

He dropped the last inch of his cigarette onto the asphalt and trod it out. "This is going to upset Dr. Webb," he observed. "Make him look all kinds of stupid."

"Yeah," I said. "I guess." I was working out distances and odds. If I just walked in off the street and headed for the annex where Rafi's cell was without going through reception first, the nurse on duty would hit an alarm. I could get to Rafi, but could I get into the cell without a key? And could I get out again afterward?

"Bound to," Paul pursued, meditatively. "Bound to ruin his day. A wanted man walks in off the street, gets through all his security, and then walks out again. That kind of thing is real hard to explain to the board of trustees."

He squared his shoulders, like a man walking back into the fray after a short, well-needed rest.

"So let's do it," he said.

Paul went first, hands swinging at his sides, looking bored and indifferent. I followed, helmet on and visor down, holding one of the film canisters because it was the only prop I had to hand.

The nurse on reception looked up, saw that it was Paul, then as she was about to return to her novel saw the other, unfamiliar figure looming behind him. She stared at me, and at what I was holding, with a quickening of interest.

"Where's Dr. Webb, Lizzie?" Paul asked her. "This guy"—hooking a thumb over his shoulder—"needs a signature for something, and it's got to be the boss man's."

"I think he's in his office," the nurse said, glancing back to Paul again. "Shall I page him?"

"Nah, I'll take him through. You sign in first though," he said to me severely. "This is a stupid time to be making a delivery in any case. Come on, move it up. Some of us have got work to do."

The nurse held out a pen and I signed the day book as Frederick Cheney LaRue, a name that had stuck with me after I read that Woodward and Bernstein book about Watergate.

"It's this way," Paul said, ambling away along the corridor. I waved to the nurse, the helmet making the gesture look more paramilitary than civil, and followed him. I wanted to look back but made myself keep right on going. I hoped for my sake that whatever chapter Lizzie was on in her book was more interesting than a weird stranger walking in out of the night to take a movie reel to her boss.

Webb's office was off to the right when you reached the annex. We went left, toward the secure cells. Paul used the Judas window to check exactly where Rafi was—a touch of caution born of long experience—and then unlocked the door for me. I stepped inside, and he followed close on my heels, swinging the door to. When I looked a question at him, he shrugged. "How'm I going to say you had a gun on me if I'm out there keeping lookout, Castor?"

"Fair point," I admitted.

Rafi was lying on a tubular steel bunk—a new addition to the cell that was in itself a vivid testimony to how much he'd changed in the last few days. When Asmodeus was in the ascendant, the cell was kept absolutely bare because you could never tell when the demon's mood would toggle from quiescent to murderously playful. Too many staff had taken hits in the early days. Webb had made Pen sign a waiver as Rafi's legal executor, and the cell had been reduced, as far as possible, to a featureless metal cube.

By contrast with those bad old days, right now it was looking almost homely. In addition to the bed there was a poster on the wall—a reproduction of Van Gogh's sunflowers—and a chest of drawers with a pencil and paper resting on top of it. Enough right there for Asmodeus to have caused some serious mayhem back in the day.

Rafi was asleep: very deeply asleep. I looked from him to Paul, and he gave a grin that was almost a snarl. "Dr. Webb says until we get the results of the new assessment back, Mr. Ditko stays on his meds. Same times, same dosages. Of course, when he was sharing the premises, so to speak, it didn't matter so much. He could shrug off the drugs whenever he needed to, seemed like. Now those two temazepam he gets at nine p.m. knock him out stone-cold until morning."

It didn't surprise me, because that was the kind of bastard Webb was: the play-it-by-the-book and my-hands-are-tied kind. Since there was nobody to explain myself to, I did what I'd come for without preamble. Taking out the scissors that I'd taken from the medicine cabinet back at the South Bank Centre, I carefully cut a lock of Rafi's hair without waking him.

"What d'you need his hair for?" Paul asked me, his face registering something like disgust.

"Sucker bait," I said, grimly. His distaste couldn't be anything like as big as mine: I knew the truth. It would be the last resort, I told myself. I wouldn't use it unless everything else failed. Anyway I probably wouldn't even get in close enough to use it in the first place. And the timing would have to be perfect, so the chances were that I'd made this detour for nothing.

I ran through that litany three times over: it didn't make me feel the slightest bit better.

I put the scissors in my pocket, tied the hair around the ring finger of my left hand, where I couldn't lose it. Then, self-conscious because Paul was still standing right behind me, staring at my back, I lowered myself to the floor and crossed my legs. With my head bowed and my eyes closed, I began to whistle softly.

It's harder without an instrument, but far from impossible: back when Juliet was still mad, bad, and fucking lethal to know, and was about to devour me body and soul, I'd dragged myself out of the jaws of death (actually it was a different part of death's anatomy, but let's not get bogged down in the technicalities) by tapping out a rhythm with my hand. Everything we ghostbreakers do is just a metaphor—visible or audible or what the hell else—for something else that's going on inside our minds. The limits are the ones we impose on ourselves.

I whistled an old tune that has a lot of different names—one of them is "The Flash Lad." It's a highwayman ballad, meant to date all the way back to the eighteenth century, and if you listen to the lyrics it ends badly. Sweet tune, though, and it seemed to be an appropriate one for what I was trying to do.

Back when Asmodeus had first invaded Rafi's body, I'd spectacularly failed to get a proper sense of him: that was why I'd screwed up so badly, and tied Rafi's soul indissolubly to the demon's essence. But I'd played my tin whistle for Rafi a hundred times since then, playing the demon down to sleep so that my friend could have a few hours' respite from the hell I'd bestowed on him. So I knew Asmodeus quite well by this time; knew how he felt in my fingers; knew how he sounded in my mind; knew the tune of him.

I teased the very edges of a summons, and I felt the demon respond. Faintly—ever so faintly—but unmistakably. Quickly I changed the rhythm and the pitch. I couldn't just break off, but I could ease away, like a fisherman easing the tension on a line to let the fish pull free and escape. I didn't want to face Asmodeus again in this narrow cell; very much indeed I didn't want it. But I did want to be sure that he was there. That although the bulk of this monster's being was embedded in the cold stones of St. Michael's, there was a corner of him still here in the soul of Rafael Ditko.

I had what I needed, and Rafi hadn't even stirred. I let the tune fade down into silence and stood, wincing at a sharp pain in my left leg. It felt like I was bruised there—probably from when Gwillam and his werewolves threw me into the storeroom while I was unconscious.

That was when Rafi opened his eyes. For a moment or two, they didn't focus—or maybe they focused past me, on something from his dreams that he was still seeing. Then he blinked, and something registered.

"Fix," he muttered thickly.

"Hello, Rafi," I said.

"That was fucking weird. I was just talking to you."

"You were?"

"Must've dreamed it. Everything okay?"

"Everything's fine, Rafi."

He closed his eyes again, and in a second a change in the quality of his breathing made it clear that he was asleep again.

"Thanks, Paul," I said, turning back to the burly nurse, who'd been watching me with a sort of glum fascination.

"That was it? You got what you wanted?"

"More or less. Do you carry a mobile?"

"Sure."

"Can I borrow it?"

"Sure. But it's a piece of shit."

He reached a big hand into his pocket and brought out a cute little silver cell phone that he could have worn as an earring. I took it, and checked the battery charge before pocketing it.

"And your lighter," I said.

Paul breathed out heavily enough for it to count as a sigh. But he handed the lighter over, too.

I gave him an appraising look. "You want me to lock you in here or something so you look more like a victim and less like you were in on it?" I asked him.

He made a dismissive gesture. "Yeah, go for it," he said. "Tell you the truth, though, I've been thinking of looking for another job. One where I won't have to swallow so much bullshit. Mind how you go, Castor."

"Thanks, Paul. I owe you one."

"You owe me somewhere between six and ten. Tell me where you drink, I'll come over some night and collect."

"The Jerusalem in Britton Street would be a good bet."

"Okay. I'll see you there."

I let myself out, remembering to ditch the film canister under Rafi's bunk so it would look like I'd made my delivery. The thing about lying is that it gets to be a habit, like anything else.

And then you have to remind yourself to stop.

Chapter Twenty-one

The great thing about riding a motorbike at stupid, reckless speed through the streets of a busy city at night is that it stops you from thinking about anything very much else. If you let your mind stray for more than a second or so, you're likely to end up attached so intimately to a wall that nothing short of a scraper and a bucket will get you off again.

That almost didn't stop me, though. I was in a weird state of mind, keyed up for a fight that might never happen—or that might already be over. If Fanke had gone ahead and completed his summoning ritual, then Abbie's soul had been struck like a match and used up to light Asmodeus's way into the world of men—after two unscheduled stop-overs in Rafi Ditko and St. Michael's Church. Or if Fanke had set up his kit at St. Michael's but been interrupted by Gwillam and his hairy Catholic apostates, then probably the satanists were all dead by now— the upside—but Abbie would have been exorcised by the people who thought of themselves as the good guys—the downside. Either way, she was gone forever and the promise I'd made to Peace was blowing in the wind along with the answers to Bob Dylan's coy little riddles.

No, the only hope here, the only way I could make the smallest dif-ference, was if Fanke hadn't started the ritual yet and the Anathemata didn't know where it was going to happen. I had to hope both that the logistics of satanism were more complicated than they seemed to be from the outside and that I'd passed out before Gwillam's needle loosened my tongue too far.

I rode straight past St. Michael's so I could look it over without committing myself. No lights on, and no sign of life: either it was all over or the fun hadn't started yet. Or maybe Fanke just preferred to work in the dark, which would make a certain kind of sense.

I ditched the bike three blocks up and walked back, the bundle of film canisters under one arm and the other hand in the pocket of the leather jacket, gripping the gun hard. Despair would make me weak, so I tried to turn what I was feeling into anger—which brought problems of its own in terms of planning ahead and keeping a clear perspective on things.

It had to be here. If it hadn't already happened, this was where Fanke was going to come. What I had to do was to stop him before he succeeded in raising Asmodeus; before he spread the psychic poison that the congregants of St. Michael's had already swallowed to the city as a whole; and before he consumed the soul of Abbie Torrington.

I put my chances pretty high: right up there with a white Christmas, the second coming, and the Beatles (living and dead) getting together again.

The lych-gate of the church was locked, as always. I took a quick look up and down the street to see if anyone was staking the place out, then shinnied over it and dropped down into the graveyard beyond. On a moonless night, and with the church itself still mantled in darkness, there was enough natural cover here so that I didn't need to worry too much about stealth. I just circled around to a position from which I could watch the presbytery without being seen myself.

Sitting under the ancient oak, with my back against its broad trunk, I settled in for the long haul. But as it turned out, my threadbare patience wasn't tested very much at all. Barely an hour after I arrived, the clanking of a chain drew my attention from the church back to the gate. It was followed a second or so later by the grinding clack of a bolt cutter biting through thick steel. The gate swung open and three figures stepped silently through. One of them threw the chain and padlock negligently down on the ground, just inside the gate.

I was completely hidden where I sat by the deep shadows under the tree and by the unrelieved blackness of the night. Not only was it dark of the moon but it was a clear night, so there were no clouds to bounce back the muddied radiance of the streetlights. Contrary to popular belief, there isn't much that you can see by starlight.

Two of the three men—at least, their height suggested they were men—went on around to the vestry door, the third stationed himself at the gate, either on guard duty or maybe carrying out some more ceremonial function.

The men had brought crowbars with them, but they didn't need them because the vestry door was still hanging on one hinge from Juliet's assault on it the night before. They pushed it all the way open and stepped inside.

By this time, more people were filing silently in through the gate, past the man on watch. Some of them were carrying sports bags or shoulder bags: one carried a long case of some kind slung across his back that looked as though it could contain a fishing rod. It was a regular field-and-stream meet, to judge by appearances.

I counted about two dozen of them in all as they trickled past in twos and threes over the next ten minutes or so. They must be staggering their arrival so that anybody passing in the street would be less likely to pay them any attention. It had probably been the same drill the week before, at the Quaker meeting house. Discretion is the watchword of the modern necromancer: mustn't upset the neighbors, or you'll never be invited back. I wondered, fleetingly, what sort of people thought it was a great idea to spend their weekends murdering children to hasten the rule of hell on earth, but I gave it up pretty quickly. The less I knew about them the better I liked it.

Fanke himself, when he arrived, was unmistakable. It wasn't that his build was so distinctive: it was the fawning servility of the men who walked at his side, or rather a couple of paces behind him on either hand, and the way the guard on the gate bowed low as he passed. He didn't deign to notice this act of self-abasement: he sailed on by, his arrogance ringing him like a visible halo. I fingered the gun again. If I'd been sure that Fanke's death would have stopped the ritual, and if I'd had more confidence in my aim, I would have emptied the clip at him. But it would have been depressing to do that and miss, and then to have to watch while the bastards got their infernal groove on. No, the gun was more useful in my hands as a deterrent than as an actual weapon; so long as I didn't use it, nobody would guess what a lousy shot I was.

When the last few stragglers had made their way inside, the guard on the gate pulled it to and tied it off with a short length of rope, or maybe wire—from my vantage point I couldn't quite see. I was hoping and expecting him to join his friends at the altar, but he didn't. He leaned against the wall, peering out into the street through the crack where the gate hung slightly loose on its new moorings. Glancing across toward the presbytery, I thought I saw the faintest hint of movement in the darkness just inside the doorway. Then the lights went on in the nave and the man standing there was outlined clearly.

Two guards. No clear line of sight between them, but I couldn't approach either one without revealing my position to the other. And I really didn't want Fanke knowing I was there before I was ready to face him. So I had to take these guys out, quietly, without raising an alarm inside the church—and I had to do it fast, before the ritual got too far along to be stopped.

I considered a few variations on thrown stones and improvised diversions before I finally noticed that there was a way up onto the presbytery roof. From where I was, I could carry on around to the far right, shinny up onto the far wall of the cemetery and from there onto the sloping slates. If they took my weight, I could get in close to the guy in the doorway without the one at the gate seeing me coming.

Okay, so that was the plan—if I could call it that without breaching the trades descriptions act. But before I put it into action, there was one more thing I had to do. I took Paul's mobile out and keyed out a number in the dark, using the raised bump on the number "5" to guide my thumb. The ring tone sounded loud in my ear—but only in my ear, thank God.

"Emergency. Which service, please?" A woman's voice, brisk and impersonal.

"Police," I murmured throatily.

"Routing you through, caller."

I waited. After ten seconds or so, the silence turned into another ring tone. A man picked up. "Bowater Street police station, how can I help?"

"You can patch me through to Uxbridge Road," I growled.

There was a fractional pause. "I'm sorry, caller, I didn't get that. How can I help?"

"Put me through to Uxbridge Road," I repeated. "This is an emergency."

I waited some more. This wasn't how emergency calls were supposed to go, but I knew that the main station on any switchboard had direct lines to all of the others. If the guy tried to pump me for information, I'd just have to leave a message with him. Otherwise . . .

"This is Uxbridge Road. Do you have a problem, sir?"

"I've got a message," I said, "for Detective Sergeant Basquiat. Tell her it's Felix Castor. Tell her I'm at St. Michael's Church, on Du Cane Road, and that Anton Fanke is here, too. Tell her to come right now—and mob-handed."

I hung up, and put the phone away. I'd played two wild cards now, and that ought to be enough for any hand. Whatever happened next, and whatever happened to me, I took some comfort in the thought that Fanke and his religiously inverted friends were going to have a hard time getting out of the building alive and free.

I stood up, as slowly and smoothly as I could, and slipped away between the gravestones with my knees bent so that my head wouldn't show against the skyline. For the first ten yards or so, I was in both men's line of sight if they chanced to turn around. I was counting on the dense shadows to hide my movements and the distant traffic noises from the street to conceal any sound I might make. All the same, I went as carefully as I could, barely lifting my feet off the ground in case they came down on a twig or a discarded Coke can and gave my presence away.

Once I got far enough around for the presbytery wall to give me cover, I relaxed a little. I straightened my back and picked up speed, reaching the wall in a few nearly normal strides. Climbing it in the dark was harder than I expected, because a good foothold at the bottom could still leave you stranded and groping seven or eight feet up, pinned to the wall with your arms splayed out like Christ's dumb understudy. Once a loose chunk of stone slid away under my foot and fell to the ground below with an audible *thump*. I froze in place, straining my ears for sounds of approaching footsteps, but nobody came. I resumed the climb, teeth gritted, suddenly aware that there might be razor wire or broken glass or some other bullshit at the top of the wall that I'd seen in daylight but not registered or remembered.

There wasn't. The stones at the top were uneven, but they were wide enough for me to stand and walk along without much difficulty. And the roof was no trouble at all: the guttering was old, of solid metal rather than uPVC, and it took my weight with a reassuring lack of give.

Leaning into the pitch of the tiles, I edged along from the back of the presbytery to the front. Now I could look around and down and see the doorway below me, a faint glow filtering out from it to light up a keystone-shaped area of gravel in pale gold. Within that lighted space, a dark blob just off center showed me where Fanke's watchman was standing just inside the doorway, but the man himself I couldn't see.

There was no time for bluff, finesse, or actual cleverness. All I could think of doing was to reach out and scrape the end of the gun barrel against the stone of the wall. The first time got no response, and neither did the second: traffic sounds from the street drowned the faint noise out. The third time was the charm. Below me in the dark, a darker figure stepped out and a pale face looked up. I launched myself into space.

The guy never knew what hit him, and he might never wake up to find out. As I landed on top of him I struck down hard with the butt of the gun, letting gravity and momentum add their force to mine. It smacked into his skull with a solid, slightly sickening sound and he crumpled underneath me, providing me with a much softer landing than I was expecting.

Not that I stayed down for long. I rolled and came up already moving, heading along the back wall of the church toward the corner where the lych-gate was. My feet were crunching on the gravel, but I couldn't help that: I had to assume that the man at the gate had heard me touch down, and would want to know what the hell the commotion was about.

I reached the corner of the building just as he came around it. That worked out pretty well, because I was expecting him and he wasn't really expecting me. He wasn't expecting the fist that slammed into his stomach, either: he folded with a strangled, truncated grunt. I spun him round with a hand on his shoulder and slammed his head into a conveniently placed tombstone once, twice, three times. After three he looked like he'd lost interest in the altercation. I let go and he slumped bonelessly to the ground.

So far so good. I rolled him on his back, gun in hand, to make sure he wasn't faking it. He was deeply unconscious, his slack mouth trailing blood and saliva from one corner. There was blood on the crown of his head, too.

Well, what the hell. In the absence of the Lord, vengeance would just have to be mine.

I went to the foot of the oak tree and retrieved the film canisters, then crossed back to the presbytery door, skirting around the body of the first guard. I weighed up the idea of moving the bodies off the path, in among the graves, but a clock was ticking inside my head. In any case, the windows of the church were stained glass: nobody was going to see the downed men unless they came in through the lych-gate and walked around to enter the church from the back. And if they did that they'd have the drop on me already.

I listened for a moment at the door, then slipped inside. The presbytery itself was empty, as I'd expected it to be. I crossed to the other door, which led into the church. It stood open. A distant murmur of voices came through it, and the *clop-clop* whisper of soft but echoing footsteps, but from this vantage point there was nothing to see; the chancel was deserted, as I'd hoped it would be. Hopefully whatever was happening in there, it was in the nave close to the high altar.

There was a carpet in the vestry, for soft, priestly feet: before stepping out into the chancel, I kicked off my shoes. I didn't want the excellent acoustics of St. Michael's to betray me before I had a chance to set my stall out.

The stone was so cold I almost gave myself away even more embarrassingly, by yelling out. It felt like some parasitic plant of the frozen tundra was growing up through the soles of my feet into my trembling legs. I regretted the shoes now, but it was too late for that.

I stole along the chancel to the big box junction where it met the main drag of the nave. The light was coming from one end of the cavernous space—the altar end, as I'd guessed: satanists are all about transgression, bless their little hearts. They're so fucking predictable it's not even funny. So where I was, there was a fair amount of deep shadow, and I felt reasonably confident that if I peered round the angle of the wall I wouldn't be seen.

They were still setting up. The robed figures were moving chairs around to make a broad, bare space just below the altar. One of them—Fanke himself, judging by the red robes that Peace had already described to me—was on his knees in the center of the space, and a scratching, rasping sound gave me a strong hint as to what he was doing: drawing the vicious circle.

So one way and another, the kiddies were all entertained. If they'd already started intoning and dancing in a ring, I'd have fired a warning shot into somebody's back and gone in like thunder—an action replay of Peace's moment of glory the week before—but as it was I took the time to set up my little ace in the hole. I went down on all fours; or rather on all threes, because I was hugging the film canisters to my chest with my left arm, tightly enough so they couldn't scrape against each other and give me away. I crab-scuttled out of the shadows of the chancel and across to the nearest row of pews, sliding in among them with as little sound as I could manage. Then I set down my burden with elaborate caution, and unpacked.

As already noted, old movie film is pretty much the most flammable thing on earth. With a Molotov cocktail you need a bottle, a piece of rag, all sorts of paraphernalia. Movie film just burns, turning instantly into boiling plastic, searing smoke, and blue-white flame like the flame of a dirty blowtorch: drop a match on it and you'd better be somewhere else when it hits.

By way of a fuse I used a votive candle that I'd picked up from the floor on my way down the transept: it was one of the ones that had rolled and scattered when I knocked the table over the night before. The thing was an inch and a half thick, but I broke it in my hands, muffling the sound inside my jacket, and pulled away the solid, almost translucent chunks of it to leave the shiny, rigid wand of the wick itself—a makeshift taper, stiff and saturated with solid wax.

The nature of the sounds I was hearing from the front of the church had changed now. The footsteps had ceased, and a rhythmic chanting had begun. I hoped the satanist liturgy was as prolix as the regular one; I needed a couple of minutes more.

I slid the film canisters open, found the ends, and hauled out a foot or so of each, which I tied together like the five intertwined tails of the rat king in the old folk legend. I slid the lower end of my taper in among them, balanced so that it stood nearly upright, then lit the business end. It burned brightly at first, then started to fade almost at once as the chill and the hate locked in the stones began to focus on the little point of light. I watched it with glowering suspicion for a moment or two, but it steadied. I couldn't be sure that it would last long enough to burn all the way down to the film, but it was the best I could do.

A single voice had risen up above the murmured responses of the acolytes: Fanke's voice, low and thrilling and solemn. I was expecting some bit of late medieval guff about how Lucifer is a good old boy and he'd just love to reach out and touch you, but this sounded older—and my classical Greek gives out after "which way to the bathroom?" and "I want mine with retsina."

"Aberamenthô oulerthexa n axethreluo ôthnemareba," Fanke boomed out, his voice rising now both in pitch and volume. *"Iaô Sabaôth Iaeô pakenpsôth pakenbraôth sabarbatiaôth sabarbatianê sabarbaphai. Satana. Beelzebub. Asmode."*

I couldn't have picked a better time to make my entrance. Standing up in the cheap seats, I fired one shot at the ceiling, and it roared around the room like the voice of God. The satanists spun round with their mouths hanging open, and Fanke faltered in his recitation. I stepped out into the aisle, leveling the gun at his chest.

"Hey, Anton," I said, strolling unhurriedly toward him. "Steve. Dylan. Whatever the fuck you call yourself on a Saturday. How's it hanging? I know how this one ends, if you're interested. The next words are 'I surrender.' And then you turn around, put your hands on the altar rail, and assume the position."

The acolytes backed away from me on either side. The last time they'd faced a self-righteous nutcase with a gun they'd found themselves transformed from chorus line to moving targets, and that experience seemed to have left its mark. Fanke stood his ground, though, and the look on his face didn't change, except to add an overlay of sneering contempt to the cold superiority that was already there. That got my goat a little.

"Step away from the circle," I said, close enough now so that I didn't have to raise my voice. I tried to keep the stooges in my peripheral vision in case they went through their pockets and found out where they'd left their balls, but the first bullet was for Fanke in any case: and the second, third, and fourth, if it came to that.

He didn't move. He was standing a little stiffly, his left shoulder a little higher than his right. I remembered him giving that spastic jerk when Peace fired his second shot: Fanke had taken a bullet, either in the shoulder itself or high up on his right arm. But he was a trooper, and the show had to go on.

"Castor," he said, with pitying condescension. "I gave you your life. True, I took away from you a great many other things, but still the overall balance, I thought, was maintained. Yet here you are. And perhaps, after all, it's fitting that you should be here to welcome my lord Asmodeus when he comes."

"He missed his train," I snapped. "He said to send his love. Now step away from the fucking circle, Fanke, or I swear on my sainted mother's grave I am putting enough holes through you so I can see the deposition of Christ in that central panel behind you."

"No." Fanke shook his head, lowering his gaze to the ground as if he were meditating on human folly. "You're not. Patience?" I took this last word to be a piece of supercilious advice, until a woman's voice from off to my left answered shakily, "Yes, magister?"

"Tell Mr. Castor how many sacrifices we've got lined up for this evening."

"Thr-three, magister. There are three."

"And what's the order of play?"

"First the chi—the spirit. The spirit already dedicated. Then the demon. Last the woman."

Eyes left, just momentarily, and with my finger tense on the trigger so that if Fanke moved at all I could still cut loose at him. That quick glance was enough to confirm what I already more or less knew. The woman who was speaking was the woman who I'd met a week ago in my office—the woman with the badly bruised face, who'd been introduced to me as Melanie Torrington. Then I was looking at Fanke again, and he raised his eyes to meet my gaze.

He wasn't smug, exactly. His expression said that he didn't think it was any great feat to outthink me.

"I wanted to be sure this time," he murmured. "The child's spirit ought to complete the summoning, and free my dread lord from this . . . place. But just in case, I thought it would be best to have a hecateum—a three-way offering, covering living and dead, male and female, spirit and flesh."

I took another step toward him and actually poked the barrel of the gun into his chest. This time he gave, slightly, and his back bumped against the altar rail. I was gratified to have gotten some kind of reaction out of him at last.

"Show me," I suggested.

"No. Put the gun away."

I held his gaze and said it again, with a very final emphasis. "Show me. Or you and me are both going to hell a little earlier than we expected."

Fanke turned to glance across at the woman. "Bring them forward," he said, the command sounding as negligent and world-weary as he could make it. He'd seen in my eyes that I was ready to shoot, and he'd changed his mind about bluffing me. That was something.

There was a bustle of activity as robed figures ran to do his bidding. If I were going to join a cult, I'd want to go in at officer level: there's fuck all job satisfaction at the bottom of the tree.

I followed the proceedings out of the corner of my eye. Pen and Juliet weren't even in another room, they were just in the shadows under the pulpit, laid side by side on the ground. Juliet was still in her coma/trance/whatever state, and didn't react at all as she was carried forward and laid down just behind and to the right of Fanke. Pen was bound, gagged, conscious, and mad as hell. She managed to kick one satanist in a part he'd probably already consecrated to the dark lord: he doubled up with an unmanly yelp and dropped her legs. Two other men stepped in and completed the task of hauling her out for my inspection. They laid her down to Fanke's left-hand side, so that from my point of view he was bookended by comely hostages.

Then, with a consummate sense of theater, he held out his clenched fist to me as if in salute, before opening it wide to show Peace's locket—on a new chain—dangling from his index finger. *"Veni, puella,"* he murmured. Abbie's ghost materialized around his hand, very abruptly, looking startled and terrified. She cast her eyes from side to side, from face to face, taking in the massed ranks of the satanists surrounding her, and me facing her across the magic circle. On me her eyes rested for longest, big and wide and full of hate.

"I don't lie for effect, Castor," Fanke said, speaking to me through her translucent body. "I lie to achieve specific goals. In this case, as you can see, I've told the truth. Now put the gun down—unless you think that my death is a fair exchange for Pamela's. Because my death is all you can hope to achieve: the ceremony will go on, and will be completed, in any case."

"Where's your male?" I demanded, still buying seconds.

Fanke actually smiled. "I don't have one," he admitted. "I'd decided to use your zombie friend—Nicholas Heath. Yes, I know about him. I know everything there is to know about your life: I've been close to you for a long time, after all. But when my people went to fetch the zombie, they found this other creature, and I yielded to temptation. My lord doesn't favor the succubi. There's something appropriate about feeding one of that kindred to the flame to set him free."

His eyes stared into mine, mocking and malevolent: the eyes of a man who was damn sure he was holding all the cards.

"A male would still be useful," he said, "for the sake of balance. But it's up to you. You can play out this film noir pantomime, if you like. Or you can take Pamela Bruckner's place and die inside our circle. I'll allow that. If you put the gun down right now, and aplogize to me for your disrespect."

I hesitated. He was lying, of course, but then time was what I was playing for here on a lot of different levels.

"Where's Nicky now?" I demanded, buying a few more seconds. I guess the wax on that candle was thicker than I thought; I guess Basquiat hadn't called in to check her messages; I guess my luck was running pretty much true to form, after all.

Fanke frowned. "Your dead friend, I believe, is still extant," he said. "But the details get a little abstruse. He locked himself into a room on the first floor of the cinema. When my people tried to open the door—" He stopped, seeing I was grinning. "Well, perhaps you already know about his security arrangements. In any case, the succubus made a more than acceptable substitute. Hiring you was the best decision I ever made, Castor. At the time I thought I was just keeping things in the family—but it brought so many incidental benefits. But now we're delaying proceedings, and they've been delayed too long already. Please—your decision."

Fanke was looking at me expectantly, and I could see in his eyes that—unlike me—he hadn't had to bluff at all. He was going to see this through, even if it meant me rearranging his innards with the aid of hollow-point ammunition. One way or another, the show was going to go on.

Trying to ignore Abbie, whose dead gaze still skewered me, I nodded.

"All right," I said. "Let Pen go, give her five minutes to get clear, and then I'll hand over the gun."

"No," said Fanke, tersely. "You hand over the gun now, and you accept my word that she won't be harmed. No more procrastinations. Decide."

I waited in vain for an explosion from the back pews, or for a hammering on the knocker and "This is the police!" from the church's main doors. The silence, in which Asmodeus's hostile attention was like a raw overlay of subliminal hypersonics, remained unbroken.

After a long pause, and just as Fanke opened his mouth to speak again—to his subordinates, not to me, because his head snapped round to face them—I turned the gun in my hand and held it out to him, butt first. He gave a nod, quietly satisfied, and took it. Then he passed it on to a tall, cadaverous acolyte who appeared at his shoulder.

"And the apology?" he asked, looking round at me again like a coaxing schoolmaster who doesn't want to have to resort to the cane.

"You'll have to whistle for that," I said. "You know how to whistle, don't you? If not, I can teach you."

He gave me the coldest smile I've ever seen.

"Grip, keep the gun trained on Mr. Castor," he said, "and bring him to the circle. In fact, have someone pass a loop of piano wire around his throat, too, to make sure he stays exactly where he's put. He has the look of a man who wants to go back on his word."

The robed minions closed in on all sides, finding their courage all of a sudden, and a great many hands were laid on me. I was manhandled to the edge of the circle, which I saw clearly now for the first time. It seemed to be identical to the ruined one I'd seen in the Quaker hall, but complete, uninterrupted by any chewed-up arc of pulped floorboards. In fact, this one was drawn on stone—and drawn with the tip of a knife blade, rather than in paint or chalk. Various half-formed schemes that had been forming in the forefront of my mind got discouraged and left.

The man Fanke had called Grip shoved the gun into the small of my back more emphatically than was necessary, and kept it there while another robed figure—a tall, heavyset woman—passed a loop of piano wire very carefully around my neck. The care was for her own fingers; as soon as it was in place she pulled it tight, and I felt it bite into the flesh below my Adam's apple. The two loose ends of the wire had been tied around wooden blocks: she held one in each hand, like a paramedic with the charged plates of a defibrillator, but what she was actually holding, in effect, was the drawstring of a guillotine. If I moved from this spot, my head was going to stay right where it was while my body did its best to make shift without it.

Fanke walked around the circle to stand opposite me. Abbie went with him, dangling weightlessly in the air, his clenched fist wrapped around where her heart would be if she were alive and still had one. Her confusion and fear were terrible to see.

The robed acolytes—except for Grip and the woman with the piano wire—took their stations with solemn faces all around in a wider circle that extended from the altar rail to the ragged heap of displaced pews, and to the aisle on either side. There were more of them than I'd thought: at least forty. Some of them must have come in through the main doors after the rest had set up shop and opened up for them, which explained why I hadn't seen Pen and Juliet being brought in. One of them was the little doctor with the Scottish accent who'd given me my tetanus shots after I passed out in Pen's hallway.

The crucified Christ stared down at us, looking dubious about the whole proceeding.

"I'd prefer to start with you," Fanke said, without animosity. "Like Pamela, you're a little out of place here. In many ways, beneath the dignity of the occasion. But the child's spirit must be sundered. That won't wait. To attempt any other sacrifice before the one that raised my lord is concluded would be unwise. So you'll have to wait your turn, Castor. And you'll have to watch your efforts and machinations come to nothing before you're allowed to slink away into death. This isn't cruelty on my part, you understand. Just . . . logistics."

"Well if it's just logistics, I don't mind," I said. "I was starting to think you didn't like me." The wire tightened fractionally around my throat.

"Marmarauôth marmarachtha marmarachthaa amarda maribeôth," Fanke said, in a singsong voice. The acolytes came in on the chorus. *"Satana! Beelzebub! Asmode!"* They threw out their hands, then drew them in and clasped them together in what was clearly a ritual gesture.

"Iattheoun iatreoun salbiouth aôth aôth sabathiouth iattherath Adônaiai isar suria bibibe bibiouth nattho Sabaoth aianapha amourachthê. Satana. Beelzebub. Asmode." More hand-wringing. An acolyte at Fanke's left hand held out a candle, and one on his right lit it with a taper. Fanke took it in his left hand without dropping a syllable. *"Ablanathanalba, aeêiouô, iaeôbaphrenemoun. Aberamenthô oulerthexa n axethreluo ôthnemareba."* Even though most of the room was already steeped in darkness, the area around us seemed to be getting darker still. I made the mistake of looking up, as though the church had some internal sun that was being eclipsed. Something hung above us in the gloom—something like black smoke, except that it was shot through with branching filaments of deeper dark like veins and capillaries. It was spreading out from a point directly above Fanke's head, and it was descending toward us. Or rather toward Abbie, who saw it coming and struggled like a fly in a web, her thrashing movements buying her no headway at all. "Please!" she whispered. "Oh please!"

He looks a lot smaller in the medieval woodcuts, but I knew who it was that we were looking at: Asmodeus, coalescing out of the stone in answer to Fanke's summons. The cold came with him, concentrating around us with such suddenness and intensity that I felt the skin on my face stretch taut.

Fanke held the locket up in his right hand, on a level with the candle flame. *"Phôkensepseu earektathou misonktaich,"* he said. *"Uesemmeigadôn Satana. Uesemmeigadôn Beelzebub. Uesemmeigadôn Asmode, Asmode atheresphilauô."*

He brought his hands together to let the locket meet the flame. Or at least he tried to, but it didn't come. Abbie dug her heels into nothing and strained backward against him, and although his hand trembled like a struck lightning rod, for a moment it didn't move. His right arm was the injured one—the one where Peace had shot him—and I'd seen before that his movements with that hand and arm were stiff and jerky. Maybe that gave the desperate ghost some hint of purchase. Whatever it was, Fanke was startled: he turned to glare at her, pulled harder. His wrist spasmed once, twice, and began to move again.

But before the locket and the flame could touch, I thrust out my own hand and put my ring finger into the candle's corona. Rafi's hair, which was still tied there in a tight loop knot, singed and sizzled.

"Amen," I growled, gritting my teeth against the pain so it looked like I was enjoying a private joke.

The piano wire tightened around my throat, and the church exploded.

Chapter Twenty-two

The noise was like nothing I can describe. If you could imagine a full brass band had packed their instruments with TNT and blown themselves to hell on the final bar of "The Floral Dance," then you'd be off to a good start. But that was just background noise: the film canisters being ripped into red-hot gobbets that ricocheted off the walls and scythed over our heads as the ignited film spools gushed out a geyser of flame and gas that expanded too fast for them to get out of its way.

It was Asmodeus's scream that really made the moment special.

Dennis Peace had tried to describe it to me when he told me about what had gone down at the meeting house, but he didn't do it justice. It was as though you were hearing it through every inch of your skin, on a pitch that made your internal organs vibrate and scream in sympathy: as though you'd become a taut membrane on which broken glass was showering down, playing notes by tearing random holes in you.

I held my hand in the flame for a second or so longer, until the pain became too great to bear. Then I lurched back, which should have been the end of me—but the woman with the piano wire had lost the plot, too, slamming her hands unavailingly to her ears. The wooden chocks on either end of the wire fell free, and their weight made the wire bite a little more deeply into my throat, but the sensation was drowned out in the all-over-body migraine effect of Asmodeus's bellowed pain and rage.

Fanke was still standing his ground on the far side of the circle, and his mouth was open as if he was yelling something. There was no sign of Abbie: I wasn't sure exactly when she'd winked out, but she was no longer wrapped around his clenched fist. Everyone else was collapsing to their knees or trying to run on suddenly rubberized legs. A gout of oily black smoke erupted up the center aisle, creeping low along the ground at first but rising and opening out as though it was alive and hungry, flickers of flame winking on and off within it like eyes.

I looked up at Asmodeus—I mean, at the clotted shadow thing that was condensing over our heads. In a different way, I knew, the whole building was Asmodeus. The thing was spasming arrhythmically, the veinlike tendrils drawn in to the heart and then spat out again in whiplash curves, tightening on themselves with audible cracks. That meant my ears were working again, at least: in the initial shock after the movie canisters blew, I was afraid my eardrums had burst.

First things first. I shrugged off the piano wire, feeling it pull and then give, releasing a shower of blood droplets where it had been partially embedded in the flesh of my throat. Letting it fall, I leaned forward across the magic circle and hauled off with a punch that hit Fanke full in the face. It sent a thrill of agony through my burned fingers, but it also sent him flailing backward into the altar rail. Jumping over the circle, I followed up with a low blow that doubled him up and made him drop Abbie's locket. Good enough. I snatched the little golden heart up off the flags, and as I straightened again I brought my knee up into the bridge of Fanke's nose for good measure. That should give him plenty to think about while I took care of Pen and Juliet.

Of course, how I was going to carry two women out of a burning building was a question that I hadn't really thought through to any firm conclusions. But turning around with the locket clasped in my injured left hand, I discovered that it was unlikely to become an issue.

In spite of the flames billowing up toward the ceiling at the back of the church, and the filaments of smoke crawling forward along the aisles, Fanke's followers had rallied and were running to the defense of their master. The first reached me just as I turned, throwing a clumsy punch that I clumsily blocked. I caught him on the rebound with a head butt that he didn't see coming. The second had a knife, and he stepped in around his injured colleague so that he could use it. But a couple of other robed figures surging up behind him knocked him off balance, and I was able to do a step-and-roll over the altar rail and back away from the charge.

They scrambled after me, fanning out along the length of the rail so that there was nowhere I could run to. This was the last place any of us wanted to be if the fire spread to cut us off from the main doors, but Fanke's acolytes obviously cared more about completing the ritual than they did about their own safety. That's what I've never been able to get about religion: that charmless combination of altruism and insanity. Give me a cynical, self-interested bastard any day of the week; at least you can play chicken with him and know he'll stick to the rules.

I sprinted for the altar, but only because there was nowhere else to sprint. It was a lousy place for a last stand, as the crucified Christ had already discovered. I tried to vault up onto it, but since my left hand was out of action I had to use my right, which as a southpaw I'm a lot less handy with. I didn't quite clear the marble top of the altar, which projected out about six inches from the base all around: instead I caught it with my knee, slipped, and fell back to the floor in a sprawling heap.

The satanists converged on me, too many to fight and too damn stupid to scare. Then, amazingly, instead of trampling me down and tearing me apart in the time-honored way of religious zealots everywhere, they hesitated and came to a stumbling halt, staring past me across the altar. I saw why a moment later, as something scratched and skittered along its upper surface, and a set of long, slender talons gripped the stone rim just above my head.

Then the thing that was up there jumped into the midst of the satanists. It looked like a greyhound at first—but that was because the two overriding impressions were of gray fur and emaciated slenderness. It was nothing like a greyhound in the way it moved: it arced like a striking snake, mewled like a cat, swiping out to left and right with hands from which claws bristled like racks of scalpels lovingly ranged by size. One of the satanists screamed, but the scream was cut short as blood plumed from his severed throat. Another staggered back clutching both hands to his face, purple gouts welling up between his splayed fingers. A third had a gun already in his hand, and fired, but the shot went wide and broke one arm off the Christ above the altar. It crashed down behind me, unheeded.

The satanists broke to either side, the gray thing dancing like a dervish between them. I saw its face, and that was a horror with its own special resonance, even in the midst of this symphony of horrors: partly because of the misshapen snout forced into an insane grin by canines too large for it to contain, but mainly because it was Zucker's face, and I saw the man within the beast.

I tightened my grip on the locket, but my charred fingers wouldn't close all the way, and the loup-garou's eyes had already been drawn to the flash of incongruous gold from my blackened hand. He tensed to jump, but then the man with the gun fired again, and one of the beast's legs gave way under it. Zucker made a squalling shriek, turning to face the new threat. It had already been dealt with, as Po—in human form—strode forward out of the smoke, took the gunman's head in both of his hands and twisted it until it faced the wrong way on his neck.

I followed the example of most of the surviving satanists and ran for it. Unfortunately, we were running into a storm: Fanke's followers fell like threshed wheat as the sound of gunfire spread across the church. They seemed to prefer gunfire to what was behind them; several of them drew guns of their own and fired back. Dimly, through the spreading smoke, I saw black-robed figures moving up from the back of the church, skirting around the ceiling-high pyre in the center where the film cans had exploded. Then a bullet whanged past on my left-hand side, knocking a fist-size hole in the back of a pew, and I hit the deck.

I considered the merits of staying there until the whole thing played itself out. Fanke couldn't do anything without the locket, and that was still safe in my fire-blackened hand. But Gwillam's church commandos were after the same thing, and if they got it they'd exorcise Abbie without a second thought. I didn't want to give them that chance. Admittedly, it was my fault they were here at all: the note I'd left stuffed into Sallis's pants back at the South Bank Centre had invited them to join me here for an informal chat and a little light jihad. I'd hoped that their arrival—or Basquiat's—might come at a point where I needed a diversion. The age-old game of "let's you and him fight" is one I've always liked.

But this was getting too hot for my liking—in the literal sense as well as the other. Pen and Juliet were still out in the open, where a stray bullet could hit them at any moment, and even without that, the thickening smoke suggested that the fire was taking hold and spreading. Whatever happened, I didn't have the luxury of just staying put.

At least the smoke would give me a little cover: it was also choking me, making my eyes water and my lungs ache and spasm with each breath, but you can't have everything. I crawled on hands and knees to the end of the pew and then sprinted across to the outer aisle, where a line of pillars provided something more solid to hide behind. I snaked forward from one to the next, making for the open area in front of the altar rail where Pen and Juliet were lying.

The smoke was thick enough now so that I didn't have to worry too much about hiding: gunfire was still echoing and re-echoing through the church, but if a bullet hit me it would only be by accident. Nobody could target through this, even by night-sight: on a night scope, the church would be one large splodge of undifferentiated red, like spilled blood.

I found Pen first. She was unconscious, which didn't surprise me. Hooking my hands under her shoulders, I hauled her toward where I remembered the doors were. I was out by a few yards, but there was a clear corridor right up against the outer wall, caused by some freakish thermocline, so once I got there I could see where I was going. I dragged her along to the narthex—a lobby area barely ten feet across—and inside, relaxing in spite of myself to be in such a relatively small space after the terrible exposure of the church proper.

If I'd been thinking about it, of course, I'd have realized that someone on Gwillam's team had to be watching the doors. It would be out of character for him to miss a trick like that. As I laid Pen down with her head right up against the doors, where clean, breathable air was filtering in from outside, Po lumbered out of the roiling blackness, backlit by the fires of hell, effectively barring my way back into the nave. He was no longer even remotely human: He was the hyena thing that I'd seen at the Thames Collective and then again at the Whittington, his front limbs twice as long as his back ones so that he stood almost like an ape.

He loped toward me, grinning. It wasn't a grin of amusement: it was more a question of unsheathing his main weaponry, which jutted from his jaws like steak knives. I watched him closely, tensing to jump when he did, but there wasn't enough room in the narrow narthex to do much more than duck. Wherever I went, there wasn't anywhere that was out of his reach.

Then a second figure appeared at his shoulder, walking unhurriedly toward him out of the growing inferno. She looked—well, right then she looked so good I would have cried, if I hadn't already been crying because of the smoke.

"You should have woken me, Castor," Juliet said reproachfully, a harsh rasp in back of her voice. "I almost missed this."

Po turned and jumped in one movement, giving out a terrifying roar. He hit Juliet like a fanged and clawed meteorite, his muscular back limbs raking up from below to disembowel her even as his jaws fastened around her head.

That was the plan, anyway. She bent under him, sinuous and graceful, caught him on her hands, and threw him, using his own momentum, into the nearest row of pews. He was up again in an instant, but Juliet was quicker. As he advanced on her again she lifted up one of the pews, judging the balance perfectly and completely untroubled by the weight. She brought it down across his head and shoulders so fast it blurred.

Amazingly, there was still some fight in him: I suspect there might have been more, if it hadn't been for what he was breathing. He closed with her and they both went down together as a gust of smoke and flame hid them from my sight.

I left Juliet to look after herself, knowing that she could. With the collapse of the ritual, Asmodeus seemed to have loosed whatever hold he had on her. I suspected there was nothing left of him in the church at all now. If there was, he certainly wasn't on fighting form right then.

I went back to Pen, kicked the main doors of the church open, and dragged her out onto the cobbles outside. Then I slumped to my knees beside her, sucking in the cool air as if it was wine. Like wine, it made my head spin and a feeling of almost unbearable lightness expand inside my tortured chest.

The bubble burst as a gun muzzle was laid alongside my head.

"Give me the locket," Fanke wheezed, his voice all the more terrifying for the bubbling sound of organic damage at the back of it. Even without turning to look at him, I could tell that this was a man with very little left to lose.

"I haven't got it," I said.

"Stand up. Spread your arms. Now, Castor!"

Maybe I'm just paranoid, but it seemed to me right then that my life expectancy was exactly as long as I could keep Fanke guessing. Once he had the locket, he'd be wanting to deal out some payback for his ruined ritual and his lost good looks. I took a gamble on his line of sight, letting the locket slide out of my hand into the space between Pen's arm and body. Then I stood, very slowly, putting out my arms to either side, fingers spread.

Fanke's hands patted down my pockets. His breathing was painful to hear: an uneven, drawn-out skirl with that liquid undertow which suggested vital fluids leaking into places where they weren't meant to be. He went through my coat, then my trousers. When he came up empty, he pressed the gun a little more tightly against my cheek.

"Where is it?" he demanded.

"I think I left it inside," I suggested. "On the altar."

The gun scraped against my cheekbone as Fanke thumbed off the safety. "Then I think you're dead," he growled.

Certainly one of us was. There was a sound like someone ripping a silk scarf, and the gun clattered to the cobbles. Twisting my head I saw Fanke stiffen, his eyes wide in surprise, and take a step backward. He looked down at his stomach. His red robes hid the stains well, but blood began to patter and then to pour from out underneath them, pooling and then running in the gaps between the cobblestones to make a spreading grid pattern of red on black. Fanke touched his left side with a trembling hand; his robes seemed to be torn there, in several parallel slashes. They seemed to have just appeared there, as if by some magical agency, but the blood gave away the truth: they'd just been made from behind, passing straight through his body.

Fanke gave a sound that was like an incredulous laugh, and then his lips parted as he murmured something that reached me only as a formless sigh: maybe it was the satanist equivalent of "Father, into thy hands . . ." He folded up on himself like an accordion—although that's a lousy image because when you fold an accordion it doesn't leak dark, arterial red from every infold. He fell forward onto the cobbles, his head hitting the stones with enough force to shatter bone, but that didn't matter much anymore.

Zucker, still in animal form, limped around the body, staring at me with mad eyes. He could only use one of his front paws: the other was bent back against his chest. He must have sat on his haunches when he took that swipe at Fanke from behind—cutting right through the man's torso below the ribs and turning his internal organs into rough-chopped chuck.

I took a step to the right, leading Zucker away from Pen. He followed, a trickle of drool hanging from his jaw. He was in a bad way, and it wasn't just the bullet wound. His claws, so terrifying in a fight, slid on the cobbles as if he was having trouble staying upright. But he snarled deep in his throat as he advanced on me, and his eyes narrowed on some image of sweet murder.

I kept on backing, kept on shifting ground so he had to turn as he advanced to keep me in sight. His movements were getting slower and more uncoordinated. His chest rose and fell like a sheet cracking in the wind, but with barely any sound apart from a creak as though his jaws were grinding against each other at the corners.

"You know which company is the biggest consumer of silver in the whole world?" I asked him conversationally. He didn't answer. His good front leg buckled under him and he sank to the ground as if he were bowing to me.

"Eastman Kodak," I said gently. "That's what you've been breathing."

His eyes closed, but his chest kept pumping prodigiously. He might even ride the poison out, but he was finished as far as this fight was concerned.

I went back to Pen. I had to kneel again, fighting off a wave of blackness that came out of nowhere. I was still in that position, just starting to struggle with the layers of duct tape around Pen's wrists, when Juliet came out of the church. At a distance behind her and on either side came two of Gwillam's men. They had automatic rifles leveled at her, but they didn't make any attempt to use them. They must have seen what she'd done to Po, and if they had then they almost certainly didn't fancy their own chances against her very much.

But right then Juliet didn't look too healthy. She'd been breathing silver, too, and it wasn't agreeing with her any better than it had with Zucker. Of course, unlike Zucker she hadn't taken any metal in the more handy .45 hollow-point form, so she was still on her feet. But there was a sway to her walk that wasn't entirely voluntary, and her clenched teeth were visible between her slightly parted lips.

She crossed to me, looking down at Pen's bound form with distant curiosity.

"Is this a new hobby?" she asked me.

"Do me a fucking favor," I rasped, my voice as harsh as my mum's in the morning back when she was on thirty a day. "Is there anyone still alive in there?"

Juliet glanced back toward the doors of the church, from which smoke was still issuing in thick, uneven gouts like blood from a wound. "The ones in priests' robes are all dead," she said. "The werewolf, too. Most of these"—she nodded toward Gwillam's men—"seem to have survived. Who are they?"

"The Sisters of Mercy," I said weakly. "Well, one of those church organizations, anyway."

Juliet bared her teeth in a grimace. She doesn't like religion any better than I do.

There was a clatter on the cobbles and I looked up to see Gwillam heading across to us, flanked by two more men with machine rifles. He made a sign that could almost have been a benediction, but it wasn't: it was an order for the men to fan out, so that if they had to shoot us they'd bracket us from as wide an arc as possible. They obeyed silently, the barrels of their squat, ugly weapons all converging on me and on Juliet. She looked indifferent: I felt, I have to admit it, a little exposed.

Gwillam himself walked past us to where Zucker lay on the cobbles. He squatted down beside the corpse, which looked small and pathetic and undignified the way we all do in death, and put a hand on its forehead. His lips worked in silence, and I didn't try to read them.

Then he stood again and turned to face me.

"You're not human, are you?" he asked, and I realized that it was actually Juliet he was addressing.

"No." She shook her head. "What about you?"

Gwillam's brow furrowed. "Tell me your name and lineage," he snapped. *"In nominibus angelorum qui habent potestatem in aere atque—"* He broke off as Juliet laughed a rich, suggestive laugh. Either she was recovering from the silver poisoning more quickly than I would have believed possible, or she was putting up a hell of a good front: but then, she always did that.

"I was old when your religion was young, O man," she murmured in her throat. "I do not fear your god, and I will not come to heel like a bitch when you call on me, whether you know my name or not."

"Then I'll tell my men to shoot," Gwillam said.

"And I will walk through the bullets and feed upon their hearts, new-ripped from their chests," she said. "But you I will kill after the manner of my kind, for I am succubus and mazzikim. I will make you love me, and be lost."

Gwillam's face went pale, and I could see that that threat had gone home. It struck me, though, that Juliet was actually making the threat at all rather than just going ahead and doing it. Subtlety isn't her strong point, as a rule. I wondered whether the silver she'd inhaled and the time she'd spent in thrall to Asmodeus had left her weaker than she looked.

With an effort, and slowly, Gwillam turned his attention to me.

"You killed the girl?" he demanded. "Snuffed out her spirit? Was that why the ritual failed?"

"You tell me," I suggested.

His eyes narrowed, and he stared down at my hands as I fished the locket back up from where it lay in the crook of Pen's armpit.

"No," he said. "She's still there."

"If he goes for his Bible," I said to Juliet without looking up, "feel free to rip his throat out."

I stood, slowly.

"If I can prove to you that Abbie Torrington isn't a threat anymore, then will you walk away?" I asked Gwillam.

"If you can prove that, yes," he said, without a pause. "You have my word, Castor. I wouldn't snuff out an innocent soul without powerful reason."

I nodded. Good enough.

"Asmodeus already has a human host," I said.

"I know that," said Gwillam. "We assessed that situation two years ago, and decided that it was better not to act: to kill Rafael Ditko might simply set Asmodeus free to act on the human plane."

"And you'd have to do it," I reminded him bluntly, a bit annoyed by the supercilious tone. "With Asmodeus bonded to his flesh and spirit, killing him wouldn't be anyone's idea of a picnic."

Gwillam acknowledged the point with an impatient wave of the hand.

"I cut a lock of his hair," I said, hesitating slightly because I shied away from saying this—from bringing what I'd just done out of hiding and nailing it down with words for other people to see. "Rafi's hair. I tied it around my finger. And then when Fanke had made his invocation—when he'd summoned Asmodeus to feast on the sacrifice inside the circle—I got there first. It was Rafi's hair that burned, not Abbie's. It was Rafi's soul that was consecrated and offered up, and it was Rafi's soul that Asmodeus got a mouthful of as he came down to feed."

Gwillam stared at me in dead silence, waiting for me to go on. Juliet was looking at me, too, her expression unreadable.

"Asmodeus had never entirely left Rafi. Part of him was stuck inside the stones here, waiting to be released by the offering of Abbie's soul: the other half was still where it's been for the past two years—stuck like shrapnel in Rafi Ditko's flesh and spirit."

Gwillam's expression was one of profound shock. "So the demon—?"

"—was starting to eat *itself*. It's like a very nasty version of trying to lift yourself up by your bootstraps. If Asmodeus devoured Rafi's soul instead of Abbie's, the ritual that was meant to free him was going to consume him at the same time. He had no choice but to back off, even if bailing out in the middle of the show aborted the ritual and undid everything that Fanke had managed to achieve. That was why it all fell apart in there. And that's why Abbie doesn't matter now—at least as a weapon in your fucking holy war. Asmodeus severed the link, and went scuttling back to the prison he was trying to escape from in the first place."

"Rafael Ditko."

"Rafi Ditko," I agreed. My friend, who I'd just betrayed for the second time. And as if to make things worse than they were already, I saw that Pen's eyes were open and she was hearing this. The gag taped across her mouth prevented her from commenting, except with her eyes—but they were eloquent enough.

Gwillam seemed impressed. "I have to congratulate you, Castor," he said, with a solemn edge to his voice. "You're easily ruthless enough to serve with the Anathemata, if you ever found the light. But"— he hesitated, massaging the bridge of his nose as if he was raising a slightly delicate subject with as much tact as he could—"why should that change my feelings about Abbie Torrington's soul? She was consecrated to Asmodeus. What is there to stop some other adept, as ruthless and as lost to human feeling as Fanke, from finishing what he's started?"

The question took me off guard, but I improvised as well as I could. "Nobody else knows about her," I said. "You've just killed all of Fanke's crew, and Zucker took care of Fanke himself."

"True. But what has he written about this on his message boards? Whom has he confided in? What will his . . . parishioners in the satanist church do when they learn of his failure? No, you dealt very cleverly with the immediate problem, but in the longer term the threat still stands. The girl's soul is still a detonator looking for the right bomb. Render unto Caesar that which is Caesar's. Render unto God that which is God's."

I opened my mouth to tell him to take his sanctimonious shit somewhere private and render it unto himself, but he hadn't quite finished. "Yehoshua!" he said, almost in a singsong voice. "Yehoshua, of all men king and of all men brother, I praise thee and live in thine eyes! The vessels being diverse, one from another. What shall we do unto her, according to the law? And when it was day, he departed. Even unto Simon's house."

I was too slow out of the gate. I didn't guess what he was doing until I glanced sideways at Juliet, realizing suddenly that there was a tension in her stillness. She was standing rigidly erect, completely unmoving, though the muscles in her neck stood out like cords.

"That was the cantrip that binds her," Gwillam said. "Should I speak the cantrip that destroys her?"

I took an involuntary step toward him. The machine rifles converged on me like the eyes of snakes, targeting on movement. I stopped, realizing that I wouldn't reach him alive.

"Should I speak the—?"

"No," I said. "Don't. Don't do that."

I would never have believed that he could get the measure of her so fast. But Juliet's very power lay in filling your eyes and your nose and your mind with her essence: if you're dealing with an exorcist, that's a high-risk strategy. You take him out quickly, or you find that you've given him all the ammo he needs.

"Then give me the locket," said Gwillam.

I looked down at the locket in my hand, but did nothing. The tableau stood for the space of three heartbeats.

"Castor—" Gwillam murmured warningly.

"You take the locket, and then you leave?"

"As opposed to killing both you and your demon whore, which I so clearly could? Yes. Take it. It's the best offer you're going to get."

He was right there. I threw the locket across to him and he caught it one-handed. Juliet's eyes narrowed, but that was the only move she made: the only move she *could* make.

Gwillam signaled to his men—a clockwise rotation of his index finger in the air that clearly meant "pack up the tents." They started to file away in good order, two of them carrying Zucker, just as the stained glass windows to either side of the church door blew out in party-colored shards, vomiting smoke and fire up into the night.

Gwillam went last of all, and he lingered for a moment as if there was something else on his mind.

"I told you that we investigated Ditko, two years ago—very shortly after you signed him in at the Charles Stanger clinic," he said.

"Yeah. You told me that."

"It might make you feel a little better about your part in all of this if I tell you something we found out at that time." I didn't say anything that could have been interpreted as "oh, do tell" but he went on anyway, looking at me thoughtfully. "Fanke had a mistress back then—dead now. In his sexual liaisons he's always favored the young and stupid. He seems—seemed, I should say—to take a certain pleasure in imprinting his own will on people too weak or vapid to resist.

"Her name was Jane—plain Jane—but she'd rechristened herself Guinevere when she joined the satanist church. Obviously she was living out some romantic fantasy of her own. Most people still called her Jane, in spite of all her efforts, but Rafael Ditko was introduced to her as Guinevere and usually shortened it to Ginny."

Memory sideswiped me like a truck. *Did Ginny see all this? Where is she? Is she outside?*

"My Christ!" I breathed.

Gwillam nodded, seeing that I'd made the connection. "When Ditko raised Asmodeus that night, it was a move in a game—a game that Fanke was playing against God. Abbie Torrington was another such move. Perhaps she was originally destined to be sacrificed on a different altar, to a different devil. But Ditko failed, and you . . . well, you did what you did. He chose his own path, of course, but your choices were made for you a long time ago, Castor. You're one of heaven's soldiers, too, whether you believe that or not. You're the brand that he takes from the fire, already burning, to smite his foes. Perhaps when he's done with you there'll still be something left to save."

"Go fuck yourself," I snarled. As clever ripostes go, I had to admit, it lacked something. Actually, it lacked pretty much everything.

Gwillam turned and walked away, his steps ringing on the cobbles until the *whoop* of approaching sirens drowned them out. It sounded like Detective Sergeant Basquiat had finally checked her messages.

I took out my whistle and played a few bars for Juliet, ragged and halting: the notes that cut the strings Gwillam had laid on her. When she could, she turned to face me, her gaze deep and searching.

"Debriefing comes later," I said. "No smutty double meanings intended. Right now, if I were you, I'd be somewhere else."

She glanced at the first of the police cars as it turned the corner and came belting toward us. Then, in the glare of its headlights, she turned back to me and nodded once, as if to say that there'd be answers she'd insist on.

When the cars rattled to a halt on the cobbles to either side of me, I was the last man standing.

Chapter Twenty-three

In the secure unit at Whittington's, I'd at least had a magazine—along with a phone on a wheely trolley, all the small change I could pick off the floor, and a werewolf-themed cabaret. In the remand cells at the Uxbridge Road cop shop, all I had was the clothes I stood up in, minus belt and jacket.

The graffiti on the cell wall were varied and imaginative, but even they palled after a while. Kicking on the door got no response except for muffled swear words from the guy in the cell next door, who muttered and raved to himself in a variety of different voices in between times. Even the cockroaches, bred in the wild and proud of spirit, refused to race. After three hours or so, I began to understand why they'd taken the belt: if I'd still had it, I'd have hanged myself. Alternatively, if there'd been any sheets on the cot bunk, I'd have slept.

Basquiat arrived some time toward morning, with Field tagging along as usual to hold her coat and feed her straight lines. The guard on duty unlocked the door for her and signed her in, then set one of the interview tape recorders down on the floor and left, giving her a respectful nod.

She left the tape recorder where it was, though, signaling for me to sit down on my bunk while she took the edge of the table and Field stood by the door, ignored.

"So," she said.

I waited for something more solid to go on.

"A burning church full of dead men in black gowns. Another one, in red, lying dead outside. And you, kneeling next to a woman who's been tied up with duct tape."

"I admit that looks fairly suspicious at first glance," I said.

Basquiat smiled coldly. "Just a little, yeah. But then we start to look at the small print. The guy in red checks out as Anton Fanke, so I guess he got tired of Belgium."

"A man who's tired of Belgium . . ."

"Don't get smart, Castor. I like you better when you're scared and desperate. And besides, I didn't get to the good part yet. Fanke was carrying a gun that my friends in ballistics greeted like a long-lost friend. It's the one that killed Melanie Torrington. And one of the corpses in the church had a knife with Abigail Torrington's blood on the blade. A whole lot of fingerprints, including Fanke's—but not yours.

"So my case against you for those earlier murders starts to look a little shaky. I've still got you for Peace, of course—you at the scene of the crime, and your prints on the gun that killed him. But that duct-taped woman has been telling us all kinds of things about the late Mr. Fanke. Stuff that you wouldn't believe."

The mention of Pen made me wince. "I think I'd believe most of it," I said.

"Yeah, maybe you would at that. Anyway, it seems like he was looking for Peace even before you were—looking in some of the same places, like that club in Soho Square. So maybe your story about him hiring you to do his legwork makes a little more sense now."

The first thing that Bourbon Bryant had said to me when I asked him about Peace: *Seems like he's flavor of the month all of a sudden.* Why the hell hadn't I made the connection, and asked him who else had been sniffing around?

"And he's got more of a motive, because he and Peace had some kind of legal skirmish a few years back, and it turns out Peace has been chasing him all around Europe ever since. Something about parental visiting rights to a little girl named Abigail Jeffers. Was that—?"

"Abigail Torrington. Yeah, it was."

"Thought so. Otherwise we'd have been talking about a hell of a lot of weird coincidences. So Fanke murdered Abbie, but Peace—what? I'm a little hazy on this part."

"The idea was to do more than just murder her, Basquiat. She was going to be used up, body and soul, to bring the demon Asmodeus onto the mortal plane. But Peace stepped in before Fanke could finish the ritual—broke the circle and took away Abbie's ghost. Her spirit. That was what Fanke was looking for. And that was what he took away with him after he killed Peace."

"So last night's gig at St. Michael's was in the nature of an action replay?"

"You could call it that."

"I *did* call it that, Castor. The question is, what would you call it?"

"Well, since they both ended in violent fiascos and a lot of dead bodies, I guess 'action replay' is as good as anything."

Basquiat scowled, clearly not appreciating the beating about the bush. She opened her mouth, but I forestalled her. "Yeah, Fanke was trying to finish what he started. He had the locket with Abbie's hair in it—the physical anchor for her ghost. He was going to burn it, inside another magic circle. That would have been enough."

"But it didn't happen."

"No."

"Because—?"

And that was about as far as I wanted to take it. "There was an interruption," I said, deadpan. "An all-singing, all-dancing interruption, as I'm sure you know by now. A dozen or so men with machine guns, a couple of loup-garous in a really bad mood, and most of the cast from *The Producers* over on Drury Lane. I don't know how many DOAs you ended up with—"

"Forty-two," Basquiat threw in quietly.

"—but I'm sure there were enough to convince you that this wasn't a one-man show."

Basquiat blew out her cheek reflectively. "All these show business metaphors. You got stars in your eyes?"

"A guy can dream." I was getting the impression from all this that the detective sergeant's opinion of me had warmed somewhat. One way or another, she seemed to have decided—like Gwillam, although for very different reasons—that I was on the side of the angels after all.

But she still had a job to do. She stood up from the edge of the table where she'd been leaning and threw a nod to Field. He flexed his muscles in a way that was frankly threatening for a moment, but all he did was to lift the tape recorder off the floor and set it down in the center of the table.

"Body count of forty-two," Basquiat said, sounding apologetic. "I've got to do this by the book. But unless you do something stupid like confess, you'll be out of here sometime tomorrow."

Field pressed the record button, so all I could do in reply was nod.

"Detective Sergeant Basquiat and Detective Constable Field," Field intoned, "interviewing Felix Castor, Friday, May twelfth, 6:32 a.m."

And they did, for the better part of an hour, but on the whole it was friendly fire. A couple of times I almost nodded off. The only time it got edgy was when the talk turned to how I'd gotten out of the secure unit at the Whittington. Two cops had been badly injured in that fracas, and then there was the security guard that Po had taken down. Fortunately, Zucker had stepped in before that particular incident got out of hand. A memory of Po with a satanist's head between his jaws intervened at this point, and once again I gave thanks to the god I don't believe in. On top of that there was a lot of property damage and a whole lot of people got the shit scared out of them. But the commando-style operation that Gwillam had mounted at St. Michael's inclined Basquiat to buy my story that the raid on the hospital had been a kidnapping rather than a rescue, so she wasn't putting any of that directly down to me.

When they'd talked me through the past seven days, and I'd unburdened myself of everything I was going to, Field turned off the tape recorder and took out the tape, which he labeled and pocketed. Basquiat headed for the door and hammered on it. She turned back to me as the key turned in the lock and the door opened.

"Anything I can get you?" she asked.

"My tin whistle, if you've still got it," I said. "It would be with the stuff I had on me when you arrested me the first time."

She pulled a face and shrugged. "What with everything that went down over there, I don't think it ever got claimed. It must still be there—along with your clothes and everything—but Christ knows where. I don't have time to go looking for it right now, or anyone I can send."

"Never mind," I said. "I can work around it. Thanks for everything, detective sergeant."

"Including knocking you on your arse the first time I met you? You're welcome, Castor. Have a good one."

She went out, Field trailing along behind her like a broad-beamed freighter behind a tug. I listened to their footsteps retreat up the corridor, and then to the cell block door being slid on its runners.

Once I was certain they weren't coming back, I leaned forward and put my hand down inside my sock. It was easy to find the little lock of hair because it had been itching the hell out of me ever since I'd put it down there. It was back in the church, around about the time when the bullets started flying. I threw myself down between the pews while the satanists and Gwillam's holy crusaders got physical with each other, and I reasoned that this might be a good time for Abbie and the locket to part company. Empty, the locket might be as useful to me as a swinging watch is to a hypnotist: something pretty and shiny that the rubes can look at while you do what you need to do.

And when Gwillam made his play, I was proved right. I was just lucky that he hadn't checked the goods before he left—probably because of the approaching sirens.

As I've already said, it's always easier for me to do my little party

trick if I've got a tin whistle in my hands. But the whistle is just a channel: the music comes from within me, and I can make it on my own
if I have to. Particularly if, as now, I was dealing with a ghost I already
knew pretty well.

Sitting on the edge of the bunk, I closed my eyes and whistled the
tune that, for me, had become synonymous with Abbie. I started low
and let the sound build as it seemed to want to, gradually but inexorably. The guy in the next cell yelled a protest, but he was outside the
infolded loop of reality that joined me to the tune, so whatever he said
fell on my ears like an abstract pattern, fell away again in unheeded
fragments.

Abbie materialized in front of me, about a foot above the ground,
and so slowly that at first she was like a trick of the light—like one of
those accidental objects that can only be seen from one angle when the
light falls just right. It wasn't surprising: after all she'd been through
in her life, and then in her death, I could understand her not wanting
to be dragged up by her heels one more time. When she saw me, her
reluctance became even greater. She fought against my call, fading out
into near invisibility time after time, but coming back each time a little
more sharply defined, a little more vivid and visible, as my sense of her
straightened and I tied the knots of my calling around her soul.

"Let me go!" she cried, in a thin voice that seemed to come across
vast distances. "Let me go!"

I stopped whistling at last and paused a moment or two to get my
breath back. It had been as hard work as any tune I'd ever played, except for one, and I wasn't up to thinking about Rafi right then.

"That's what I intend to do, Abbie," I assured her. "But first I want to
tell you how your dad died. What you missed. So you'll understand."

She was staring at me, her phantom fists clenched in tension and
defiance. I told her how the ambush at the Oriflamme had played
out, and how Dennis Peace had died defending her against her wicked
stepfather. She didn't look as though she believed me—but then the
last two times she'd seen me it had been standing right alongside Fanke
in circumstances that stank up to heaven.

Then I told her about the church, and why I'd put my hand into the fire. I showed her my burned fingers to prove my point, and I think perhaps she did believe me then. At any rate she forgot her hate and fear and grieved for her father, with dry eyes because ghosts can't cry. Sometimes they can mimic tears they cried in life, but they have no moisture of their own.

"Perhaps you'll see him again," I told her, offering her the only crumb of consolation I could think of. "If there's something after this life, and after this death, then I bet he'll find you there if anybody can. He hasn't let anything stop him so far."

She didn't respond. Turning slightly as though in a wind I couldn't feel, she cast her eyes around the narrow confines of the cell. It wasn't the first prison she'd seen in her brief, constricted life: with any luck, though, it would be the last.

I started to whistle again. Not the summoning this time, and not the exorcism, but the unbinding. I whistled the notes that would set her free from the lock of hair to go where she would, unmolested by the Fankes and Gwillams of this sublunary sinkhole.

But she didn't leave. I guess there wasn't anywhere she could think of to go, anywhere where she would have felt safe, or wanted. The only man who had ever loved her or tried to make her happy was dead. She could go back to the Oriflamme and wait for him there, but not everyone rises, and when they do you can't always tell where they'll go. It was a long shot. All that was left to her now was long shots.

I thought through the options. You don't get to have a happy ending when you're dead: this was just damage limitation, nothing more.

"Good-bye, Abbie," I said, standing up and shifting my ground to face east. Not toward Mecca: toward somewhere else entirely, on the other side of the city. "Good-bye, and good luck. I hope it all works out for you."

I whistled again, a tune I hadn't played for a good long while now: "Henry Martin." An electric prickle played down my arms to the tips of my fingers.

The Charles Stanger clinic was a good few miles away, but ghosts—

when they travel at all—aren't limited to light speed. All the same, I'd gotten through two complete renditions of the song and well into the third before I felt their presence stealing upon me, approaching on some vector that had nothing to do with north, south, east, or west. I didn't look around. I felt, in some weird way, as though the dead girls might not take to Abbie if they saw me talking to her, as though the taint of the living might cling to her and make her seem alien to them.

There was a whispering of sound that had no words in it I could make out. Then there was silence, and the silence lengthened. The feeling of their nearness faded from me, leaving behind a more acute awareness of how cold the stone was under my stockinged feet, and how stale the air smelled.

When the last echoes of the tune had died from the air and from my mind, I turned around again.

I was alone in the cell—and more tired than I'd ever been.

Chapter Twenty-four

Basquiat was as good as her word. The charges were dropped and I was released back onto the street in the middle of Saturday afternoon. The clothes I'd left at the Whittington hadn't turned up, though, so I was still stuck in the natty outfit I'd taken from Sallis. It was smelling even riper than when I inherited it.

The first thing I did was to go out to Walthamstow and check on Nicky, because I didn't believe Fanke's bland assurances that his cultists had left my favorite dead man in one piece. But Nicky was none the worse for wear, and even inclined to be a little smug—even though most of the cinema apart from his inner sanctum up in the projection booth had been comprehensively trashed.

"See, Castor," he said, "I got everything here insured eight ways from Sunday, and I already put in the claims—through proxy companies, naturally; got to keep that footprint small. Anyway, I'm gonna build it up again ten times better. I mean, fuck air-conditioning. I've got a freezer on order from a place in Germany that fits out hospital morgues. You're not gonna know this place."

I looked at the outside of the projection booth's door. The wood had been split with axes or crowbars—but all that had done was to reveal the metal underneath.

"It must have been a hell of a siege," I said.

Nicky shrugged, some of his good mood evaporating. "Yeah, it was fucking scary, all right. I had to watch while they smashed everything up. Then they spotted the cameras and took them out, so I couldn't even do that. It was . . . I dunno . . . like having scabies, or something, like watching little insects crawling around under your fucking skin.

"Hey, I'm sorry about your friend. You know that, right? If there'd been anything I could've done, then I would've done it. They brought fucking blowtorches in, for Christ's sake. Nothing to stop them, once they had me shut in up here. I tried to call you again when they took her, but by that time they'd brought one of those phone jammers in, so all I got was static."

He hesitated, as if realizing belatedly that he should have covered this part of the conversation first. "So is she okay?"

"Juliet?"

"Ajulutsikael. Don't anthropomorphize her. That'll get you in trouble somewhere down the line."

"Doesn't the use of a female pronoun already anthropomorphize her?" I asked.

Nicky scowled. "Anyone who can give a dead man an erection has earned that pronoun, Castor. Consider it an honorific."

"She's fine, Nicky. Thanks for asking. Back to her old self by this time, I'm sure."

"And my payment? You know, the five questions?" He looked at me hopefully.

I shrugged. "All I can do is ask her. The deal was that you'd keep her safe, Nicky. She may take the view that you're in breach of contract."

"Breach of—?" He flared up. "Hey, I was invaded, Castor. I kept my part of the deal, ten times over."

He had a point. I said I'd get back to him, and left him choosing thermostatic valves out of a catalog. They've got some really nice ones these days.

At Pen's, to my far from huge surprise, I found all my worldly goods stacked up out in the driveway. I tried my key in the lock and it didn't fit. Quick work, under the circumstances.

I rang the bell, and Pen's sister Antoinette answered. She folded her arms in a *no pasaran* stance, which she does pretty well despite being only an inch or so taller than Pen. She's got Pen's coloring, too, but she went into politics, stood for local councillor, lost three times, and got herself a hatchet face that never cracks a smile.

"Hey, Tony," I said. "Can I talk to her?"

"If she wanted to talk to you, Castor, she wouldn't have changed the locks."

"Why don't you ask her?"

"Because I don't want to have to talk her down from another round of hysterics. Why don't you e-mail her?"

"No computer."

"Heliograph, then."

I looked up at the heavy overcast sky. Antoinette did, too.

"Looks like you're fucked," she observed, and closed the door.

———

Over at the Stanger, Rafi was under deep sedation after smashing his head against the door of his cell until he left half of his face on it. He'd recover, of course: Asmodeus was back in residence, so he once again had a strong interest in making sure his home away from home was kept in good order.

But under the circumstances, the follow-up hearing to determine whether or not Rafi's sectioning should remain in force had been postponed sine die.

"That means 'watch this space,'" Dr. Webb translated helpfully. "You now have twenty-one days, Castor. If you don't come up with anything within that time, I'm going to consult with Professor Mulbridge with a view to signing Ditko over into the care of the MOU at Paddington."

"Watch your back," I suggested.

Missing my point, he swiveled to look behind him. We were standing in the main corridor of the Stanger, just outside Rafi's cell, and the corridor was clear. Webb turned back to me, slightly annoyed, as if I'd just played a silly practical joke.

"I meant," I explained patiently, "watch your back if you throw Rafi to Jenna-Jane. Because if you do that I'm definitely going to break both of your arms and both of your legs."

Almost in disbelief, Webb looked at the two male nurses who were flanking him to either side—his usual tragic chorus. "I have witnesses," he said, "who heard you make that threat."

"I'm sure their testimony will be invaluable," I agreed. "But you'll still be quadriplegic."

Maybe that was a tactless thing to say, but in many ways it was seeming like a long and fairly stressful day. And there was still the question of where I was going to sleep that night.

Juliet and I met up in the evening at a pavement café close to the refuge where she lives. She arrived late, without apology. One of the other residents had a problem with an abusive husband, she told me, and this guy had turned up out of the blue and tried to make his wife leave with him. "So I had to step in and help."

"What, you mean you ate him?" I asked.

"In front of everybody? No, of course not. I have to go on living there, Felix."

"What, then?"

She drank her espresso in a single swallow, wiped her lips with her hand. "I showed the other women how to do it."

"How to—?"

"Impose their will on a man."

"Ah." I fished for more, starting with what Juliet was best at. "By employing their feminine wiles?"

"By employing their boots, mostly. And I think an empty bottle was used at one point."

"Right, right." Violence, of course. The *other* thing that Juliet was best at.

There was something on her mind, I could see: something she found hard to say. I tried to make it easier for her.

"Thanks for getting that werewolf off my back," I said. "It always puts a crimp in my day if someone rips my spine out through my throat."

"It was my pleasure," said Juliet, meaning it. "I . . ." She hesitated, feeling her way around social niceties that had no meaning for her. "I should thank you, too. The thought that I rendered myself helpless—that I placed myself so entirely within Asmodeus's power—is very hard to bear. But you kept me safe, as far as you could. And you brought me back."

"Brilliant improvisation," I said modestly. "Include me in your memoirs. And in your will."

"And in my vagina?"

A large mouthful of café latte went the wrong way in best Hollywood comedy fashion: refusing to endorse the cliché by coughing and spluttering, I went red in the face and waited for the scalding stuff to go down.

"Would I still have my soul afterwards?" I asked her wheezily once the attack had subsided.

Juliet looked thoughtful. "Probably," she said slowly. "That depends, really, on how much self-control I could muster. At the very least it would have bite marks on it."

What's life about if it's not about taking risks? I opened my mouth to say yes, but Juliet was still speaking.

"We'll need to wait a while, though," she said. "Tonight I'm trying something new."

"Something new?" I repeated, struggling to keep the chagrin and frustration out of my voice. "You're way past your seventeen thousandth birthday, Juliet. Is there anything new?"

She grinned. "For most of that time," she reminded me, "I came to earth only at the hest of magicians powerful enough or stupid enough to summon me. They used me either to satiate their own desires—in which case they died, whatever protections they tried to deploy—or to destroy their enemies, in which case other men died. But if the intention was to destroy a woman, then it was my cousins, the incubi, who were called upon. In all that time I was never sent against a woman. Or raised by one."

I suddenly saw where this was going.

"Well, it's mostly the same hormones in different concentrations," I said offhandedly. The bored tone took a supreme effort, though: I was getting a sinking feeling that started in my stomach, gathered momentum in my crotch, and kept on heading due south.

"For me," Juliet said, "it's different. Or at least, I think it might be different. To enjoy lust—pure lust—without the impulse to hunt and kill and eat intervening . . ."

"How do you know it won't intervene?" I asked, looking at my fingernails as if I were worried about how dirty they were.

"I don't. But I think I'd like to try."

"All right, so try," I said desperately, "but does it have to be right this very—"

"What a lovely place," said a voice from behind me. As I turned, biting my tongue, Susan Book took a chair from one of the other tables and set it down in between the two of us. "It's so nice to be able to eat right out on the street. So continental. Is there anything you like better, Mr. Castor?"

I told her, insincerely, that there was nothing I liked better than eating on the street. I didn't add that I was probably going to be sleeping there, too.

She looked very much her old self again: shy and diffident and apologetic about a whole bunch of things that weren't her fault. She told us about how her case was going, and how her solicitor thought he could get her sentence very substantially commuted on a plea of temporary insanity. It had been a riot, after all. Most of the people there were solid citizens who had no previous history.

"No previous history," she repeated dreamily. "When he said that—about me—I suddenly realized that he was right. I had no history of anything at all. No past, because I'd never had the courage to go out and have a present."

"And your religious beliefs?" I asked. I know how that sounds: you'll just have to believe me when I say the tone wasn't quite so snide as the words.

"I still believe in God," she assured me earnestly. "But—I don't think that I have a vocation for the church. I'm going to go back to my old job, and try to live a little more in the world."

"What was your old job?" I asked.

"I was a librarian in Stepney."

Ordinarily I wouldn't have touched a straight line like that for a free weekend in Las Vegas. But tonight didn't have an ordinary feel to it. "Yeah," I agreed. "That's really going to—"

"We should be moving," Juliet said.

She stood, and Susan followed suit, giving her a smile of radiant admiration.

"I'll see you, Felix," Juliet said.

"Sure."

"Good night, Mr. Castor."

This time I just nodded. Mine's not going to be half as good as yours, I thought gloomily.

They left, arm in arm. All along the pavement as far as I was able to keep them in sight, men walked into walls and into each other and almost under cars as they turned to watch.

They say that if you suffer in this life you'll come back as something better in the next.

I'm coming back as God.

Chapter Twenty-five

I saw her one more time, a few months later. Not Juliet, I mean, Abbie.

I was coming home late from some night of debauchery in Farringdon. I think it was the night that Paul finally made it down to the Jerusalem and called in my marker, but maybe that was a different time altogether. Anyway, I found myself walking along Old Street at one in the morning, dead drunk and more or less at peace with the world.

A small, wild quartet of ghosts burst through a shop front ahead of me in a storm of shrieks and giggles, saw me watching them and stopped. All of them were girls, ranging in age from ten to about sixteen. They tried to compose their faces, like living girls faced suddenly with a stern teacher or a scary headmaster, and like living girls they couldn't quite do it. One of them set the others off again and they fled, laughing like birds, across Golden Lane into a narrow alley between two office blocks. Three of them dissolved there into sudden, evanescent motes of light. Abbie lingered a moment, head bowed, as if fighting a brief battle with herself. I hoped she might look back so I could wave, but I guess she didn't want to be left behind. She picked up her steps and faded into the dark.

Not everyone gets the ending they deserve. Rafi deserves to have his evil twin ripped out and sent back to hell with firecrackers tied to his tail. Pen deserves Rafi. Father Gwillam deserves martyrdom. Someone up above or maybe down below deals out destinies without ever giving us a chance to watch the shuffle or cut the deck. It's not fair, but then nobody ever told us it was going to be.

I whispered her name like an incantation.

Abbie Jeffers.

Fanke.

Torrington.

Peace.

Acknowledgments

In the UK edition of this book I thanked my editor, Darren, my agent, Meg, publicist George Walkley, desk editor Gabriella Nemeth, copy editor Nick Austin, and my wife, Lin, all of whom played crucial roles in its creation. I'm thanking them again now, but this time with a Damon Runyon–style New York accent.

And because the American edition has been through an entirely different alchemical process, I'd also like to thank Grand Central Publishing editor Jaime Levine and publicist extraordinaire Lisa Sciambra, both for making the U.S. edition happen and for all of their heroic efforts during my recent ten-city U.S. book tour (which included keeping me alive and sane). They go into the box labeled "people I feel privileged to have met." So do Charlotte Oria, Claire Friedman and her totally amazing family (Jeff, Jeremy, and Jacob), James Sime and Kirsten Baldock, Tad Williams, Richard Morgan, Chris Golden, Alan and Jude of Borderlands, Kristine and Jeannie and their colleagues at the Encino Barnes and Noble, and Doselle Young (whom I also have to thank for one of the most memorable games of pool I've ever lost).

Sometimes I love this job.

extras

orbit

meet the author

MIKE CAREY has been making up stories for most of his life. His novel *The Girl With All the Gifts*, written as M. R. Carey, was a *USA Today* bestseller and a major motion picture based on his BAFTA-nominated screenplay. Mike Carey has written for both DC and Marvel, including critically acclaimed runs on *X-Men* and *Fantastic Four*, Marvel's flagship superhero titles. His creator-owned books regularly appear in the *New York Times* bestseller list. He also has several previous novels, two radio plays, and a number of TV and movie screenplays to his credit.

if you enjoyed
VICIOUS CIRCLE
look out for

DEAD MEN'S BOOTS
Felix Castor: Book Three

by

Mike Carey

Author of The Girl With All the Gifts *Mike Carey presents
the third book in his hip supernatural thriller series
featuring freelance exorcist Felix Castor.*

*You might think that helping a friend's widow to stop a lawyer
from stealing her husband's corpse would be the strangest thing on
your To-Do list. But life is rarely that simple for Felix Castor.*

*A brutal murder in the heart of London bears all the hallmarks
of a long-dead American serial killer, and it takes more good*

sense than Castor possesses not to get involved. He's also fighting a legal battle over the body—if not the soul—of his possessed friend, Rafi, and can't shake the feeling that his three problems might be related.

With the help of the succubus Juliet and paranoid zombie data-fence Nicky Heath, Castor just might have a chance of fitting the pieces together before someone drops him down an elevator shaft or rips his throat out.

Or not....

ONE

I don't do funerals all that often, and when I do, I prefer to be either falling-down drunk or dosed up on some herbal fuzz-bomb like salvinorin to the point where I start to lose feeling from the feet on up, like a kind of rising damp of the central nervous system. Today I was as sober as a judge, and that was only the start of it. The cemetery was freezing cold—cold enough to chill me even through the Russian-army greatcoat I was wearing (I never fought, but poor bloody infantry is a state of mind). The sun was still locked up for winter, a gusty east wind was stropping itself sharp on my face, and guilt was working its slow way through my mind like a weighted cheese wire through a block of ice.

Ashes to ashes, the priest said, or at least that was what it boiled down to. His hair and his skin were ash-pale in the February cold. The pallbearers stepped forward just as the wind sprang up again, and the shroud on top of the coffin bellied like a sail. It was a short voyage, though: Two steps brought them alongside the neat, rectangular hole in the ground, where they bent as one and laid the coffin down on a pair of canvas straps held in place by four burly sextons. Then the sextons stepped in from either side, in synchrony, and the coffin slid silently down into the ground.

Rest in peace, John Gittings. The mortal part of you, anyway; for the rest, it was going to be a case of wait-and-see. Maybe that was why John's widow, Carla, looked so strained and tense as she stood directly opposite me in her funereal finery. Her outfit incorporated a brooch made from a sweep of midnight-dark feathers, and staring at it made me momentarily imagine that I was looking down from a great height, the black of her dress becoming the black of an asphalt highway, the remains of a dead bird lying there like roadkill.

The priest started up again, the wind stealing his voice and distributing it piecemeal among us so that everyone got a beggar's share of the wisdom and consolation. Sunk in my own thoughts, which were fixed on mortality and resurrection to the exclusion of redemption, I looked around at the other mourners. It was a who's who of the London exorcist community: Reggie Tang, Therese O'Driscoll, and Greg Lockyear were there, representing the Thames Collective; Bourbon Bryant and his hatchet-faced new wife, Cath; Larry Tallowhill and Louise Beddows, Larry looking like a walking corpse himself with the white of his cheekbones showing through his skin like a flame through a paper lantern; Bill Schofield, known for reasons both complicated and obscene as Jonah; Ade Underwood, Sita Lovejoy, Michelle Mooney, all up from the beautiful South (Elephant and Castle, or thereabouts); and among the also-rans, a very striking, very young woman with shoulder-length white-blond hair who kept staring at me all the way through the service. There was something both familiar and unsettling about her face, but I couldn't place it. That uncertainty did nothing to improve my mood, and neither did the absence of the one London exorcist I'd been hoping to see at this shindig. But then Juliet Salazar never did hold with cheap sentiment. In fact, she probably didn't have any to sell even at the market price.

Meanwhile, seeing as how this was a cemetery, the dead had turned up in considerable force. They clustered around us at a safe distance, sensing the power gathered here and what it could do to them, but so starved of sensation that they couldn't keep away. It was hard not to look at the sad multitude, even though looking at ghosts often makes them come in closer, as though your attention is a gradient they slide down toward you. There were dozens, if not hundreds, packed so closely together that they overlapped, thrusting their heads through one another's limbs and torsos to get a better look at us and maybe at the new kid on the block. The ghosts of the most recent vintage still carried the marks of their death on them in wasted flesh, oddly angled limbs, and in one case, a gaping chest hole that was almost certainly a bullet wound. The tenants of longer standing had either learned or forgotten enough to look more like themselves in life, or else they'd started to fade to the point where some of the more gruesome details had been lost or smudged over.

The priest seemed oblivious to his larger audience, which was probably a good thing: He looked old enough and frail enough that he might not weather the shock. But people in my profession have the sight whether they like it or not, and it's not something you can turn on and off. At one point during the funeral oration, Bourbon Bryant reached into his pocket and half drew out the book of matches he always carried there—the particular tool he uses to get the whip hand on the invisible kingdoms, just as a tin whistle (Clarke Sweetone, key of D) is mine.

I put a hand on his arm and shook my head. "Not the time," I said tersely, speaking out of the corner of my mouth.

"I'll just torch one or two, Fix," he muttered back. "The rest will scatter like pigeons."

"I'll break your jaw if you do," I said equably. He shot me a surprised, affronted look, read my own expression accurately, and put away the matches.

Why hadn't I gotten drunk before coming here? Judging by the faces around me, I sure as hell wouldn't have been the only one. Exorcists often resort to booze to stifle their death perception, just as a lot of them use speed when they want to put a particular edge on it. But I'm careful about how I deploy my crutches. Today that would have felt like I was hiding from something specific I was ashamed to face, rather than just dulling unpleasant distractions. Bad precedent.

I defocused as far as I could, staring through the massed ranks of the dead toward the cemetery's high wrought-iron fence, which was topped with very un-Christian razor wire. No respite there, though; the Breath of Life protesters were pressed up against the bars like tourists at the zoo, shouting abuse at us that we were too far away to decipher. The Breathers, as we dismissively call them, are radical dead-rights extremists, and they view us ghostbreakers in much the same light in which staunch Catholics tend to see abortionists: You can always rely on them to break up the funeral of an exorcist if they get a tip-off that it's going down. Most likely, the priest or one of the sextons was a closet sympathizer and had sent the word down the line.

Things were starting to wind down now. Carla threw some earth into her husband's grave, and a few other people got in line to do the same. Then the sextons took over for the serious shoveling. Now that we'd made that ritualistic nod toward plowing the fields, we were free to scatter as soon as was decent. Carla's earlier plan for a post-funeral gathering at her house in Mill Hill had been canceled at the last moment for reasons that weren't entirely clear—and the service, which on the black-edged invitations had been set for three p.m., had been moved forward to one-thirty without explanation. Maybe that was why Juliet hadn't shown.

But just as I was congratulating myself on getting away easy, a shout from the main gates made me turn my head in that direction. There was a man there, running toward us at a flat-out sprint that sat oddly with his immaculately cut Italian suit. By and large, people don't wear Enzo Tovare to go jogging. All the muck sweat's not good for that delicate stitching.

This Johnny-come-lately looked pretty striking in other ways, too. His mid-brown hair was back-combed into an Errol Flynn–style college cut, and he had the Hollywood face to go with it—hard to get without plastic surgery or sterling-silver genes. He looked to be about thirty, but there was something in his face that read as either premature experience or some kind of innate calm and seriousness. He was old for his age, but he wore it pretty well.

He had a folded sheet of paper in his hand that he was holding up for our appreciation like Neville Chamberlain. That plus the sharp suit made it less likely that he was what I'd taken him to be at first: one of the Breath of Life guys trying to disrupt proceedings with a paint bomb or a noisemaker.

He slowed down as he got in among us, and I noticed as he passed me that he wasn't breathing hard despite the run. I wondered if he worked out in Italian linen, too.

"Mrs. Gittings," he said, offering the paper to Carla. "This is a warrant executed this morning by Judge Tilney at Hendon Magistrates' court. Will you please read it?"

Carla smacked the paper out of the man's hand so that he had to flail briefly to catch it again before it fell into the grave.

"Go away, Mr. Todd," she said coldly. "You've got no business being here. No business at all."

"I have to disagree," Italian-suit guy said politely enough, unfolding the paper and showing it to Carla. "You know what my business is, Mrs. Gittings, and you know why I couldn't just allow this to happen. What you're doing here is illegal. This warrant forbids you from burying the mortal remains of the late Jonathan Gittings, and it requires you to appear at—"

He ran out of steam very abruptly. He was looking into the grave, and he clearly registered the fact that it was already occupied and half full of earth. There was maybe a second when he seemed false-footed: all dressed up, writ in hand, and nowhere to go. Then he refolded his warrant and tucked it away in his breast pocket with a decisive motion, his expression somber.

"Obviously, I'm already too late," he said. "I was under the impression that this service was scheduled to start at three o'clock. I'm sure that was what I was told when I called the funeral parlor this morning. Perhaps there was a last-minute cancellation?" Carla flushed red, opened her mouth to speak, but Todd raised his hands in surrender. "I'm not going to try to interrupt a funeral that's already in progress—and I apologize for disturbing the solemnity of the occasion. If I'd been in time to stop the burial, it was my legal duty to do so. Now...I'll retire and consider the other avenues available to me. We'll talk again, Mrs. Gittings. And you can expect an exhumation order in the fullness of time."

Carla gave a short cry of pain, as if the words had physically wounded her. Then Reggie Tang—an unlikely Galahad—

stepped in between her and the lawyer, fixing him with a look full of violent promise.

"Can I see your invitation, mate?" he demanded. At the same time I saw Reggie's deceptively scrawny-looking friend Greg Lockyear moving in behind Todd, looking to Reggie for his cue. I couldn't believe they were planning to lay some hurt on a lawyer in front of fifty witnesses, but the grim set of Reggie's face was impossible to misread. Like most of us, he knew John from way back, and like most of us, he'd teamed up with him a fair few times when there was nothing better on offer. That tended to be how it worked, and I guessed that maybe, like me, he was feeling some belated pangs of guilt that he'd only ever seen John as a last resort. So maybe beating up a man in a sharp suit seemed like an easy way to burn off some of the bad karma.

Stepping forward as much to my own surprise as anyone else's, I put a hand on Reggie's shoulder. He turned his glare on me, surprised and indignant to be interrupted when he was still warming up.

"Behave yourself, Reggie," I said. "You're doing no one a favor starting a fight here, least of all Carla."

We held each other's eyes for a moment longer, and I was half convinced he was going to take a swing at me. I took a step to the left to keep Greg Lockyear in view, because that way, at least, I wouldn't be fighting on two fronts; but the moment passed, and Reggie turned away with a disgusted shrug.

"Frigging parasites," he said. "Have it your way, Fix. But if he doesn't get the fuck out of here, I'm gonna put something through his face."

I gave Todd a look that asked him what he was waiting for. "Mrs. Gittings will be in touch," I said.

"I'm sure," he agreed. "But I really need to proceed with—"

"You need to pick your time. She'll be in touch. Leave it until then, eh?"

Todd looked at the grim faces ringing him and probably did some calculations. He glanced around for Carla, but she'd stepped back into the supportive crowd and was being comforted by Cath and Therese. "I'm prepared to wait a day or so," he said, "out of respect. A day or so—no longer."

"Good plan," I agreed.

With a wry nod to me, Todd turned on his heel. He took the path back to the gate a lot more slowly and stayed in sight for the better part of a minute, further dampening the already tense mood.

We broke up by inches and ounces, swapping halfhearted conversation at the turning circle by the car park because nobody wanted to seem in an indecent hurry to escape. I said hello to Louise, whom I hadn't seen in a year or more, and we played the "ain't it awful" game, trading stories about the Breathers.

"They're running ambushes now," Louise said in her lugubrious Tyneside drawl, igniting a cigarette with a gold lighter shaped like a tiny revolver. "Picking us off. Can you believe it? Stu Langley got a call in the early hours of the morning. Some woman saying she'd just moved into a new house and there was a ghost in the bloody downstairs lavvy. He told her he'd come the next morning, but she started crying and pleading. Laying it on thicker and thicker, she was, and Stu's too polite to hang up on her. So in the end he got dressed and went out there. I'd have told her to hold it in or piss out the window.

"Anyway, he gets to this place out in Gypsy Hill somewhere, and look at that. There's a house with a for-sale sign up, exactly where she said it would be, and the front door's open. So he went on in, like a bloody idiot. Didn't stop to ask himself why there were no lights on, or why the sign still said for sale if this whining old biddy had already moved in.

"There were four of them, with baseball bats. They laid into him so hard they put him in a coma. He lasted for a week, and then they turned the machine off. I'm telling you, Fix, they won't be happy until they've killed us all."

"Won't do them much good if they do," I observed, shaking my head as she offered me a drag on the cigarette. "Exorcism is in the human genome now. Probably always was, only it didn't show itself until there was something there to use it on. Killing us doesn't make the problem go away."

She blew smoke out of her nose, hard. "No, but beating the shit out of a few of us gives the rest of us something to think about."

Another knot of mourners walked past us, heading for their cars. One of them was the acid-blond girl, walking alongside two guys I didn't know, and she gave me another killing look as she passed.

"Any idea who that is?" I asked Louise, rolling my eyes to indicate who I meant without being too obvious about it.

"Which one?"

"The girl."

Louise expelled breath in a forced sigh, made a weary face. "Dana McClennan."

"McClennan?" Something inside me lurched and settled at an odd angle. "Any relation to the late, great Gabriel McClennan?"

"Daughter," said Louise. "And she's following on in the family tradition, Fix. Bigger arsehole than he was, if anything. When she found out Larry was HIV-positive, she backed off at a hundred miles an hour. You'd think he'd tried to give her a

Frenchie or something. Or maybe she thinks you can catch it by talking about it, like my mum."

I didn't answer. The mention of Gabe McClennan's name had triggered a whole lot of very unpleasant memories, most of them dating from the night when I'd killed him. Okay, it was kind of by proxy: Actually, I just made it really easy for someone else to kill him. It wasn't like he left me much choice, either, since he was out for my blood; and the wolf I threw him to was one he'd brought to the party himself, so you could say what goes around comes around. Lots of great arguments to mix and match. None of them made me feel any better about it, though, and there was no way I'd ever be able to explain it to the wife and kid he'd left behind.

"So what's she doing here?" I asked.

"She came with Bourbon. I think he put the word out at the Oriflamme that John was going into the ground today—said he'd lay on cars for any exorcists who wanted to come along."

"She's a ghostbreaker?"

Louise shrugged. "That's what she's calling herself, yes. Following in her father's footsteps. I don't know if she's any good or not."

I took it on the chin, but it wasn't great news. If Gabe's daughter was in the same line of business as me now, and if she was operating in London, then we were going to keep running across each other's trail whether we liked it or not. Not a happy prospect. I watched Gabe's daughter down to the gates—saw her stop, her two escorts walking on without her, and exchange words with the Breathers on picket duty. Someone ought to have a word with her about that: It wasn't a great idea to encourage the lunatic fringe.

"How's the music going?" I asked in a ham-fisted effort to raise the mood. Louise played bass in a band that had had many more names than gigs. I had a vague feeling that their current nom de soundstage was something vaguely punk, like All-Star Wank, but it would be something different tomorrow.

"It's good," Louise said. "It's going good. We've got a new manager. He reckons he can get us in at the Spitz."

Larry Tallowhill came up alongside Louise at this point and slid an arm around her waist. "Felix Castor," he said with mock sternness. "Leave my fucking woman alone."

"Can I help it if I'm irresistible?" I asked. "How are the new drugs working?"

Larry shrugged expansively. "They're great," he said. "I'll live until something else kills me. Can't ask for more than that."

Larry was always amazingly upbeat about his condition, which was the result of the sort of arbitrary bad luck that would fill most people with rage or despair to the slopping-over-the-top, foaming-at-the-mouth point. He'd contracted HIV from a bite he got when he was trying to subdue a loup-garou—you might call it a werewolf, except that the animal component here was something leaner and longer-limbed and altogether stranger than that word suggests. It wasn't even a paying job; he just saw this monster chasing a bunch of kids across a Sainsbury's car park, and stepped in without even thinking about it. The thing was looking to feed, but it turned its attention to Larry as soon as it realized he was a threat, and like I said, it was sleek and fast and very, very mean. Larry took the damage, finished the job with one arm hanging off in strips, then walked a mile and a half to the hospital to get himself patched up. They did a great job: stabilized him, took the severed finger he'd brought with him and sewed it back on, stopped him from bleeding to death or getting tetanus, and eventually restored 95 percent of nervous function. About ten or eleven months later, he got the bad news.

For an exorcist, it all falls under the heading of occupational hazard. There aren't very many of us who get to die of old age.

I changed the subject, which sooner or later was going to bring us around to the even more painful issue of how John Gittings had died—locked in the bathroom with the business end of a shotgun in his mouth. I'm not squeamish, but I'd been shying away from that particular image all afternoon.

"Business good?" I asked, falling back once more on the old conversational staples.

"It's great," Larry said. "Best it's ever been."

"Three bloody jobs all at once yesterday," Louise confirmed. "He's fast." She nodded at Larry. "You know how fast he is, but even he can't do three in a day. They get in the way of each other. The second's harder than the first, and the third's impossible. So I did the middle one, and of course, that was the one that turned out to be an absolute bastard. Old woman—very tough. Fought back, and I lost my lunch all over the client's carpet."

"Your breakfast," Larry corrected. "It was only eleven o'clock."

"My brunch. And this bloke—company director or something, lives in Regent Quarter—he says, 'I hope you're going to clean that up before you go.' And I would have done, too, but not after he said that. I hit him with the standard terms and conditions and walked out. Now he's saying he won't pay, but he sodding will. One way or another, he will."

As changes of subject go, it hadn't gotten us very far away from death. But that's exorcists' shoptalk for you.

After a few more pleasantries, Lou and Larry strolled away arm in arm, and I walked back over to the grave to say my goodbyes. Carla was now standing in deep conversation with the priest—maybe a little too deep for comfort. At any rate, she took the opportunity as I walked up to extricate herself, thank him, and disengage.

"I'm heading out," I said. "Take care of yourself, Carla. I'll be in touch, okay?" But she was holding something out to me, and the something turned out to be her car keys.

"Fix," she said apologetically, "could you drive me home? I really don't feel up to it. And there's something I want to ask you about."

I hesitated. They say misery loves company, but I'm the kind of misery who usually doesn't. On the other hand, I'd missed Bourbon's charabanc, and I needed a lift back into town. Maybe a half-second too late to look generous, I nodded and took the keys. "Thanks again, Father," Carla called over her shoulder. I glanced back. The priest was watching us as we walked away, the expression on his face slightly troubled.

"He asked me if I had any doubts," Carla said, catching the movement as I looked around. "Any bits of doctrine I wanted to talk over with him. Then, before I could get a word in, he was pumping me for clues."

"Men of the cloth are the worst," I agreed. "They don't approve, but they have to look. It's the same principle as the *News of the World*." That was slightly unfair, but it's something you come across a lot. People assume that we're sitting on a big secret: We have to be, because how could we do what we do without knowing how it's done? But it's not like that at all. Would you ask Steve Davis for an explanation of Brownian motion, or Torvill and Dean how ice crystals form? We've got a skill set, not the big book of answers.

Carla's car was the only one left in the car park: a big, roomy old Vectra GLS in a dark gray that showed off the splatter stains of old bird shit to good effect. I let Carla in—no central locking—and walked around to the driver's side, taking an appraising look at her in the process. She was calmer now that it was all over, but she looked a little tired and a little old. That wasn't surprising: Having someone you love commit suicide has to be one of the nastiest low blows life can throw at you. In other respects, she was still very much the woman I'd known back in the early nineties, before she'd ever met John—when she was a brassy, loud blonde I'd met at a poker session and almost gone to bed with, except that my fear of intimacy and her preference for older men had kicked in at about the same time and turned a promising fumble into an awkward conversation about micro-limit hold 'em. There's a line in a Yeats poem where he asks whether your imagination lingers longest on a woman you won or a woman you lost. While you're puzzling over that one, you can maybe give him an estimate on how long a piece of string is. If things had worked out differently, Carla and me could have gotten a whole Mrs. Robinson thing going, although even in those days, I was less of a Benjamin Braddock and more of a Ratso Rizzo.

I started the car and pulled away, noticing that the priest followed us with his sad eyes as we drove by. I sympathized up to a point. It couldn't be an easy way to earn a living these days.

We eased our way out between the pickets, collecting a fair share of abuse and ridicule along the way but no actual missiles or threats. Most of the people waving placards and chanting rhythmically were in their teens or early twenties. What did they know about death? They hadn't even gotten all that far with life yet.

The cemetery was all the way out in Waltham Abbey, and John and Carla lived—or rather, Carla still lived and John didn't anymore—on Aldermans Hill just outside of Southgate, in a flat over a dress shop. It was going to be a long haul, and the Vectra handled like a half-swamped raft. Turning in to the traffic, I remembered the half-bottle of metaxa in my inside pocket, fished it out one-handed, and passed it across to Carla. She took it without a word, unscrewed the lid, and downed a long swallow. It made her shudder; probably it made her eyes water, too, but there were plenty of other explanations available for why she rubbed the heel of her hand quickly across her face.

Looking in the rearview mirror, I noticed that we'd picked up a tail. I swore under my breath. It was one of the vans that the Breathers had arrived in—a big high-sided delivery truck that someone must have borrowed from work, deep blue and with the words BOWYER'S CLEANING SERVICES written in reverse script over the windscreen—because a good idea is a good idea, even if the emergency services think of it first. I didn't mention it to Carla: I just switched lanes whenever I could to make life harder for them. I was confident that I could lose them long before we got back into London.

"So what was all that shit with the lawyer?" I asked. It sounds tactless, put like that, but I've always found anger a good corrective to grief. Grief paralyzes you, where a good head of hacked-off biliousness keeps you moving right along, although it's not so great for making you look where you're going.

Carla shook her head, as though she didn't want to talk about it, and I was going to let it lie. But then she took a second pull on the brandy bottle, and away she went.

"John had always said he wanted to be buried at Waltham Abbey, next to his sister, Hailey," she muttered. "Always. She was the only person he ever loved, apart from me. But he wasn't himself, Fix. Not for months before he died. He wasn't anyone I recognized." She sighed deeply and a little raggedly. "There's a condition—EOA, it's called. Early-onset Alzheimer's. It got John's dad when he was only forty-eight, and by the time he turned fifty, he couldn't even dress himself. John was convinced that Hailey was starting to get it just before she died, and he was always terrified he was going to go the same way. He tried to make me promise once that I'd give him pills if it ever took him. If he ever got to the point where—you know, where there was nothing left of him. But I couldn't, and I told him I couldn't.

"Anyway, just because it *can* run in families doesn't mean it will. You don't know, do you? There's no point running halfway to meet trouble. But he'd have days when he couldn't move, hardly, for brooding about it. I tried to jolly him along when he was in one of those moods. Wait for him to pull out of it again, and then most times he'd say he was sorry he'd worried me, and that'd be that.

"But a couple of months before Christmas, he went through a bad time. He had a job on—something that was going to pay really well, but it seemed to prey on his mind a lot."

"What sort of job?" I asked, sounding a lot more casual than I felt. This was where my guilt was stemming from, in case you were wondering. I'd already heard a few hints about John's last big earner, and I had good reason to feel uneasy about it.

"He wouldn't say. But he put a grand in my hand, sometime back in November, it was, and told me to bank it—and he said there'd be more later. Well, you know how it is, Fix. Most of the time, no offense, you just work for rent money, don't you? Oh yeah, for young men, it's lovely. Two or three hundred quid for a couple of days' work, you're laughing. When you're a bit older, it gets to be different, and you never really have a chance to lay anything by. So I was over the moon for him, I really was. I said, 'What, is there a ghost in Buckingham Palace or something? Can we say we're by royal appointment now?' And he laughed and said something about East End royalty, but he wouldn't tell me what he meant.

"I think the truth was, whatever this job was all about, he didn't know if he could handle it. He called those two on the Collective—Reggie and that friend of his who never washes. But they wouldn't work with him anymore. They said he was too sloppy, and they wouldn't trust him if things went bad on a job."

She hesitated as if she thought I might want to jump in at this point and defend John's reputation, but I made no comment. Because if Reggie had said that, Reggie was right. John had never been the most focused of men, and he'd gotten worse as he got older. Having him at your back was far from reassuring: generally, it just gave you one more thing to worry about.

But I didn't feel comfortable thinking those thoughts, because John hadn't called only Reggie. He'd called me, too, three times in the space of a week. The messages were still on my answerphone, since I never bother to wipe the tape. Three times I'd sat there and listened to him telling me he might have some work to put my way, and three times I hadn't even picked up because life's too short and you tend to avoid things that might make it shorter still.

Then I got a call from Bourbon, the de facto godfather of London's ghostbusters, with the news that John had kissed a loaded shotgun.

"Did he say who he was working for?" I asked Carla, crashing the gears as we turned onto the M25 sliproad. The blue van was still in back of us, but I wasn't worried; I hadn't even begun to fight.

Carla shook her head. "I asked him. He didn't want to talk about it. He just said it was big, and that when it was done, he'd be in the history books. 'One for the books,' he kept on saying. Something nobody's ever done before.

"And it changed him. He started to get really fretful and

really paranoid about forgetting things. He'd make himself little notes—lists of names, lists of places—and he'd hide them all around the house. I'd open the tea caddy, and there'd be a bit of paper all folded up inside the lid. Just names. Then the next day he'd go around and collect them all up again. And burn them. For the first time ever, I started to think he might have been right all along. You know, about the Alzheimer's. I thought maybe the stress had brought it on or something."

She rubbed her eyes again. "It was a terrible time, Fix. I didn't know who to talk to about it. When Hailey was alive, I'd have called her over, and we'd have had it out with him all together. But I couldn't get near him. He started to fly off the handle whenever I even hinted that he was acting strangely. It got so I had to pretend everything was all right even when he was sneaking around like a spy in a film, picking up secret messages that he'd left for himself.

"Then one night he got into bed and started to talk about death. Said he thought his time would be coming soon, and he'd changed his mind about what kind of send-off he wanted. 'Forget about Waltham Abbey, Carla. You've got to cremate me.' Well, I didn't know what to say. What about Hailey? What about the plot he'd already paid for, right next to her? It was the disease talking. It wasn't him. So I did just what I did that time when he tried to make me promise to poison him. I kept shtumm. I didn't say a word. I wasn't going to make a promise that I didn't mean to keep.

"And then after he"—she saw the word looming, swerved away from it—"after he did it, I got this letter from a solicitor. Mr. Maynard Todd from some company with three names, and one of the names is him. He said John had come to him before he died and written a new will. Still left all his money to me, but he wanted to make sure he'd be burned instead of buried.

Even picked out someplace over in the East End—Grace something. He'd put it all down in black and white. And he'd written a bit at the end about how he'd had to go to a stranger because he couldn't trust his own wife to do right by him."

"So what did you do?"

"Nothing," Carla said with bitter satisfaction. "I ignored it. I thought, Fuck it, let the bastard sue me. I'll do what my John wanted when he was still in his right mind. So I went ahead with the funeral, even though this Maynard Todd said he was going to stop me, and I moved the time from three back to one-thirty so he'd miss it and get there too late. Which he did." Her voice had been getting thicker, and now she burst into shuddering sobs. "But it doesn't matter anymore, Fix. I don't care what they do to John's body. I just want him to be at peace. Oh God, let him find some peace!"

There wasn't anything I could say to that, so I didn't try. I just concentrated on making life hideous for the driver of the blue van. The League Against Cruel Sports wouldn't approve, but if you know you're being tailed, there are all sorts of subtle torments and indignities you can inflict on the guy who's chasing you. By the time we'd reached the Stag Hill turnoff, I'd shaken him loose and relieved some of my own tensions in the process.

I drove on in silence, exiting the motorway and coaxing the uncooperative car through the congested streets of Cockfosters and Southgate. Meanwhile, Carla went through three handkerchiefs and most of what was left in the bottle.

When I pulled up at Aldermans Hill, she was more than half drunk. I parked in front of the costume shop, which was closed for Sunday, leaving the car on a double-yellow line because it seemed more important right then to get her back onto home turf and more or less settled.

The flat was on the first floor, up an external flight of steps with a dogleg. On the door frame there were a good half-dozen wards against the dead, ranging from a sprig of silver birch bound with white thread to a crudely drawn magic circle with the word *ekpiptein* written across it in Greek script. That translates as "bugger off until you're wanted, you bodiless bastards." Greek is a very concise language.

Carla fumbled with her keys, and I noticed that her hands were trembling. I was quite keen to get out of there now that I'd done my civic duty. I'm fuck-all use as a shoulder to cry on.

"I'm sure he is," I said clumsily—and belatedly. "At peace, I mean. John was a good man, Carla. He didn't have any enemies in this world. You know I don't believe in heaven, but if anyone deserved—"

I stopped because she was looking at me with the sort of expression you give to dangerous madmen.

"No," she said bluntly. "He's not in heaven, Fix, or anywhere else. He's here. He's still here."

She turned the key and shoved the door open, but she made no move to go in. I stepped past her into the small hallway, smelling a slightly musty, unused smell, as though nobody had been there in a few days.

Three steps took me into the living room, and I stopped dead, if you'll pardon the expression, taking in a scene of devastation and ruin. Most of the furniture was overturned. The television lay in the corner like a poleaxed drunk, staring blindly up at the ceiling. Three deep dents scarred the screen, a fish-scale pattern of fracture marks spreading out from each one. Broken glass crunched under my feet.

And then a framed photo of John and Carla smiling, arm in arm, leaped up from the broken-legged dresser and shot through the air, spinning like a shuriken, to explode against the wall just inches from my head.

With a muttered oath, I dodged back around the corner and turned to stare at Carla in dazed disbelief. She gave me a curt nod, her face bitter and despairing.

Despite his faults, most of which I've already mentioned, John had always been a pretty easygoing sort of guy. But that was when he was alive.

In death, it was painfully obvious, he'd gone geist.

if you enjoyed
VICIOUS CIRCLE

look out for

THE LAST DAYS OF JACK SPARKS

by

Jason Arnopp

"Ingenious and funny…Magnificent."—Alan Moore,
creator of Watchmen *and* V for Vendetta

Jack Sparks died while writing this book.

It was no secret that journalist Jack Sparks had been researching
the occult for his new book. No stranger to controversy,
he'd already triggered a furious Twitter storm
by mocking an exorcism he witnessed.

extras

*Then there was that video: forty seconds of chilling footage
that Jack repeatedly claimed was not of his making,
yet was posted from his own YouTube account.*

*Nobody knew what happened to Jack in the days that
followed—until now.*

"Wow. Seriously hard to put down."—M. R. Carey,
author of The Girl With All the Gifts

CHAPTER ONE

Before we vanish into Satan's gaping mouth, Bex wants to get something straight.

Sitting beside me in a very small car, she says, "So your new book's going to be about the supernatural. Which you don't believe in. At all."

"It's already riling people," I tell her. "Did you see the bust-up yesterday?"

She scrunches her face. "Why can't you accept that social media isn't a part of my life?"

"Because I don't believe you."

"Last time I looked, in about 2009, social media was one big room full of people not listening to each other, shouting, 'My life's great!' I doubt this has changed."

"So why are you still *on* there?"[1]

---

1 Jack very rarely named specific social media sites in his books. According to his agent, Murray Chambers, this policy was his "revenge" against sites who refused to pay him for name-checking them. —*Alistair*

Bex makes her frustrated, dismissive noise: the sound of a brief, chaotic catfight. "I have *profiles*, Jack, so old friends can catch up, but I don't read anything. Social media makes me think less of people. I'd rather not know all the self-obsessed shit in their heads."

"How selfish of you."

"Won't this book be kind of *short*? Just a great big atheist travelling round the world saying 'Bullshit' a lot?"

I frown at her underestimation of the concept. "Obviously I'm going to keep it rational. But I'll also keep a completely open mind. Social media's full of people who think ghosts are real, so I'll give them a chance to guide me in the right direction. I've got this ongoing list of hypotheses for paranormal phenomena, which I'm calling SPOOKS. That's short for—"

"I think I can do without knowing."

"And when the book's done, I can at least tell all the mad believers, 'Look, you had your chance to convince me and you blew it.'"

"How very magnanimous of you."

My hopeless love for Bex intensifies when she employs long words and sarcasm together. Long-time readers will recall her as the late-twenties fitness instructor I've known and shared a flat with too long for anything to happen between us. They'll also know I've found it challenging to listen to her banging men in an adjacent bedroom. This may explain why my books tend to involve travel. (By the way, she doesn't bang loads of men. She's not like that. She's been seeing a guy called Lawrence for six months, even if he is a smarmy, chinless loser. And he is.)

I can openly discuss this love of mine because Bex doesn't actually read my books. "Jack, I *live* with you," she once said while we half watched *EastEnders* and fully ate Chinese food on our big fat yellow sofa. "I don't actually need to read these books. Why would I want to relive you overdosing on coke in our toilet?"

Apart from making the mistake of not reading my books, Bex is the most sensible person I know. In truth, I always seek her approval on my book ideas. Which makes me want to win her around on this one.

A burst of power makes our very small car rattle and hum. We roll forwards with a creak.

"So," she says. "How was Greece?"

"*Italy*," I say, forced to raise my voice as people start squealing behind us. "It caused the big bust-up. I did a bad thing and got yelled at by an exorcist."

"On Halloween. Perfect."

"Then I saw this weird YouTube video."

Bex processes all this information. As our car gains speed, she settles on a question: "What video?"

"I'll tell you after this."

And into the mouth we go.

So I'm deep in rural Italy, over twenty-four hours ago. The first stop on my epic journey into the supernatural world, which will see me visit a combat magician in Hong Kong, a ??? in ??? and a ??? in ???, not to mention a ??? in ??? *(Eleanor: I'll fill these in later, once I know who I'm actually meeting and where I'm going. If I forget, you can do the honours.)*

I am about to enter a church.

The ancient building sits isolated and forlorn on a hill that becomes a sheer cliff face on one side. Hurl a stone from up here and it vanishes halfway down, caught by the twisted, arthritic fingers of bare trees. This church, this stone sentinel, keeps watch over dense woodland and clustered hills that mark the horizon.

Inside, it is functional, relatively bare bones. There are still a few of the usual looming statues calculated to intimidate and belittle, plus a few glistening symbols of opulence and power. Yet the most elaborate feature is the stained-glass window in the back wall, shot through with winter sun.

I always think the beauty of stained-glass windows is wasted on a church.

Everything is so quiet and serene, you'd scarcely credit the fact that in ninety minutes we'll need an ambulance.

Arriving half an hour late at 1:30 p.m., I barrel in looking windswept and interesting. Eighty-year-old Father Primo Di Stefano greets me with a stiff smile and matching handshake. Sporting a large black frock, he is flanked by two frosty aides, who are both short and stocky, in black shirts and grey trousers. The only real visual difference between these two is that one has facial hair, so let's call them Beard and Beardless. I also have a handy Italian translator at my disposal, named Tony. So he'll be Translator Tony, obviously. Despite his werewolf-hairy hands, a monobrow crowning shifty brown eyes, and teeth you could ride a Kawasaki between, Tony's the only halfway personable guy here. We bond over a cigarette outside, when he admires my brass Zippo. A dull, tarnished old thing these days, but it does the job.

Di Stefano does not run this church. To all intents and purposes, the priest is a guest here, like me. One of the Pope's most trusted foot soldiers, he is based in Rome and has travelled many miles to commandeer the place on a mission of mercy. Specifically, he has come to drive the Devil out of a thirteen-year-old girl with the use of words, gestures and a great deal of biblical *Sturm und Drang*. This man claims to have carried out over two hundred exorcisms. As a purely incidental side effect, this has provided him with material for a lucrative string of books detailing his crusades. The titles include *At War with the Devil*, *My Lifelong Battle with the Antichrist* and of course *Satan & I*. That last title is my favourite, like a wacky sitcom. "In this week's episode of *Satan & I*, Father Di Stefano attempts to throw a house party for friends, only for his mischievous flatmate Satan to slay them all while denouncing God!"

Bitterly cold winds sail up and down the aisle as Father Di Stefano, Translator Tony and I literally pull up a pew for a chat. We have time to kill before the subject of the priest's latest ritual arrives.

Exorcism can be traced back through millennia to the dawn of civilisation. Right from the word go, man was all too keen to ascribe sickness, whether physical or psychological, to evil spirits. And of course people from the ancient Babylonian priests onwards were all too keen to present themselves as exorcists. As saviours. The most famous was allegedly Jesus Christ, who couldn't get enough of it.

Di Stefano considers exorcism more vital than ever in the online age. "The internet," he tells me via Tony, "has made it much easier to share information, but not always good information. People experiment with Ouija boards and get themselves in trouble. And then they call us, asking for help."

This man has the lived-in face and manner of a mastiff dog. There is not the faintest flicker of humour in his dark eyes. He is barely tolerating me. His aides hover within earshot, which always irritates me during interviews. I ask for them to move further away, but the request is rudely ignored. I soon discover that Di Stefano's hearing is poor when he wants it to be—when I ask a challenging question, for instance. At other times, when I say something he wants to pounce on, his ears sharpen the hell up.

Di Stefano has granted a fair few interviews over the years—most notably when he's had a new book out—but as far as I can tell, no journalist has been allowed to watch him perform an exorcism. Today feels like a concession to the modern media, a canny PR exercise: if the Church is seen to be helping people, it stays relevant in the eyes of the world. And if there's one thing religion should be worried about these days, it's relevance. There's no question that converting Jack Sparks would be quite the coup.

I can't help but picture Di Stefano conducting an exorcism with an entirely straight face, then bursting into uncontrollable fits later on, the moment he shuts his front door behind him. Just *hooting* at the nonsense he gets away with on a daily basis. But there's undoubtedly a very serious side to all this. After all, Di Stefano deals with often quite severely distressed people of all ages (except babies, seemingly. Babies are so consistently insane that it's hard to tell if they're possessed, unless they start floating about). The lion's share of these people arguably suffer from some form of mental illness, or have experienced abuse.

"That is true," allows Di Stefano, to my surprise. "Very often we realise, you know, that a person does have a mental illness or there is some other history there. In those cases, a demon is not to blame after all. When this happens, of course, the person will be sent for the correct treatment. The need for an exorcism is actually very rare."

"How can you tell when an exorcism is required?" I ask.

Di Stefano looks down his nose at me, regarding me like the rank amateur I am. His stare is unyielding, those eyes dead as a cod's. "You get to know the sign of a true demonic possession," he says. "You can feel it. The feeling is completely different."

So far, so vague. "How *exactly* does it feel when it's a real demon?" I persist.

"The air feels . . . thick," he says, with distaste. "And black, like oil. It is . . ." He rubs his forefinger and thumb together as he searches for the word. Then he exchanges rapid-fire Italian with Tony, who provides the word on the tip of Di Stefano's tongue: "Oppressive."

"Also," the priest continues, "you can see it in the subject's eyes. The eyes, you know, are the windows to the soul. You can see who, or what, is living inside."

"How do you know it isn't all in *your* head?" I ask.

That mastiff face crumples. No mean feat when your face is already a sponsored crumple-thon. He doesn't enjoy this line of questioning, no doubt because it could just as easily be applied to religion as a whole. Still, he gamely indulges me. "As far as I know, I am perfectly sane. So are my exorcist colleagues. The things we have seen . . . the way people have behaved with demons within them . . . this is no make-believe." He gestures around the church. "You will see today, I think."

"Have you seen *The Exorcist*?" I ask.

"The movie? A long time ago. I don't remember too much about—"

"Are exorcisms anything like that?"

"Sometimes they are," he says wearily. As if anticipating my next question, he adds, "But you know, exorcism existed for a long time before that movie. The movie took its cue from exorcisms before it. But I must say, I have seen things far more terrible in real life."

I lean forward, quote-hungry. "Could you give me an example?"

Di Stefano recalls a middle-aged single mother in Florence who would cry blood. Her skin turned sickly green and broke out in open sores. When he tried to expel her demons in an attic room, she whispered the Lord's Prayer backwards as she gouged out one of her own eyeballs with a rusty antique spoon. Di Stefano (then a mere assistant, in the late seventies) and his exorcism instructor restrained her, encased the eye in ice and rushed her to hospital. Despite a five-hour emergency operation, the eyeball could not be reinstated. Still, Di Stefano claims that they eventually exorcised the demon from this woman, who was reunited with her children.

When pushed for his very worst memory, he reluctantly dredges up the 2009 case of a ten-year-old boy in Milan. As he speaks of this boy, his full-bodied voice becomes little more than a murmur.

"The first time I tried to exorcise him, he laughed in my face, as he broke each of his fingers one by one."

"Just the fingers on one hand?" I ask, genuinely curious. "He couldn't do both, right?"

Di Stefano glares at me, as if I'm trying to be funny.

He bows his head. "I could not save him. The demons had such a firm hold. I think they wanted to make a point, to scare me away from my life's mission. During exorcism number three, the boy smashed his face against the corner of a glass table, blood everywhere. In number five, he threatened my nieces' lives. He said he would cut all the skin from their faces as I watched, then force me to eat it."

Translator Tony pops a square of nicotine gum into his mouth.

Di Stefano takes a moment to compose himself. "Two nights later, I had one of my visions."

Ah yes, Di Stefano's famous visions. His books are full of them. These visions physically root him to the spot and flood his mind with astonishing psychic sights. Interestingly, he rarely seems to tell anyone about them *before* their real-life counterparts occur. Why, it's almost as if he pretends to have had the vision in retrospect.

"In my mind, I saw the boy murder his sleeping stepfather with a hammer, then jump out of the window. And this actually happened, thirty minutes later. The boy, he jumped ten floors down to the busy road. Such a terrible, terrible . . . People said he screamed blasphemy as he fell."

Satisfied that I can't come back with a smart answer to such a grim story—or worried that I might ask for more information about that stepfather—he stands, ending our cosy chat. He needs, he says, to pray and mentally prepare.

As I leave him to kneel before the altar, I wonder how many exorcisms actually take place in churches. Aren't the possessed supposed to burn up when they walk through the door, or at least protest and writhe around? Have these people never seen *The Omen*?

I open my notepad and review the SPOOKS List I've created . . .

THE SPOOKS LIST (Sparks' Permanently Ongoing Overview of Kooky Shit) (Full disclosure: I had to ask social media's hive mind to help with the "K" word. Prior to that I only had "Kreepy," which simply wasn't good enough.)

People claim to have witnessed supernatural phenomena for the following reasons:

(1) They're trying to deceive others
(2) They've been deceived by others

Those, then, are the only two *viable* explanations as I see them, in top-down order from most to least likely. It won't surprise you to learn that I don't consider "Ghosts are real" to be a viable hypothesis. Neither can I entertain the notion that people can be deceived by their own minds to the extent that they "see" a ghost. Not without the use of LSD, anyway, and in such cases the drug is clearly the mother of total delusion. I should know this better than most, after the incident with the dive-bombing spider-geese.[2]

What I'll be looking to do, both here today and throughout this book, is to fit everything I see to one of the two explanations above. Should neither of them fit, I'll potentially add a third explanation to the list.

That's highly unlikely, I'm saying, but let's get stuck in.

Thirteen-year-old Maria Corvi arrives on foot, alongside her fifty-something mother Maddelena. The frigid Halloween air converts their breath to vapour. They live somewhere off in all those forbidding woods, which offer few helpful footpaths. During the last hour and a half of my drive out here, I saw neither towns nor villages—just the occasional run-down cottage or cabin set far back from recklessly winding dirt roads. If this little church ever served a bustling community, then such a thing has long since dissolved.

At first sight Maria doesn't strike me as demonic. Neither is she all cute-as-a-button smiley like Linda Blair's *Exorcist* character, Regan MacNeil, who was one year younger. Maria Corvi radiates the sullen nonchalance of your typical teenager who's doing her best to mask fear. Look closer and you see that, like her mother, Maria is quietly desperate. The pair are decked out in the same plain, practical blue smocks and boots they wear for their work as farm labourers. Maria is pretty and worryingly thin. Gaunt, too, and those dark-ringed eyes suggest

---

2 *Jack Sparks on Drugs* (Erubis Books, 2014), p.146. —*Alistair*

sleepless nights. Her unwashed black hair hangs halfway down her back.

Apart from a splash of grey up top, Maddelena is so self-evidently Maria's mother that they could be nesting Russian dolls.

I watch Maria carefully as she crosses the threshold into the church. Her flesh does not burn and she does not shriek. She does, however, bring a hand up to her throat and swallow hard, as if resisting the urge to be sick. Catching my eye awkwardly, almost shyly, she looks away and continues with her mother towards Di Stefano as if nothing has happened.

The priest greets Maria and Maddelena by launching into a formal speech in Italian. It reminds me of company reps who read legal tedium over the phone, while you play Candy Crush and say "Yes" every thirty seconds. It very clearly reconfirms, no doubt partly for my information, that Maria and her mother have agreed to this rite. The Church, stresses Di Stefano, would only force such a thing on someone if they had harmed others or were deemed to be at risk of doing so.

"Please do not be afraid," he tells the women. "Today, Maria, you will be free of the negativity that has no business within you." I later learn that "negativity" is a euphemism the Church often employs. They claim it helps to avoid leading the subject through the power of suggestion. Which seems unusually sensible of them.

Maria nods, her expression neutral. I can't tell whether she believes in this stuff, or is going through the motions for her mother's sake. Did Maddelena find an Ozzy Osbourne album on Maria's iPod and hurriedly dial the Vatican's 1-800-DEVILCHILD hotline?

Di Stefano briefly explains why I'm present. Then he leads Maria to the strip of dusty floor that passes in front of the altar.

Her mother signs legal papers handed to her by Beard (oh yes, legal papers—the Church likes being sued about as much as any other multinational corporation). Then he and Beardless usher her, along with me and Translator Tony, to our designated pew five rows back from the front.

Maddelena chews what's left of her fingernails while Tony translates her. "I know this has to be done. But . . . she is my baby, you know? I do not understand. Why has Satan chosen her?"

It doesn't seem the right time to tell her Satan doesn't exist. Or indeed to ask if, you know, Maria might just be your average teenager who seems a bit nuts—especially against the backdrop of a quiet rural expanse like this. Instead, I ask what led Maddelena to hire an exorcist.

"Maria started to sleepwalk," she says, never taking her eyes off her daughter as Di Stefano gives the girl a final briefing in hushed tones. "Or at least I thought she was sleepwalking. In the middle of the night I found her standing outside our home, at the edge of the clearing . . ."

Maddelena flicks her eyes around the church before continuing. "She was naked, in the freezing cold. I thought she was asleep, so I said to her, 'Maria, please wake up.' But she turned her head, with her eyes wide open. And she smiled. I'd never seen a crazy smile on her face like that. She said to me, 'I *am* awake.' And then . . ."

Maddelena looks set to cry, but steels herself. When she lowers her voice, Translator Tony follows suit. "*And then* . . . she slapped my face and said, '*You* wake up, you Christ-loving whore, before I rip out your fucking heart.'"

After that night, Maria's nocturnal wanderings escalated. Maddelena claims she tried locking both of the house's external doors and hiding the keys, but still her daughter managed to break out. One time, Maddelena and a search party of friends found Maria a mile away from home, in the dead of night. She was writhing around, naked again, covered in the blood of a deer that she'd slain with a butcher's knife taken from the kitchen.

"She was laughing when we found her," says Maddelena with a shudder. "After that, I felt so lost. I knew that only the Church could help with something like this. The old pastor who owns this church helped me make contact with Father Di Stefano in Rome. The good father sent an assistant to meet Maria, then it was decided that a blessing would be best."

Another euphemism, there. It's so much easier to agree to a blessing than an exorcism. When I ask if Maddelena ever considered medical help for her daughter, her face suggests that she trusts doctors and science about as much as I trust priests and religion.

"If this does not work, then *maybe* . . ." she says, as if that really would be the last resort.

I'm unprepared for the transformation of Maria Corvi. I just didn't expect this skinny kid to have it in her.

Sitting on a simple, creaky wooden chair in front of the altar, she appears withdrawn but compliant, her head bowed, hands clasped on her lap. The only small sign of any real emotion comes when she glances over at her mother. I would place good money on it being a look of resentment. A look that says, "Happy now? I'm doing it."

Maria's mother doesn't seem to interpret this look the same way. She smiles back encouragingly and wrings her bony hands in anticipation, as if her daughter is about to audition for *The X Factor*.

Father Di Stefano stands before Maria, an ancient leather-bound Bible spread across his palms. Beard and Beardless position themselves at either far side, hands behind their backs.

Di Stefano reads interminable passages from the book. His words echo darkly around the ceiling. Maria looks embarrassed, as if wondering what she's supposed to do. It's weirdly hypnotic. Thanks to a late night out in Rome, my eyes lose focus and I drift into a dreamlike state . . .

Maria's whole body goes electric-shock rigid. Her eyes bulge and her hands and feet shoot out in all directions. I can't see her toes from here, but her trembling fingers are spread wide. She holds this bizarre position for no more than a second before the chair beneath her gives way, breaking with a loud crack.

Maria falls to the ground, her back arching awkwardly over the pile of broken wood, her body limp. I shake my head, disappointed that the all-powerful Church has resorted to age-old slapstick ruses like sawing halfway through chair legs in order to jazz things up. Coming next: Maria and Di Stefano attempt to carry a piano up a tall flight of steps, with amusing consequences.

Beside me Maddelena gasps, a rosary gripped tight in one hand, the beads fit to burst. Beard and Beardless dash in and examine the lifeless girl, while carefully removing the pieces of chair from beneath her. They return to the sidelines: twin roadies who scurried on to fix a rogue microphone stand during a gig.

Di Stefano switches his attention from the Bible to the prone teenager. "I am addressing directly the spirit that dwells within Maria Corvi," he says. "Speak your name, before I have cause to do so myself."

On the word "myself," something dramatic happens. Something that, I'll admit, is harder to explain than the magical breaking chair.

As a kid, I owned what is generally referred to as a thumb

puppet. A small wooden donkey standing on a cylindrical base, its tiny constituent parts joined by string. When you pushed your thumb up inside this base, it made the donkey collapse. On the withdrawal of your thumb, the donkey would spring back up into its former rigid state.

Maddelena cries out in shock as Maria Corvi springs up from the church floor like my donkey used to. Her heels remain on the ground, but the rest of her rises fast, as if hoisted by some invisible pulley system. Unlike my donkey, Maria remains loose. Her body appears boneless. Eyes shut, she drifts from side to side as if underwater. I stand and peer over the pews, spotting that she's now up on her tiptoes. It doesn't seem possible for a human being to achieve this stance, or at least to maintain it for so long. Her centre of gravity is not so much *off* as non-existent. The magician David Blaine would take notes.

Father Di Stefano, of course, is not fazed. He's seen all this stuff many times before. Truth be told, he invented it. Because as he repeats his exhortations for the evil within Maria to speak its name, the truth hits me. Remember Jim Carrey's character in *The Truman Show*—the guy who discovers that the world around him is artificial? All of this is one big set-up, for my benefit. It's a feeling journalists will know well on a smaller scale: the sense that you're no longer a non-influential observer of events, but instead the spark that brought them about.

If Maria Corvi isn't an actual actress, then she and her mother have surely agreed that she will become one, no doubt in exchange for a better life. *(Eleanor: please don't kick off about libel here. I really can't be dealing with another debate like the one about Katy Perry and the bag of . . . well, you know.)* The arrangement of the pews and the space before the altar resembles audience and stage, with stage managers Beard and Beardless lurking in the wings. After all, what has the Church always been about, if not an audience flocking to watch a performance? And of course here I am, hemmed in several rows back—all the better to stop me seeing this propaganda display from the wrong angles.

Maria's eyelids flick open, revealing that her eyes now swim with some cunningly applied yellow dye. Nice touch. She's still up on her tippy-toes, and I now suspect that her conveniently oversized smock harbours some kind of body harness. Her lips stretch back over her teeth to form a sickly grin. When she speaks, her voice is lilting and childlike, in direct contrast to her words. "You cock-sucking prick," she tells the priest, thereby fulfilling the minimum post-Friedkin quota of fellatio mentions during an exorcism. Translator Tony lowers his voice reverentially as he continues to whisper her words in English: "You fuck children and yet judge me?"

Maria's laugh is slithery. If a snake could laugh, it would sound like that.

This Maria, if that really is her name? She's good.

To a man like Father Primo Di Stefano, child abuse accusations, whether from entities alive or dead, are water off a duck's back. Delving into his robes, he produces a sturdy, old-school wooden cross with a Christ figurine on it.

When he presents this trump card to Maria, it's as if she's being made to look directly into the sun. She lashes out at the priest and the cross, her fingers cramped into claws. Di Stefano takes a step back, while Beard and Beardless hurry in to restrain Maria, each gripping an arm. She struggles against them with surprising force and sends Beard tumbling to the ground.

"Maria is ours," she says. Her voice is now deep and throaty, but punctuated by freakish high notes. "We are her blood. Her flesh, her bones, her guts. We have freed her soul. By hurting us with your trinkets, you only hurt her."

Di Stefano steps back into the fray, his cross to the fore, bellowing, "That is a sacrifice I'm prepared to make in order to secure her freedom."

I wonder how Maddelena feels about Di Stefano taking that decision into his own hands. To my consternation, she seems okay with it. Oh, hey, she's in on all of this anyway. Just playing along with the script.

And so it goes on. Yellow-eyed Maria verbally abuses Di Stefano, spits, shrieks and generally misbehaves. Di Stefano remains devout and steadfast. He brandishes his religious iconography as a pepper-spray threat and mentions Jesus Christ at least three times per minute. Translator Tony struggles to keep up with them.

Now. Here's the thing. It's a universal truth that laughter becomes more insanely delicious the more wrong it is.

Taboos are funny. They just are. When you're absolutely, definitely not supposed to laugh, that's when laughter is all the more potent and combustible. As scarily inevitable as a sneeze, or an itch you just *have* to scratch, no matter how demented you'll look.

You might be sitting among heartbroken folk at a funeral. You might be sitting behind a TV news desk, staring into a camera and telling the world about the latest genocide.

Or, as in my case, witnessing a faux exorcism.

Surely I can't be the only man on earth who considers *The Exorcist* a comedy. Even when I first saw it as a child, in the late eighties, the film provoked far more chuckles than shivers. Friedkin's po-faced seriousness really tickled my ribs. "The power of Christ compels you!" became something to yell at other kids in the playground with a big grin.

As the action escalates, so does my urge to laugh at it. This whole charade is so very deadpan that laughter is the only sane response. Part of me *needs* to laugh, in order to exorcise myself of these ridiculous characters. And while I'm genuinely over-come by mirth, there's no doubt that my laughter will also be a statement. Because people's enduring belief in conveniently invisible devils makes the work of science so much harder. It slaps a leash on progress and encourages backward thinking.

In 2012, while appearing on a TV show in the Dominican Republic, U.S. magician Wayne Houchin unexpectedly had his head set on fire by a man who reportedly believed him to be a voodoo practitioner. In 2013, a YouGov poll found that over fifty per cent of Americans believe in the Devil and exorcism. And earlier this year, in his documentary about "gay cures," British doctor and TV presenter Christian Jessen encountered American teenagers who genuinely thought homosexuality was caused by demonic infestations.

Belief in the concept of Satan possessing children has led to murders around the world. Sometimes these murders are deliberate: kids have been burned and buried alive. Such things are straight out of the Dark Ages. Other deaths have resulted from misguided attempts to get those imagined demons out, often by one of those maverick exorcists. In the Philippines as recently as 2011, an anorexic girl named Dorca Beltre starved to death during a botched five-day exorcism.

And so we must laugh at this medieval crap. It is our duty to do so.

My laugh explodes out of me in a great belly-pumping blast, amplified by its own inappropriate glory.

orbit

Follow us:

f **/orbitbooksUS**

🐦 **/orbitbooks**

▶ **/orbitbooks**

Join our mailing list
to receive alerts on our
latest releases and deals.

orbitbooks.net

Enter our monthly
giveaway for the chance
to win some epic prizes.

orbitloot.com